D1628744

Sandra Benns lives in Toronto, Canada, and enjoys her passion for writing and all things literary, along with running her non-profit corporation which focuses on seniors. When asked how she balances her writing schedule, work, and family life that includes two small granddaughters, she smiled and shook her head, "Pinch me. Just pinch me. I'm living the dream."

For Dad and Great-Grandad

My father and great-grandfather were the first men in my life to love me unconditionally. Their spirits ride shotgun as I barge through the thick and thin of it.

Sandra Benns

7 RUSSELL HILL ROAD

AUSTIN MACAULEY PUBLISHERS™

LONDON * CAMBRIDGE * NEW YORK * SHARJAH

Ordering Information
Quantity sales: Special discounts are available on quantity purchases by corporations, associations, and others. For details, contact the publisher at the address below.

Publisher's Cataloging-in-Publication data
Benns, Sandra
7 Russell Hill Road

ISBN 9781643788098 (Paperback)
ISBN 9781643788104 (ePub e-book)

Library of Congress Control Number: 2020919888

www.austinmacauley.com/us

First Published (2021)
Austin Macauley Publishers LLC
40 Wall Street, 33rd Floor, Suite 3302
New York, NY 10005
USA

mail-usa@austinmacauley.com
+1 (646) 5125767

Over the years, my girlfriends and I have picked each other up, dusted each other off, and laughed and cried together so many times that I can't remember. What I do remember, however, now that the dust has settled somewhat in our lives, is my love, respect, and admiration for each and every one of these remarkable women.

Chapter 1
Humble Beginnings

At the tender age of nine years, Nigel Royal had no idea that the two-page letter he was holding in his small, brown hands was a major game-changer. His whole world as he knew it was as a boy living in an extended family household in rural Jamaica, playing cricket and attending a small public school. That, and eating a sizable portion of local fish along with goat stew most days, was all about to come to an abrupt end.

His big sister was standing there with her hands on her hips and an animated face. According to her, the postmaster had brought this letter from his mama who lived all the way up in Canada. His mama didn't write often, so he knew vaguely that the letter must be important, especially to see his sister all riled up.

"Your mama has made arrangements for you to go up to Canada to live with her!"

"What's Canada?"

"What do you mean what's Canada? You buffoon, Canada is a country! The question is: where's Canada? That's where your mama lives. She wants you to live with her there in the big house!"

"But I like it here. Who will feed Daisy? What about my cricket team?"

"Daisy is a dog, little man. She'll be just fine with the rest of us here to feed her."

"No, I can't leave her. If I go to Canada, she will have to come with me."

"I don't think so, Buster. Now sit down and read that letter from your mama again to make sure you understand. You are going to fly out in a week's time. Besides, dogs aren't allowed on airplanes. You are one lucky boy, and don't you be forgetting it. Count your blessings and forget about that damn mangy dog."

Nigel sat, as ordered, and as he focused on the second page, he put his head down on his arms to cover his tears. He couldn't leave – he just couldn't. He knew they wouldn't feed Daisy. He was the only one that loved her. And it would be the first time meeting his mama. Would she like him? Did they have a school for him to go to up in Canada? He liked his school and he liked his headmaster. Did they have books there? He always did his best to keep out of trouble for his big sister, and now she wanted to get rid of him.

***

He sat in the big, deep chair in the 'special baggage claim' office, holding on to his small brown suitcase and keeping his eye on the nice lady in the uniform that worked on the airplane.

The attendant looked over at the young unaccompanied minor who had an unfortunate, red, and angry-looking keloid scar that hooked around and under his cheekbone on the left side of his face. During the long flight, she had kept him occupied with lots of snacks and a variety of coloring books. Actually, the coloring books were way too childish for him, but he didn't whine about it. He just asked her for more after outlining and coloring in every page carefully, with no mistakes, throughout the long journey.

Nigel glanced to his left and saw a large, old woman lumber through the door. Could that be his mama?

The tall, big-boned black woman took a moment standing there, her left hand carrying a black handbag with a small wrapped package sticking out of the top of it and her right hand clutching a white cardigan that had been washed and folded a thousand times over. Face beaded with perspiration, her tidy hair was pulled back and adorned with a small, maroon-colored pillbox. She was sporting her Sunday's best white shoes with the low heel, even though it was midweek and not the Sabbath at all.

He stood up in the manner that small Jamaican boys are told to, in respect of their elders. He studied her face earnestly. She looked like she was happy to see him, and well, maybe a little relieved as well. 'She does look a little friendly, right?' he rationalized to himself. He hoped she didn't notice his scar. "Are you my mama?"

She lowered herself down, opening her arms while still clutching the black bag and the white cardigan on either side of her large frame.

Nigel's head was buried in her ample chest, and he struggled to breathe amongst his mama's hot, sweaty breasts that had been dosed liberally with 'Lily of the Valley' perfume hours beforehand. He decided that she smelled good.

Neither of them knew that the dime-store scent that she had bought at Woolworth's years ago was a fitting choice for the reunion between the mother

10

and her last-born child. In fancy script on the blue bottle, below the popular perfume's nomenclature, its byline read: *You have made my life complete.*

And so, it was on a balmy night in the summer of 1959, at Lester B. Pearson Airport in Toronto, Canada, that Saul Himmel, who had driven his housekeeper, Mavis Royal, to the airport, witnessed a young nine-year-old boy reconnect with his mama for the first time in his memory. His housekeeper hadn't laid eyes on her boy since he was a ten-month-old baby just taking his first steps. Saul blew his nose noisily and blinked to keep the tears back. Yes, he had to agree with Mavis; the boy was a sight for sore eyes.

***

The next day, his mama had allowed him to step outside her small apartment that was partitioned off from the big house behind the back stairwell, with the promise that he would not leave the property line, no matter what. He promised and found his way to the front steps of the big house located at 7 Russell Hill Road, on a leafy street in the Toronto neighborhood called Forest Hill.

Saul opened the front door to collect the morning newspaper.

"Well, hello, young man, are you all settled in?" he said from the doorway.

"I suppose." Nigel turned and looked up at the man standing in front of him. "Sir, I forgot your name, sir. I'm sorry. Don't tell my mama, or she'll give me a whooping."

"I think that you should call me Saul. Your mama will probably want you to call me Mr. Himmel, but when we are just the two of us, like now, you can call me Saul."

"Saul?" he asked quizzically.

"Yes, Saul."

"What kind of a name is that? Is that a Canadian name?"

"Well, yes, you might say so. But really, it's a Jewish name."

"What's Jewish mean?"

"That's a whole long story. We'll save it for another day. Meanwhile, back to my name, do we have a deal? When we are by ourselves, you will call me Saul and I will call you Nigel." He extended his hand to the boy.

"Yes, sir. I mean Saul." He jumped up to meet the outstretched hand.

"Let's both go around to your mama's door and ask if I can take you down to the Dutch Dreams Ice cream Parlor and we'll get a cone."

With Mavis giving her son last-minute instructions on how to behave all the way down the driveway, the man carefully held on to the boy's hand. They walked across to Bathurst Street, crossed over St. Clair Avenue, and they discovered that both of them thought chocolate was the best flavor in the world, even as far away as Jamaica.

As Saul sat across from the small boy, with the ice cream cone wrapped neatly in the supplied napkin, he leaned over and said to the seemingly happy, squirming boy sitting across from him, "What's the other guy look like?"

"What do you mean, Saul?" Nigel asked as chocolate began to drip down his chin and onto the collar of his worn but clean and ironed shirt.

Saul smiled as he realized the boy was a little young for his age-old quip, so he went into detail to explain the nuance of conversation.

"Well, when someone asks you about a scar that you may have on your face, you don't necessarily have to tell the real story. You can add a little humor and a little charm, and all you say in response to the question is y*ou should see the other guy.* It seems to work especially well with girls."

"Oh, oh! I get it! It's kind of like a joke! Okay, okay," he enthused, bouncing up and down. "Saul, later, when we're walking home, you ask me about my scar. Okay with you, Saul?"

"Okay with me, Nigel," Saul offered from his smiling face.

The two new friends chatted easily in between Saul's admonishments to wipe the chocolate up before it reached the table. Nigel caught on quickly, and licked the ice cream mostly direct from the source, but there were many carefully angled licks to his right hand and up and down the chocolate mess that oozed from between his fingers.

It was there sitting in the booth that Nigel confided in Saul his worst fears that Daisy wasn't getting enough to eat back home.

"Who is Daisy?" asked Saul in an alarmed voice.

"She's my dog," Nigel explained.

On the way home, Saul casually mentioned to the boy that he was thinking of getting a dog and could Nigel possibly help take care of the new pup by feeding him and taking him out for walks, with his mama's permission of course, and with a small allowance of course.

"What's an allowance, Saul?"

"It's a little bit of pocket money to buy an ice cream cone once in a while."

"Count me in, Saul." Nigel shot his sticky brown hand out to cement the deal before Saul had a chance to rethink the whole dog idea. How was he going to explain this to his wife? She had maintained a strict 'no-animals-in-the-house' policy for all the years they had been married. He had an uneasy feeling this rash move was going to cost him. He looked down at Nigel's beaming face and threw his caution to the wind.

"We'll have to come up with a good name for the pup, Nigel."

"I know! I know!" Nigel said as his hand went up automatically, like he was back in his Jamaican classroom, and then back down quickly as he realized where he was. "We could call her Little Daisy if that's okay with you, Saul."

As they were turning the corner at Heath Street and Russell Hill Road, with small sticky fingers firmly under the grasp of the larger hand, Saul leaned over and said, "How did you get that scar?"

"You should see the other guy!" quipped the laughing boy, jumping up and down in delight with his newly minted joke. He shook loose of Saul's grip, and his long, thin arms boxed the air, calling out to Saul, "Float like a butterfly. Sting like a bee – just like Muhammad Ali says. Right, Saul?"

They parted ways at the driveway, Saul using the front door and Nigel running around to the back of the house, shouting all the way, "Mama! Mama! Mr. Himmel is getting a dog and I'm going to take care of it! Can I, Mama? Can I?"

Saul entered the cool, quiet house. After washing his sticky hands, he went into his office to phone around to his friends and colleagues in a quest to find the best pediatric plastic surgeon that the city had to offer. He got out his notebook to jot down a few thoughts on the keloid scar that was so evident on the young boy's face.

It seemed that the well-established, middle-aged lawyer, with absolutely no experience with children at all, was acting on new, bold ideas that were to define his sense of purpose that lasted the rest of his lifetime.

And Nigel had no idea at that time that twenty-one years later, in the summer of 1980, as he buried his mama's kind and benevolent employer, he would still be claiming the Retired Supreme Court Justice Saul Himmel as the very best father-figure in the whole world.

***

It was June in 2004, and Nigel limped along. He had hastily left the Aroma Espresso Bar on Spadina Road after bailing out and stumbling down the step with his face burning with humiliation. His dignity was in tatters. He slammed his cane into the sidewalk with each painful step forward. He just wanted to get home and gather his composure.

It was all because of a woman! It wasn't just any woman. Usually, he never noticed the women around him, but there was something about that girl with the mane of dark, tousled hair that had caused the whole embarrassment. He had been minding his own business, reading the *Globe and Mail* as usual and enjoying his cup of java when she burst into the café.

She was wearing a pair of summer sweats, sneakers, and a long-sleeved, thin, pink cotton tee-shirt. It was obvious to him that she avoided the sun; her skin was white, very white. Her dark hair definitely needed some work, and it was piled on top of her head, held together with a big plastic clip of some sort. In one hand, she was carrying a binder and a smaller red notebook made up of a multitude of dog-eared pages held together with a thick elastic band. Her other hand was full with a beat-up, old-fashioned pencil case. He pegged her at around forty years old. She wasn't a kid. And he couldn't take his eyes off her.

"What the fuck," he chided himself, "I haven't had a hard-on like this in years! Who the hell is she, and what's really going on here!?"

He had watched her survey the crowd, her eyes searching for a table where she could spread out the binder and the notebook. Her eyes circled around to his table, and he felt his face flush as her big, round, gray eyes met his. Her eyes seemed to widen a bit, and much to his alarm, she seemed to just pause there. She slowly took in every inch of his face. She seemed to look right through his soul.

'Shit, shit, shit!' he thought to himself. She must have seen that he had been staring at her. He carefully lowered his *Globe and Mail* newspaper on to his lap to cover his bulge which was now completely out of control. He jerked his head to the side to stare out the window. 'This is ridiculous,' he thought, 'even my heart is pounding. What the hell!' Out of his peripheral vision, he eyed her as best he could, as she set up camp at a table twenty feet away from him, positioning herself directly in front of his table, so he could watch her but she also could watch him.

He finally was able to retrieve his newspaper from his lap, gave in to his fascination, and began studying her while she busied herself with her opened binder of paperwork. It was a quiet cat-and-mouse affair. Every time her big, soulful, gray eyes slowly lifted to see that he was looking at her, his face would flush with embarrassment, but he just couldn't help himself. He was a goner.

All hell broke loose when she idly pulled a pencil from out of her topknot which must have loosened the plastic clip. The plastic clip took on a life of its own; it sprang open and escaped from the mound of long brunette hair that tumbled down everywhere. The clip bounced, bounced, and then bounced again on the floor and skittered to a stop right in front of his table.

'Oh my God, what am I going to do now!?' he whimpered silently to himself.

He sprang up from his chair at the same time she sprang up from hers. They stood in front of each other for a split second while the runaway clip lay between them. They both leaned over to retrieve the clip, her reaching the runaway barrette first. He was so engrossed with his nose practically in the midst of that glorious, scented, brunette heaven that when she came up from the floor, the top of her head met his chin with a terrible crack.

"Ohhhh!" he wailed out loud. She was mortified, but it was nothing compared to his horror and complete humiliation. "Oh, I'm fine. I'm so sorry. I'm so sorry," he repeated in a hushed, deep voice, just wanting to get out and away from the forewarned train wreck. He backed up, hand on chin, as if to run away and inadvertently tipped his metal cane off the back of his chair, which noisily clattered across the tile floor.

She noticed that the moving cane looked like it was heading for the door all on its own accord. "No, I'm sorry," she apologized. Her gray eyes turned back to meet his once again. "Are you going to be okay?" she asked him in a concerned voice as it registered with her that he was using a cane to get around. "Please take care of yourself," she admonished him softly and gently as if she was talking to her elderly grandfather.

Nigel stooped down and with his long arms claimed the annoyance. He quickly gathered up his damaged dignity to proceed toward the door in a hasty exit. He swore to himself that with this nightmare that he just couldn't wake up from, he would never darken the café's doorstep again. "Fuck, man," he said to himself, "there is no second chance at a first impression. She must think I'm an old, disabled pensioner."

After he left, and unknown to him, the brunette went back to her booth, with her paperwork scattered haphazardly over the tabletop. She sat there staring into space, disappointed that she didn't get the handsome stranger's name. Over the course of the hour earlier, she had had time to look him over and surmised his age to be around her own or maybe he had a few years on her. The surprise cane that had appeared at the end of their shy *tête-à-tête* belied his younger appearance. Perhaps he would return tomorrow. She knew she would. It was worth a chance. It wasn't every day she was so attracted to a man, and she was taken aback with her reaction to the tallish, lanky, intellectual type with the black brows that framed gorgeous, dark brown eyes. She rationalized to herself that it wasn't just a one-sided attraction. She had felt a definite spark between them just before the fated collision.

***

By the time he had reached the corner of Heath Street and Russell Hill Road, he began to see the humor in the situation and was almost congratulating himself on the terrific erection that had come upon him. "Old man, indeed! Not on my watch!" he claimed as he limped onto the pavers and under the portico at 7 Russell Hill Road, admiring the variety of flowering hedges and gardens that lined his property.

He blamed the whole mishegoss that was that morning on the damn cane and he vowed to ditch it as soon as he could. He challenged himself to work a little harder with his new rehab team to overcome the temporary sciatica attack that he had experienced the week before. Ever since he went under the Canadian Witness Protection Program, he could feel himself ageing from day to day. Living under the radar and not being able to work in the courts any longer took its toll every day, both physically and mentally. He jumped at the chance when an old colleague had asked him to cover for him the next week to wrap up a simple case in court. The system approved it, as long as his name was not on the roll call list as being the presiding judge. He was determined to work hard with the rehab as he simply could not be getting around town looking like an old, used-up, retired judge another day.

One thing he didn't want to ditch was the sight and scent of Ms. Brunette, and he regretted not wrapping up the misadventure by at least getting her name so he could invite her out for lunch or something. There was that glint of intelligence in those big, beautiful gray eyes.

But back in the recess of his mind, a few haunting, painful memories of messing with white girls in his youth were fighting to come out to the forefront. He tamped them down and focused on the woman at hand.

Beauty and intelligence are a dangerous combination in any case. The much-quoted definition of the classic Irish Faerie came to mind – *The Irish Faerie, both delicate and dangerous, sometimes known as a woodland sprite.*

As he opened the front door, he called out to the boys, "Madison, Stéphane, are you up and out of bed yet?" his deep baritone bellowed.

"Yeah, Uncle Nigey, we're in here having some cereal. How's your leg coming along today? Oh yeah, Dad called. He's going to be in town on the twenty-seventh, a week before we go home. He's meeting Uncle George here and wants to know if they can stay overnight."

Nigel looked in through the kitchen door and smiled at his two teenage houseguests that were engrossed with their phones and bowls of cereal, still in their pajama bottoms and tee-shirts, perched around the big kitchen island. MTV was blaring out from the flat-screen on the wall above them, and all was well with the world once again.

"I'm going to hide out in my office to read over a case that I'm presiding over next week, boys. And later – any interest in going out for pizza tonight? We could buzz down to Queen Street if you like. Might be able to check out some girls for you."

"We're down with that, Uncle Nigie, but can we go over to Little Italy? Remember that place over there with the good pizza?"

"Whatever floats your boat, boys. But just refresh my memory; was it the pizza that was so good or was it those cute little dark-haired Italian girls that were giggling away in the corner? We'll leave early, around six, to beat the rush. Are we all good?"

"Yep, we're all good," the boys said in unison, heads still down in rapt attention as their thumbs competed for annihilation of the video game challenge in front of them.

Nigel entered his office, grabbed the file from his desk, tipped back the old oak swivel chair and gingerly swung his feet up over the corner of the desk.

He surveyed the room that he had been adamant over all the years that the designers didn't touch. It had been Saul's office before him, and it was the only part of the whole house that hadn't been primped, painted, and renovated to the inch of its long life. He didn't have any need whatsoever to mess around with the last of Saul's memory. After all, he had been with him every step of the way – first through his childhood, teenage years, all through university, and law school. Thank God that he had died before his pitiful, short-lived marriage to Mercedes so many years ago. Saul had always been his biggest fan and the closest thing to a father that Nigel had ever known. Saul had proudly and joyfully reveled in the fact that he had followed in his footsteps. It was a shame, though, that he had died before he had reached the esteemed office of supreme court justice himself, just as Saul himself had many years before.

He cracked open the file and began to read:

Denise Allen, plaintiff v/s Lori Driessen, defendant

It was a simple case of an estate gone wrong and with the executor, Lori Driessen, being found on the wrong side of the law – for not dispensing the late mother's estate according to the law.

He flipped back through the file to make sure that the actual last will and testament was bona fide. As he read through the simple document, he was struck with the thought that the mother's wishes seemed to be harshly one-sided, leaving all her personal belongings to the two sisters and definitely nothing except an even one-third share of the money for the third sister, the plaintiff, namely Denise Allen. He was puzzled by this division of assets, as he had read and re-read the plaintiff's well-written plea to the court to uphold her mother's wishes and father's legacy of equality. The sense of purpose idea was a bold, innovative approach that the courts did not see very often in these

17

small, rather insignificant estate cases. And surprisingly, she had represented herself throughout the whole process.

It didn't sound at all like the plaintiff had an ax to grind. She merely wanted to establish grounds that her parents deserved to be respected. It wasn't like she was asking for money or personal *tchotchkes*; her whole case was based on the fact that she herself had lost her sense of purpose, which, in fact, was to ensure that her parents' wishes and legacy were both carried out properly. She had even called the last will and testament a 'love document.' Apparently, the mother had secretly switched the executorship from the plaintiff to her sister, just before she died.

'Troubling, to say the least,' he thought to himself. 'Family dynamics. You just never know.'

He closed the file. Since it was to be the final day of the case, all he had to do was to deliver the verdict and announce that Denise Allen was to collect her share of the $420,000 that seemed to have slipped through the cracks. He was impressed with the pleadings written by this plaintiff. She was clear, concise, and pled a full case based on her suffering due to the mishandling of the estate.

He wrote a note to the clerk and paperclipped it to the file. In the note, he requested a short meeting with the plaintiff after his decision had been handed down so he could personally applaud her for her carefully crafted and clever approach in the court of law. Ethical and moral values should not go unnoticed, and this particular plaintiff had established and proven moral obligation that one doesn't see every day.

"Hmmm, a sense of purpose," the retired judge mused. "That's what I need in my own life at this point now that I'm retired. Yes, a new sense of purpose deserves closer inspection. Thank you, Ms. Denise Allen, or whoever you are, for the brilliant idea. No, wait a minute. Hmm, maybe what I really need in my life is an Irish faerie. Yeah, with beautiful gray eyes and thick brunette hair. No! No, man, give yourself a shake! There is a big difference between needing something and wanting something. Now which is it? And be honest with yourself," he challenged the more reasonable, right side of his brain.

And that side of his brain answered him back with memories that he hadn't thought of for years – painful memories.

***

Back in the day, just after wrestling his way through puberty, he realized for the first time that the teenaged white girls at the high school dances in the predominantly Jewish neighborhood were friendly enough until it came time to separate a little from the crowd and perhaps take in a Saturday afternoon movie. His mama tried to warn him, Saul tried to protect him, and the girls' parents simply wouldn't have it. End of discussion. It wasn't because he wasn't a Jew. Saul had taken him to synagogue over the years enough that Nigel was well versed in the religion as well as the culture. No, it was simply because he was a black boy from Jamaica. He limped through high school with great social success in the middle of the crowd, but flying solo with an actual girlfriend for the smart, good-looking kid with the nice manners just wasn't meant to be. A deep shyness settled in that would define his persona for the years to come. University wasn't much better, but he buried himself in his studies and ended up as the youngest graduate from the University of Toronto to pass the bar. He had become a lawyer, to Saul and his mother's greatest pride.

Time went on, and as he situated himself in a law firm, he volunteered for every committee, every social agency, and every club that there was. He had applied to volunteer as a lawyer at the Nobel Prize Awards in Stockholm and was delighted when he was accepted to represent Canada and to attend the awards in 1974 as part of the global legal community.

***

It had been a hectic week in Stockholm. Although he had thoroughly enjoyed it, he was ready to head back home on the red-eye later that evening. He rang room service from his hotel late in the afternoon, and shortly afterward, there was a knock on his door.

"Come in!"

There was another knock a minute later. "Come in!"

Another knock came.

"Oh! Hello, you didn't hear me?" he said as he opened the door in exasperation.

To his surprise, a stunningly beautiful girl with long, straight, pale golden hair and blue eyes looked directly into his face and signed. Yes, signed. She followed up with pantomime that she was deaf.

"Oh, oh, sorry!"

She rolled the cart into the room and stood in front of him. He understood from her signing and gesturing that she was deaf and that she did not speak either, but that she did read lips.

He stood there looking directly into her face and he was awash with her beauty. In the lapse of the next five minutes, he had managed to understand that she usually did not deliver food to the rooms. She just worked in the kitchen, but her shift was over and she was doing a favor for a busy colleague. She was on her way home.

He insisted that she share his soup and sandwich, and over the shared lunch, he grabbed the hotel's notepad and pen and wrote his name and where he was from. "What's your name?" he asked, carefully enunciating every syllable. She studied the note paper but showed no comprehension at all. She didn't offer her name. She picked up the note paper, folded it carefully in half, and put it in her pocket.

As he watched her, it occurred to him that perhaps she only spoke Swedish and wouldn't even be able to decipher his English. Maybe he should try French. He certainly didn't know the Swedish language.

The radio was playing, and to his delight, some American blues filled the room. Nigel took her hand and walked her to the radio that was on top of the bureau and mirror. Holding her hand on the small speaker, he cranked it up with full force. Her face lit up and he held her from behind, both of them swaying back and forth to the music. The tall, slim black man with his arms around a beautiful blond woman smiled back at them through the reflection of the dresser mirror. It wasn't long before they were dancing all over the room, with him coaxing her into a simple two-step while holding her ever so gently.

Her beautiful, trusting eyes that never left his face seemed to free him from his painful shyness. As Ray Charles sang, *You Don't Know Me,* Nigel looked down at her and sang softly and directly into her face, hoping that she could understand his every word,

You give your hand to me
And then you say hello
And I can hardly speak
My heart is beating so
And anyone could tell
You think you know me well
But you don't know me

As he continued with his serenade, he had to admit that although the singing and the dancing were smooth moves on his part, Ray's words 'afraid and shy' couldn't be more fitting.

I never knew
The art of making love
Though my heart aches
With love for you
Afraid and shy
I let my chance go by

The chance to you might
Love me too
You gave your hand to me
And then you say goodbye
I watch you walk away
And then in my heart I cried
You'll never, never know
The one who loves you so
No, you don't know me

As the song finished the very last note, she looked from his lips into his dark brown eyes. She didn't sign. She didn't pantomime. She just began unbuttoning his shirt slowly and nodding her head slightly in the affirmative. Nigel silently thanked God for the luminous, golden angel that was offering herself up to him.

He lifted her up in his arms and carried her to the bed. The ages-old male pattern of pheromones and musk took the lead to guide the two inexperienced lovers into an intimate world that neither of them had ever been to before.

Hours later, as he untangled himself from her legs and arms, he checked his watch and jumped from the bed, saying, "Oh no, oh no, I'm going to miss my plane!" That, of course, fell upon deaf ears. He grabbed his air ticket and waved it in front of her. She was dressed and standing at the door as he came out of the bathroom, just standing there, her eyes watching his every move. He stood in front of her, both of them spellbound, serious, and silent.

As he was spinning around to get some bills out of his wallet, he said, "Oh my God, where are my manners!? Please let me give you some taxi fare."

She was unaware as to what he was saying; he had turned his head away when he had faced the other way to retrieve his wallet. She didn't hear a word of his polite offer of taxi fare.

As he came forward, standing in front of her, his hand outstretched with the folded bills, she looked at the money and then up to his face in disbelief. They stood there facing each other, with him saying, "What is it? What's wrong? What's wrong?"

With sickening realization, she thought that she was being paid for sex. She had been labeled a whore by a handsome stranger that she had freely and stupidly given herself to. All of her sadness, all of her unrealized passion, and all the lonely years of being undervalued showed on her face as she slapped his face so hard that it made him reel backwards. And she was gone.

He sat in the hotel room's single guest chair with his elbows on his knees, his face in his hands, and sobbed loudly. His deep, out-loud, gut-wrenching cries spoke to his own loneliness and his own years of struggling through his painful encounters with girls, especially white girls that couldn't seem to see beyond his brown skin. He had no idea that she hadn't heard his offer for taxi money. The last singular idea that he did have, however, was based on his past experience with girls. He concluded that once again, race had played its ugly hand in his love life which never seemed to get off the ground.

He stared into the mirror. He called himself a fool. Stripped of his naivety, he accepted the hard, cold fact that in the eyes of white girls, his brown skin was nothing but a condemnation.

The short magical afternoon that had ended in devastating tragedy was to shape both of their lives for all their years to come.

***

It was mid-December, 1974, when he arrived back in his safe, small, one-bedroom condo that he had bought himself a year earlier. He didn't tell a soul what had happened in Stockholm, and he hunkered down MIA to map out a plan to reinvent himself. He was sick and tired of being the nice, polite, shy, twenty-four-year-old man with the brilliant career on fast-track and absolutely no social life whatsoever. His life's lesson in Stockholm had toughened him up and had given him a new edge. He vowed to get on with his life, find a nice black girl, get married, and settle down. The single man-about-town scene was not for him. He had grabbed a notepad, tipped his chair back, got his feet up, and began to evaluate the almost-over year of 1974.

His first two questions on his notepad stared back at him, demanding his attention over the next two days. They asked:

"Who am I, and what do I want? Fuck the roles that I play. Just who am I?"

"What is my sense of purpose? Who am I and what do I want?"

Spring arrived, and recognizing that Saul and his mother were getting on in years, he had an apartment built over Saul's garage. He had hired a young immigrant couple from Vietnam to live there. The husband, Chi, took care of the cars and gardens, and the wife, Nuyen, took care of the housework and cooking. It wasn't long before they were pregnant, and Saul and his mama had a new lease on life. It was a perfect fit for all of them. The gardener husband and his pregnant housekeeper wife lived in the apartment over the garage. Saul, now a widower, lived in the big house, and his mama, now semi-retired but still on Saul's payroll, continued to live in the apartment behind the back stairs where he had grown up. He had felt a little guilty on leaving home when he had bought his condo downtown, and this was the perfect solution that eased the guilt that only-children carry when they leave the doting, lonely parents behind.

His thoughtful duties as a son were completed in a timely matter, but the plan to find a nice black girl and settle down would take a lot longer than he ever anticipated.

***

Chapter 2
My Day in Court

I arrived early, and I settled in up front at the plaintiff's table in the near-empty courtroom. Today, Tuesday, June 15, 2004, was my big day. Ms. Denise Allen, plaintiff, had a good ring to it. The battle was over, and I was here today just to hear the final gavel go down in my favor. It had been a long haul, and I was so happy to be done with this sad and sorry state of affairs. After all, it was a court case, and that in itself denoted that all was not well, but I was proud of my work done and the outcome of it.

I had always had a fairly good moral compass, and as crazy as it all sounded to many of my friends, I couldn't drop it that my sister, who was the executor of Mom's estate, was not willing to give me a copy of the will or to share the proceeds of the estate with me.

The only thing I had from my family life was a handful of old photographs that Dad had given me before he died many years ago and a triple-strand of pearls that I had by default. Mom had begrudgingly loaned them to me years ago to wear to a function, and I had simply forgotten to give them back to her. So, I had to sue my sister to get a copy of the will and find out what had happened to Mom's money and corresponding 'personality,' as the court called it. I called it her jewelry and *tchotchkes*. I simply had to persevere through the court process in order to see that my mother's will and my father's legacy was wrapped up in a dignified manner instead of it being swept under the rug like a pile of dirt.

Now it was time to get on with my life – time to take care of myself. I wasn't getting any younger, and I had faced the music a couple of years before when I turned the big forty that I had to take care of myself, as there was simply no one out there that was going to do it for me.

I arranged my notes in front of me. I had carefully handwritten one of my favorite sayings by Alex Colville, one of Canada's master painters, on the top of the first page in bold, red ink:

I choose to think of things as beginning rather than ending.

I had planned on using this if and when the judge offered me the chance to add a final remark after he gave his verdict. The saying was, on one hand, uplifting, but on the other hand, it intimated that I was ready with a change of heart to start anew with my younger sister. Or was I?

Glancing at my watch, I reached into my briefcase and took out my small red leather notebook that I carried everywhere. I smoothed out a few of the dog-eared pages in the well-thumbed ragtag journal, turned to a fresh page, and sketched a rectangular box and neatly printed inside it:

How Did I Get to Where I Am Now?

I had spent my whole life just knocking around, pulling up, and moving on when the going got tough because of either a man in my life or the lack of one. It was time to put down some real roots. I had had a nice apartment in the city for over a year now, and it felt like home to me. It was time I put my footloose and fancy-free days behind me.

My small settlement from my second marriage along with my instructional design and curriculum contract business kept me afloat, and I had done okay with flipping houses and condos as I floated around from place to place. I had left teaching English as a second language a few years earlier, and developing curriculum for the school board was not grabbing my attention like it used to. I was toying with the idea of writing a novel. Yeah, I would pen a big, sprawling saga. I had thought of using this court settlement to finance me over the next two years.

Yes indeed, I had written about losing my sense of purpose in my court documents, and it was time to map out a new one. I printed out in my red notebook both the questions and the answers:

Who Am I? I am God's child.
How to live? No fear, no anger, no enemies, no conflict.
Life's lesson: There is no coincidence – ever.
Changes necessary: Change your thoughts; change your life.
Going forward: Forget the past. Move forward.
Acceptance: Acceptance is the key.
What to do with my life? Tell my stories; write a novel.
How to do it? Just get on with it and stop procrastinating.

'Am I up to the task?' I asked myself.

My thoughts were interrupted with, "The court will come to order. All stand."

I stood and deliberately chose to ignore my sister, who had quietly taken her place in the defendant's chair, to the left of me. I focused on the door at the front of the courtroom, casually wondering if the judge would be a male or female.

My heart stopped and then started back up again, pounding madly right out of my chest. It was him! The handsome man from the café! It was him, only this time he was presenting in the court robes of an officiating judge! One and the same! The man that took one on the chin as I hastily rose from the floor only to collide literally head-on with him! Oh my God! Could it be?

I stared, not allowing myself to blink in case it was just a dream. I followed his every step forward into the courtroom as he solemnly scanned the rows of seats in front of him. It was him! As he gazed over to my side of the courtroom, in less than a millisecond, I witnessed some unknown horror registering over his face, and then all of a sudden, he disappeared behind the raised witness box that stood on the right side of his elevated desk and chair.

A court clerk, her eye on the judge, quickly disappeared along with him. What had happened?

I craned my neck to see and was rewarded a minute later as the court clerk stood up, both hands full of papers that the judge had obviously dropped while he was surveying his courtroom.

He rose from behind the witness box, also holding his file folder in one hand and loose papers in the other. But it was definitely him. Maybe he had tripped over his cane which was nowhere in sight.

The judge settled in his chair, and the court clerk shouted a loud, "Please be seated!" We sat.

He avoided looking at me as he addressed the courtroom in a deep baritone, "Sorry, folks. I am so clumsy. Please grant me a minute or two to sort things out here."

It was all over within thirty minutes. I had the opportunity to speak at the end of the case, as I had anticipated. I rose and spoke, looking directly at the judge who had chosen not to register any recognition of me or our doomed previous encounter throughout the whole proceeding. He kept his eyes down as he listened to me.

Feeling the sting of the judge's obvious rejection of our first shy meeting was slowly and painfully registering in my heart. I spat out my prepared words, unable to offer any softness or condolence to my sister throughout my delivery. 'What kind of idiot is he?' I answered my own question with, 'A handsome, heartbreaker idiot. That's what kind of idiot he is.'

"Court adjourned. All stand."

We stood.

The court clerk waived me over to the side of the courtroom. "Ms. Allen, the judge would like to see you in chambers in fifteen minutes."

"Absolutely," I responded as I made my way to the women's bathroom.

I refreshed my lipstick, adjusted my jacket, smoothed down my black pencil skirt, and purposely undid the top three buttons of my white shirt. I tucked it down tight into my skirt to show him my best assets. Throwing my shoulders back, I sauntered forward to chambers' closed door.

I wasn't about to give him a second chance to forget me so easily.

Chambers was a small, almost-empty room, with dark, paneled walls and barely furnished. There was a narrow table in the middle of the room. To encourage a meeting of the minds, I supposed. I took a seat on one side of the table and breathed slowly and deeply to prepare for meeting the handsome supreme court justice face to face.

The inner chamber door swung open, and he strode in, no cane in sight. I took in a deep breath to calm myself.

He had taken off his courtroom robes, so I didn't stand when he entered the room. He wore a dark blue suit with a very faint Tattersall check, white shirt, and traditional red silk power tie. And he wore the ensemble extremely well. He was definitely older than me, hovering around middle-age but with a smooth, pampered look. Yes, middle-aged eye candy, and I promptly marked him as a ten out of ten on the sex-appeal scale.

After his graceful entrance, he took a chair in his big brown hand and smoothly pulled himself up to the table. Offering his handshake casually over the table, he introduced himself simply as Nigel Royal.

I responded with a very brief, "Hello. Denise. My friends call me Denni." I left it at that, as I was taken aback with his scent. Could it possibly be? Could this sophisticated man be wearing my dad's old-fashioned Yardley's Old Spice? No, I must be mistaken. They didn't even make it anymore, did they? All I knew for sure was that my heart stopped for a minute when my nose caught that first whiff from my childhood that I hadn't smelled for over twenty years. It was like Dad was right there looking over me, making sure I was okay.

He laid out his agenda in a couple of sentences, "Ms. Allen, I asked for your time in chambers this morning in order to congratulate you on your well-prepared case. It was actually a first for me. I've never dealt with an estate which was brilliantly based on what you called the 'love document' that outlined your mother's last will and testament and your father's legacy of equality and inclusivity. And you claimed your loss was not based on the financials; it was based on your loss of your sense of purpose. If we look at the pleading in a deeper sense, it demonstrates that your ethical and moral values are deeply ingrained in your persona. Perhaps we can attribute that to your late parents. So, kudos to you for a job well done!"

"Thank you!" I said. I was a little taken aback with his personal opinion of my ethics and morality. He definitely had skills for reading between the lines.

He continued, "Although the court cannot do anything about your broken family, I hope you are happy with the financial settlement that the court has awarded to you."

"Well, your Honor, you are exactly right about the broken family part of the case, but I put that all behind me last year, right after my mother died. However, I'm sorry, but I have to argue your other point about the court awarding me the financial settlement."

"Oh?" His eyebrows shot up, and he sounded surprised. "Do you mean you think you should have been awarded more?"

"No. Not at all. It's my opinion that the Canadian Supreme Court of Canada didn't award the settlement to me. My settlement comes straight from the law of divine compensation. As we both know, the law of the universe is self-correcting, and this material manifestation is simply payment for me upholding my parents' loving wishes."

His eyes widened even more with my response, and there was a brief second before he threw his head back and erupted into laughter. "Well done, counselor, well done!"

I couldn't help but disarm, as his nearness melted away the perceived slight I had suffered as I sat in the plaintiff's chair thirty minutes earlier. I told myself that perhaps he actually hadn't recognized me as the idiot in the café the week beforehand. His close proximity coaxed me to give him the benefit of the doubt.

He continued on in his deep baritone, pointing out pertinent parts of my side of the case that in his opinion were particularly well done. His friendly manner put me at ease, and I found myself joining in, enjoying the small talk that took place between the two of us.

As we maneuvered the delicate dance of conversation between two introverts living in an extroverted world, my confidence grew as I confirmed to myself that yes, a spark between us had initiated during that first clumsy meeting whether he remembered it or not. This was beginning to be world-class interesting. We seemed to be in sync as he did most of the talking, and I did most of the listening. His presence wasn't what I'd call intimidating, but I could see that he was used to being the person in control of the situation.

Either that or he had prepared well.

He brought his courtroom voice down to an intimate level as if to share his theory of some sort of a developing conspiracy. He leaned in. His smiling deep brown eyes and his handsome brown face with the faint outline of a large hooked scar on his left cheek met my fluttering, curled, and tinted eyelashes head-on.

"I feel, Ms. Allen, that it's your time to forget the old and shine with a brilliant, brand-new sense of purpose."

"Yes, Your Honor," I smiled as I mirrored him with an ever-so-slight lean in to meet his encouragement and growing interest in my wellbeing. I tilted my head down and lifted my eyes to meet his. "Actually, I think I feel one coming on."

His beautiful, dark brown eyes held mine, and I noticed his face was beginning to flush. He straightened up a little to pull away from the heat and lifted both big, brown, well-manicured hands up and then down, giving the table a resounding slap.

I instinctively knew that my little response had forced him to forge ahead with his carefully mapped-out plan of action.

I too sat back and drew in a slow breath and held it in anticipation – his move.

"How about lunch next week? We can discuss your options," he said as he took back control of the events that were playing out. "Let's say Ruth's Chris Steak House on Tuesday, the 22nd?"

"Perfect plan, your Honor." I smiled as I stood up.

He rose to stand up, as old-school etiquette demands, before I was out of my seat.

"May I send a car to pick you up?"

I detected a slight hint of eagerness in his polite ask, and I quickly snatched back the control that was obviously up for grabs between the two of us.

"No need. I know the place. It's on Richmond, near Queen. I'll meet you there at twelve o'clock." I wanted to show him that I was just as much of a player as he was. I sauntered toward the door, knowing that he would have his eyes on what my mama gave me.

"Have a wonderful day, Ms. Allen. I'm looking forward to next Tuesday."

"Likewise, your Honor."

As I closed the door softly, I allowed myself a last quick look at him as he sat back in his chair. I noticed he looked a little flustered. 'No more than me,' I thought to myself. I hoped to hell that I had played my cards right. 'This may be a very interesting luncheon ahead,' I mused. But really? An old-fashioned steakhouse? That's where the old powerhouses take their old cronies for lunch. Maybe I had read him wrong. A warning bell went off in my head that he may be a bit of a controller. Well, buster, not with this girl. Been there, done that, and it's not my scene. I re-buttoned my shirt and headed toward the elevator.

I just had to get home to peace and quiet to revel in my courtroom success but also to digest the game-changing news that the universe had tossed my way. The tall, dark, and handsome stranger in the café last week was not a stranger any longer. And according to the way he played the conversation, he didn't recognize me as the shy, clumsy girl in the café the week before. '*Hallelujah*, there is a God! How could this possibly be happening to little old me?' I asked myself.

There was one small, niggling thought that I wasn't really ready to consider yet. It was his scent. I'm a sucker for a man's scent, and I picked it up loud and clear when he swooshed the door open and shut as he came into chambers while I was sitting down waiting for him in the small room. I hadn't smelled that scent for many, many years. It had immediately swept over my heart like a warm blanket on a chilly evening – Yardley's Old Spice. 'Oh, Dad, I miss you,' I thought to myself. Was I prepared to factor that kind of sentiment into the upcoming luncheon? I nervously put the thought aside. My past told me that I didn't fare well when it came to affairs of the heart. Sex, yes. Bring it on. But love, well, no, that was a different matter altogether.

'Oh, note to self,' I thought. 'I must ask him about the scar on his cheek. I bet that's a story and a half.'

***

The court clerk tapped on the door twice and began to open it slowly.

"Not now, Jessica," his baritone boomed. "Thank you, though. I'll close up when I leave."

He sat there alone, leaning back on the small chair in front of the empty table. His shirt was wet all the way down his back and his chest too as he loosened the red silk tie.

'Now this is going to take some planning. This girl that presented today with the beautiful gray eyes is much, much more complicated than the same girl that I watched in the café. There was a definite wariness behind the witty repartee. Smart. And savvy. Yes, as smart as a whip,' the judge thought to himself. He reached into the inside pocket of his made-to-measure suit and pulled out a slim, black leather notebook with gold letters of '*N.R.*' embossed in the lower right-hand corner. A pen was clipped over the front cover. He double-clicked and began to jot down his main points that would help him define the woman who had just left the building.

1. Intelligent – hell yes
2. Honest – yes
3. Street-smart – definitely
4. Motivated by money – no
5. Free spirit – absolutely
6. Vulnerable – too early to tell
7. Interesting – very
8. Interested – yes
9. Beautiful – in spades
10. Sexy – indisputably
11. Drama Queen – tamped down but yes
12. Seeking emotional intimacy – if so, buried deep with issues
13. Worth the effort – no question
14. Scale of one to ten – eleven

He looked through his phone to find the number and tapped it.

"Good morning, Ruth's Chris Steak House. My name is Gerard. How may I help you?"

"And good morning back to you, Gerard. My name is Nigel Royal," his voice boomed, "and I'd like to reserve your very best table for two, set a little apart so that I can enjoy a private conversation away from the bustle of your busy dining room, next Tuesday, at noon sharp."

"Oh! It's you, Mr. Royal! It's a pleasure to hear your voice! We haven't had the pleasure in the last little while. Absolutely, and we look forward to serving you and your guest next Tuesday, at noon sharp. Would you like the chef to prepare a special meal for the two of you?"

"No, we will order from the menu, but thank you. Oh, of course, the menu without the prices printed on it for the lady, right?"

"Of course, Mr. Royal. Will there be anything else?"

"I think we've got it under control, Gerard. And thank you."

He stood up while tucking his phone in his jacket's inner pocket and deftly shut off the lights before closing chambers' door behind him, half-whistling and half-singing the old Temptations' song, *Get Ready Here I Come* all the way to the elevator.

***

The next Tuesday, I entered the cool, dark, well-established steakhouse a few minutes after noon and announced to the *Maître d'* that I was expected at Nigel Royal's table.

'Had I put on too much perfume?' I fussed to myself as he ushered me through the restaurant, down to the table in a quiet corner.

Nigel, looking as handsome as ever in a dark blue summer weight suit with a white shirt and blue and pink paisley tie, rose from his chair to greet me as the *Maître d'* pulled out mine.

In order to avoid my characteristic clumsiness, I walked up close to my date. I was inches away from his chest as I realized that I was right last week when I noted that his scent was the old-fashioned, out-of-date Yardley's Old Spice. I lifted my face and tilted my head to the side in a confident, age-old manner to allow him a small kiss on my cheek.

***

Nigel Royal, on his first date in many years, complied with the woman's sophisticated gesture. As he tilted his head down to kiss her cheek, he instinctively breathed her in slowly. His little brain was telling him to linger, and his big brain was telling him that he was a damn old fool and to sit down. He knew better than to tempt fate, especially with her. He waited until she was seated and without taking his eyes off her, he sat down safely, without incident.

***

Two tall glasses of ice water with lemon appeared, and after Nigel leaned over and asked my preference to red or white, he ordered a bottle of *Châteauneuf du Pape*, vintage 1995, without looking at the wine menu.

We settled into easy conversation, and I simply could not keep my eyes away from his. His lowered baritone voice purred on, explaining that his life's work was complicated by his unpopular idea that the court should change parts of the system rather than trying to change the people. And he had just accepted a publisher's offer to write his memoirs of his time spent serving the court as a supreme court justice.

"It's actually a sobering look as I look back through all the cases, Denise – may I call you Denni?" He continued with my quick nod, "It seems that our big, sprawling country, and especially our city, is slowly but surely showing that we are well on our way to keeping up with other big cities in terms of crime stats. And to top it all off, the world of the petty thief is shrinking, and the world of sophisticated cartels and mafia-type crime is growing," he paused, taking his wine glass in hand.

"But enough about business! I'm sure you don't want to hear about the woes of a retired justice man."

He raised his glass slightly and his baritone softened, "Here's to the beautiful gray eyes that are making me forget mid-sentence what I'm saying."

"Well!" I smiled, "thank you. And I want to return the toast to welcome you into the world of writing. So, you're going to write your memoirs! It's a tough go, but I have a feeling that you're up to the task. May I ask, though, aren't you a little young to be retiring?"

"Flattery will get you everywhere," he laughed. "Damn, I can feel my face flushing with all this attention." He turned to look away, still laughing, putting one big hand up to his cheek that was indeed a little pink under his closely shaved profile.

I relished this face-to-face time, and I came to the conclusion that his killer looks were a mix of the dark black, thick brows and the corresponding graying-just-a-little Afro hair that he wore a little longer and fuller than most men his age. His natural, spikey curls and waves spiraled up into perfectly messy, sexy unison. It looked like his hair guy had applied some kind of double-process dark lowlights to accent the gray, wiry spirals. The end effect was a perfect execution of what the salons call a 'loose and casual' look. I wondered if they also promoted the new 'silent haircut' that so many introverts were clamoring to sign up for. My luncheon date certainly didn't appear as the chatty, gossipy kind of guy that shared his every move with his hairdresser. His tan-colored skin and his narrow, straight, and aristocratic-looking nose could be a biracial thing. His look, in some ways, was similar to Canadians from the Nova Scotian Africville community where the Native Canadians, *Métis*, and the French had intermarried with the black population that had resulted in exceptionally good-looking children. As I continued to listen to his Canadian-accented deep baritone, I still had no idea as to his heritage.

As if reading my mind, he asked, "So I'm thinking that your beautiful pale skin and brunette hair originates from say, Ireland? Am I wrong?"

"Well, yes and no is the answer to your question, Nigel. You see, I just got my Ancestry.ca kit back, and I was so surprised at the outcome. It turns out that my paternal earliest male gene is marked and registered as coming from Iraq, of all places, where this Middle-Eastern man traveled to hook up with a female gene who was part of the original Celtic tribe living in Germany. On my mother's side, my genes originated in Norway, who met their match when they hooked up with the native Pics in Scotland in the year eight-hundred-something. So yes, Dad's side immigrated to Canada as farmers from Ireland in 1840. Been here ever since. To make a long story short, Dad's from Ireland and Mom's from Scotland. How about you? Were you born in Canada too?"

Nigel proceeded to tell a simplified version of his story, starting with an early childhood spent in rural Jamaica and immigrating to Canada at the age nine to live with his mother who was a housekeeper to a very kind and benevolent employer, namely, Saul Himmel. He had lived in the small apartment with his mother, which was behind the main house located on Russell Hill Road.

He continued the story, telling the tale of being taken under Saul's wing. His first attempt at public school did not go well, he said. He explained that it was 1959, and his brown skin and Jamaican accent was a high hurdle for the predominantly Jewish upper-income neighborhood school to accept.

After struggling to fit in during his first year, Saul took the matter in hand and had registered him in private school. St. Michael's College School was located a short walk from the big house on Russell Hill Road. It was all easy-peasy for the young immigrant from there on. He wrapped it up at University of Toronto, wrote his bar exam, and never looked back.

"I owe my whole happy existence to Saul. He was my father-figure, and there isn't a day when I don't think back to all the love and kindness that he bestowed upon me," he said quietly.

"But never mind my sentimental story," he said, brightening up. "I had thought perhaps you were of Irish descent. You see, I watched you as you entered the restaurant. I summed you up as a beautiful brunette, a delicate flower daintily walking toward me in a perfect, girly-girl pink silk dress. Turns out you are a true-blue Scots-Irish Canadian femme fatale. The fiery Scots and the poetic Irish, all wrapped in one beautiful package. I hereby acknowledge that I have been forewarned," he said with his smile reaching from side to side.

I looked down at my plate, shaking my head in silent protest. I wasn't used to this admiring, intense scrutiny, and my shyness forced me to turn the conversation back his way.

"However, you missed out on a little detail that I'm curious about, Nigel," I ventured on. "May I ask what happened here?" I said, motioning to my cheek and outlining a hook with my finger.

"Oh, that," he grinned. "Nah, that's nothin'," he said as his left hand rose to his face to acknowledge the old scar. "You should see the other guy."

I laughed, delighted with his charming rendition of the old joke, and I noticed he was soaking up every little bit of my approval. Hmm, maybe he wasn't a controller after all. Could it be that he was a pleaser? A man in his position? And at his age? A rare combination if it was the case. Probably it was just his shyness.

I continued in the same vein, "Okay, okay, so I'll never know about that, but there is something I really want to know. I've noticed that your manicure is better than mine! I'm jealous! Where do you get your nails done? No, no, don't try to put me off! I'm complimenting you on your beautiful nails! I'm serious!" I said, laughing as his face colored up again with my close observation.

"You're the first person ever to ask me that one, I must admit. And I will tell you my little secret if I must. I go to the Elmwood Spa, you know, near Yonge Street," he motioned with his hand in the direction of the street. "If I happen to splurge for a massage, they throw in a free manicure. They treat me like a king, and I've gotten used to it."

"Oh! So! You're gay!"

"Court's out of order! Out of order! Enough out of you, Ms. Brunette!"

As we both settled down from our kibitzing, his face became sober, and he looked straight into my face. "All joking aside, Denni, I have a confession to make."

"Oh, and what would that be, Nigel?" I said lightly, trying to keep hold of the playful banter that had graced over us the whole time. Instantly, my wife-radar came into play. 'No, no, no, please tell me there isn't a wife to be factored into this fairytale,' I silently pleaded to the Gods above.

"I'm so sorry for not acknowledging our awkward first encounter that happened a week ago in the Aroma Espresso Café," he said contritely. "When I saw you in the courtroom, I couldn't believe my eyes. I had made such a fool of myself in the café in front of you and my humiliation and embarrassment just took over as I saw you, the girl with the glorious brunette hair and the beautiful gray eyes staring out at me from the plaintiff's chair. I was so shocked that I dropped my file, and I just couldn't look at you during the whole time, as I was so rattled. I was acting like a clumsy teenager, and to complicate matters even further, I'm a fairly shy person who lives a fairly solitary lifestyle. I just couldn't recover with you sitting right there before me in the courtroom. Forgive me."

He offered his big hand over the table, and I responded with mine. He took my hand in both of his and raised it to his lips.

I said softly, "Silly you. Absolutely nothing to forgive. And just to let you know, I too live alone and have had to learn to enjoy my own company over all the years. But think about it; we are both currently working in the very solitary world of writing. No wonder I find myself talking to the television!" I laughed. "Honestly, though, it takes its toll, doesn't it?"

He nodded in a silent agreement, and I raised my glass.

"Here's to fated encounters."

He beamed, "Fated encounters indeed!"

I quickly changed my tune to end the intimacy that was now at a crazy, dangerous level. It made me feel panicky. I just couldn't handle it. "Oh my, I just realized we haven't even looked at the menu. I'm absolutely starved!" I said briskly. "What's your absolute fave here?"

I didn't know if he was just ordering the same as me or if I was just following his lead. We both had the chop salad, the petite filets, although I ordered mine with classic béarnaise sauce and he opted for the tangy Cajun served on the side. I shared my Brussels sprouts with him and he traded back with some of his asparagus. It was like we had been doing this for years. After the long, delicious entrée, I found myself just nodding my head no to the dessert menu, not wanting to break the conversation we were in. He didn't look at the menu either. He simply ordered one serving of plain chocolate ice cream with two spoons.

"Would you like coffee, or maybe a tea, Denni?"

"I'd love just a plain black tea with lemon, please. Nigel, speaking of things to drink, I must tell you that you've impressed me with your choice of *Châteauneuf du pape*. Do you know that region of France or are you schooled as a sommelier or something?"

"Oh no, I'm no expert. That's for sure. But to answer your question directly, I have spent a little time in the south of France with my brother and his wife who are in the wine business. Sort of. Not really. What about you? Do you have a favorite wine?"

I looked at him while mulling over his modest answer. Anyone that knew how to order a 1995 bottle of vintage wine like that was definitely lying straight to my face about his sophisticated choice. Perhaps he was accustomed to wining and dining lots of ladies about town. Or was it simply his modesty or shyness that had caused his downplayed explanation?

I responded with, "I don't know much about wines. I do know that I like red better than white. The only reason that I recognized your *Châteauneuf du pape*, is because one time, many years ago, I was on a train heading to Avignon, and I met a nice young man whose family owned that particular type of vineyard near la Ville d'Orange. We met up a few weeks later at his vineyard, and he and his young wife had me sampling all their vintages right out of their old oak barrels. So, it's become my favorite over the years. It's simply out of my price range. That's for sure. You know how it is."

He was grinning from ear to ear as he leaned over the table and said softly, "So, does that mean you're in the poorhouse?"

I knew that he was well aware of my recent inheritance from my mother's estate and that he was just teasing me. I continued to stare him down with a straight face and I retorted, "So does that mean that you're rich?"

He threw back his head and tried his best to tone down his big baritone as he laughed with delight at my saucy response.

"*Touché.* I'm teasing you. And I must add, I'm not surprised in the least that you are well aware that I was just showing off with my wine choice. I was trying my hardest to impress you. I find out now that you're not an easy target for my bad manners. But really, Denni, I'm just a shy, humble kind of guy."

"Yeah. Sure. The Honorable Nigel Royal is shy and humble. Still just a little country boy from rural Jamaica. And you bought that suit on sale, right off the discount rack at Sears, right?"

"I'll have you know that I bought my suit at the same place you bought that pink silk ladies-who-lunch dress that fits you so well."

I was laughing at his compliment and I conceded the point, "Okay, okay, you win. Have it your way. So now we know that we are both shy and that we both come from humble, rural beginnings."

"And you, my dear, tend to shop at Holt Renfrew's flagship store on Bloor Street."

"But wait, wait. Think about it. Although we both live in the big city, we were both born and spent our childhoods in the country, you in rural Jamaica, and me on an old farm just north of Toronto. Is it possible that we're both just country bumpkins dressed up in fancy clothes? We can't forget where we came from, can we?"

He smiled and leaned over the table a little and said, "Right at this very moment, Ms. Brunette, I'm enjoying living in the moment. Let's leave the past for another time."

"You're absolutely right, Nigel. The past is definitely a big, fat waste of time. There's no time like the present."

The tea arrived, and I said, "You mentioned that you have been to the south of France a few times. Do you like to travel?" I asked.

"Yes and no. The yes part of my answer is that I love to travel to see the world, especially the big urban centers like New York and London. However, to tell you the honest truth, my problem is that I'm a single, nerdy type of man, and traveling solo tends to be just too lonely for me. And I find that casual conversation is not one of my strengths either. So, I end up staying at home, reading my law books, taking notes down, all in my own little comfort zone."

He broke his sensitive admission as he reached into his inside suit pocket. He brought out a small, black leather notebook and held it up for me to see. "Just look at me. I like to document everything. It's crazy. I'm such an observer that meanwhile, life just passes me by! I can safely say that right after dinner tonight, I will be in my home office, detailing the red wine and meal we've had today like it is the most important document I have ever written." He laughed a little ruefully as he put the notebook back into his suit.

I was taken aback with his sensitive and personal admission. Oh my, he really was shy and humble, and totally honest. "I hear you," I said softly. "Although it seems I do have gypsy blood in me and I've lived out of a suitcase my whole adult life knocking around from place to place, I feel that loneliness too. But I find that it tends to be less lonely in the big urban centers where you can just meld into the crowds somehow," I continued, trying to summarize and close the intimate talk that was getting way, way too close to home for comfort. "I've got a brilliant solution for you! You should just go online and find a travel companion!"

He gave me an *Are-you-out-of-your-mind look* and said, "Denni, there isn't enough of our favorite wine barreled in the whole of France to get me to that point."

"That's just my weird sense of humor coming through. Me too, I just can't muster up the courage to venture into that world. But if you don't mind, I have a question for you regarding your little black notebook, and what you are going to be writing in it tonight."

"Shoot."

"Am I going to be in it?"

"Yeah. Five words."

"Being?"

"Be afraid. Be very afraid."

I laughed at his clever little quip and sat back in my chair to assess the current situation. I found myself thinking about that old country song with the message that girls get prettier around closing time. Nigel Royal was getting cuter and sweeter and more adorable by the moment. I mentally rewound the conversation back a paragraph or two. 'He had said, *OUR favorite wine.* As in not just him, but him and me together, as in a couple. Oh, my God. Pinch me. Just pinch me.'

The afternoon whiled away as we continued our nuanced, back-and-forth information-seeking as well as gathering. He seemed very eager to find all common ground that could possibly lead us to continuing this newfound friendship. I simply couldn't believe my luck and kept pinching myself (figuratively) to ensure that this was really, really happening.

He continued on to tell me the story behind his ill-fated cane that he had been sporting at the café the week before. He had suffered from a sciatica attack which was under control now, but he was starting a new exercise regime which included a prescribed daily evening walk around the neighborhood to protect against another attack. He wondered if I would like to join him.

I agreed wholeheartedly to join in, to help whip him back into shape.

He explained that his young teenaged nephew, along with a friend, was staying with him for a couple of weeks. Although they were no trouble at all, it required a little background supervision, as the two boys had gladly taken over the guest quarters' apartment in the basement and were reveling in their freedom, away from the parents and their rules and restrictions.

I smiled at the affection in his voice as he continued the conversation, "I'll tell you what. We'll start the exercise regime tomorrow evening at 7:30 p.m. Just ring my doorbell, and I'll be ready to go. Oh no, no, change of plans," he quickly interjected upon himself. "Why don't you come in for a moment, on our way out for the walk, as I want the boys to meet you? I mean it's not every day I have a beautiful woman knocking on my door to drag me out for some exercise."

"You're on, babysitter extraordinaire. But first you have to give me your address. You mentioned you live on Russell Hill Road, but I haven't had the urge to stalk you from behind your privacy hedge yet, so I need all the details."

"I'm at Number Seven, 7 Russell Hill Road."

"Oh yes, I think I can find it, thanks. So yes, we're on for 7:30. I'll have my brand-new Nike trainers on, and I plan on leaving you in the dust."

"Now, now. Don't count me out just yet. I'll get some pointers from the boys to keep up with you."

As I sat there, going back to his address, I thought, 'That's strange. I think that's my favorite house on that block. Does this mean that my newly found Mr. Wonderful has been right there under my nose through all those lonely walks by myself?'

We continued on in our own little bubble, completely unaware of what was stirring up at the front of the restaurant.

"No! No way!" the experienced waiter argued with the *Maître d'*, "I know Mr. Royal, and he's a very big tipper. He's cool, man. He's totally into this chick, and she's hanging on to every one of his words like there's no tomorrow. He usually comes here with an Asian guy. I always thought he was gay. If you think I'm going to break up his little rendezvous just so you can set up for the early dinner crowd, you've got another thing coming. Aw, come on, man, give the old man a break."

The *maître d'* threw up his hands and rolled his eyes. He had to admit that he too was a sucker for romance.

At the end of our luncheon, he signaled to the wait staff and then eased out from behind the small table, rather close to where I was still sitting. For the second before the waiter had a chance to pull out my chair for me to rise, my eyes rested on the huge bulge pushing out of the front of his pants. I couldn't help it as my eyes widened at the situation presenting itself to me, directly at eyelevel. As the waiter silently pulled out my chair, I met the occasion by boldly standing up straight, right in front of Nigel. I looked up into his face and paused just to let him know that I was ladylike enough to pretend I hadn't noticed his erection.

I had no idea if he was aware that I was aware. We stood there, eyes locked in the moment, both intent on playing our best game forward.

As the not-so-subtle game of who blinks first stretched out, we just stood there silently, holding our ground, both of us unable to pull ourselves away from the heat. The two of us could have burned Ruth's Chris Steak House down to the ground. It was definitely time to get out of Dodge.

It had been a long, long time since I had been interested in a man that much. By the size of his arousal, I surmised he felt the same way about me. I also had no idea that he was about to be very aware of another telltale sign of what was really happening over the polite and charming luncheon that we had shared.

As I sashayed in front of him through the now-empty restaurant toward the door, he had seized the moment to check out my curves as he followed me from behind. His eyes roamed and then rested on an unladylike wet-spot that was beginning to seep through the ass of my demure pale pink dress. My naughty 'lady-bits' excitement that had been brought on by this handsome, very sexy man had unfortunately soaked through my skimpy panty, allowing him to see how I really felt about him.

***

As we stood out in the late afternoon's summer heat, he hailed a cab for me, explaining that he had a little business to take care of and would I mind traveling home solo. Opening the backdoor of the cab for me, he leaned close to kiss me on my cheek. His lips were very soft and very warm, and he prolonged the tender touch just a little longer than necessary. "Gotta find out the name of that fragrance," he whispered to himself, just loud enough to make sure I heard his little compliment.

It was the killer punch to a four-hour round. I couldn't even speak. He slipped the cabbie some folded bills and stepped away.

I leaned back and closed my eyes to gather my wits.

***

I put the phone to my ear, with eyes still closed, covers still way up over my shoulders, and his booming voice answered my soft and sleepy good morning.

"Did I wake you, Ms. Brunette?"

"No, of course not," I lied, "but I bet you're standing there still in your pj's, aren't you? However, besides that, I'm glad to hear your voice. About yesterday's luncheon."

"Yes?" he sounded a little anxious.

"I just wanted to tell you how much I enjoyed your company yesterday over lunch. It was a delightful afternoon, and it was all because of you and your thoughtful ways. Thank you."

"Oh," he laughed, definitely sounding relieved, "I thought for a moment you had had second thoughts about our seven-thirty date for tonight! Whew, dodged a bullet!"

"Now, really. I gave you my word. Who else is going to be willing to coax and cajole you around the block with your new exercise regime? It's a tough job, but I'm determined to see the job through to the bitter end. And yes, to confirm, I'll see you at 7:30."

"I can't wait. *Ciao*, Denni Allen."

"*Ciao* back to you, Nigel Royal, and meanwhile, you'd better limber up for what's to come," I playfully admonished.

"What's to come indeed!" and the laughing baritone ended the conversation with, "I'm shaking in my boots!"

That afternoon, my buzzer rang, and I waited at the door for the delivery. It was a beautiful floral arrangement, not the usual traditional hothouse roses, no, not at all. The exquisite bouquet was a glorious mix of perfectly unpretentious field flowers. There were delicate blue forget-me-nots, yellow daisies, snap-dragons, blue-bells, and white lilies-of-the-valley with roots, shoots, and grasses among the rest of the colorful flowers. They were all sturdily set into a round, moss-covered, hand-thrown piece of blue-gray pottery.

The card had been handwritten. He had used a fountain pen that was loaded with purple ink.

The card read, *Flowers for a country girl.* It was signed, *A country boy.*

***

Chapter 3

Houseguests

After a sleepless night after the luncheon date, reliving every word of every sentence over and over in my mind and admiring my flowers every five minutes, I rang the doorbell at 7 Russell Hill Road at 7:30 sharp. I noticed an old mezuzah on the door's millwork, and I wondered if Nigel was a Jew.

I carefully stepped back a little so that I could either go forward into the house if he invited me or back down safely if he trotted out all ready to go without knocking either of us over in the process. I didn't want to repeat the mistakes made in the café.

The door opened and two teenage boys gave me a very obvious onceover from the top of my head to the bottom of my new trainers.

The one with the Asian face was first to stick out his hand. "Hello, I'm Uncle Nigel's nephew. My name is Madison. Please come in." He nudged the other to remember his manners. An intense-looking boy with white skin, blue eyes, and a shock of long black hair extended his hand and said simply, *"Je m'appelle Stéphane. Entré vous, si'l vous plaît."*

"Merci," I offered. "Good to meet you two. My name is Denise, or Denni, whatever you prefer. I'm here to coax your uncle out for a walk around the block. Actually, I'm going to challenge him to a race, and I intend to beat the pants off him."

The two boys started laughing and telling me that their Uncle Nigel was too old to be running out and around the neighborhood. They advised me to take it easy on the old guy.

At that point, Mr. Wonderful appeared, looking as handsome as ever in gray sweats and a dark blue tee-shirt that was a little tight across his pecs. He gave me a quick kiss on the cheek as he said hello. He was laced up and ready to go but not before he shadow-boxed around Madison, who seemed to be used to the affectionate horseplay.

As we hit the sidewalk, he gave me the basic outline of the three kilometers' walk that he had mapped out, and we were off to a good start.

Once again, he did most of the talking, and I followed with most of the listening. It seemed to me that he was the type of man to plan everything out carefully beforehand to cover for his shyness. 'Oh yes, I can understand that completely,' I mused as I looked back and remembered how many outfits I had tried on and how many talking points I had mulled over just to be able to get up the courage to ring his doorbell earlier that evening.

"I'm curious as to the Asian connection in your family," I prompted.

"Oh yes, we have that look of a typical Canadian mishmash of race and color, don't we? Once you meet the rest of the family, you will really be confused. You see, Madison isn't the only Asian face we have in the family. You haven't met Chi yet. Chi is my old friend, and he lives over the garage. Been there for over thirty years now. His wife Nguyen died a few years back, but they had a son, François, that I'm very close to. He's kind of like the son I never had. Actually, I'm his godfather. François lives downtown, and he's a young lawyer."

He continued, "But, back to Madison. Just to clarify, Madison's dad is not my biological brother. He is simply an old friend that I met years ago when he was working in Toronto and needed a lawyer for a little misunderstanding that he found himself in the middle of. I was just starting out in a new firm, and a more experienced lawyer passed the file over to me to handle. Turns out he's now as much a brother to me as anyone could be. He's a year or two younger than me. He's not Asian like his son, and he's not black like me either. He can be a pain in the ass at times, and I've seen him through a million girls and more entanglements than I choose to remember. He has always been a party boy and a little prone to having a girl in every port, as they say. But finally, he settled down somewhat as a family man once he met his wife and her baby son. She keeps him in line most of the time. They all moved to France years ago but they still have the house in L.A. But you know, Denni, truth be told, I owe him a lot. I was always very, very shy with the ladies, and he took me under his wing to show me the ways of the birds and the bees you might say."

"So, I guess we can say that you were a late bloomer just like me, is that right?"

He looked over at me and smiled. "If you say so, Ms. Brunette."

"Yes, I remember you mentioned at lunch that you had a brother and sister-in-law that lived in the south of France. Same one?"

"Yes. They have six children now, and they have a busy life, so I don't see them as often as I'd like to."

***

He couldn't have known that at that very moment that same younger brother in a pair of well-worn cut-offs and an old tee-shirt from back in the day was not feeling much like the party boy of days gone by. Sitting alone poolside out in L.A., he was re-reading for the fourth time a very private and very confidential report from his no-name burner phone. The report was based on his big brother's years of lofty ideals and uncompromising principles that the court had handed down back east, and that someone who had felt the full effects of this brilliance was now wanting payback from the judge who had ruled against him. This was the first red flag noted within the otherwise quiet, routinely, monthly surveillance reports of every movement around 7 Russell Hill Road in Toronto, Canada, that he had cautiously read through and kept secret from his brother for over the past ten years.

He keyed, "Photos?"

Intelligence typed back, "Not yet."

"Shit! Fuck man! I'm going to have to break it to the poor, naive bastard that retribution is a bitch. Somebody wants him dead." He sat there, trying not to panic, laying out a plan that would keep his brother, his hero, safe from harm. He sat there, mentally sorting through his A-list of people that owed him a favor, somebody that would know about such matters.

***

I listened as Nigel continued discussing the two teenagers as we walked through the quiet, tree-lined streets of Forest Hill. "Now that Madison is older, he and his young friend Stéphane have been coming over to holiday in Toronto by themselves, just the two of them, over the past few years. They are like two peas in a pod and have been best friends since they were in kindergarten."

I looked over at him as his voice became sober, "It just so happens that Stéphane has been suffering with some mental health issues this past year, and his parents are beside themselves with worry. It's not just the usual teenage angst, and it breaks my heart to see him like this, but what can you do?" As he continued to confide in me, he threw up his hands in despair. "I've got him set up with a good shrink here in Toronto to tide him over until he gets home to France, just to reassure his folks that I've got him covered during his holiday. He's been here with me lots of times with Madison, so we established a pretty good bond years ago. And Madison is very good with him."

"Yes, yes, I hear you. Mental health issues are difficult," I said.

"Uh huh. While we are on a serious note, Denni, of course you understand that I have told you this in complete confidence. I guess it stems from me spending so many years in the courts, holding onto confidential information, but even though I'm retired now, I still run my house a little like Las Vegas. You know – what happens in Vegas stays in Vegas. Although we don't know each other very well yet, I feel that I can trust you implicitly."

I laughed out loud at his life-to-Vegas comparison. "Of course!" I exclaimed. "I understand completely, but it does make a girl wonder exactly how many skeletons are in all those closets in your big house. Don't you worry a teensy-weensy bit. My lips are sealed regarding all convos that we share. Your trust has not been misplaced, Mr. Holder-of-Many-Secrets," I teased as he grinned at my flippant retort to his serious request for privacy.

Something told me to file away his quietly stated request in the back of my mind, as my intuition told me that there was more to his story than what he was divulging.

I picked up the pace so I could report back to the two boys that the old guy was completely winded at the two-kilometer mark, which may be a tad exaggerated, but I realized if I wanted this walk to become a regular routine, I would have to ingratiate myself into his family first.

We neared his walkway that led up to the house, and I followed my planned exit with precision. I didn't want him to feel obligated to ask me in, so I said, "Oh my God, I'm running late. Time for me to get home to watch my favorite show! *Ciao, mon ami!*" as I reached up and gave him a quick peck on his surprised cheek. I broke into a run, heading up the street.

"But won't you come in, at least for a minute? The boys will want to see you!" he called out to no avail. I waved my goodbye over my head and did not turn around once.

You've just gotta know when to hold 'em and when to fold 'em.

***

Once again, the next morning, I picked up the ringing phone, eyes still closed, with my blankets pulled up over my head.

"Okay, I'm putting my foot down. I insist that you come in after our walk tonight so the boys can at the very least make you a smoothie. They were so disappointed last night when you hightailed it up the street," the deep baritone pleaded his case.

"Good morning to you too! It sounds to me like you are just a little embarrassed that I beat the pants off you last night. Am I right? Never mind with your excuses; you are just going to have to try a little harder in the future."

"Don't even go there, wannabe track star. Just tell me are we on for at least a smoothie tonight?"

"Yes. Meanwhile, please say good morning to the boys and mention that I like my smoothie with yogurt, banana, strawberry, and none of that health-food additive crap in it at all. See you at 7:30?"

"You are a handful, Ms. Brunette."

"And you are one lucky man, your Honor. Now I'm going to hang up after I wish you a wonderful morning ahead of us."

I clicked my phone off, tossed the covers aside, and stretched out, flexing my toes down and fingers up as far as they would reach. It seemed to me that my plan was coming together without a hitch in sight. What could possibly go wrong? Everything was tickety-boo.

The phone insisted on ringing a second later. "Hello, did you forget something?" I said into the phone, fully expecting that it was Nigel again.

"Hello, Denni? Is that you? It's Kurt."

"Kurt! Oh, Kurt! It's so good to hear from you! Where are you? Are you okay?"

"Yes, it seems I'm going to live to tell the tale. Are you free to meet me this morning for a coffee somewhere along the line? I'm at my mom's house right now on St. Mary, you know, just below Bloor."

"Oh, of course. How about the Aroma Espresso Bar? It's in the village, right on Spadina Avenue. Does that work for you? Can you bring the kids?"

"No to the kids, but yes to the location. See you at, say 10:00?"

"Can't wait," I said with relief as I clicked off the phone. My poor friend had been through the wringer. He had been teaching in China and for some reason, he had been arrested and held in detention by the Chinese over the last six months. I couldn't wait to see him once again, safe and sound and back in Canada.

***

The next evening, after our huff-puff around the neighborhood, Nigel and I looked on as the two boys took charge of the kitchen. We pulled up two of the barstools to the white and gray marble kitchen island to watch the flourish and tomfoolery that was behind the smoothie-making.

The flat screen was blaring with MTV, and the boys, for reasons unknown, had decided to wear old cowboy hats, a little worse for wear, along with somebody's cast-off cowboy boots that had been broken in somewhere south of twenty years beforehand.

They clomped around in the size-twelve boots, curling their toes to keep their size-eight feet firmly on the floor. As the blaring music emanated with

MTV, once in a while Madison would break loose with a loud hee-haw, I suppose in reference to his cowboy attire.

"Oh, here it is again! Listen up, here's Gretchen Wilson with Redneck Woman!" and the two boys, pointing at me, joined MTV with the chorus while pointing at me.

'Cause I'm a redneck woman,

I ain't no high-class broad

I'm just a product of my rasin'

And I say hey y'all and yee haw…

I was completely charmed with their antics and mimicry of the latest country tune that had hit the sound waves that summer, and they rolled on the floor with laughter as I sang right along with Gretchen with the last line, *let me give a big hell yeah from the redneck girls like me.*

I joined in the giddy state of affairs, with my story of living up country, on my old, broken down farm years ago, and learning how to milk a cow old-style, sitting on the three-legged stool and squeezing Bessy's teats until my fingers couldn't squeeze any longer.

"If the smoothies are really, really good, and I mean exceptionally good, I think I could even arrange a day trip down to the old farm if anyone would be interested."

The three urbanites, the two younger ones wearing the hats, and the older one wearing the ear-to-ear grin all clamored their shouts of, "Please, please! When can we go?"

So, it was settled. Nigel promptly added details to the newly-hatched plan and suggested that we take the big Benz so that we would all have legroom. Chi would do the driving, he said.

"Oh, right, Chi. He lives here, right?"

Madison chimed in that Uncle Chi was Nigel's right-hand man who lived in the apartment over the garage.

Madison continued, "He's chill, Denni. You'll really like him. I've known him my whole life. Him and his son François. They're part of the family."

So, I promptly got on my cell to make the arrangements right then and there. I explained to Ann-Marie, who was one of my oldest and most trusted friends, that I wanted to book a table in her main dining room so that we could eat our main meal at noon on the day of our visit. She had been running the old Marlbank Hotel for over forty years and was renowned for her big roast beef dinners and apple pie that finished the meal off to perfection.

Her beloved husband, Walt, was also renowned for running the opposite side of the hotel, which comprised of a long, well-worn bar with old booths that had seen better days. The booths ran down the pine-paneled wall that divided the fine diners from the seasoned drinkers. He, too, had also served their small farming community well over the years.

"Now don't 'cha be worrying about a thing, Denni. I'll fix you up with something real special for you and your friends. I just can't wait to see your smiling face down in these parts once again. I've missed you terribly over all these years. What took yah so long, girlfriend?" her voice boomed out.

Our plan had come together, and as they say down on the farm, it was done like dinner.

***

It wasn't until later as I hopped into bed that I realized that in all the planning for the boys' road trip, I had totally forgotten to tell Nigel about Kurt's nightmare of spending six months in a Chinese prison. Poor guy! If the prison treatment had turned his otherwise dark hair snow-white, what had it done to his brain?

***

'Right on schedule,' I thought, as I rolled over to answer the ring the next morning. I was surprised to learn that it wasn't Nigel.

"Hello, Denni," the voice said hesitantly. "Uncle Nigel said I would probably get better results if I called you myself, so here goes with my reason for calling so early in the morning." He quickly continued as if he feared I would hang up on him, "My dad is arriving this morning, but he's only staying over until tomorrow, and I was wondering if you would please come in before your walk with Uncle Nigel so Dad can meet you. I promise I won't cut into your time with Uncle Nigel; I just want you to meet my dad so he will say okay to me and Stéphane going with you to the farm next week. Mom and he keep pretty close tabs on me, even when I'm with Uncle Nigel. Can you do me this one favor, Denni?"

"Of course. Rest assured, I'll lay on a really good impression, and I promise I'll be on my best behavior in front of your dad. That being said, I will pop in at say 7:15, but only for a few minutes, as I have to keep your Uncle Nigel on schedule for his seven-thirty walk around the block," I said, giving myself a quick and easy way out of a prolonged meeting with the boy's protective parent.

"Oh, good! I'm so relieved. I'll let Uncle Nigel know we're all set for 7:15 sharp. Oh, yeah, I think my dad's best friend is planning on meeting him here at Uncle Nigel's today at some point. We're planning a boy's night in, just the seven of us. Just the boys. It's not often we can all get together at the same time. Even Chi and François are coming. You know, a couple of hands of poker and all."

I smiled at the perfect oxymoron that was oblivious to the speaker. The young, earnest plea versus the casual reference to the 'couple of hands of poker and all' was all I needed to quickly add in, "Sounds like fun all the way around. See you at 7:15 and meanwhile, let your uncle know that I'm planning on leaving him in my dust tonight."

I had taken time to dress, in my ongoing quest to please Nigel, and rang his doorbell, confident that he would take a second look at my new, tight, cropped sweats with matching-colored short-sleeved cotton tee-shirt. I purposely wore a sexy, *La Perla* bra and the delicate lace of it showed up well under the pale tee-shirt, especially over my breasts. My hair was down around my shoulders, and I had a scrunchie on my wrist for the run. I had more mascara on than six girls out on a Friday-night bar hop.

Nigel opened the door with a face that I suspected was some sort of an apology for something that hadn't happened yet. He offered no explanation but gave me a kiss on the cheek before leading me toward the kitchen. He had put his arm around my shoulders as if I needed protection or something.

I turned the corner to enter the kitchen. Oh! In a flash, I understood what Nigel's apologetic look was all about.

His younger brother stood there with a half-shy but wide smile on his Hollywood-handsome face. He moved smoothly out from behind the kitchen island and glided toward me. His eyes were crinkling at the corners due to his wide smile, and he opened his arms a little to indicate silently that a hug was in order rather than a handshake. "So happy to meet you, Denni. I'm Brad."

I complied. I tried to recover from my surprise privately while my face was buried in his chest. I paused, took a deep breath, stepped back out of the warm welcome, and felt the safe comfort of Nigel's protective arm slipping around my shoulders once again.

"It's so nice to meet you, Brad. I feel like I know you somehow," I said as I joined in the laughter of everyone else in the room. I looked up at Nigel with mock annoyance on my face and to let the crowd know that he hadn't betrayed his family's Hollywood connection. Nigel's dark brown eyes, all squinched up with laughter, told me that he was proud of my ability to go with the flow. I now understood that his home was a safe haven for the hounded and hassled celebrity of his small, private family unit.

I looked out again beyond the island to see Brad's best friend stepping forward to introduce himself. Emboldened with my last success, I stepped out from Nigel's protection, opened my arms, and cried out, "And you! Yes, you! My God, I slept with your picture under my pillow for years!"

Madison and Stéphane were jumping up and down by then with my antics and howling from behind the island. Nigel had his arm around Brad's shoulders, and his head was thrown back in laughter.

George responded amidst all the hoopla. "I'm pleased to meet you, Ms. Brunette." His arms loosely corralled me to give me a light peck on my cheek. The two of us joined in the laughter at my agile response to their lifestyle that required all of them to fly under the radar so much of the time.

As I peeked out from under George's embrace, my eyes focused on the two brothers. 'Hmm,' I thought. 'They say that the fairer sex is the vain one. I don't think so,' I mused to myself as I examined the two brothers standing there in front of me with their ever-so-casual shaggy yet perfect hair crowning their good looks. The blond one was with the dark brown lowlights and ragtag golden locks, and the other with the brown skin had the soft black lowlights and corresponding spirals and spikes of gray and silver shooting upwards in random disregard. The fairer sex indeed. They had nothing on these two closet prima donnas.

Once George had gallantly handed me back to my protector, Nigel kept his arm tightly around my shoulders as he motioned for the boys to set up some glasses to toast the lady in their midst. His arm never left my shoulders the whole of the thirty-minute meet-and-greet. As they raised their glasses to, "Here's to Denni," I felt like I had passed the indoctrination into a very special and very private club.

George started the teasing as they all chimed in with the silly sing-song, arms around each other, swaying back and forth. "Nigie's got a girlfriend. Nigie's got a girlfriend," they sung out like a band of ten-year-old boys in the schoolyard.

I grabbed Nigel's hand, and we ran up the hallway to make our getaway. They were still chanting as Nigel closed the door behind us to head out for our nightly walk.

As the cool night air hit our faces, we left the walkway and onto the sidewalk, I teased him, "Now really, Nigie, how do you expect to get results while you are just wimping along, holding onto my shoulders like there's no tomorrow?"

He grabbed me and pulled me in close. He held me tight for a moment. "Call me a wimp, eh? I'll show you who's a wimp." He jumped ahead and started an easy jog as I just stood there watching his easy stride make distance between us.

I was momentarily stunned and electrified all at the same time, and all from the feel of the big bulge in his sweatpants during his tight, intimate press-up against me beforehand.

'Snap out of it, girl!' I hissed at myself as I jumped back into action. As I closed the gap between us, I smiled as I said to myself, 'Oh, now that must be an uncomfortable little package for him to jog along with.' I caught up with him and we buried the bantering, slowing down to an easy hand-holding walk through the rest of the neighborhood.

We never mentioned his houseguests during the whole walk, and I was secretly pleased that he had graciously allowed me the opportunity to act as cool and hip as the rest of the crowd that had gathered around his big, white, and gray marble kitchen island on that memorable summer's night.

As I left him at his walkway, he gave me a quick kiss on the cheek, and as he turned me around so that I was facing my homeward stretch, he whispered softly in my ear, "Nice ass!"

Sticking to my game plan, I did not turn around to acknowledge his boyish compliment. I simply waved my arm up in a blind goodbye and carried on, but I knew that his eyes were on that same ass every step that I took, until I turned the corner and headed across Heath Street. Hours later, as I clicked off the television, I thought to myself, 'You couldn't make this up if you tried. Truth is always stranger than fiction.'

I tossed and turned into the wee hours of the morning. But it wasn't meeting the famous Hollywood eye candy that was keeping me awake. Oh no, not at all.

Thoughts of Nigel's recurring big erections had me reeling, hot and bothered, as they say, down on the farm.

***

Chapter 4
Marlbank

It was after eight in the morning when we pulled out of the driveway. Nigel was riding shotgun with Chi in the driver's seat. I glanced to my right to see a big smile on Madison's face, and then to the left of me, I saw Stéphane's somber look. He was gazing out the window, obviously to avoid communication.

'Note to self,' I thought, 'give this boy some space this morning.'

I felt a little uneasy and chided myself silently for starting our day-trip down to the farm just waiting for a black cloud to come to fruition.

The boys had stored their cowboy hats in the trunk, but they both wore their old, scuffed up, hand-me-down western boots, ready for what the farm had in store for them. Of course, I was dressing for Nigel, the male fashionista, but I was happy with myself for taking the time to go down to my locker earlier in the week to dust off some real McCoys – tan-colored 'Dale Evans' leather boots that I had bought years ago at the Calgary Stampede.

The big Benz slipped uptown and then seamlessly headed east along the 401. I anticipated that we would reach the farm, this side of Kingston, just before lunch.

It was my first trip in Nigel's bigger vehicle that was usually sitting idle, housed in his garage. He said he kept it for occasions exactly like this one, and Chi was obviously enjoying handling this big, elegant powerhouse. Mostly in conversation with Nigel, Chi was constantly checking his passengers, especially Madison, in the rearview mirror. I noticed that his face brightened whenever the teenager engaged him in a conversation. He had met this teenager about fifteen years ago when Madison was a toddler, and the two had bonded instantly. Perhaps it was that they both shared the Asian face and the lean and wiry build, albeit Madison was born in Cambodia and Chi was born in Vietnam. Or perhaps it was just one of those things. Chi had a son, now in his thirties, who was busy with his career, always striving to make partner with the big-city law firm downtown. His Uncle Nigel was his mentor, and they had spent many, many hours together in Saul's old office talking shop. When he was born, his parents gave him a French-Canadian name in honor of their *Québécois* roots and their own native language. His name was François Tran. He hadn't settled down with a wife and children yet, so Chi's family was sparse, especially since his wife, Duyen, had died years before of cancer.

Chi had arrived in Canada with his wife in the mid-seventies as a member of the storied and documented boat people from Vietnam. As French was their first language, they were sponsored way up north of Montreal, as many of the boat people were in a small French-Canadian farming community to begin his life anew.

Once settled, he joined in the community, attending English as a second-language class and then on to night school, working toward his GED with university in mind. Once again with food and basic lodgings, the young immigrant couple made plans to work, to save, and to move to either Montréal or Toronto, as they thought they had a better chance of settling down and having a family of their own in a large urban center in their new country. They knew there was no going back and played their cards with grace and humility, living with the all-white French-speaking community and grieving their lost lives privately as to not seem ungrateful. It was a tough road for them both to put the obliteration of their world as they had known it and the horrors of the boat migration behind them.

They eventually moved to Montréal, armed with their native French and their newly acquired night-school English language skills. Duyen worked in a hotel, and Chi as a FedEx delivery person. He met Nigel quite by coincidence, while delivering a court file to Nigel, who was practicing law in Toronto but had to appear in Montréal's courts for a case he was working on.

The rest is history, as they say. Nearly thirty years later, Chi still lived in the apartment over Nigel's garage, although his duties of houseman, gardener, and driver had diminished to an 'on-call' basis years ago. Chi and Duyen's son, François, born at Women's College Hospital in Toronto, had enjoyed all the privileges of a doting 'Uncle Nigie' who by then was a prominent lawyer on the fast track for becoming one of Canada's Supreme Court judges. Nigel had the heart to match his deep pockets that paid for the young man's law degree and post-graduate work in the Canadian penal system, while his parents had the security of a home and the blessing of a good employer the whole of their working lives.

After Duyen lost her battle to cancer, Nigel and Chi aged into their respective lifestyles, living separate lives but within the close proximity of the house and the attached garage upstairs apartment.

Who could have guessed back in 1955 that a skinny, black, five-year-old, standing barefoot in a dirt-floored kitchen in Jamaica, and a healthy, smiling child of crop farmers in Vietnam would share their lives, their hopes, and dreams for over thirty years at 7 Russell Hill Road? They were family.

Stéphane abruptly came out of himself, and during a pause in Chi and Nigel's commentary, announced in tones more of a statement rather than a question, "Do you know that I'm a Jew?"

"Yes, of course we do, Stéphane," Nigel responded. He continued, "Now let's clarify that a little; tell us all the story about your bubby who survived the Holocaust. Was this bubby on your dad's side or your mother's side of the family?"

"It doesn't matter; she's dead now."

I piped in, "Well, I didn't know until just now that you are a Jew, Stéphane. Some of my friends' mothers were Holocaust Survivors. Do you practice your faith on a regular basis?"

"No," Stéphane responded dully. "That's just it. I have just decided that I want to visit a Rabbi as soon as I can. It's my new sense of purpose. L'oncle Nigel, do you know anyone you can call for me?"

"Oh! Now there's a lofty term – a sense of purpose. And spoken in perfect English too! Good for you, my man. And yes, of course, tomorrow morning I'll phone Rabbi Klieman, Saul's old Rabbi. We'll see what we can arrange. You know, Stéphane, if Saul had had his way, I'd be a Jew today. He used to take me to synagogue all the time, but my mama was a straight-laced Baptist, and she made sure that I was sitting in a pew in her Baptist church as often as I was in synagogue. She was the queen of that castle, and Saul knew not to cross her. Actually though, I had the best of both worlds."

Madison added, "Yeah, Mom especially takes care to make sure all us kids know all the cultures and religions. It's all good. But, Stéphane, meanwhile, lighten up, man! We're off to the farm where the cows don't give a damn about your newfound sense of purpose!" exclaimed Madison, trying to lift Stéphane out of his funk. He reached over me, sitting between the two of them to give Stéphane a soft punch on the shoulder.

I sensed that Madison too felt a little anxious with his friend's solemn manner.

A week before, the day after I had first met all of them, Stéphane and Madison first, and then Brad and George, I recalled that Nigel had filled me in a little on Madison's longtime friend. Stéphane had had a few years of suffering serious bouts of depression and anxiety. He had been in and out of care, and in fact, with his parents' permission, Nigel had set him up with a psychiatrist in Toronto to keep a close watch on him while he was holidaying in Canada with his buddy.

As we all attempted to change the mood and the conversation, I noticed with a sideways glance that Stéphane had once again turned slightly to look away and out the window, his eyes closed. We all quietly settled into idle chitchat and focused on teasing Madison about his favorite 'le foot' team and his futile attempts to get a steady girlfriend back in France.

Unlike his friend, Madison had a savvy retort for every tease, and he gave as good as he got. Beyond the banter, though, there was a maturity and soulfulness that belied his seventeen years. Yes, a savvy kid was a good way to define him. He was on his way to growing into what women call a 'charmer.' 'The apple doesn't fall far from the tree,' I thought to myself.

We all voted against a pit stop, and without further incident, the big Benz carried us closer to our day at the farm. It turned out to be a day that none of us would ever forget.

We pulled up to turn into the parking lot of the Marlbank Hotel. Nothing had changed. The old hitching posts, more for decoration now than anything, stood aside the worn timber holding up the front porch. A faded tin Canadian Club Whisky ad was nailed onto one side of the main door, with *DRAFT SERVED* on the other. Not a lick of paint left on the exterior, but the flowers' window boxes were barn-red and blooming as if just waiting for our arrival. An old bicycle was leaning against the steps as if the rider had dropped it and dashed in for a quick pint before the lunch crowd got there.

Ann-Marie was standing there on the step, with fresh apron and sensible shoes on, just like I remembered her from years earlier.

All of a sudden, the boys were too shy to wear the cowboy hats, so Chi closed the trunk and the five of us were enveloped with hugs and laughter.

Ann-Marie's husband, Walt, ambled over from the big old rocker on the front porch and joined Ann-Marie in ushering us in to the more formal dining room area of the old hotel. We were all seated around a big round table, and there were no other guests at the few separate smaller tables. The dining room walls were still covered in the old dark red Victorian printed wallpaper, and the linoleum floor had a worn path leading to the darkened, long hallway where the 'ladies' and 'gents' rooms were. Our table was set up just within view of the more casual bar on the other side of the big door that was always propped open. Country folk tend to be friendly and inclusive in most social situations on their own turf. Some people call it being plain nosey and I could imagine the party-line was buzzing from farm to farm at the sight of the big Benz sitting in the side gravel parking lot.

Of course, Walt was trying to sneak in a draft for the boys, and they were all laughing at my antics of trying to fake-call the police as the boys were underage and seriously under my wing for the day.

I had arranged with Ann-Marie ahead of time to have our main meal then and there before actually going to my old farm. We would come back after our visit to the old homestead for pie and coffee before heading back to the city. I had e-transferred her enough money to cover the bill; I certainly didn't want Nigel to think that I expected him to pay.

Lunch was served, and Ann-Marie didn't disappoint. There were no menus, just a big platter presenting a perfect roast of beef, crispy-crusted and pink in the middle, with homemade rolls covered up with a linen cloth in a basket, and a jug of brown gravy on the side. Nigel's face was beaming as he eyed the plate of catfish and boiled potatoes that Walt held, with his shirt sleeves now rolled up. Catfish, the epitome of country life around the world, reminded him of back home in Jamaica when he was a young boy where fish was a big part of the staple diet. Ann-Marie, face flushed with serving her big-city guests, explained that the bowl of rice wasn't usually something that she cooked, but added simply and naively, "Denni told me on the phone that some of her friends were not from these parts, so I whipped up this bowl of rice special just for you all," as she beamed at Chi and Madison.

I realized how much I had missed her genuine niceness over the years and vowed to myself to keep in touch a little more often.

After lunch, we made our way to the farm, with me sitting up front with Chi. The farm was situated just around the corner from the hotel, and as we turned up the long lane, I was momentarily mortified at how shabby the old place really was. Walt and Ann-Marie had warned me about the sad sight of the remains of my old farmhouse that had burned down a few years ago, but to tell you the truth, my heart sank with that first sighting.

First view of the old outbuildings on the left and the old weathered barn on the right of us told me it hadn't changed a bit. It was me that had changed, I supposed.

The first old drive-shed stood on the left, with its roof caved in, just as it was after Hurricane Hazel took it out in 1955. The 'new' drive-shed was in better condition and it's two wide doors were closed firmly with the sliding plank of barn board in place, and the tin roof was burnished brown and red-gold from all the years of hot summers and cold winters. A few pieces of old, large farm equipment rusted silently beside the outbuildings, amongst the remains of a once-fruitful hay field. Through the wild grasses sidling up to the yellow hay, my eye caught the overgrown apple orchard behind the weathered gray barn board that made up the collection of two driving sheds and the chicken coops. The pond lay behind the small knoll, and the slope met last year's brown bull-rushes lying half-mast, with the fresh crop of weeds and algae giving the frogs and water-life a green and safe haven for the time being.

Even as I remembered years ago picking apples there to make my first ever apple pie, and all the skinny-dipping in the pond with Joe, my first husband, I couldn't see an ounce of romance as my eyes took in the landscape. It was gone. All gone. A real pang of regret that I had come back 'home' hit me deep and hard. Yes, true, it was because I was a little embarrassed having my new friends, especially Nigel, witness the present state of affairs, but really, the loss I felt was due to the immediate obliteration of all the memories of good times and laughter that I had been holding on to over the past lonely years. Definitely all had gone in one cruel swoop.

I put my hand up to my chest, closed my eyes, and took a deep, sorry breath to relinquish the past.

His touch startled me, and I opened my eyes as I felt Nigel's hand on my shoulder. I turned my head toward the backseat to see him quietly leaning forward, watching me, with his face full of understanding.

"Holy mogul!" Stéphane said quietly to himself.

I collected myself, and I laughed out loud at his skiing reference aimed at the rutted laneway.

"There's the barn!" Madison shouted. "Stop! Stop the car!" he yelled. "Where's the barn door, Denni? Let me out. I'll run ahead!"

"Whoa! Easy boy," Nigel advised.

"Yes, looks like we will park in front of the drive-shed." Chi was calmly navigating as the boys were hanging their heads out the window.

I bailed out with the boys and ran toward the barn doors as Chi and Nigel parked and strolled behind. I reached the doors and turned around, facing the boys with my arms outstretched to block their entrance.

"Wait! Stop! There is a very special sight here; we all have to go in at the same time!" I exclaimed. The four of them stopped up and when we were all together, I gathered myself up and explained to them in my best drama-queen fashion the romance of opening a barn door. They all listened intently, and Chi was smiling from ear to ear.

"You must be quiet, and it will take your eyes a second or two to adjust to the dim light. Quietly, look up. Look up. Quietly. You will see the silver shards of light through the interstices of the barn board, and it will light up the hay up high in the loft, and it will also light up the hay on the floor. Drink it all in. Pure silver ribbons running down the walls, pure golden pools up in the loft and down on the floor. There is no light more beautiful than this in the world, only to be found in a barn on a summer afternoon. Just stand there quietly and look and then I'll whistle. The barn swallows will all rise and fly up and away. There is no sound like this, only to be found in a barn. Okay, are we ready?"

I turned around, facing the doors, keeping my arms out as if to block them from entering while Nigel, playing his part, leaned over me and slowly and silently pulled the bar from the black iron handles to loosen the door. We single-filed in while Nigel held the door to manipulate the dim light. It was exactly like I had described. And we stood there, drinking it all in for the moment. I whistled. The whoosh from the rising barn swallows was like it was emanating from Bose speakers.

After the symphony of the birds, Chi sprinted forward, claiming that he would give the demonstration on how to swing on the rope. We all laughed, surprised at how this usually quiet man who had lived in the city for the last thirty years or so knew the technique of this age-old country pastime as he nimbly made his way up the ladder to the hayloft to catch the rope. He stood there, a little out of breath and excited, testing the rope with his weight, and then, with a crazy 1950s-inspired Tarzan yodel, he soared off the ledge of the loft, over the floor of the barn, tilting up and into his flight and swinging back, angling his legs up just in time to catch the loft's floor ledge to safety.

We all had a go at it, trying to outdo each other with our versions of Tarzan and Jane callouts, and we all agreed hands-down that Chi was the best.

Chi, Nigel, and I left the boys to their antics, and we made our way over to the remains of the farmhouse where I had once lived and loved years before. The clapboard century farmhouse had burned to the ground a few years earlier, and it was definitely a sad sight but still fascinating to see the old stone floors and cellar walls made from the local marl still intact. You could see where the first building was erected, back in 1847, and then the new addition added in 1901.

We sat on the ramparts of the old farmhouse and looked over the back fields, and Chi told us where he learned all about the intricacies of haylofts. After their escape from Vietnam in 1975, the Government of Canada had placed him and his wife, Duyen, in a farming community in Quebec where they lived on a farm. It took an old barn in Quebec to show them the ways of loving and living in the frozen north country that they had claimed as their future.

Chi reached over and took my hand and said, "My trip to your old farm is the greatest gift I could ever receive. Thank you for reminding me of my beautiful young wife and me in that old Québécois barn so many years ago. One of these days, I'll find my own farm. Well, maybe not a big farm. But there's something about the land, isn't there, Denni? It seems that the two of us are connected to the earth somehow, rather than to the sea." He continued,

"Now I know as well as you do that as we sit here, we're all city-slickers through and through, but I know deep down that I belong close to the earth. I guess that's why I enjoy the gardening at 7 Russell Hill Road so much. I'll have to show you our nice little greenhouse that we've built at the back of the apartment."

"A greenhouse? Really! Oh, my, I've always been so interested in greenhouses and the new hydroponic farming methods. Yes, please! Just let me know when you have the time, and I'll be down in a drop of a hat."

Nigel added in, "Yes, Chi has quite an operation. He supplies the local food bank all year round with fresh vegetables in the summer and canned produce in the winter."

"Yup. It keeps me busy."

As I look back now, I know that the three of us bonded in a way that we would always remember forever. Funny how the simple times turn out to be the most poignant ones when you are looking back at personal milestones long passed.

There was shouting from the boys in the background and Chi left the two of us alone to get the car turned around toward the laneway.

"Nigel, if you want to run ahead, just go. I brought down an old poem and I want to read it, right here, as I'm sitting on the burned-out shell of my old farmhouse," I explained. "My dad's favorite poet was Robert Frost, especially this one. It sounds like Robert Frost was sitting right here when he wrote it. It's about an old farmhouse that burned down, but the barn was spared. Do you mind?"

"Don't think for a minute that I would miss another performance like the one you gave at the barn doors, telling us about the barn swallows. I'm not moving. Just read, baby. Just read. I'm your biggest fan."

"Really?"

"Really."

And so, I reached into the back pocket of my jeans, unfolded the old poem, and began reading out loud the one and only verse of Robert Frost's *The Need of Being Versed in Country Things*.

The house had gone to bring again
To the midnight sky a sunset glow.
Now the chimney was all of the house that stood,
Like a pistil after the petals go.
The barn opposed across the way,
That would have joined the house in flame
Had it been the will of the wind, it was left

To bear forsaken the place's name.
No more it opened with all one end
For teams that came by the stony road
To drum on the floor with scurrying hooves
And brush the mow with the summer load.
The birds that came to it through the air
At broken windows flew out and in,
Their murmur more like the sigh we sigh
From too much dwelling on what has been.
Yet for them the lilac renewed its leaf,
And the aged elm, though touched with fire;
And the dry pump flung up an awkward arm;
And the fence post carried a strand of wire.
For them there was nothing really sad.
But though they rejoiced in the nest they kept,
One had to be versed in country things
Not to believe the phoebes wept.

The two of us sat there, not wanting to break the magic of the moment.

"What is it? What is it I hear?" He asked softly.

I looked over into his face. "Dragonflies. It's the glorious dragonflies."

"Magic." There was not even a hint of a smile or a tease.

His sincerity encouraged me to go on, "Dragonflies symbolize change. You know, like realization or emotional or spiritual growth or something. Some sort of deeper understanding of life, they say."

"You give me lots to think about, honey."

We just sat there. I breathed in the land, and I leaned back to allow my own personal little bit of heaven envelop me. It was like Chi said I seemed to belong to the earth somehow.

"But back to your poem," he took my hand as he kissed me gently on the cheek and continued, "You're right. The poem and your farm are a perfect match. And you say that this was your father's favorite poem but he had died long before you ever owned this farm?"

"Yes. Many years before. But really, we know it's not about the farm or the fire, right? Robert Frost is just talking about loss and resilience, isn't he? That's why I love the poem so much. For me, it's not just my farm I've lost; it's my dad too. I've often wondered what or who it was that my dad lost that he thought of when he read this poem. Obviously, it wasn't this particular old farmhouse." I didn't mention that it was also the loss of my first marriage where Joe and I had also swung on the rope in the old barn.

60

"Honey, you are so insightful. I agree; we all have our own burned-down farmhouse in some form or other, don't we?" Nigel sat there quietly, leaning into my face, "Thank you for this memory. I'll never forget it." He sat back and smiled a little. "And for this wonderful road trip, my Irish faerie."

"Hey, what do you mean Irish faerie? You've got me all wrong. I'm totally one hundred percent Dale Evans. Look at these cowgirl boots. I'm a very tough broad, not some little woodland sprite."

"Trust me, I know exactly who you are," he went on with one black eyebrow raised in rueful irony. "You have no idea about Irish faeries. Being both delicate and dangerous, they take special handling. I know all about them; I've been experiencing one firsthand over the past month."

"Is that a compliment or a complaint?" I quipped back.

With that, we ambled down to the Benz to get back to the Marlbank Hotel to have the belated desert and coffee before heading back to the city. The boys had popped the trunk and had put their cowboy hats on.

"Denni, take a photo!" And so, I did. As we drove down the lane, I passed back my cellphone from the front seat so everyone could take a look at the photo. I was struck at how young and vulnerable these two boys looked, not at all like the sophisticated, entitled, young-adult world travelers that I had thought they were back in the city. 'After all,' I told myself, 'they were only seventeen. And away from home as well.' Of course, they both still had boys' bodies and not even a shadow of a moustache between the two of them, but there was something about their faces in the photo. Both of them looked a little world-weary, almost like they had lost that childlike innocence, especially Stéphane. I looked at the photo a second time. The earlier sunshine had disappeared, and the photo's backdrop showed a gray cloud. It had cast a shadow over the pair of teenagers staring out of the photo back at me. 'It's not easy being a kid, even if your parents are rich and famous,' I thought to myself. I shook it off and put my phone back in my purse. No more photos. I would rather keep my rose-colored glasses on.

As we got out of the car, once again at the Marlbank Hotel, Madison hopped on the old bike, still propped up on the old hitching post.

"Hey, guys, this is how a Marlbank cowboy gets out of Dodge!" We were all laughing, and Stéphane dared him to burn a little rubber to see if it was a good getaway.

Madison gave it his best, and the gravel was flying.

Ann-Marie and Walt had gathered a few old neighbors together to welcome us, and we had just sat down to coffee and Ann-Marie's famous apple pie when Stéphane leaned over to whisper in Madison's ear.

"La merde!" he hissed, *"Ne te fais pas de souci pour moi téléphone portable dans la grange. Je m'en vais."*

"Non, non," he continued to whisper into his ear. *"J'accélérer un velo. Non, non, à tout de suite. Shhhh, shhhh."*

He shifted from Madison's ear, looked into his friend's eyes and almost inaudibly said, *"Adieu."*

"Adieu – whaddya mean *adieu*?" Madison whispered back with one eyebrow raised. "Just get your ass back before anyone notices you're gone, bro."

As someone asked Madison a question about his favorite soccer team in France, Stéphane slipped away from the table without anyone noticing.

"Oh, you mean 'le foot.'" He proceeded with his boyish exuberance and charm in describing how 'le foot' beats hockey, especially Canadian hockey, any day of the week, to the great amusement of everyone sitting around the table.

How could he have known in his youthful soccer bliss that the older man in the faded blue plaid shirt sitting across from him was no other than one of Canada's greatest hockey players, Bobby Orr. Madison would never know that the joke was on him. And all the others, including Ann-Marie, would never know that Madison had a very rich and famous set of parents, so I suppose that the score was even.

I caught Nigel's eye and he gave me a conspiratorial wink. I felt like the proverbial fly on the wall as I held my poker face and played to all sides.

Forty minutes later, Madison said, "Uncle Nigel, Stéphane isn't back yet. Would it be okay if we took the car to pick him up?"

At hearing this, Nigel motioned Chi to the doorway and then announced to us all to have a last coffee and that they would be back right away, after picking up Stéphane and the bike from the farm. As I looked out the window, I noticed that they were running toward the car with keys in hand. "Is something wrong?" my small inner voice whispered. I turned back to the conversation.

Stepping away from the table to answer my phone twenty minutes later, I heard Nigel's voice.

"Denni, please listen. I need you to do exactly what I tell you. Are you listening? Stéphane is dead by suicide. Do you hear me? Do you understand?"

I took a deep breath, closed my eyes, and said clearly, "I understand and I'm listening. Go ahead."

"One. Get Ann-Marie and her phone and tell her to drive you and Madison to the farm immediately. Two. Tell them both that Stéphane has died by suicide in the barn. Tell Madison that he has a job to do here. He must stay with the body with me until the Rabbi gets here. Back to Ann-Marie. Tell her to call the police, but no ambulance until after the Rabbi arrives. Tell the police I'm a judge, and I do not want an ambulance right now, and only two male officers. No sirens, no lights. Complete privacy. No bullshit. Do you understand?"

"Absolutely. Yes."

I lowered my phone and looked back into the room at Anne-Marie. She caught my eye and moved toward me. I didn't have to say a thing. That's how it is with old friends.

Bouncing along in the front seat of Ann-Marie's old truck, with both my arms around Madison, I could see up ahead that Chi was waving us in just beside the barnyard gate. Madison's wails continued to muffle into my chest. They did not abate until Chi grabbed him around his shoulders to help get him out of the truck.

Still in the driver's seat, Ann-Marie continued to bellow into the phone, "He's a big-time judge in the city, and a big, black son-of-a-bitch too, so don't screw this up in any way or fashion or there will be hell to pay. Two of you only, no lights, no sirens, no ambulance until I tell you any different. Do you hear me?" She motioned with her free hand for me to go.

"Go, just go," she mouthed to me as she continued to bark her instructions to the dispatcher.

I made my way to the barn, silently relieved that I had not given Ann-Marie any indication whatsoever that Madison had famous parents. We simply did not need any press getting wind of this. I walked at a measured pace, giving Chi and Madison lots of lead time. I had no desire to witness the two teens' last farewell.

Less than an hour earlier, both Nigel and Chi had worked feverishly and silently to loosen the noose that Stéphane had crafted. Then the two men took turns to meticulously time the CPR that they administered to no avail.

Nigel looked up from tending the body that was lying in the hay loft as the barn door slid open. He motioned silently for Madison and Chi to come up the ladder.

With Madison back up in the hay loft, Nigel, still holding on to the body's one hand, began to speak in his deep baritone, quietly explaining to Madison that his duty as Stéphane's best friend was to be the shomer, the man that guards the body until the Rabbi arrived. He explained to Madison that he had already called Rabbi Kleiman, an old friend of Saul, who in turn would arrange for a local Rabbi to come immediately to take care of everything.

Nigel went on to say that perhaps Madison could sit down in a comfortable position next to the body and think of all the good times he shared with Stéphane. "Kind of like an early shiva," Nigel comforted, and Madison solemnly nodded, tears dried by the immediacy of the nightmare upon him.

Madison, a little surprised at how calm his uncle was, knew instinctively to follow his lead. As his mom would often say to him, "Put your big-boy pants on when the going gets tough."

He kneeled down, not yet able to look at Stéphane's face. Knowing that it was his duty to act in a dignified manner, he looked up to his uncle for reassurance.

Madison and Nigel spent the next forty-five minutes in remembrance of all the good times the two boys had spent together over the years – growing up in France, both of them struggling to gain their bilingual fluency, their inevitable ups and downs of puberty, holidaying with his famous family and playing pranks on the press, and even sometimes traveling without the parents. It was just the two of them, hanging out with Uncle Nigel in Toronto, incognito, completely under the radar, free from paparazzi and peer pressure.

Nigel smiled at Madison's version of the two teenage pals holidaying, just the two of them, no adult supervision in sight, downstairs in his apartment, playing video games all night, sleeping in late, eating pizza for breakfast, and talking trash about girls and life in general for hours at a time. The two teenage boys seemingly were unaware of their unwritten code that they spoke French while discussing girls and nothing but English when they were using all thumbs with the video games, except for the expletives, of course. The multitudes of expletives were up for grabs in whatever language that came out first.

Meanwhile, Chi was perched on the bottom rung of the ladder, head in hands, while I stood in the center of the barn, dry-eyed with sheer anxiety. My eyes caught something peeking out from the loose hay on the floor. I approached cautiously. My heart sank. It was one of Stéphane's hand-me-down cowboy boots that he had borrowed from Brad. We had all laughed at the boots being way too big for him to wear at the time in Nigel's kitchen that night, but Stéphane insisted that they were just perfect. It must have fallen off during Stephan's last earthly flight. I picked it up and clutched it like my life depended on it.

Chi's head jerked up as Nigel's voice offered the first prayer. He slowly made his way over to me as Nigel asked God to grant perfect peace to Stéphane and to remember his good deeds. The Lord's prayer followed, with Madison, Chi, and I chiming in as this familiar old prayer was offered up to the rafters.

My tears finally flowed, and as I opened my arms to Chi, I saw the tears flowing down his face as well. We propped each other up, standing there in the middle of the old, empty gray barn, quietly sobbing into each other's shirts, not only for Stéphane's pain but also for the pain of the boy's family yet to come, and to make it worse was the realization that we would have to deliver it.

And yet, as my eyes opened and lifted up to the dim light in the shadows of the great timbered structure above, I felt at peace when I heard the steady murmuring of the teenager and his wise, measured uncle as they continued talking their way through the life and death of Stéphane Fournier.

I gave up my own silent prayer for God's mercy on his loved ones left behind.

I looked toward the barn door and said to Chi, "I'll wait outside for the police to make sure we don't have any circus out there." He nodded and started walking back toward the ladder.

Ann-Marie, still standing at the barnyard gate, had been busy making plans. "As soon as the boys in blue get here, I'll get back and bring over some coffee. Do you need anything else in there? How's everything going? How's the boy? That's one hell of a good man you've got there, Denni."

"I'll never be able to repay you for your help, but right now, thank you... thank you from the bottom of my heart," I heard my voice starting to waive once again.

"Never mind, girlfriend. Time for tears later. Oh, here they come now. I'll put them straight before they go in," she said as she narrowed her eyes to the one cruiser, with no lights and no siren, turning into the laneway.

Both of the officers took their hats off as they approached us at the barnyard gate and they said to me, "Sorry for your loss, ma'am," but nodding all the while to Ann-Marie.

"I'll take you in now. If you like, the body is lying in rest up in the hayloft. Since the boy was a Jew, we don't want the body moved, if possible, until the Rabbi has a chance to perform the basic rites of mourning."

"Absolutely, ma'am," they offered in unison.

With that, an old brown Chevy turned up the drive. The Rabbi lost no time introducing himself to the four of us and asked the two police officers' permission to have time with the body before they called the ambulance. He explained that he would not perform the complete ritual bath, the taharah, right then and there, but he would appreciate if the officers could give him a hand with his bag of supplies that he had brought to perform the basic rites of passage.

"Yes, sir. Meanwhile, to keep out of your way, we can do our paperwork to make this as smooth as possible, sir."

"Okay," Ann-Marie stated, "I'll get back now and bring over coffee etcetera for everyone. I'll set it up in the drive-shed. Would it be okay with you, Denni, if I filled Walt in on what's happening and if he came back with me?"

"Perfect plan," I said.

The two police officers and the Rabbi strode toward the barn door, and the Rabbi looked at the two of them and said, "I notice that you took your hats off in respect of the grieving women. In our culture, we keep our head covered. Would you mind putting your hats back on, or I brought a few kippas here, just in case we needed them."

The Rabbi held out two kippas, and the two officers politely left their police caps under their arms and donned the kippas.

"Good, fellas, good. We are going to witness a young Jew receiving his last blessing, and God is present above all of us."

"Yes, sir," they answered in unison.

I took the lead to open the door and usher them in, and Chi stood up in the hayloft, silently waving them forward with both arms.

As the Rabbi's eyes adjusted to the low light in the darkened barn, he followed Chi's silent directions and walked slowly, stopping for a second or two between each psalm and prayer that he offered up to God.

The chants delivered by the Rabbi in Hebrew, as old as time itself, were perfectly and hauntingly beautiful as the Rabbi paused on each rung of the old ladder. It seemed he was keeping pace on his climb, taking time with each of the Hebrew prayers and praise to God that he was emoting. I was wrong earlier, thinking that there was no romance left in this old farm. It was here. The sheer power of God and the universe was reverberating all around me.

I stayed below to allow the Rabbi and the men the traditional space and time needed for this cultural and religious process to take place. Madison asked the Rabbi quietly if he brought some kippas, and all three men respectfully clipped the bobby pins into their hair. By then, the magnificence of the pomp and ceremony of the immediate moment fell away and I stood there once again, completely overwhelmed by the horror that had presented itself.

While the men were still up in the hayloft, the Rabbi thanked Madison for being a wonderful shomer. He explained that he would ride with Stéphane's body in the back of the ambulance and that he would attend the autopsy, perform a complete taharah, and help prepare the body for the flight home to France. He would arrange for someone to stay with the body right through to France, if that was what the family wanted.

Nigel quietly confirmed, "I'm not a Jew, and I defer to your experience, and please know that I'm responsible for returning the body to his parents in France. I want it done to the highest standards. Please arrange for someone to sit with the body during the flight overseas. I'm also responsible for all costs, and I'll straighten up with you right after we finish here."

I quietly closed the big barn door behind me and looked out to the gray skies above. It wasn't long before I spied Ann-Marie's truck once again turning up the laneway.

By the time Walt, Ann-Marie, and I had set up a table fashioned from an old flat panel interior door perched on a set of sawhorses and set with a white cloth, the two police officers had joined us, just in time to waive in the ambulance.

Ann-Marie and Walt stood out in front of the drive-shed to witness the final procession make its way from the barn. I held the barnyard gate open for the men that were silently carrying the body on the stretcher, and the Rabbi asked us all if he could say a prayer in departure.

We gathered at the back of the ambulance, and I helped Walt with his kippa. I explained that it was a sign of respect at this point, and Walt nodded in agreement. "Whatever you need, Denni." I looked around at all the faces in front of me, huddled together as the Rabbi motioned for us to form an arbor in front of the opened ambulance backdoors. We lined up, with Nigel and Madison between the two police officers on one side, and myself and Ann-Marie between Chi and Walt on the other. The stretcher advanced, centered and stopped in the middle of us, and held up while we all placed a hand on each side of the stretcher.

The Rabbi asked Madison to repeat the Mourner's Kaddish after him, and Madison's voice rose to the occasion,

"May Stéphane go to his resting place in peace!" and all our amens followed.

The Rabbi solemnly issued his last simple prayer, "We ask God to grant perfect peace to the departed and to remember his good deeds."

The two police officers shook hands all around before following the quiet ambulance in their quiet squad car. I watched them drive away silently, slowing to a near stop for each rut, and I remembered Stéphane's description of the rutted laneway.

My heart followed the procession as I murmured my last goodbye.

"Watch out for the moguls, and may God bless you, my young friend!"

It was late afternoon and the gray skies started to spit as Nigel, Madison, Chi, Walt, Ann-Marie, and I entered the old drive-shed to share coffee and some of Ann-Marie's famous butter tarts. Walt quietly offered Nigel and Chi a pull from his bottle of whisky hidden away from Ann-Marie's eyes. Ann-Marie explained what was in the basket she had packed for us to take home, to have as a late supper. It included the rest of the earlier roast beef, fresh rolls, half a ham, tomatoes, a head of lettuce right out of the garden, and some big, juicy, ripe peaches. She apologized for the lack of a pie; there was nothing but crumbs left after earlier that day.

Madison spoke up and made a little speech, thanking us all for taking care of Stéphane and him and declared that he was going to be okay. He ended his brave few sentences with: "Let's toast to my best friend, Stéphane," and we all said in unison, "Here's to Stéphane," as we raised our coffee mugs. I thought to myself, 'After this is all over, I must phone his parents and tell them how proud we all were of him.'

The Benz purred along the highway toward the city, and we all deferred to a pit stop, just wanting to get as far away from the nightmare in the country as soon as possible and back to the safety and security of our relative routine lives in the big city.

Breaking the silence, Nigel piped up from the backseat, "Well, team, I have an idea. Although we have all had a very hard day, I know that we won't sleep tonight, so I'm proposing that we all take the same flight as Stéphane's body to France tonight; it leaves around midnight."

He continued to explain, "I have already arranged with Air France and the Rabbi to send the body back home on Flight 0432 tonight, so why not fly out, too, to be there to support Stéphane's family through this terrible ordeal? I haven't notified your mom and dad yet, Madison, nor Stéphane's parents, and I thought we could at least add this news in when I do make the call. I know that your mom and dad will want you home immediately anyway, Madison. What do you all think?"

"I'm down with it, Uncle Nigie."

"Me too," chimed in Chi.

"Hmm…" I said, "I'm going to bow out to keep the family's privacy intact, but I think it's a fantastic idea for the three of you to accompany the body and to be there to share the grieving. I'll stay behind and keep the home fires burning."

"You sure, Denni?"

"Absolutely. And in fact, I may just call a girlfriend to come and have a sleep over tonight. We'll crack open a bottle of good red and watch a favorite chick flick just by ourselves. I'll be just fine."

Nigel promptly got on his phone, and, speaking with his assistant, arranged for three first-class tickets on Flt. 0432, Toronto – Marseilles, which was leaving at 12:15 that very night.

"We'll sleep on the plane. Right, boys?"

"Yeah, I can always sleep on the plane," Madison piped in. "Oh yeah, I just remembered, Uncle Nigie. Thanks so much for telling the police that my name was Madison Royal, instead of my real name. Can you imagine the shit-show that would be my life if the press got wind of today!?"

"Yes, Madison, a shit-show indeed."

Although I couldn't see Nigel's tired, stressed face in the back of the dark car, as he quietly continued to make his calls, I imagined he was smiling at Madison's youthful declaration that rose up from the darkened backseat.

I turned and looked at the driver. I didn't know Chi very well, of course, but I realized perhaps I had underestimated this thoughtful, soulful, quietly efficient, handsome, and well-dressed man. I had no idea of how he and Nigel had managed to release the body from its noose but I knew for sure that it would have taken grit and sheer toughness to pull it all off. It spoke of his and his employer's many years together. I could only imagine all their shared ups and downs that life in the big city bestows upon all of us mere mortals. And, yes, of course, now I knew about Chi's greenhouse and what kept him busy. However, what I didn't know at that time was what he really did for a living.

I reached up to pull the scrunchie from my ponytail, and I sighed out loud with the release. I felt Nigel's hand come from behind to touch and smooth down my tangled long hair. My tears sprang at the tenderness of his touch and, not wanting to show him, I tucked my head down and silently reached back to offer my hand in response. I knew with his 'Irish faerie' comment earlier in the day, long before our worlds came crashing down, that he 'got me.' Yes, he really got me.

Chi motored on, the radio played some of Nigel's favorite light jazz, and we all pulled into 7 Russell Hill Road in record time. As we all fell into the foyer, so glad to be back, I insisted that I walk home right then and there to give the three of them time to shower and pack for their midnight flight.

"Denni," Madison said while giving me a hug, "I've been thinking of me calling you a redneck woman, you know, like the song we were singing the other night."

"Well, you got that right, buster. That's me!"

"No, Denni, not at all. You're wonder woman, through and through. Thank you so much for taking care of me today. I'll never forget how amazing you were through everything."

"Your parents must be so proud of you, Madison. You are one hell of a stellar guy, you know. Take care of Nigel for me in France, please, and send him home soon."

He was a little teary-eyed as I looked into his face, so I looked away quickly to save him from embarrassment. I whispered a 'thank you' to Chi as I hugged him goodbye, and Nigel stepped out under the portico with me.

He spoke quietly, "Denni," holding me rather gently and apart from him. Staring intently into my upturned face, he said, "You are the most remarkable woman I know. You are so beautiful, inside and outside. Thank you for being you. There is so much I want to tell you, to share with you, to experience with you, but right now is not the time. I want to put some separation between the nightmare that was today, and with the future happiness that all our tomorrows will bring the two of us. I will be thinking of you every moment that I'm away, but Madison is going to need my attention for the next few days, so I may not be able to call as often as I would like to. I'm missing you already."

"And I'm missing you already too, Mr. Wonderful. Just go and do what you have to do. Please give my heartfelt condolences to everyone, and please take care of yourself."

As he watched me walk across the street, he called out, "Oh, expect a call from the Elmwood tomorrow. They will set you up with a few spa days to get your mojo back. On my tab. Enjoy!"

Hearing his caring words, I breathed in deep, turned around, and started a slow walk back toward him. I stepped off the curb to cross the street. He followed my lead and also stepped off the curb. We met halfway in the middle of the quiet street. It was the longest, most emotional, and most intimate kiss I have ever known.

A car turned the corner and swerved, narrowly missing us. The car window came down.

"Get a room!" the driver shouted as he sped up and disappeared around the bend.

I don't know if it was the whole day, the mind-blowing, one-of-a-kind kiss or the near-death car swerve that undone us, but the two of us began intermittently laughing and crying uncontrollably. We were completely unraveled. We staggered to the curb and sat down to collect ourselves. Twenty minutes later, with tears dried, Nigel simply took my hand, and we breathed in the summer evening in quiet repose. We had definitely been through the war.

Nigel proceeded to walk me home to my lobby door. He kissed me lightly on the lips and whispered, "Think of me when you're listening to the dragonflies."

He stepped back into the twilight and he was gone.

***

Chapter 5

A Birthday Present

I ran to answer the phone. "Good morning," I said with fingers crossed.

"Good morning to you, Ms. Brunette," His deep baritone voice rocketed right through me. "I arrived home early this morning, and I'm hoping that you can spare me a little time to say hello in person."

"And good morning to you, Mr. Wonderful. What exactly do you have in mind?" I smiled over the phone.

"I have to pick up a new jacket that I ordered from Harry's at Yorkdale, so I thought we could take in a late brunch after that. I'm still on Euro time, so I will be due to collapse by jetlag in the early afternoon. I promise I will have you back home by two at the latest. I really just want to see you."

"Perfect planning," I said, trying to keep it light. "How about 10:30 at your front door?"

"You're an angel. Can't wait to see you."

"Me too." I hung up the phone, a knot in my stomach forming at the thought of what was to come. Over the past week's calls from France, neither of us had mentioned our kiss that we had shared in the middle of the road and I was anticipating and hoping that my absence had made his heart grow fonder. I was more than ready, I argued to myself. But, was I really? In his absence, I must admit I suffered from cold feet, running hot and cold, fighting my old instincts to bail at the first sign of real attachment.

I nervously sorted through my closet, pulling out this and that, second-guessing myself on what to wear. "For God's sake, Denise," I chastised myself out loud, "get a grip!"

I leaned on his doorbell, and to my surprise, the door opened immediately and I found myself staring into the face of a small, rather tough-looking, no-nonsense older black woman who had one hand on her hip and a tea towel in her other. My eyes followed her dark brown collar down past her slim torso that topped her two skinny, bowed legs. Her carefully laced new black Sketchers were planted firmly in front of me, framing the doorway.

"Oh! Oh, sorry, is uh… Is uh…" I stuttered.

"Be right there, Denni! Please come in!" I heard from the depths of the house. The woman moved ever so slightly aside, but not enough for me to move past her. I squared my shoulders, raised my eyes to meet hers, and settled my mouth with lips pursed and teeth clenched. I squeezed past just as Nigel bounded into the foyer.

He looked at both our faces and said, "Oh, you two have not met yet. Denise Allen, this is Matilda Mattis. Mrs. Mattis runs the house for me."

I stuck out my hand with a terse, "Pleased to meet you," and she had no option other than to begrudgingly respond with a perfunctory handshake. I looked at Nigel. He looked at Mrs. Mattis. Mrs. Mattis decided that she wasn't leaving.

I watched Nigel as he grabbed his jacket and keys before saying, "I'll run ahead to back the car out."

He left me to fend for myself. We stared each other down, and by this time, my disappointment in not even getting a welcome-home kiss from Nigel was welling up, so she could see it on my face. What was her problem? I was still in the doorway when she slammed the door behind me and literally bumped me down onto the step. I heard the door lock click loudly and I swallowed my slow burn and walked out to Nigel's car.

I hopped in the car and as we pulled away from the curb, Nigel explained, "Mrs. Mattis is a tough nut to crack. Give her a little time." He started to laugh as he described the scene set with both of our thundercloud faces staring each other down in the foyer.

"It seems she has taken ownership not only of the house, but of me too!"

I listened as he told me the story of how he had met her, along with her back-story of surviving a tough life in Kingston, Jamaica, that had had a few ups and many downs. Now the two managed their lives, quite independent of each other, with her living in the back apartment and taking care of the house and him quietly adjusting his schedule to avoid her comings and goings with the routine housekeeping duties that she had performed for him over the last few years.

"By the looks of things, she has you wrapped around her little finger. Please don't expect me to make allowances for her rude behavior."

"Aw, she's okay."

"So much yarn, so little time."

We arrived at Yorkdale and I adjusted my mood accordingly as we walked hand-in-hand, old-school style to Harry Rosen Menswear to pick up the new jacket. I was happy to notice the two of us as we walked by a large mirrored wall in the mall. We were a good-looking couple. My summer dress and sandals matched up with his dark blue pima cotton golf shirt and his white jeans and loafers. We looked like a happily married, middle-aged couple somehow.

I remember eating lunch at the Restoration Hardware Café and looking into his handsome face, with his smile lines etched deep, and the square jaw with yesterday's stubble. 'Yes,' I thought, 'he must have called me the minute he got in the door. Didn't even shave.' I smiled wide and looked deep into his eyes, and when he realized I was looking right into his soul, his face flushed and he busied himself with his glass of water. Who would blink first? Not me, that was for damn sure.

I leaned forward and held the gaze. "Electric or straight razor?"

***

"Harump! Little Miss Whitey from the neighborhood decides to come in here and take over! Harump!" She mopped the kitchen floor for the umpteenth time that morning. "She'd better not make any trouble for my boy if she knows what's good for her. I'll whoop her sorry ass all the way to kingdom come!"

Five minutes later, with a dozen wipes over the already-sparkling white marble kitchen island, she continued examining the pros and cons of her boy finally bringing a girl home. "At least she's in his age bracket. She's no spring chicken, that's for sure. I gotta give her that. But if she thinks she can waltz in here with the big smile and the bouncy hair, she's got another thing comin'. And really, what's he thinkin!? A white woman! Tsk tsk tsk. That boy needs his head read! Harump!"

She turned to the fridge and wiped it down with fervor. "And him, yah never know. A body just can't read his face at all. He hides everything down. I always say it's the damn inscrutable Chinese in 'im. Too much Chinese blood in that Jamaican boy for his own good. Nothin' but a poker face," she bitched on to herself while she puttered in the very clean kitchen. "But I must admit there was a spark between the two of them. I felt it. Better not hurt my boy, Miss Whitey! Now that's all I'm gonna say about that."

***

I buzzed Nigel's doorbell and heard a shout to come in, so I stepped once again through the doorway and into the low light of the foyer. I cautiously, but half-jokingly, looked both ways to see if Mrs. Mattis was going to jump out at me. A jacket was flung over a chair, and a beautiful pair of leather gloves lay on top of the console. I reached over and picked up the soft lambskin gloves.

73

'Nicely done,' I mused. Even in the shadows, I could feel and appreciate the handwork. Yes, no doubt about it, the man had style.

"Nice work, eh?" he smooched in my ear.

"Talking about the gloves or the kiss?"

"Both. Are you ready to walk my legs off, Ms. Brunette?"

"As always."

As I skipped down the steps, he reached for my hand and said, "Speaking of gloves, I just happen to know a wonderful *'le gantier,'* and since I know your birthday is coming up, I would like to treat you to a pair or two that I guarantee you will enjoy for a lifetime."

"Oh, what a wonderful surprise! Yes, count me in, and thank you!" I leaned in to reach up to give him a kiss on the cheek as he continued in easy banter style.

"However, it may take a little arranging, as this particular glove maker is quite busy, so leave it with me and I'll arrange everything."

***

Since Nigel had returned home from France, the two of us, with still no words spoken of the big-drama kiss that we had shared, we reverted back to our comfortable, easy pattern of a nightly walk through the neighborhood. Actually, it gave the two of us a chance to get to know each other, and with the grace of nightfall, we strode up and down the darkened streets, enjoying the night air, spilling our stories to each other in the dark, looking straight ahead or toward the variety of porticos and gardens, anywhere except at each other, which required introverts to jump a very big hurdle. What would be our motivation?

However, I must admit all along and all the while that we were chipping away slowly but surely at our inherent shyness. The walls were coming down, albeit in a rather painfully slow, brick-by-brick fashion.

These stories shared between us, two shy adults of a certain age, began to weave the warp and weft of a true intimacy that neither of us had known for many, many years, if in fact ever.

We walked on, and we both oohed and awed over the maples that were just beginning to show their fall colors. I wondered to myself if the two of us were ever going to be able to enter the next season of our relationship, never mind the damn maples getting on with their next step. This never-ending tiptoeing around what was really going on between us was beginning to wear a little thin.

I instinctively spoke up, "Nigel, there seems to be an elephant in my room, or at least on my side of the sidewalk, so I want to run it by you. It feels awkward to me somehow."

"The ball's in your court. Shoot."

"It's just that I haven't been my usual polite self with you, and I apologize for my standoffishness. You see, I'm a little shy, but it gets more complicated than just shyness with you."

"Complicated? With me?"

"Yeah. I haven't even had the manners to invite you to my home, you know, so you can get to know me a little better. You are always so welcoming, but I feel a little shy about having you in my personal space and it has nothing to do with you, however."

He laughed softly. "Oh, I get where we're going with this. You mean that you don't want to see me any longer?"

I stopped dead in my tracks. "Oh my God, Nigel, no, no, it's quite the opposite, you see. I've messed this up completely. I'm such an idiot. I don't even know how to talk to you."

"Well, Ms. Brunette, try to gather your words and explain."

I blurted it out, "It all started with that kiss we shared in the middle of the road before you went to France."

He turned and pulled me in close. "You mean the long one where our tongues met and I had the biggest erection that I've ever had in my life?"

I laughed a little. "Yeah, that's the one."

"I know, I know," he sighed. "I think of nothing else."

Squeezing my hand, he looked down into my face with a big smile. "So, finally. Finally. We're there, aren't we?"

"Oh, we're there, all right."

"What are we going to do about it?"

"Let's seal the deal with another one of those kisses, just like the one in the middle of the road."

"Okay, okay, let's go then. My house."

I looked up at him, startled. "No! No, not your house!"

He started jogging, holding my hand. "Well then, your house. Sorry, I misunderstood. I thought you said you didn't want me at your house."

I pulled him into a stop. "No, you're not listening to me! What I said was exactly what I meant. I want a big kiss right here on the sidewalk."

He stood there, eyes wide with disbelief. "What the fuck!"

"I'm sorry. That's what I'm trying to tell you. I need a little time for my head to catch up with my body. I need you. I want you, but I'm just not ready yet in my head. I'm all nervous due to my past of running away from the situation when things get too close. And I don't want that with you. I want you forever. I'm just nervous; I guess it's partly due to my shyness."

"Fuck, man! Okay, okay, so clarify for me. You were just telling me that you can't invite me into your home. And why is that? Do you have a husband hiding in the closet or something?"

"Very funny. No, it's not that simple. You see, if it was just a husband, I could just shoot him and drag his body out to the garden in the middle of the night. But my problem is with me. I'm just nervous because I like you. I really like you. And I don't want to mess this up. And I must say, the real reason is that it's been a very, very long time."

He stood there, and he put his arms around me. "I know. I know. It's been a very, very long time for me too. I do know something though, Denni. You're worth waiting for. And to tell you the truth, I have my little issue with jealousy, so I was only half kidding when I asked you about your husband. I'm just as nervous as you are, and I know I'm way shyer than you. My track record with women is so bad. I can't even talk about it. I'm sorry for rushing you. That's why I've never pressed you to come back to my house after our walks. I just can't trust myself to be a gentleman around you and I understand that you're skittish. I'm just way ahead of you. I need you, and I have since I first laid eyes on you."

I looked up at him, and we both started to smile. "Hmm, so our problem is that we both need each other too much. Not a bad problem to have, I'd say."

He grabbed my hand and put it on the big bulge in his sweats. "You see what you're missing?"

I whispered into his ear, "It's probably just a pair of extra socks you've stuffed down there for effect."

"It's all me, baby. I'm happy to get it out if you like, to prove my point."

I laughed, "Not necessary."

"You are bordering on becoming a tease, Ms. Brunette."

"I'll tell you what. Here's the deal. Tomorrow night before our walk, you come to my apartment for the cook's tour. Check all my closets for that pesky husband. And any other skeletons. They're bound to come out sooner or later anyway. And then, after the five-minute tour, and if you are a gentleman, I'll treat to ice cream down at the Dutch Dreams Ice cream Parlor down on Vaughn Road."

"Your plan is perfect. And meanwhile, I'll start making a few plans of my own."

"Like what?"

"That's for me to know and for you to find out."

I opened the door to his knock. He was holding a beautiful bouquet of the same wild flowers he had sent me after our first luncheon date.

He leaned in for a kiss on my cheek as I said, "Oh, Nigel, they are so beautiful. I love the wild flowers. They remind me of the farm. Thank you!"

As he was slipping off his shoes, he said, "And they remind me of you."

I said, "No, no, please, leave them on, and we'll only be a minute anyway. Come in. Come in. Can you get me that vase from the top shelf of the *ètagére*?"

He came into the kitchen with the vase and as he looked at the art on my kitchen wall, he exclaimed, "Oh my God, these are tremendous! Look at the color in them! This is something that I would choose for myself! Where on earth did you find the pair?"

"Yeah, I love the colors too. Very French. He's pretty well known now, but he's not that old. Igor Marceau, he lives in Provence. These art prints are from 2002. I bought them in Atlanta at an auction last year. I researched the originals and they sell for eight hundred thousand to a cool million each. Crazy, huh?"

"They're very good. They look like originals. But look at your copper pots and pans. Are they French too?"

I laughed, a little embarrassed with his enthusiasm for my old things. "Yes, and there's no doubt about it. They are original, all right. I lug them around from place to place."

I knew that I had done the right thing by inviting him into my small, humble apartment. He was simply beaming as I showed him my decorated balcony and then my bedroom. He asked me what the jumping off point in the decorating was to make me paint the feature wall behind the bed fuchsia pink.

"It was the sheets. I'm a sucker for Italian linens, and when I saw this fuchsia pink, I just had to have them, and then I color-matched the paint from there."

"A very bold choice, but brilliant. The color is all you. The modern color with the gold, ornate European headboard. Girly-girl all the way. Sexy as hell. I love it."

"Yes, it is a bold choice. And you know what they say about bold choices?"

"No, but I have a feeling you're going to tell me."

"Beware of the non-conformist."

He smiled as he said, "Forewarned is forearmed, they say."

As we made our way into the living room, he asked, "Is that a Simon Bull?"

"Yes, and that's another thing that I've had for years. I know it's not an original, but I love the color, don't you? When I moved in here, I made the drapes to go with that painting, and my desk just fits perfectly in the front window. Don't you think so? Here, please, take a seat at my computer so you will know my view, if I ever send you an email."

"Oh. So, so nice with the big tree right here in front of you. The third floor is perfect for living in the treetops, isn't it? Nice white computer. It's so streamlined. Not like my old clunker. Oh, is this where the tunes are coming from?" he said as he looked at my screen.

"Yes, easy-peasy. It's called Radio Tunes and it's free. Right now, it's tuned into Classic Motown, but you can get all the internet radio stations on it."

He twirled the swivel chair and surveyed the living room, and he said softly, "I love it here, Denni. It feels like you and it looks like you. It's artistic and you have a very good eye for design. Although your home is uniquely original, is there a specific designer that you follow?"

"Yes and no. Yes, to the designer. It's Kelly Wearstler. Are you familiar with her work? She's bold but really all about comfort and joy. And no, I can't afford a designer per se; I do everything myself, from sewing my drapes to painting my walls. But I have a few of her books here, if you'd like to take them home with you."

"Thanks. I'd love that. You know, Denni, I could be so comfy and at home here; so that does it. I will have to be on my best behavior so you will invite me here for dinner one night."

"I think we could arrange that. I'm a pretty good cook, you know."

"If you cook, I'll wash up."

"It's a deal. But right now, ice cream awaits."

***

Two days later, I had a call which was initiated downstairs from a delivery service. I buzzed the voice in, throwing a robe over my pajamas to cover up, trying to think of what I had ordered online.

"Yes. Thank you. Sign where? Oh, of course, thank you."

I swung the door shut with my foot as I slit the unfamiliar delivery packaging open.

I placed it on my desk and savored the sight. The surprise delivery package housed a dark blue gift box about twelve inches long, five inches wide, and four inches deep. There was no wrapping paper, just a wide black satin ribbon simply bow-tied around the exquisite matte finished box.

Not taking my eyes off the beautiful box, I blindly reached behind me to pull up a chair. This required my full attention. I placed the box on my lap, and I slowly pulled the ribbon open and gingerly lifted the box's lid.

I folded the layers of crisp, black tissue paper back carefully and I felt my face flushing with the revelation.

Red leather with *'Ms. Brunette'* engraved in gold lettering was on the front of the travel wallet. As I snapped the tab open, I could see through the folded, thin white paper that was tucked in the right-hand pocket. The type read:

TRAVEL ITINERARY

The appointment with M. Louis Ferrand, Le Gantier, located in the Septième Arrondissement, Paris, was listed on Day Three of the seven-day itinerary. First-class Air France tickets made out to Denise Allen and Nigel Royal were tucked into the left-side pocket of the travel wallet along with reservations for six nights in 'Le Suite du Jardine' at The Four Seasons Hotel George V. There was a small, plain white card tucked into the right-side pocket in front of the itinerary. He had once again used his fountain pen with the purple ink to write:

Happy Birthday, Baby. Love, N.

The old adage, "You've got to kiss a lot of frogs before you meet your prince," came to mind as I realized that I was about to jump into the deep end, colloquially speaking, of course.

Could this be the real deal?

***

Chapter 6
Paris

Not often was I nervous, but here I stood in the tight confines of the Air France 'toilette,' peeling off my clothes and shimmying into a set of new streamlined 'loungewear' that was being touted all over the internet as the latest and greatest thing to wear while snuggling down in first-class on an overnight flight. I assured myself that the outfit was perfect for the occasion. The flight attendant had already given both of us complimentary pajamas to wear, but my own fit me to a 't,' and it was no time to let Nigel see me in a pair of one-size-fits-all freebies. I left my new navy-blue pushup bra and matching panties on, but I would save my sexy La Perla nightwear for Paris.

I hadn't slept the night before, nervously packing and repacking, second-guessing every item I had carefully chosen for the trip. It wasn't like me to lose confidence in a situation, but this slow and steady romance had me rattled completely. I was in way, way over my head, and a part of me just couldn't handle all the happiness coming my way. It had been a long time coming, and the sex to come – oh please – I couldn't even go there! You might say that I was a nervous wreck.

Thankfully, the flight attendant and Nigel had made up both beds in our sleeper cabin while I was changing, and Nigel had thoughtfully turned down our lights. By the time I had snuggled under my covers and lay nose-to-nose with Nigel, who was fully entrenched in his own bed, we both began to giggle, and soon we were whispering about where to have our first dinner in the city of lights.

I must have dozed off. I remember opening my eyes to see Nigel still watching me, dark brown eyes soft and a slight smile on his lips.

"Stop. Stop it. Stop looking at me. Go to sleep. Now. You'll be so cranky in the morning."

"It's your snoring that's keeping me awake. And it's all the drooling from the side of your mouth. And, oh my God, your hair is such a wreck. Honestly, it's a little scary, Ms. Brunette. What have I gotten myself into?" he teased, his happy face now grinning from ear to ear.

"Stop right now or I'll call the flight attendant."

"How did I get so lucky? Please, God, tell me. How did I get so damn lucky?"

That was the last thing I heard as my lips smiled and my eyes closed.

***

"Will there be anything else, Monsieur Royal?"

"Non, et merci, Jorge," Nigel said as he placed the folded euros into the hotel attendant's palm.

I didn't know where to look first. The suite was magnificent – understated elegance and at the same time totally luxurious. The French doors in the living room opened to a small terrace and the chairs were lined up to view the top half of the Eiffel Tower from this side of the Seine. Frette sheets on the king-sized bed and traditional Fortuny patterned drapes opened to a small Juliette balcony in the bedroom.

Nigel was distancing himself a little from me. He was dancing around the living room, flipping a coin over from hand to hand. "Time to flip a coin. Heads, I win. Tails, you lose."

"What are we flipping for?"

"The ensuite bathroom. Loser takes the small one."

He flipped the coin and deftly caught it, calling out the winner before I had a chance to review his call. Half laughing and half running, I found the ensuite quickly before he changed the rules into a two-out-of-three. The bathroom was half the size of my whole apartment back home, and as I caught sight of my travel-weary face in the mirror, I stopped. I sobered. I knew there was no going back. It was show time.

I squared my shoulders, took a deep breath, turned, and stepped out of the bathroom. Straight ahead, he was standing there in the middle of the big, beautiful bedroom, watching me. His heart was written all over his face. The silence was deafening. After what seemed to be a lifetime of stillness, our feet began to move in slow motion toward each other and our arms slowly stretched out to receive each other. Our hearts were pounding out of our chests. It was heaven and it was hell, a very bad case of the nerves for both of us. With his arms wrapped around me, chest heaving, a deep, muffled moan sounded from his chest. He was struggling to take deep breaths. I realized his shirt was wet with my tears. I wiped my cheeks off, trying to calm myself so that I could calm him down. "What a pair of fated lovers we are! Romeo and Juliette have nothing on us," I anguished to myself.

We stood there, unable to climb out of our nervousness and shyness, clinging to each other, both getting our bearings. After a moment or two, he whispered calmly and quietly with his mouth in my ear.

His recovery was admirable; I still couldn't even look at him as he coaxed me, "Let's leave the unpacking for the morning. We'll catch a shower now in our respective bathrooms and I'll meet you in our big, comfy bed in five minutes. And," he quietly asserted, "baby, be prepared for the best lovemaking you have ever had in your entire life." I knew by his voice he had mustered up a smile on his big, beautiful lips as he described what I was in for.

I stood there, still unable to speak. My head down to cover my nervous tears, I nodded in agreement as he gave me a light kiss while turning me around and giving me a soft push on both shoulders toward the ensuite.

"Go! Just go!" he encouraged. "I've waited for you for one hundred and ten days, and I can't wait any longer!" his baritone came to life as his long legs strode out of the bedroom, shirt crumpling onto the floor and belt flying through the air as he broke into a few bars of Leonard Cohen's old song, *I'm Your Man.*

I put my silly schoolgirl nerves behind me and even managed a little smile. Maybe it was the promise that Leonard's famous lyrics suggested, but I was back on the right track! I quickly unzipped my suitcase to pull out the La Perla red silk short nightie set with the black lace trim. Armed with that, along with my makeup bag and body lotion under the other arm, I shut the bathroom door and had the quickest shower a girl could have under the circumstances. I brushed my teeth and slathered the George-V house lotion up my arms and down my legs. 'No Channel No. 5 tonight; natural is better,' I told myself. I glanced at the fluffy, white George-V robe hanging behind me and looked down to see matching slippers underneath it. 'Good for the morning,' I thought. I pulled my ponytail out and brushed my hair down long and straight. The red loose panty peeped out below the short top barely held together with loose, thin black straps. 'Easy to get out of,' I conspired.

I opened the ensuite's door slowly to try to make a sultry entrance of sorts, although I knew I was a little on the shy side to pull off a sexy, I-do-this-every-day-of-my-life look. I noticed Nigel had closed the heavy Fortuny drapes and lit a single candle by the bedside. It flickered, casting a shadow along the wall covering. There were two glasses of water on a small tray on the other night table and no music.

He had pulled the bedcovers down and propped himself up, head and bare chest against the padded headboard, with a pale, striped linen pajama bottom covering his long legs – sexy as hell. He obviously had been spending time in the gym. His pecks were high and full, and his abs were tight. His chest hair still looked damp and curled tight into perfect, tiny round circles on his chest. I'm a sucker for chest hair; why the younger generation of men shave their chests is beyond me. Manscaping they called it, balls too. That must hurt. In my panic, I realized my mind was racing and I took a deep breath to focus on my lover. I had to smile as I studied his handsome face. In spite of the very adult and very hot do-or-die moment that was upon us, he somehow looked like a kid on Christmas morning, about to open his favorite present.

I pulled off a catwalk strut over to the king-sized bed to try to cover my shyness, and I leaned forward and swung my one leg over his torso to straddle him. He was big and hard under his pajama, so I moved up a little around his waist to enjoy some foreplay before there was no return. I was pretty sure that he was aware that my fancy red silk panty was leaving a hot, wet spot all over his navel.

"So," I inquired with one eyebrow raised, "what, exactly, were you boasting about before our showers?"

"Baby, I was saying that I'm your man. The man that's gonna give you everything you want, and then some."

I tried to play it straight, but I was very tempted to smile through our faux boldness. "How do you know what I want, lover boy?"

"Beautiful, you are going to tell me. And I want details."

I leaned up toward his handsome face, so my breasts were front and center. I put my hands in his damp, curly, sexy hair. I could feel his hands sliding up my legs and resting on each side of my ass.

"First things first," I purred. "Start with your mouth on my breasts and simply work down. All the way down. I want it all. I want to feel your lips over every inch of my body."

He moved as if to sit up, and he quickly used one arm to wrap around me. He flipped me over on my back in one smooth move. With his other hand, he slipped my red silk panty down over my hips, and I raised my knees so he could slide them down my legs. His long arm flicked upwards, and I smiled as I saw the panty first floating up and up and then whooshing down on the floor ten feet from our big king-sized bed.

I remembered Nigel singing Leonard Cohen's *I'm Your Man* as he peeled out of his clothes a short twenty minutes ago, and I smiled as I thought, 'I've got my own song for right here, right now!' I mentally sang out Rod Stewart's *Tonight's the Night, Everything's Gonna Be Alright.* I was living the dream. I leaned back and closed my eyes, all prepared to enjoy every second of what was to come.

He settled with his one leg between mine, both hands cradling my face, with his lips almost touching mine. He whispered, "But no, no, no, Ms. Brunette. You've got it all wrong. We don't start with the breasts. You see, first we start with the mouth. I have been thinking of that one kiss we shared in the middle of the street every moment of every day since it happened. Any objections to my plan of action?"

"No, Your Honor."

"That's what I like to hear. And we won't be needing your sexy nightie either."

"Yes, Your Honor." I lifted my arms up and he slid my nightie off with one hand and tossed it over to the floor. His big full lips landed softly on my mouth, and I mentally declassified our first kiss in the middle of that street down to nothing but child's play. This kiss was an absolute stunner. I opened my mouth for more.

He was magnificent. He played me like a fiddle. And I was eager to match his every move.

Long, long after the candle had burned lower, then finally out, and we were absolutely exhausted, my amazing lover said in hushed wonderment, "Here we are, and it's now well documented. I'm a crier, and you're a screamer. Who knew?"

Nigel spooned us into a deep, deep sleep.

***

My eyes adjusted to the dim light of the room and I checked the bedside table clock quietly as to not wake Nigel. Oh my God, it was eleven p.m. Paris time, and I was starving! I was still on Toronto time. I lay there thinking if I could possibly sneak out of bed to reach the big bowl of fruit on the dining room table that I had noticed when we had checked in. I inched my way out of the bed and changed my route. I slipped into the big ensuite, as I realized it was my only time to get into the shower and wash my hair before Nigel would see me with no makeup and wet hair up in a towel. Not wanting to turn on the light in case I would wake him, I left the door ajar and clicked on the small night light beside the vanity.

As I squished the shampoo back and forth through my long hair, I heard his voice softly call in from the bathroom doorway, "Is there room for me in there?"

I stuck my head around the glass wall and said, "What are you waiting for?"

As I made room for his long legs to get in and over the tub, he was shyly confessing that he had never done this before, that is, never showered with a girl. As I quickly looked up to read his face, I was a little taken aback to see that he was being honest about being a 'shower virgin' of sorts. My heart went out to his vulnerability, and I made a mental note to add this little tidbit to my notes on this handsome, sophisticated, but complex introvert that I was simply having a little fling with.

If the truth be known, I should have been asking myself, 'Who's kidding whom here? Why am I so afraid to admit that this 'little fling' may, in fact, be the real deal?' I deep-sixed that nagging little thought within the blink of an eye and came out of my head with my usual bantering cover.

"Okay, so, first things first," I said in my best matter-of-fact teacher's voice. "Before you start any project, you ensure that your tools have been plugged in and charged up." I placed both my hands around his long and currently flaccid penis. "Do you understand?"

"Yes, miss. Check. What comes next, miss?"

I started laughing as he continued his part in our little classroom skit. "Miss, wait! Miss! We have to name this old but trusted tool if that's okay with you. What's it going to be? Just another run-of-the-mill Johnson? Or how about Vlad the Impaler?"

"Well," I said, "that old tool, as you fondly call it, just went from a wet noodle to the Bone Ranger in less than three seconds. I'm impressed. But I'm going to leave his nomenclature up to you."

"You're impressed? And you've just met him today. He's going to really impress the hell out of you over the next week. You have no idea."

"I might have just met him today, but I've been dreaming of him ever since I saw his big erection on our first luncheon date."

As his long arms went under my ass to lift me up, I wrapped my legs around his hips. I raised my arms around his shoulders and rubbed my breasts against his chest so my nipples could feel his chest hair. He held me up against the shower wall with one hand while his other hand guided himself into me.

"Do you like this, baby?"

I cried out, "More! I want more! I want it all!"

***

He ordered room service in perfect French as we stood there at midnight, Paris time, both in our George-V big fluffy white bathrobes and matching slippers. We had decided it was the perfect time to unpack and he took the left side of the dresser drawers, and I took the right without so much of a word, just like married folks.

He was dancing around, acting like a goof, and he ran over to the Fortuny drapes, took the cord from the side, and was lassoing it all the way back to the dresser.

I couldn't help but laugh; he was like a little boy with the big grin on his face. I asked him, "What are you doing now? Surely, you're not going to tie me up like in *Fifty Shades of Grey* or anything like that!"

He laid the cord carefully down on the carpet in front of the center of the dresser. "This is the line in the sand, baby. My side and your side. Get it?"

I immediately stuck my foot out an inch or so over the line, all the while laughing at his silliness. I stuck out my tongue as he shook his head to warn me of dire consequences, and before I knew it, he had scooped me up, sat on the bed, and threw me over his knee in order to spank me. He cried, "Say uncle! Say uncle!"

And as I cried right back, "Never!" the door chime sounded. Our late-night supper was soon laid out on the dining room table with white linens and all.

We were both still giggling away as he danced around the table, pouring the red for me and the white for him. We delved into the room service *potage du poulet* and *croque messieurs* with gusto. He had his trademark wide grin plastered all over his face as he gently wiped the melted, gooey *gruyère* from my chin. I realized that that moment, that very moment, was the happiest moment of my whole life.

***

I woke up slowly and rolled over to find that I had been sleeping by myself. I listened. The morning light was filtering in from the living room. I heard some light jazz playing, and I could hear the rustle of a newspaper page being turned.

I ducked into the ensuite and freshened up a little. I was tender from all the sex the night before, but with any luck, I told myself, I would be good to go by this evening. I brushed my hair up in a high pony, and I put on a white stretch-lace teddy under my pale pink silk pajamas that I had bought in New York a few years earlier. They were new-looking, of course, as I was always short on occasion to wear them, and as the delicate silk slipped over my shoulders, I knew that I had nailed it. I left the top of the silk pajama unbuttoned to take the 'prim and proper' out of the ensemble itself, and I slipped on my old ballet slippers to meet my new world comprising of a suite at the George-V, a handsome lover and some light jazz.

As I entered the living room, I was suddenly overwhelmed by the whole crazy situation, and in shyness, I quickly sat down in a big armchair that was facing the sofa, where Nigel was sprawled, enjoying the *'Le Monde'* and a cup of coffee that he had poured from a tall, silver coffee pot that was resting on the coffee table.

He put the newspaper down on his stomach and said softly, "Good morning, sleepyhead. I hope I didn't wake you. It's just after eight. I've ordered breakfast in this morning; it should be here soon. Would you like coffee, baby?"

The doorbell sounded before I could answer, and he stood up, grabbed his robe to put on over his pajama bottom, and came over to my chair. He cupped my face in his hands and gently, ever so gently, kissed me on the lips. As he turned to walk to the door, I grabbed onto his robe's belt. He looked back and stopped. I pulled the belt in to return his kiss and I offered him a "Good morning, Mr. Wonderful" before releasing him to get the door on the third ring. I watched him stride down the hall, tying his robe closed to hide the rise under his pajama bottom before he had to open the door.

Nigel decided we would eat breakfast casual-style, and the wait staff set up the full American breakfast complete with white linens right on the coffee table, instead of on the formal dining room table. He sat on the sofa, and I continued to sit in the big armchair and pulled up a little closer to the full breakfast that included eggs Florentine.

We both wolfed down the breakfast, laughing all the while, with me teasing Nigel that he couldn't trust himself to have me sit beside him on the sofa.

"You're damn right, sugar. You are going to have to keep your safe distance, or we will never leave this room for the next six days."

We both put our feet up on our respective sides of the big, round coffee table. We shared the two Paris newspapers, *Le Monde* and *Le Figaro*, and circled a few restaurant reviews, gallery hours of operation, and which department stores were having which sale. We made a loose plan to see *The Thinker* in the Musée Rodin Garden and Monet's water lilies in the Musée d'Orlay at some point, and both of us nixed the Moulin Rouge for some reason. He reminded me that our appointment with the glove-maker was coming up on Day Three.

We were going to take it easy that first day, as jetlag would probably present itself in the afternoon. The plan was to just walk down to the Eiffel Tower and on the way back have a browse through the many, many bouquinistes that line the Seine, where they sell thousands and thousands of second-hand books from their individual tables and stalls. The lazy morning start was as close to heaven as one can get. It gave both of us a chance to climatize a little from our foray into amazing sex, in order not to sink back into that painfully shy world that we mostly lived in.

As I moved through my *Le Figaro* page by page, I looked over at him. He had tossed his robe off earlier and had thrown his newspaper on the carpet. He was just lying there all stretched out on the sofa, watching me. I couldn't help but look at his sexy bare chest and the huge bulge in his pajama bottom.

My newspaper slipped from my fingers and I walked over and kneeled down beside him. He put his hands in my hair to release the ponytail clip, and my hair fell all over his bare hips as I slid his pajama down. My hands held his big erection, and I opened my mouth to give him relief from our long, sexy breakfast tease.

***

We stood there, taking in the long view of the Eiffel Tower, and we both agreed that it hadn't changed a bit, but it just seemed to be at its most beautiful that particular day. Maybe it was us that had changed since we had individually visited the famous monument years before. As we headed back to the bouquinistes, I explained my whole theory about how it was a different world when traveling with a partner rather than traveling solo. I gave him many examples of me traipsing around the world always on my own and always wishing I had someone to share it with.

"Exactly!" Nigel exclaimed. He explained that was why he didn't travel very much. He couldn't stand the aloneness of it all. He added, "But back to your theory. Well done, by the way, with all your own personal examples of traveling alone. Your summary points to the solution that all you have to do is to travel with a mate. However, it doesn't include the magic potion. A potion that you may not even be aware of."

"Oh. So, are you saying that I don't know what I'm talking about?"

He looked down at me and grinned. "Now, now. It's way too early in our holiday to be having our first fight."

I laughed. "Oh. Oh. Did I sound a little defensive there?"

"Not really. I'm teasing you. It's just that I have the advantage over you here. You see, I'm on the receiving end of this particular magic potion that you may not have recognized before."

"Magic potion? Such as?"

"Faerie dust."

"Are you kidding me?" I could feel my face starting to flush. "What are you talking about?"

He stopped and pulled me close and whispered in my ear, "My capricious little Irish faerie, you come complete with faerie dust, which you sprinkle out on whim. You have no idea what you do to me."

We lost ourselves in the world of second-hand books, and a few times I would look up and he would be down the row a little, lost in a volume. I smiled to myself as I watched him look up as if he had just realized where he was, and his eyes would search up and down the row until he spotted me. He would wave to me excitedly as if he had found a first edition that was worth a million dollars or something. It was obvious he was having the time of his life as I was. How was it possible that we both loved the same things so much of the time? I had to drag him away to get a bite to eat for our late lunch.

We sat outdoors of a small *pâtisserie*, eating our jambon-beurres down to the last crumbs. He grabbed my hand over the table as we ordered a coffee, and I knew by the serious look on his face that something was on his mind. "Baby," he said in a quiet voice as he leaned in to me, "are you okay? Are you a little sore from our lovemaking last night? I'm sorry if I was a little rough in the shower. You just make me crazy. I'll try to take it easy."

"Yes, I'm a little tender. But that's normal. But please know; *taking it easy* are not words in my sex vocabulary, except for when you're doing one thing in particular." I had to smile at his eagerness to continue the conversation; he plainly just wanted to talk about sex.

He half-rose from his chair, keeping his napkin over the bulge in his jeans and slid his chair over next to mine. He put his one arm around my shoulders, held my hand, and said softly, "Tell me, baby, when do you like it easy?"

I half-laughed and said, "I'm not sure if this is the right time and place for this discussion. You really want to get into it right here, right now?"

"Yeah, baby, right now," he said eagerly. "I can't resist you. And I want to know how I can please you."

"Nigel, look around us. Look where we are and what we're doing. And just the fact that my side of the conversation includes 'we' instead of 'I' says it all. All of this is what pleases me."

"What!? All of a sudden, my beautiful Irish Faerie is shy? No, no, no. Talk to me," he whispered in my ear.

"Well, okay, I'll tell you if you really want me to. You see," I said softly, looking straight into his sincere, eager face, "I like it nice and slow and easy when you are going down on me, and I put my hands in your beautiful hair to push you down further, you know, like last night. And then you use both hands to spread me wide open where I'm all wet for you, you know, before you start kissing my clitoris with your lips and your tongue. And that's exactly when I like it easy."

He straightened out his long legs and pressed his napkin down into his lap. "You are such a handful! Oh, my God! Now what am I going to do with all this?"

"You asked!" I smiled and whispered into his ear, "Do you want me to tell you now when I like it rough?"

"Don't you dare! One more word out of you, and I'm going to have to walk around the streets of Paris this afternoon with a big, wet stain on the front of my jeans. It's going to take me another thirty minutes just to be able to stand up."

"Whatever you say, darling. You sit here and have another coffee and just chill while I do a little window-shopping right here beside us."

He whispered into my ear before kissing me on the cheek, "And I'd better not look at your ass as you walk away. Not once, or I'm in big trouble."

As Nigel got out his cell to call my favorite restaurant to make a dinner reservation, I walked the few steps to the small shop right next door to us, with beautiful gold foil signage written on the glass of the front window. It read: *'Letterai.'* They sold special stationery, handmade writing paper, Mont Blanc fountain pens, and the like. The window display was exquisite. It was the gloves that caught my attention at first. The whole display was set as a 1930s woman's *boudoir* with a Louis-sixteenth lady's writing desk up front and center. A pair of vintage ivory, hand-tatted, three-quarter-length gloves lay beside a dark red tam on one side of the antique desk, with a fur stole draped casually over the small chair. It looked like the woman had just arrived home from a night at the opera and was compelled to write her *'merci'* note immediately. A variety of handmade notepapers and fountain pens with a small, clear glass bottle of opened purple ink lay amongst the envelopes on the right side. There was a variety of delicate pages, all handwritten, of course, in French in the same purple ink, but I couldn't read the fancy, old-fashioned French script that outlined the perceived 'thank you.'

Nigel had finally calmed down, and he clicked off his phone from booking the restaurant before joining me at the window display. "We're all set for tonight," he said as I started to point out the vintage gloves and the penned thank-you notes written in the same purple ink that he used at home.

Meanwhile, from inside the shop, the French shopkeeper, wearing her dark hair up in a French twist and Channel Red on her lips, crossed her arms in contempt as she watched the couple perusing her window display. She knew by the woman's animated expressions and their dress that they were not Parisienne. "Fucking arrogant Americans. They think they rule the world. Them and their US dollars. Well, not this one. Not on my watch. They come over here with their loud voices and horrible accents, demanding this and demanding that. They let their mouthy kids run roughshod in our restaurants and always want a discount. I'm going to jack up the price by twenty percent if they dare to open my door."

I stood there with Nigel's arm around my shoulders, pointing out all the fine details of the display, "Look, Nigel, it's the same purple ink that you use!" But it was the vintage, hand-tatted ivory gloves that I kept going back to.

"Well, let's go in and try them on."

"Oh, babe, it's just a display. They only sell paper goods here. But I do want to go in and get you a few of those little notebooks that you are always carrying around."

As the small doorbell tinkled to announce our arrival, I sized up the shopkeeper's haughty attitude immediately. I turned my back to her and mouthed the words to Nigel, "She thinks we're Americans."

In response, Nigel's eyebrows went up as if to say, "What the hell are you talking about?"

We browsed. She watched. We browsed some more. Not a word was spoken. Finally, I said in my broken French, "I'd love to see some of your handmade notepaper. Would you be kind enough to show me the blue and white?"

She plopped it down in front of me, tapping her red lacquered nails on the display case while gazing out of the window.

"Oh, *c'est beau. Très, très beau. Merci. Nous sommes Canadiens. Je désolé avec ma française. Mais.* It's just so nice to be here in Paris. *Nous visitons votre la ville lumière pour la semaine.*"

"Oh. Oh. Oui. Je comprendre. N'est-ce pas l'Américain?"

I tittered softly, "Oh. No. No, we live in Toronto. We hardly ever go to the USA. It's just not our cup of tea. We find that the Canadian culture is much more in line with the European way of life."

At the first mention of our Canadian identity, the bitchy French shopkeeper morphed into the most charming woman I had ever met in my whole life and began to speak English like it was her first language.

Nigel and I enjoyed a full hour of her showing us every scrap of paper in her store, along with the beautiful Mont Blanc pens, notebooks, embossing possibilities, and leather desk sets, right down to telling us all the ins and outs of her exquisite window display. She even allowed me to try on the vintage gloves that, sadly, were not for sale.

Nigel insisted on buying me a red Mont Blanc fountain pen and a bottle of the purple ink to go with it. I bought him a half dozen of his small black leather notebooks that he always used. She proposed that we leave our purchases with her until the following day so that she could have the Mont Blanc pen engraved and Nigel's black leather notebooks embossed. We agreed wholeheartedly. Nigel laughed all the way back to the hotel at his Irish faerie's sly efforts to get some decent service.

Our jetlag had kicked in as anticipated, and Nigel set his alarm so we wouldn't miss our 8:00 p.m. dinner reservation. We fell onto the bed in exhaustion, and the next thing I heard two hours later was a faraway sound of beep, beep, beep, and feeling Nigel's lips on the back of my neck.

***

Le Grand Colbert was exactly as I had remembered. It was still situated down the little laneway of sorts, hence the name 'Colbert,' meaning passageway. There were lots of small galleries and shops nearby, so we had taken our time strolling down to the big glass doors of the famous eatery.

The French brasserie was frozen in the old Belle-Epoque Paris-style, and, in fact, was quite similar to Balthazar's in New York City. I was amused with Nigel being ever so charming in his nerdy way as he discussed the menu with me in great length, and throughout the meal, he would bring out his little notebook and jot down thoughts on our choices as they were presented, one at a time, with great fanfare.

As the wait staff brought our courses out, still in the steaming-hot copper pots, Nigel exclaimed, "Denni, these are exactly like your pots and pans at home!"

"Yes, you're right. My old pots and pans and me – we're the real deal, you know."

We shared our meals like lovers do, and I had to pinch myself. So, this was how the other half lived; that was, the half that was not single. But there was another difference of us being just lovers. We were new lovers. It was written in our starry eyes. We had very little conversation actually, just two happy faces devouring the other, totally engrossed in every little eyebrow raise and laugh line. He had the curried salmon with lentils, and I had the duck confit with garlicky potatoes. We shared the warm chocolate fondant for dessert. It was perfect.

"Guess what I brought along in my purse?"

"A revolver?"

"No, silly. A lock."

"Oh, a lock. Of course. Imagine me guessing a gun. Now, inform me, darling. What could we possibly need a lock for?"

"We're in Paris. And we're lovers. I want us to go somewhere on the way home tonight where we're going to use it."

"I'm afraid to ask, my Irish faerie."

"Now, now. It's a very romantic gesture I'm offering to you. We're going to the Pont des Arts."

His smile could have lit up the whole city. "Oh, I see. My beautiful, eccentric femme fatale is showing a softer side of herself here."

"I also brought a permanent marker with me so you can write something on your side. I've already written mine. And I'm just wondering if we'll write something similar to each other. Shall I bring it out right here and now for you to complete your side? Now, I don't want you to see what I've written until after you write. Deal?"

"Deal. Lay it on me."

He wrote without hesitation. I watched him form a heart and put our initials inside it. Below, he wrote the date. We finished our wine as the ink dried, and then I flipped it over for him to read my inscription.

"Same," he said softly. Grabbing my hands over the table, he leaned in to give me a soft kiss on my lips. "So now we're going to lock our initials onto the bridge along with all the other lovers that have ever come to Paris."

"Exactly."

***

The actual locking of our lock brought a whole different vibe to the otherwise happy, upbeat night. I wasn't expecting it, and Nigel didn't appear to be ready for it either.

It happened after we finally found a spot on the bridge where we could squeeze our lock in among the thousands of others. It was down low, and we were both crouched down so that we could snap it into place with his big hand covering mine. We were laughing a little, and as we stooped down, I raised my face close to his so that we could kiss to seal the deal. However, the moment our lips touched, it became all too serious, and the two of us were taken aback but not willing to break the spell either. We breathed into each other's mouth, and after a long, tender kiss, I looked up and saw that he had tears in his eyes, the same as mine. I felt his hand squeeze down on mine, and we heard our lock click in finality.

Without a word between us, as we stood up, he opened his jacket to keep me warm, and the heat from his chest melted my heart like never before. For some reason, I hesitated on throwing the key into the Seine. Something told me just to hold on to it, to keep it safe somehow.

"Throw it, darling," he urged. I threw it down… down… down into the blackness that was the river.

93

We walked back across the bridge in silence. "Coffee?" he asked.

"No, thanks. Is that okay with you?"

"Whatever you want, baby."

We rode the elevator up in silence, simply holding hands, with our bodies stuck like glue from my shoulder down through my hip. Looking in the antiqued mirror that lined the elevator car, the reflection showed a middle-aged couple, both looking a little solemn. I think we were both still jetlagged and a little overwhelmed with all the emotional output over the last twenty-four hours. I noticed that the elevator operator, the same one who took us downstairs earlier that evening, was averting our eyes, but he could not wipe the wide smile off his face. 'Ah,' I thought, 'love is a permeable, palpable entity. It seeps into the small cracks and breaks through the tough scars that all hearts bear, even if you are simply a third party to a great love affair. And here I am, right in the thick of it.'

I just stood quietly there in our foyer as Nigel unwound both of our scarves and unbuttoned and hung up our coats. No words were spoken. In the quiet, he took me by the hand and led me directly into our big bedroom and sat me down on the edge of the bed. The staff had come in in our absence and dressed the bed with a fresh set of beautiful, white Frette sheets, all ready, made up, and turned down. A single long-stemmed red rose lay on the crisp white pillow.

I put my hands in his hair as he kneeled down to remove my boots and to tug down my skirt. As my skirt fell to the floor, I heard his breath suck in as his eyes hit my lace garter belt, holding up my fishnets. He bent down and kissed my bare thighs as he unclipped the stockings, and he rolled them down slowly and carefully over my legs down to my ankles. He kissed and licked my bare insteps as my toes curled under with sensitivity, and his hands reversed all the way back up my legs to my waist. I quietly raised my arms so he could lift off my dark blue cashmere sweater. He lifted my legs up and swiveled me so that I lay back on top of the covers just in my bra and matching panty.

I watched him as he stepped back. With one arm, he silently and slowly pulled his sweater up from behind and over his head in true Chippindale-dancer fashion, all the while holding my eyes with his. He slowly pulled his belt through the loops and dropped it on the floor. With black jeans lying underneath his feet, his briefs came off with one hand when modesty overcame him and forced him to half-support and half-cover his erection with the other. Or maybe it was just part of the well-executed striptease. And still, not a word was said. As he made his way toward me, that same vulnerability that I saw in the shower the night before was written all over his face. I felt my own melt away a little, but I was extremely anxious about this overwhelming intimacy that was growing between us. I was pretty sure that the pounding and pumping of both our hearts must be audible all the way across the Seine to the Moulin Rouge.

Nigel pulled off my panty and unclipped my bra. He gently lay down on top of me in the old-fashioned missionary position that you still read about in old Harlequin romance novels. We lay there mouth to mouth, and he broke the silence.

"You're beautiful."

Only two words were spoken. And it was all so hot and sexy that the two of us could have burned down the whole hotel in about thirty seconds. He simply took my one hand in his, and we both guided his big, hard erection into me. He gently raised both my arms up, his hands taking my hands over my head as he moved ever so slightly to accommodate himself and I lifted my legs to meet him.

"Don't move. Don't move. Please don't move. I want this to last forever. Oh, baby, please don't move," he whispered.

I knew exactly what to do and what not to do as every woman since the beginning of time before me has known as well. I moved ever so slightly.

Remembering what he had said the night before about him being a crier and me being a screamer, I buried my mouth into his throat to muffle my noise. He struggled to hold back the tears as he clenched his hands into my tangled hair.

That night, our freshly unfurled hearts bonded with our quiet, old-fashioned four-minute-tops lovemaking. We were rewarded with that astounding intimacy that we both had needed so badly. Why had I fought it for so long?

Looking back, I think that's the moment we actually and honestly gave in to the fate that was ours. We had fallen in love.

We had no idea of the pain and heartbreak that it was to cause both of us over the year ahead.

***

A few days later, we stood there at the counter as the clerk patiently waited for us to count up how many boxes of chocolates and macaroons that we wanted sent back to the hotel. We were in Jean-Paul Hévin for a *chocolat chaud* mid-afternoon, and Nigel had suggested that I take some treats back home for my girlfriends. 'Pinch me,' I thought to myself. 'Just pinch me.'

As we finished our hot chocolate, Nigel leaned over the small bistro table and said, "So, did you like Monsieur Ferrand's service this morning?"

"Oh my God, he was the best. I felt like a queen as he took every small measurement. And all the leathers and the colors. Amazing. I've never had a dress made for me, let alone gloves. And you spoil me. I didn't need all that. But I do love the red ones especially. And I can't believe that he will have them all ready for us before we go home."

"But, baby, although I appreciate the matching scarves that you bought for both of us there, there's really no need for you to be spending your money on our treats. Please, let me take care of everything. I'm a little embarrassed to tell you now, three days into our holiday, but I did bring euro cash and a euro VISA card just for you for your own personal spending money, and then I was too worried on the plane to give it to you in case you would be offended. I didn't want to embarrass you, as I know that you're a very independent woman. I don't have any experience in these matters, on top of my shyness. However, in my defense, I also know from your court case that you do have enough money to take care of yourself. Please know it's not a control issue or anything like that with me. I just want to make you happy."

"Okay, okay, so here's what we're going to do. We are going to go shopping, and I'm going to buy you a cashmere turtleneck with my own money, and I'm going to pick the color. You, on the other hand, are going to be the gracious gentleman and simply say thank you. Please indulge me here. After all, we both know that it isn't money that's coming into play on this glorious holiday that you've treated me to. Oh no, it's not money at all. So please don't worry. We're doing just fine in the money department. And every other department. It's a deal?"

"Okay honey, whatever you want. It's a deal." He reached into his jacket's inside pocket. "But just in case you need it, here, take the card at least."

"Don't you dare, sugar daddy. I'm not that kind of girl." I leaned over and gave him a kiss on his cheek to break his embarrassment of trying to offer a woman money. "But thank you, Nigel, for being the generous and caring man you are."

His face was flushed as he said quietly to himself, 'Ouch! She called me sugar daddy! That one hurts!'

The week went by in a happy blur. Mornings were spent over a big breakfast in our suite to give us the time new lovers need to make leisurely love in the morning before a day of tramping the streets of Paris, browsing all the little shops as well as the *Galeries Lafayette, Printemps, and Le Bon Marché,* where we bought each other sweaters and scarves for our upcoming winter back in Canada. Nigel was very fussy about quality, and he knew his stuff when it came to both fashion and quality in both the men's and ladies' departments.

We were walking along the Rue du Faubourg Saint-Honoré and he pulled me into Hermès. He spoke in his perfect French to the middle-aged shopkeeper as we stood admiring the display at the scarf counter. *"Bonjour, madame. Mon nom est Nigel, et c'est Denni. Nous avon Canadien. Vous avez un très beau magasin. Je voudrais l'éscharpes, s'il vous plaît."* He looked over at me as he grabbed me around my waist to give me a quick kiss on my cheek, and he continued in English, speaking to both of us, "You know how it is, nothing but the best for my girl."

She looked at the two of us and said politely, *"Enchanté and bienvenue, madame et monsieur."* She smiled. *"Vous êtes Canadien? D'accord."* She proceeded to pull out several trays of beautiful silk scarves. *"Je m'appelle Antoinette."* She arranged the trays right along with the famous wallets, handbags, and belts for us to peruse as a whole collection. She murmured a small, quiet *'excusez-moi'* as she turned her back to reach up into the locked cabinet behind her to take out her prize. It was a beautiful, rich, dark brown Kelly bag which she carefully placed directly in front of us as she loosely tied a gold and burned-orange silk scarf through the handles of the bag. I was not surprised to see that there was no price tag on it. It's like they say, *"If you have to ask, you can't afford it."* Antoinette had had a chance to size us up and was not about to let an obvious sugar daddy's live VISA card out of her sight by simply purchasing a 'onesie.' No way. She was going to upsell the hell out of the good-looking, happy couple standing in front of her.

Nigel was enjoying himself immensely, standing there with his new, bright blue cashmere scarf that I had bought him earlier in the day wrapped around his neck, Euro-style. My heart went out to this beautiful man who was so earnestly trying to impress me. I smiled and stepped up to the plate, playing to his testosterone-led tendencies. The shopkeeper played the game as well, aware of the fact that her weekly sales quota was about to be met. She spoke to Nigel in French and spoke to me in English. She knew who carried the credit card, and she knew exactly how to get her hands on it. She made herself very busy draping the scarves around my neck and arranged a beautiful crossover bag across my chest, all the while nodding her soft *'oui, oui,'* to Nigel and asking him for his preference of the light or the dark in the scarves and for his opinion of what looked best with my brunette hair and fair complexion.

"Thank you, darling." I smooched his face all over as the experienced salesclerk turned away for a moment to give the sugar daddy and his girl time to seal the deal.

"Honey, honey, enough already. You're getting me all excited again," he whispered with his face all flushed and happy.

I slowly unwrapped his too-warm cashmere scarf to give him a little air, and I gave him one last kiss on his exposed throat.

He said in my ear, "You're killing me, Ms. Brunette. Stay away from me or we're going to have to get a room somewhere."

Madame Antoinette carefully wrapped up my new traditional, patterned blue and yellow silk scarf and the brown belt with the big gold 'H' that fashioned the buckle that Nigel had insisted on. She placed them into two separate Hermès-orange boxes and tied them individually with thick, black satin ribbon carefully before placing the wrapped boxes into a large orange Hermès shopping bag.

As we were leaving the department, Madame's colleague came over to her counter to help her put away the scarves and to lock up the unsold Kelly bag. She said to Antoinette, "Too bad that he didn't bite for the Kelly. I thought for sure you were going to get that sale."

Antoinette sighed and responded, "At first, I thought so too. He wanted to, but she wouldn't have any part of it. I caught her eye, and she's not your run-of-the-mill gold-digger. There was an integrity there. As crazy as she was about him, she wasn't for sale. I don't think he's her sugar daddy somehow, although he acted the part. She was a little on the old side for that little game anyway, and besides, they were Canadian. You know, nice. Yes, my sales approach was right on; my problem was that she was a nice girl. That's the only reason I wasn't able to sell him on the Kelly."

***

When we got out onto the street, Nigel grabbed my hand and said with a little laugh, "Did you see that the doorman was laughing at me?"

I stopped and looked up at him in concern. "What do you mean?"

He grinned ruefully, "Man, the whole world could see my big erection that I was trying to hide behind the shopping bag. That's why I was carrying it in front of me like that. Baby, you are such a tease. Just like at home, when you run away from me after our walk and I'm compelled, in total frustration, to watch your beautiful ass all the way up to the corner."

"Good thing we didn't go into the lingerie department."

He looked down at me and warned me, "Don't even go there, missy."

I laughed. "But seriously, babe, I have the solution for your dilemma at home when you're watching me run away from you."

"Oh, oh. I feel like your supposedly innocent advice is going to be similar to your little story that got me into that big mess at the outdoor table in front of the Letterai shop the other day."

"So, you don't want to hear my solution?"

He smiled and kissed me on the lips. "I'm really fucked here, aren't I?" He threw his hands up in the air. "Okay, Irish faerie, tell me. Out with it."

I leaned into his ear and whispered, "Okay, okay, here's what to do about watching my ass run away from you. Once you get in the house, pretend. Just pretend. Take your big, hard erection in your hands and masturbate to my ass. Just close your eyes, and it will make you feel good, baby."

He cried out, "Taxi! Taxi!" He unceremoniously shoved me into the cab that had spotted the handsome, middle-aged man's urgent flag.

We never made it into the bedroom. He was still lying on top of me, down on the big, square, ornate Persian carpet in the hallway, just inside the front door of our suite. He had his hands up in my hair, and I was still grappling his beautiful bare ass. We both started to laugh.

He looked up and around us and said, "Let's hope the afternoon maid isn't in the bedroom changing our linens right now. We're quite a sight."

As we showered together, I noticed that sometime over the last few days, my nails had made marks down his back. "I'm sorry for the scratches on your back, Nigel."

He grinned and said, "You are a wild and crazy girl, all right. And I wouldn't have it any other way."

As I watched him douse his curls with shampoo, I had an epiphany. Ah ha! That was what it was! Finally, I had it figured out! That was what it took to get past the intimacy that I was struggling with. I just couldn't get enough of the sex that we shared, but the intimacy that developed when we were having sex in the quiet, slow, and easy way that he seemed to prefer was simply too much for me. That was why I was always playing the tease when we were out and about. I just wanted the sex, but here I was with a lover that wanted the intimacy. (Thinking back on the situation though, I had no idea that I was playing against a loaded deck. We were both way, way beyond being fuck buddies, but I just wasn't emotionally mature enough to accept it.) I stood there quietly as my lover took the big, fluffy facecloth and slowly and gently washed me under my arms, one at a time, as if I was a cherished, newborn infant.

As it happened, housekeeping had indeed been in earlier in the day. She had placed our purchases from the Letterai shop on the dining room table and Nigel beamed as I carefully opened each individually wrapped package. He had surprised me with a set of beautiful red leather notebooks, with D.A. embossed in gold in the lower corner, just like the black ones that I had treated him to. I was curious about the last box however; I couldn't remember us ordering anything else other than my Mont Blanc pen, purple ink, and the notebooks for him. It was a long, rectangular box, too big for a pen and not the right size for stationery.

I cried out as I lifted the vintage, ivory, hand-tatted, three-quarter-length gloves from the tissue. "Nigel, oh Nigel." I couldn't say anything else. I was overwhelmed with his thoughtfulness.

**

We spent our last day acting like the locals by taking the Line-four metro out to the Les Puces, the big flea market and antique mecca in Paris. Nigel wanted to go there mainly for the jazz café where we would have lunch. The old flea market is more formally known as Les Puces de Saint-Ouen, and I had never been there before. Nigel had asked me to leave my purse at the hotel and to just wear a money belt around my waist as we were leaving the affluent and touristy part of Paris and going to the eighteenth arrondissement. He didn't want me to get pickpocketed, he explained.

We navigated the metro easily and delved into the vast flea market to realize that we both loved all the same things.

"You're just being nice to me. That's all. Surely, we can't like everything the same. Show me something you absolutely hate."

"That. Over there. That's hideous."

"Oh. No, no. That's not going to work. I agree with you wholeheartedly. It's baroque-ugly and it's ridiculous." We both laughed at our compatibility and walked on.

I bought him an old silver picture frame that I saw him admiring, and he dragged me away from a silver-topped walking cane that I wanted to buy him, just in case his sciatica came back.

"All week long, I've felt like a teenager, and now you're wanting to buy me an old man's cane. No way, José."

We wandered into a small antique stall full of old Victorian-style toiletries for both men and women. He picked out three beautiful, vintage art deco hairclips. Carefully holding each up against my hair and asking the shop attendant for her advice, he had all three wrapped up to go as I stood there shyly, holding his hand and thanking him. Over the whole trip, I'd never seen him happier.

He ushered me into a shabby, old music stall and asked me to help him look through the old bins and stacks of jazz to add to his collection at home. He allowed me to pay for a couple of CDs that he found, and you'd think he had found a three-pound gold ingot or something by the wide grin on his face.

Over lunch in the jazz café, he had taken off his leather jacket and put it over the back of his chair. He studiously took notes in one of his new notebooks as the little quartet played throughout our soup and sandwich. I leaned back, watching him in blatant admiration; I was just so happy to be sitting there with him. I could have stayed another whole week right there, sitting in the little, dingy café, just watching him jot down his notes and tapping his foot to the jazz that floated across the small space. Pinch me, just pinch me.

Nigel had wanted to have our last night's dinner at Le Cinq, downstairs in the George-V, so we taxied back from 'le fleas' in time to nap beforehand.

We dressed up. I put on my high heels along with a form-fitting red dress that was ladylike enough to hit just below my knees but Jezebel enough to show off my assets. I wore the infamous lacy garter-belt underneath it, in anticipation of what may transpire after dinner.

I looked over the top of my menu to admire him. My God! He was the most handsome man in the whole restaurant. He was wearing all black and looked sexier than ever. The suit was an Italian fine wool, and the jacket left no doubt that it was made-to-measure, just a little tight over his biceps. Underneath the jacket was a black silk twill shirt. He had nixed the tie that night and wore his three top buttons undone. He wore no jewelry as usual. The overall effect was a sexy Euro image, just bordering on a bad-boy, dangerous look.

He looked up and caught my admiring gaze. "You like the shirt? Is it a little too much?" he asked shyly. "The problem is," he continued, "you make me feel all man, and I've never in my whole life had that feeling before now. And I fear that my newfound testosterone is taking over my wardrobe too."

"It's a perfect look for you, baby. I love it. And actually, we look like a real couple tonight, don't we? Your black and my red together."

He leaned in and confessed, "You know, honey, this is our first holiday together, and I'm not used to dressing in front of anybody. I'm shy. You know how it is. I love it that you're the same. I know your body and you know mine inside-out now, but somehow, it seems to suit the both of us that we still dress apart. I hope it never changes. I love that shyness about you. You're shy one minute, and you're ripping the clothes off me the next. What gets into you, my little tiger?" By this time, he was grinning, and I was blushing.

"It's not only the dressing really. Girls need their time alone, especially for their hair and makeup. We're just silly that way."

"Don't ever change. And please know, with or without the war paint, baby, I can't take my eyes off you."

"Well, you'd better take your eyes off me long enough to read the menu. I'm starving, aren't you?"

As I teased him unmercifully about jotting down the nuance of every course of the delicious meal, he was crafty enough to drag me into the culinary discussions, and I found myself thinking back to our first luncheon in Toronto a few short months ago. As I looked over at my handsome lover, I was turned on in this restaurant even more, as I knew what was to come once we made it back to our big bed upstairs.

The quartet had a great singer, and as we danced a slow dance, I asked him, "Why did you bring a banana with you to dinner at Le Cinq?"

"It's not a banana, honey. I'm packing heat tonight. Just in case a fight breaks out and I have to protect my girl."

"Yeah, you're packing heat, all right. I can feel it. It's hot."

"Don't start with me, Ms. Brunette. I have to keep my wits about me tonight. You see, tonight we're playing by my rules, and I'm not going to rush into any of your crazy, exciting, mind-blowing sex tonight. I'm sick and tired of being under your spell, acting like one of Pavlov's dogs, drooling all down my shirt the moment you decide to sound your little bell. No, no, no. I'm in charge here. Tonight, I'm going to show you a new way of doing things that you're going to be begging me for, for the rest of our lives."

I looked up at him in surprise. It was like he had been reading my mind in the shower the day before and that he had caught on to my way of shying away from the intimacy. I felt nervous, and I was a little taken aback with his know-it-all assessment.

The dance floor was fairly crowded, but we seemed to be in a world of our own. I shook out of the classic waltz pose with my one arm resting lightly on his back. I put both my hands up around his neck and moved in tight. I smiled confidently into his face and said, "Tell me all about it, big boy."

He snatched my hand back from his neck and put it into position straight out to the side, out and above my shoulder. I felt his thigh push between my legs as he led into a salsa position. I spread my fishnets, stepped my one leg back, and raised my other leg up to his waist. I submissively leaned back as his big, strong hand supported the small of my back.

He whispered into my face, "You are going down, sugar, and there's not a damn thing you can do about it."

"So, you can dance," I taunted. "What else can you do for me?"

His mouth was a millimeter from mine, and he delivered his two-word plan of action to take me down. "Multiple orgasms."

To this day, I don't remember a thing about the rest of that dinner. I know I sat through dessert and coffee, and I know I felt him hold me through a whole set of dancing, but he had me completely brain-fogged over what was to come once we got back upstairs in our suite.

He undressed me slowly, and once we were in bed, he kept me reigned in. He kept it sexy, slow and easy, teasing me out just the way he liked it and just the way I was beginning to accept that he had been right about all along. The eureka moment that I had had in the shower the day before, of wanting him to just fuck me, was a thing of the past. 'No, no, no!' I screamed silently to myself. 'This is what I really wanted. This is what I really needed,' I tried to explain to my sex-befuddled mind.

I had never been that wet or slick for a man in my whole life. He had me exactly where he wanted me and all I could do was whimper and whisper, begging him not to stop. A few times he had to pull away from me to control himself, and as I reached out to touch him, he flinched back with a whisper, "No, no, don't touch me; I'm too close." He held my wrists down with one hand as his mouth and tongue once again worked their magic. And that was how it all happened. I had never in my whole life felt that much intense, drawn-out pleasure, and I've never felt it since. Wave after wave crested and washed over me as he continued his touch all through my orgasms, and finally, as I cried out with sensitivity and emotion, I whispered for him to stop. Afterward, face to face, he entered me and cried out in his deep baritone. His tears were all over my face, and I felt his ribcage heaving against my chest. I smoothed his damp hair down gently to calm him.

As we lay there recovering, I said quietly, "Baby, can we just move over a little? The bed seems to be all wet under my feet."

"Sorry, honey, that's my fault. I came all over the sheets while I was making you feel good."

***

The next morning, and for the first time on our holiday, I woke up before him. We were still entangled in each other's arms and legs. I breathed deep into his chest, and I could smell his sexy pheromones and sweat from the night before. It was glorious, and I couldn't get enough of it. I just lay there in my own little world.

I had no idea that it was to be my last few minutes of Nigel-induced heaven for a long, long time to come.

The moment I stood up and got out of bed, I knew I just wasn't my usual happy self, although I should have been. I felt uneasy and unsettled. Nigel had his ever-watchful eye on me, and I didn't want to alarm him. I just chalked it up to my disappointment that our fairytale holiday had come to an end.

We stayed in our George-V robes and slippers as we started our packing, sipping away at our coffee that Nigel made us in our little kitchen. I heard him ordering the usual big breakfast up to our room.

He smoothed my hair down with his hands and looked deep into my eyes, "You okay, honey? You seem quiet."

"I'm fine. I'm fine. I must be just a little sad that our glorious holiday is coming to an end. We've had such a wonderful time, haven't we?"

"Listen, I can finish up here. Do you want to slip up to the spa for a massage or something on your own? Was it too much for you last night?"

I smiled at his caring gesture, and I confessed, "Yes, you may be right about last night. I think I'm just feeling a little overwhelmed. That's all."

I simply couldn't face the beautifully prepared breakfast that the staff had laid out for us on the coffee table as Nigel liked it. I picked away at a brioche roll and a bowl of berries. Nigel continued to fuss over me, asking if he could order something else up for me.

Later, after my shower, I padded out to the living room with a big towel wrapped around my shampooed hair and said to Nigel, "Yes, thinking about it, there is something that you can do for me."

"Anything, babe. How can I help?"

"I'm well aware of all the money that you've spent over our holiday, and at the very least, I want you to allow me to take care of the tip for the housekeepers, our concierge, and the elevator man that have all been so good to us here at the hotel."

"Okay, baby, but here's the deal. Only if you promise never to call me a sugar daddy again for as long as we live. I almost died in the café when you labeled me. And, of course, like an idiot, I didn't learn my lesson. Oh no, I had to barge into Hermès and try to buy you a Kelly bag, and I embarrassed you to no end in front of the all-too-knowing store clerk." He threw his hands up in the air in resignation and explained, "It's my first time in Paris with a beautiful woman and I just don't know how to behave."

I couldn't help but laugh at his earnest confession. As I jumped onto the sofa and into his arms, I murmured, "Yeah, you're a real pain in the ass, I must say. But don't you dare ever, ever change. Please, just be you. And me! I'm the worst! I'm sorry about name-calling you. That was probably just my own weird reaction to all your love and generosity over the holiday. I'm sorry. And just for the record, it's my first time in Paris with a handsome man, and from now on, I'll try to be more of a lady and less of a tease when we're out in public."

"Like you just said, don't you ever change. I love you the way you are."

Later, he eagerly pulled up a chair beside mine as I sat in front of our suite's beautiful antique Louis-XV1 desk, carefully writing on the hotel stationery the individual notes to attach to the euros that I had counted out in little piles for each of the staff members that had taken such good care of us. I signed each one, *Denise and Nigel, Toronto, Canada,* before Nigel folded each package and wrote the names on the fronts of each envelope.

***

During our flight home, and for reasons that I fully did not understand at the time, I broached the subject of my plan for going forward with Nigel. Ever since our lovemaking had become so serious, and especially after last night, I was suffering with my old 'fight or flight' issues that had dogged me ever since I began dabbling into the crazy world of men.

"Nigel, please hear me out."

"Sure, baby, what's up?"

"I know this sounds a little crazy, and I can't really explain why, but once we get home and get settled back into our respective lives, I feel like I just need a few days on my own to settle in."

He looked at me and hesitated before saying softly, "Well, baby, I don't recollect asking you to move in with me, so I guess it's your call."

"Please don't be hurt, darling. I'm just so overwhelmed by all our closeness in Paris, and I need a couple of days to sort through all the love that we've shared. I guess I'm a little panic-stricken or something. I just don't feel like myself somehow."

"Denni, you are a grown-ass woman. Act like one. If it's over between us, just tell me."

"No, no, not at all," I cried out. "Please. Quite the opposite. As the old saying goes, *it's not you, it's me!*"

The hurt was written all over his face, and I dropped the joke like a hot potato. I acknowledged his order to grow up and said, "I'm sorry, I'm an idiot. I'm not making myself clear, and I'm hurting you with my childish insecurities. Nigel, it's been a very, very long time since I have allowed myself to jump in the deep end in a relationship, and I just need some time to decompress so I can enjoy what we have together."

His face masked the hurt, and he looked like the experienced judge that he was in real life, in complete control of the situation. He sat there, quiet for a moment, staring into my face, completely on top of his game. "Out with it. No bullshit. What's the real deal here, Denise?"

I was completely vulnerable and unable to control my real feelings any longer. I answered him truthfully. "The real deal is that, Nigel, I love you."

"And I love you."

"But you never said so, and I have been thinking that I was in the deep end all on my own!"

He laughed and as he folded me into his big arms, he said, "Oh yeah, I was right there, right beside you. Ever since the day I watched you watching me with your big gray eyes in the Aroma Expresso Bar on Spadina Avenue. I have always been way, way ahead of you, and I didn't want to rush you." He pulled back a little and, looking directly into my face, said, "Now, wait a minute. Think about it. You very well know that if I had told you that I loved you in Paris, you would have been on the first flight out of there without blinking an eye. Am I right?"

I didn't answer him and said, "So, it's okay with you if I take a couple of days on my own?"

"Baby, I'm in. I will gladly ignore you for, let's say, three days, starting the minute we touch down." He laughed confidently. "Doll, you have no idea how much you are going to miss me."

As I smiled at his confidence, he continued on a more serious note, "I must tell you though that our holiday allowed me to confirm my suspicions about you."

"Which are?"

"That your affections aren't based on my bank account or my court appointment or my skin color. I thought from our first meeting in chambers that money and skin color didn't matter to you, and I'm happy to find out that my intuition proved correct."

"So, what then? If it's not your millions, what could it be? It certainly couldn't be your looks, you being such a pitifully homely man, now could it?"

"Honey, don't mess with me." He took my hand and laid it on his lap and pushed down. "I know as well as you do; it's my big package here that gets you every time."

I laughed. "That's where you're wrong. It's your big brain that makes me crazy, not your big Johnson. I'm a sucker for the sensitive, nerdy, note-taking, intellectual type."

"Whatever you say, honey."

***

We touched down. Nigel made a big fanfare out of resetting both our phones and clicking on the alert to beep seventy-two hours later.

But no matter how much I tried to convince myself that everything was okay between us, I knew the whole stupid, impulsive request for timeout had hurt him deeply and had left a bitter taste in his mouth. And furthermore, what kind of an idiot I was, telling a man that I loved him that forced him to return the sentiment. Shit. Shit. Shit.

As our limo pulled out from the airport, Nigel mused to himself in a voice that he made sure I could hear, "Yeah, I can fill in three days on my own quite nicely."

I felt a pang of regret as I realized that the intimacy of Paris was all gone. We were back to our normal *tête à tête* relationship and I had no one to blame except myself.

Deep down in the pit of my stomach, a prescient was forming as to what was yet to come.

***

I unlocked my door, suitcase, and carry-on in tow, breathing in the much-needed solitude that my own apartment offered up to me.

I was alone with my thoughts at last. All I wanted was to get rid of the uneasy feeling I had in the pit of my stomach that I had had since the moment I had asked Nigel to give me some space. I unpacked, opened a tin of Campbell's tomato soup, unwrapped a few Saltines for a light supper, and I was in my own bed at 8:00 p.m., Toronto time.

As I was drifting off, it occurred to me that Nigel hadn't called me to say goodnight. I supposed he was keeping his side of our agreement.

***

Chapter 7
Addendum: Nigel

He woke up after a good night's sleep that sleeping alone in his own bed had afforded him. After a quick shower and big breakfast, he went downtown to his old condo, which he used as an 'under-the-radar' office to alert his assistant that he was back in town and to take care of any mail and correspondence from the previous week that she had dropped off for him in his absence.

With chair tilted back and feet up on the desk, he grabbed the big, brown envelope on top of the in-basket. He slit the top edge open.

He stopped breathing as his eyes slowly took in the contents. With his heart pounding, he desperately looked again in the envelope, telling himself that there was a reason, any reason. "Please God, tell me what's going on here?"

The photos were of two people standing in bright daylight, in a close embrace in the middle of a sidewalk. There were also several photos of an intimate conversation in the café, holding each other's hands and leaning forward. One photo showed the man's face and the back of the woman's head. She was holding his face in her hands.

The man in the photo appeared to be about forty-five years old, tall, and very thin, with a pale, drawn face – good-looking but haggard. He had an unusual shock of pure white hair that you would usually see on a man much older than him.

The woman was Denise Allen.

It took a minute for his nightmare to register. Then his chair crashed over as he ran to the toilet so that he wouldn't throw up all over the cream-colored broadloom.

***

He spent the next few days in solitude, living and reliving the horror that the brown envelope had bestowed upon him.

As he painfully and slowly evolved into survival mode, he wrote on his notepad once again, *"Who am I and how did I get here?"*

He went back in time, with meticulous and painful detail after detail, reliving his failures that had dogged him since his first attempts to be a boyfriend to one of the many nice, Jewish high school girls that were not within his reach, and then, that fateful afternoon in Stockholm with the beautiful, deaf, and mute golden angel thirty years ago.

The worst time ever, though, was the end of his short marriage to Mercedes. He leaned back as if this episode in his life was almost too much to bear. He started his recall with the day that he met her, way back in 1981, just after Saul and his mother had died.

She had walked into the office, and by the time he had shaken the beautiful laughing woman's hand, he was smitten. She was an articling student that had come on board. Her résumé was a little light, but she was a hustler through and through and knew exactly how to get on top of any situation that presented itself. She was a black woman, a natural beauty who made the most out of her lanky shape, long legs, and shoulder-length, straightened hair. Her hometown was Kingston, Jamaica, and her brains got her a placement in the esteemed lineup to write her bar exam in Toronto. She made no bones about kicking ass, both in her professional life and her personal life as well. She was single and was on the make for a husband. She wanted it all. She sized up the black, good-looking, brainy, well-dressed lawyer from back home and plucked him out of his introverted, studious, and lonely existence. He simply couldn't help himself.

Their first date ended by her showing him how to striptease for a woman. On the dates to follow, she groomed him into a magnificent lover, and both of them were into the game with heart and soul. Every touch and every move was orchestrated to perfection; she was a very knowledgeable teacher and he was a very willing student.

He was in a daze. He couldn't sleep. He couldn't eat. He could only count the hours until they were, once again, out of their clothes and meshed together in his small, one-bedroom condo.

Like a big cat following her prey, she struck. "Nigel," she purred, "it's time we got married. You have no family, I have no family, and we make such a good couple. We're not getting any younger, and we need to settle down and have a family."

That's all he needed to hear. Mercedes decided over the next twenty minutes how and when they would become Mr. and Mrs. Royal. It was to be a simple beach wedding in Jamaica, with just a few of her old friends present, and of course, anyone that Nigel wanted to bring along.

One month later, in the Jamaican sunset, Nigel and Mercedes were standing in the surf, her in a white lace, short, flirty wedding dress, with long brown legs ankle-deep in the surf, and his white tuxedo pant legs carefully rolled up against the wet.

He had stood there alone, hands in pockets, watching the guests dance to the reggae band. Mercedes was flitting from one dance partner to another, casually pouring the champagne into the raised glasses as he surveyed the crowd of about twenty of her friends. Actually, he had been embarrassed to tell his colleagues and few friends, including Chi and Nuyen, that he was taking the leap so early into the relationship, so he had planned on announcing the nuptials once they got back home from the wedding and short honeymoon in Jamaica. He hadn't asked anyone back home to be his best man, and Brad was in the middle of a well-deserved break at home in Provence after shooting in India. His mother and Saul had died earlier in the year within six months of each other. Little Daisy, who had become affectionately known to all as Old Daisy, had followed them two weeks later at the ripe old age of sixteen people-years.

Heaven would host them all, the Jew, the Baptist, and the dog as the family from 7 Russell Hill Road.

So, it turned out that Nigel Royal was alone at his wedding, standing like a wall flower and watching the gaiety from outside looking in.

Feeling his old shyness beginning to overwhelm him, he slipped away down to the beach. He walked with his hands in pockets and feet in the surf. He wondered what Saul would think of all of this. He lingered, not really wanting to go back to the party. Perhaps he could get his bride to end the evening with a walk, just the two of them, down here in the moonlight. 'Yes,' he smiled to himself, 'they would consummate the marriage Jamaican-style and bare-assed right on the sandy beach.'

He got back to the dance floor, and Mercedes was nowhere in sight. He thought perhaps she had the same idea for private time on the beach and that she had gone up to the room to change out of the wedding dress. God only knew it had cost him enough. Only the best for his bride. He had paid for the works, including the dress from Holts, his new white tux, the flights, the party, the band, and the many, many bottles of champagne, all for a little piece of paper that simply meant in Canadian terms that she now owned fifty percent of everything that he owned.

As he left the party to try and catch his bride up in the bridal suite, he went around the back way to avoid the party. Just before he opened the stairwell door, he heard something, or someone, in the darkness behind the thick, flowering bougainvillea hedges on the slope that led down to the shuttered tennis courts. His head told him to follow the sounds, and his heart was pleading with him to mind his own business and to go straight up the stairs.

His eyes strained through the dark and the quarter-moon seemed to point the way to the couple. Her long brown legs were straddling her partner and her hands were in his long dreads. He was sitting on a lawn chair beneath her, with shirt open and pants down around his bare feet. The moon beam caught the short, white-laced dress as it flounced up and down to the rhythm of his thrusts.

He didn't remember silently backing up and away from the gut-wrenching sight. He made it to the bridal suite, packed his bag, and was in a local taxi heading for the airport before he realized that he was trembling from head to toe. He took the first available seat heading north and as he settled back in the privacy that first-class offered, he asked the flight attendant to keep the fresh coffee coming. He opened his notebook and got out his pen to draft his annulment papers.

***

Over twenty years later, as he sat there in his small, quiet condo, he realized that the wound was as fresh that day as it had been back then. He had a new determination building in his gut to never to get caught in the clutches of another woman as long as he lived. He blamed himself for being taken in by the Irish faerie who had completely mesmerized him over the past few whirlwind months.

He wrote his plan of action on a fresh sheet in his notepad:

1. *Be a man, and master your circumstances.*
2. *Take a leave of absence. Yes, for sure.*
3. *Meet up with Brad on set and get lost in some Hollywood hype to pass the time.*
4. *Hike in Nepal?*
5. *Study British law at Oxford?*
6. *Visit the kids in France.*
7. *Move away from 7 Russell Hill? No, never.*
8. *Ditch my phone number. Yes, definitely.*
9. *Treat Madison to a trip back to Cambodia?*

A small, rueful smile came over his face as he thought, 'Shit, how am I going to tell Brad about this fucking mess? He'll never let me live this one down. I think this time I've got him beaten when it comes to woman troubles.'

He checked his international clock to see what time it was in France and grabbed his phone to call him, ready to accept the brotherly ridicule like a man.

After forty-five minutes of mostly tears and sobbing from Nigel's end, Brad said quietly, "When did you win the lottery?"

"What you mean when did I win the lottery?"

"Dry your eyes and look out the window. You are in Toronto and I'm in Provence. This call is costing you a fortune. For Christ's sake! Is she worth it? Now listen up. Here's the plan and here's what you're going to do. Take your studious little notes down, bro. I'm back in LA, starting a new gig next week. Give me a chance to unwind. Then you are going to come out to the coast. I'm sending you to boot camp. You've got to lick your wounds and get back to being the smart, calm, and collected dude that I know you are."

"Boot camp? Seriously?"

"Seriously. Don't give me any lip. Thinking about it though, man, you're going to like this six-week program. It's a tough go, but I remember you telling me your hero as a kid was Muhammad Ali, and this is a boxing camp. It's strictly one-on-one, and you live, eat, breathe, and sleep right there. Intensive, gritty, but very, very good for the mind, body, and soul. It's called Gerri's Gym, and it's not a joke. You have to be in pretty good shape to even be considered for a placement. It's just up from the beach. Trust me, it's not fancy. You'll probably sleep in a bunk, but there will be lots and lots of serious food because you're going to bulk up a little. The team that runs it takes their work very seriously. I've checked in myself over the years to get toned up for a new role. All my buddies go there. I'll have all your gear ready for you. Don't be running out buying boxing boots or shorts or anything. And certainly not a red silk-lined cape like Ali used to cavort in. And, oh, don't worry. I remember, for your jockstraps, you take a thirty-four waist and an extra small cup, right?"

"Very funny, bozo. Will the kids be in L.A. too?"

"No, the kids are still in school for the semester. But you won't have time for social shit anyway. This is an intense program, believe me. In fact, I'll tell you what. This one's on me. I'll pick up the tab for the six-week program, and you'll get notification from my assistant when to pick up your air tickets at Lester B. Pearson."

"Shit! Did you hear that!?"

"What?"

"It was my left jab breaking the sound barrier!" It was Nigel's first joke since he left Paris.

"Now that's what I like to hear." Brad chuckled with relief. "Remember, just pack a light bag. We're not going to be out doing the town. All you need is some running shoes for your beach run, a pair of cross-trainers, and a couple of pairs of shorts. Part of your daily routine will be running the beach early every morning."

"Thanks, Brad. I love you, man."

"Back at 'cha, bro. Now get some sleep."

* * *

Nigel sat in the passenger's seat of the souped-up, muffler-amped 1970 bright orange, V-8 Plymouth Duster, with his arm up and out the window as Brad dialed in some old Motown over the old car's radio. He looked down over his clothes that his brother had set out for him the night before when the two of them packed his bag for his stay at the gym. He hardly knew himself. A vintage tee-shirt sported Bob Marley, with sleeves ripped out at the shoulders and faded with too many wears and washings. The cut off sweats had car-battery burns down along one side, but they did fit his ass nicely, he had to admit. He wasn't complaining. No, not at all. He was in his brother's world now, being driven to boot camp, and Nigel was up for playing any part at all. He was just happy to be hanging with Brad in his *'car du jour,'* just thankful that his bad-boy Hollywood brother didn't want to take the big Harley down to the gym.

They parked in the back lane, and Brad gave a loud shout as he pushed the backdoor of an old, clapboard, two-story building with his shoulder. An older, rough-looking black man with a boxer's nose was hugging Brad in a bear-hug and at the same time reaching over to shake Nigel's hand. "Call me Joey."

Just then, a dead-ringer Grace Jones' lookalike strutted into the gym. She was a six-footer, with black, broad, muscled shoulders, and her afro was clipped very short to her head.

"Gerri, meet my brother, Nigel Royal."

Nigel turned his head and whispered to Brad, his voice squeaking with surprise, "When you said Gerri over the phone, I thought that you meant Jerry! She's a woman! Fuck, man, you could have warned me!"

She stepped back after shaking his hand like a man and stood there, sizing him up. She circled him, studying his arm reach, calf muscles, back and buttocks, and then she stepped forward. Pursing her lips and leaning back a little as if to check him under the hood, she used one finger to slowly lift Bob Marley up to check out his abs. "Needs some work," she said. As she continued to lift the shirt up, she finger-tapped his pecs.

Nigel, in instantaneous fight-or-flight response to her touch, caught her wrist in his right hand and growled, "Don't touch the merchandise, sister. Who the fuck do you think you're dealing with?"

Brad was stunned, and he looked on, eyes and mouth wide open, alarmed at Nigel's intensity.

Gerri's sharp eyes zeroed in on Nigel's manicured nails, and she danced around him, ricochet-jabbing into his left shoulder. "So, we're dealing with a mama's boy here. A fucking pussy. Well, buster, you're going to get that shit kicked out of you over the next six weeks. Welcome to my world."

"Fuck you! Just fuck you!"

She laughed and jeered right back into his face. "Not on my watch, asshole. You gotta grow up and be a man to get into my pants."

As Joey led Nigel down to the office to get him sized up for boots and headgear, Brad anxiously said to Gerri, "Geez, Ger, you think you may have been a little hard on him?"

The strikingly beautiful forty-year-old athlete, who had turned pro over twenty years beforehand, put her arm gently around Brad's shoulders. "Trust me, Brad, your brother is going to be okay. I wanted to see if he still had a little fire in his belly, and the good news is it's there big-time. I promise you that we'll take very good care of him. Mind, body, and soul, remember what we talked about? We're going to build him back up, from the inside out. His schedule includes a five-mile run along the beach every morning, sparring with Joey during the day, and with me taking a little time with him at the end of the afternoon, before his masseuse takes over. The cook will keep him proteined up twenty-four-seven. Early to bed. Alone. No worries. I have never let you down before, and I'm not about to start now. But I do have one question for you."

"Anything, Ger. Shoot."

"How the hell does a pretty white boy like you get a handsome piece of chocolate like that for a brother? And what's he do for a living? Hands like that, looks like he's a surgeon." She added, "I'll make sure he's taped up good before the gloves go on."

"He's a Canuck, lives in Toronto. And he's my brother down to the core. We're both pretty much colorblind, I suppose, but that's how it's done up in Canada. Everyone seems to meld into the mix up there. He got me out of more than a few scrapes in the past when I was a little asshole shooting my first pitiful little movie up north, and we've been tight through thick and thin ever since. Steph and the kids just love Uncle Nigie. And no, he's not a surgeon, but he does have a brilliant, analytical mind. He likes to keep his profession to himself, and trust me, you don't need to know."

"A cop?" she said in an alarmed voice.

"Please. Ger. Really. Give me a break. Would I have a fucking cop for a brother?"

"You're right. I don't need to know. If you say he's okay, he's okay by me. He's going to be one hell of a good-looker once we get a little muscle on him. So, what happened to him? He doesn't look like a user or a boozer. Just how fragile is he? Does he have mental health issues? How about that big hooked scar under his one cheekbone? What the hell happened there? I'm just guessing that something has hurt him bad; it's showing just below the surface of that good-looking face of his. I don't want to push him over the edge or anything. We don't need him cresting and crashing right here on the mat."

"No, no, he's not a psych-ward case. And the big scar below his cheekbone was due to a childhood accident. A cricket bat walloped him right in the face. It was a woman that did the real number on him. He fell hard, real hard, for a beautiful white girl with big gray eyes."

"Oh shit, woman troubles, and you say she was a white woman on top of it. So, he's fighting double demons then."

"Not really, Ger. It really isn't entirely all about the white girl at all. Many, many years ago, Nigel married a black woman, a hustler. She was a real piece of work. He caught her getting it on with a member of the band in the middle of their wedding reception."

"You playin' with me?"

"Honest to God. I can't even remember her name right now, but she was a black hustler bitch if there ever was one. Nigel never really recovered from it. I honestly don't think he had been with a woman after that marriage disaster so many years ago, until just recently when this new little cutie-pie white girl popped up out of nowhere a few months ago. I met her, and I still can't believe Nigel's story that he caught her out and about with another dude. There must be some sort of reason or a misunderstanding there. I have a hunch it's a replay of the classic old Romeo and Juliette tale. But they made such a good couple, and he called her Ms. Brunette. Cute, huh? I've never seen two people more in love with each other. Ger, I mean the real deal, like you used to read about in fairytale books as a kid. They hadn't even had sex at that time. That's the problem too; they're both romantics. He whisked her off to Paris for their first big night in the sack. They were just so perfect together. They both had that elitist, uppity Canadian speech pattern. You know, that slight sound of the Queen's English with the crisp consonants and all. In fact, especially Nigel, as he was born in Jamaica where they all used to speak like Brits. But my well educated and brainy brother left his poor country roots behind him long ago, and there's no talkin' jive for him. He's worked hard to develop that classy image. Yeah, Ms. Brunette and Nigel, those two were the real deal."

"Is she a looker too, like Nigel?"

"Hmm... not to Hollywood standards. That is, she's had no work done. But there's something about her. It's the eyes and the long, dark hair. Nice body, and she's got soul. And that same intellectual curiosity that Nigel has is written all over her."

"But wait, wait. Thinking back to the black bitch-wife for a minute. Do you think that maybe when I was all up in his face, he was going through some sort of psychological transference or something? That may explain his hostile and explosive *fuck-you, fuck-you* response to my teasing him."

"You might be on to something there. I remember my shrink talking to Steph and me about that shit before. It can screw up all your interpersonal relationships, and I think I remember the doc saying it's a chronic condition. Shit. Will you keep your eye on it? All I know is that he is not himself. He has always been the slow, steady one. Now he's crying one minute and cracking jokes the next. Just too close to the edge, if you know what I mean."

"Yeah, I hear you. I'll bring Joey up to date in any event so he can work in a little extra psych-101 into his part of the program as well. But enough about the poor bastard for now. I haven't even thanked you yet for paying his bill in full and upfront last week. Brad, you're a good brother to him, and you're a good friend to me. Relax, he's in good hands," she said as she hugged him goodbye.

"You're the best. Love you, honey."

"Love you too. Say hi to the kids for me and bring Madison in next time he's back in town."

***

Nigel sat on the edge of the old chair with the ripped leatherette seat. He put his hands up over his face, with elbows resting on Joey's desk. He moaned, "Oh my God, I'm so sorry for my behavior back there. I just feel sick. I've never spoken to anyone like that before, let alone a woman. What's happening to me?"

The two men sat there hunched over the desk as Muhammad Ali looked down from the old signed poster that was thumbtacked to the wall. Joey knew exactly what to do for the fragile man sitting across from him. His low, quiet voice was the soothing touch that Nigel's jangled nerves needed.

"Yer no different than any other man that has been thrown into our training program here, Nigel. Trust me, I've been with Gerri for over twenty years now, and I've seen it all. Gerri runs a pretty tight ship, but you'll see she gets results, and you are going to be one helluva happy man six weeks from now. Just focus on you and me, yah hear? We're going to work together very closely, and you

116

only have to deal with Gerri for a half hour in the afternoon. Now, you look like an intelligent man to me, someone that likes to keep things organized. Here's a brand-new loose-leaf notebook, and here's a pen. Every day when we're outside the ring, I'm going to ramble on through our daily tips and pointers, and I want you to take notes. And the cook will want you to keep track of your calorie count, etc. We're a team. In fact, no time like the present. Take down the list of what I want you gather up for your first lesson tomorrow morning before we meet up in the ring at 8:00 a.m. sharp, and be damn sure you have your equipment right beside you. I'll get you outfitted later on tonight after your first supper, but jot down your list now so you are ready to go tomorrow morning. Ready? Yer jump rope, bag gloves, hand wraps, sparring gloves, headgear, and mouth guard. Of course, be wearing your jockstrap and boots."

After quickly taking down Joey's notes, Nigel asked, "Do I wear anything over the jockstrap, boss?"

"Oh, so yer a comic." Joey smiled a little as he slapped his hands down on the desk and said, "Don't 'cha be letting me down now, yah hear?"

He got up from behind the desk and motioned for Nigel to follow. He grabbed a set of car keys off the hook by the door and explained that they were going to go down to the beach right then and there to check out the route of the daily five-mile morning run.

"Pay no attention to the smashed window on your side there." He shrugged his shoulders as he coaxed the old beat-up Ford to start. "What can you do? When they want the radio, they take it. And by the way, help yourself to the car keys off the hook in the office every morning to get you back and forth to the beach. No need to check in with me. Just take 'em. Just be back, standing in the small ring, with your boots on, head gear on, ready to go at 8:00 a.m. First breakfast is at 6:00 a.m., so you've got enough time there. It's very important to stay on our training schedule. On time, but slow and easy."

Joey offered his new student a quiet little remembrance from his youth. "Yup. Slow and easy. Come to think of it, I used to know a cute little girl back in the day and that's the way she liked it," and he winked at Nigel with a boyish grin.

"Count yourself a lucky man. Slow and easy is good. I seem to only get the wild ones."

By the time they had motored down to the beach, Nigel was almost smiling. He knew everything was going to be okay. He was in good hands with Joey. He looked down at Brad's old tee-shirt and pulled the Bob Marley face down tight and said out loud, "Bob, what the fuck have you done to me?!" and Joey and Nigel shared their first laugh of many to come.

"You're gonna be okay, Nigel. Like they say, 'Don't worry. Be happy,'" Joey said assuredly.

"No, no, you're wrong, Joey. That's a different singer altogether," and with that little bit of wit, the new two friends began their friendship that would last the rest of their lives.

"Oh-oh. Spoke too soon," Joey said quietly as both men spotted the flashing cruiser pulling up beside them. "Sorry, man, yah know what to do? Yah know the drill?"

Nigel nodded, and Joey pulled over. Both men silently put both hands on the dash and stared straight ahead as two cops with guns drawn opened both the driver's side and passenger-side doors simultaneously.

"Slow and steady, boys. Out. Hands up over the hood of this shit-box."

Nigel and Joey, both leaning over the hood of the car, endured the head-to-toe frisk, and both answered the cop's askance for I.D. together as if they had rehearsed it.

"Back pocket, sir."

One officer took the driver's licenses to the cruiser to radio-scan while the other officer stood ten feet behind them, both arms out straight ahead of him, both hands on his gun, loaded and cocked on target.

"Turn around slowly. Arms down." The officer handed Joey's I.D. back to him and said, "Keep your nose clean. You're free to go."

He turned toward Nigel and said, "Sorry, Your Honor, I had no way of knowing that you're with us." The officer cocked his head toward Joey. "Does he know who you are?"

"No, sir, Joey is my coach at Gerri's Gym."

"Gerri's Gym! How the hell did you end up there?"

"My brother booked me in. He's a local resident here in L.A."

"Yeah, I know, the scanner filled me in. Just checking," he said as he gave a little smile. "Meanwhile, here's my card. If you need anything, and I mean anything, call me. I've got you covered."

As Joey continued driving down to the beach in silence, his big, strong hands gripped the steering wheel tightly to stop their shaking.

Nigel turned his head to the Ford's taped up window, trying to catch the elusive peace and serenity tied into the smell and sound of the saltwater surf that was always just a little out of his reach.

Joey parked and turned the car off. He turned to Nigel and threw up both hands and asked, "Who the fuck are you?"

There was a thirty-second pause before the two black men, who had just survived what all black men in America go through every day of their lives, burst into gales of laughter, howling with relief and Joey's comic inquiry as to Nigel's real identity.

Nigel wriggled all ten fingers in Joey's face. "Look, Joey, ten fingers and ten toes. You're right. I'm going to be okay!"

"No, really, there's a good chance you just saved my life back there. Fess up, and it'll stay between you and me."

Nigel proceeded to tell his coach his story of becoming a sitting duck in the courts up north. He spoke of all his inherent shyness, coupled with the loneliness that the Canadian Witness Protection Program had forced on him, his inability to connect with a good woman and the sheer boredom of not being able to work any longer in the judicial system.

"But something that the cop said has me puzzled," Nigel mused. "He indicated that I was with them. Did you hear that, Joey? He said exactly *you're with us*. What did he mean by that?"

"Maybe he was referring to you being on their side of the law. Don't worry about it. The outcome couldn't have been better for you."

"Oh, don't get me wrong. I know, I know. But it just made me wonder. It's bad enough being under the Canadian Witness Protection Program; I sure as hell don't want to be under an international one."

As they settled into a silent, easy jog along the boardwalk, Nigel was feeling better after sharing his sadness and anxiety with his coach.

Joey was mentally tweaking his client's workout schedule to add in more bag exercises to allow him extra venting time. 'Shit,' he thought to himself, 'I thought I had problems!'

***

Nigel settled into the new routine with ease. He loved the early mornings especially. The cook took him under her wing, ordering him to eat everything on his plate, as he was just too skinny for her liking. He pegged the large, black, gruff woman at about sixty-five years old; in fact, she was quite similar to his mama both in build and character. The cook always served him first and saw to it that there were extra helpings for him, keeping warm on the back of the big six-burner stove. It wasn't long before he was labeled as *'cook's sucky baby'* and he took the teasing in good stride, lapping up all the extra attention like a ten-year-old boy.

He got a kick out of sneaking into the office, grabbing the keys and cruising down to the beach for his run in the old Ford, arm hanging out of the cranked-down window. The beach offered him alone time, the chance to clear his mind as his slim, lanky frame adapted to the five-mile beach run.

At the end of the day, after the masseuse had rolled the kinks out of him, he was bone-tired. He appreciated his private, small room, with the small three-piece en-suite and double bed that his feet hung over as he stretched out to sleep. A row of six pegs mounted on the wall acted as a closet, and a small, three-drawer bureau with a lamp perched on the top of it completed the décor. He was secretly pleased to see that his pecs were taking shape and that his arms were blowing up, even after only two weeks of the routine.

He did as Joey had ordered and focused on his routine. He was constantly surprised at how the simple skip rope was as big a challenge as all the more strenuous upper-body work. The days slipped by, and the only real problem for Nigel was the half-hour spar with Gerri. He found himself with a tight gut even thinking about it as the clock ticked toward 3:30 p.m. when she would be up front and personal, her gloves nipping at him from all angles and talking trash into his sweating face. He kept his mouth shut, bearing down on his mouth guard throughout her drill and found he was sweating like a pig before they even got started. What really sickened him, though, was his reaction to her taunting face right outside his headgear. Every day, he swore he had it under control, to no avail. He ended each session with her with an uncomfortable erection that he simply didn't understand, and he hated himself right along with her for his body's betrayal. His greatest fear was that her routine taunt was based on her knowledge of his adverse reaction and unwanted attraction to her. His resentment built, day after day.

It all came to a terrible head at the end of Week Two when Gerri had stepped up her banter and he lost his cool. He spat out his mouth-guard with such force that Joey heard it from behind his desk in the office. Joey came running with a towel in hand.

Nigel was horrified to hear himself bellowing and espousing a long, two-minute rant, cursing his opponent out, calling her every name he could think of, and then some that he had never spoken before in his lifetime.

Gerri, still dancing, stepped back, and with contempt and pity written all over her face, she said softly, "Yah talkin' to me? Oh, baby, you are going down." Like all pro fighters, she calmly mapped out the distance to her target, located just behind and dead center to his headgear. She shot one deadly, on-target right-hook and you could hear the crack of his bone cartilage collapsing like a deck of cards. There was a thud as Nigel hit the mat with blood spurting from his nose.

Joey saw it all go down, and he stood back on the ropes as Gerri calmly stepped up to Nigel. She looked down at her trophy. She was a pro, however, and as she bent forward, she checked his pupils from her distance to make sure he wasn't in concussion. Nope, clear. Just a clean pop to give his perfect nose a little character going forward and to wipe the arrogant, elitist look clean off his handsome face.

She stood over him and watched his eyes, full of fury and hate, hold hers as the gusher ran freely down across his cheeks into the crease of his neck. "Gotta give him that. He's got balls," she said to herself and she slowly raised her boot and placed it in the middle his solar plexus with enough weight to make him tighten his abs. He didn't flinch one iota, and he took it like a man. She leaned over his face and hissed:

"If you come at the king
You'd better not miss. Asshole."

As Joey moved forward from his vantage point on the ropes, he had his phone to his face, calling Doc Rosen to come in right away to pack a nose.

Doc, as they all called him, had been working with Gerri's Gym now for over five years. A lot of movie people had been through that old gym ever since Brad had come on the scene and began filtering his movie-star buddies through the system. And Hollywood paid good money for him to patch up these pretty boys.

Gerri, on the other hand, had left the ring immediately after her parting words of wisdom. She leaned up against the wall in the long hallway to call Brad to let him know his brother's breakdown had crested and crashed as tears of sympathy for her fragile student's pain rolled down her cheeks.

***

Nigel lay there flat on his back in the ring quietly, as Joey ordered, and he felt a cold pack go over his face and his boots being unlaced and taken off.

Dr. Rosen arrived in ten minutes, and his nurse quickly set up the portable examination bed down on the floor, in between the small and large rings. A large surgical lamp set up beside the head of the bed. She arranged supplies and instruments out on her table and stood there quietly, holding the blood pressure cuff and waiting for the patient to be moved ever so carefully by Joey and the doctor down to the examination table.

Doc was puzzled. He peered into the man's face as he quietly asked the routine questions. The patient just didn't fit the Hollywood image at all – very well spoken, no L.A. jazz evident in his speech, and a little older than most that he had patched up in this gym. There was an intelligent look about his face. He had good hair that looked like he had expert lowlights and took care

121

of himself. He was tough though; he didn't flinch as the nurse cleaned him up so that they could take a better look at the nasal septum.

"The nurse needs a little time here, Nigel, before I can pack your nose, so we've got a minute to assess the situation. Don't speak out too loudly, just take your time, and a nod will suffice here and there. I'm really checking to assess if you are in shock or if Geri's right-hook rattled your brain." He gave a rueful smile.

Nigel nodded.

"Which studio are you with?"

"No, Doctor Rosen," Nigel said softly. "I'm not part of the Hollywood scene at all. My brother Brad booked me in here. My name is Nigel Royal, and I am a retired Supreme Court Justice up north in Toronto. I'm under the Canadian Witness Protection Program, and I live a quiet life under the radar up in Canada. I simply have no business being in a Hollywood gym, and I seem to be going through some sort of a mental breakdown. I take full responsibility for what has happened here today."

"Now I've heard everything."

"Yes, I know. It's does sound a little like a Hollywood script, doesn't it?"

"No, no, judge. It's not your background I'm talking about. It's your admitting that the current situation is of your own making. That's very rare indeed. I'm talking to a man who knows how to man up. A real man."

"Trust me, Doctor Rosen, over all my years sitting in the courts, I've heard all the excuses you could ever dream of. Excuses only prolong the pain, and I'm very interested in getting to the bottom of my own."

"I can help you, judge. Now here's what we're going to do. We're going to complete a soft psych examination, and at the same time, the nurse and I will be analyzing how to get the best results for your new nose. The said nose will never be quite the same. You're too good-looking anyway; this new nose will give your face a little character, kind of like your hooked scar under your cheekbone," he explained. "But first, what happened there?" he asked as he nodded towards Nigel's scar.

"You should see the other guy."

Doctor Rosen chuckled. "I can see that you're on the mend. But really, the work that you have had done on it is very, very good. Toronto does have an excellent roster of specialists, that's for sure."

"I was a youngster living in Jamaica when I got in the way of a cricket bat. I moved up north and as a teenager, a good plastic surgeon did his best with numerous tweaks to get me to this point."

"Okay, so that takes care of the physical part of the exam. And you're lucky to be blessed with that athletic body. Take care of it. The nurse and I have decided on how to pack your nose, but first, before the local anesthetic, we'll look under the hood."

"Booze?"

"No."

"Drugs?"

"No."

"Money problems?"

"No."

"Gay or straight?"

"Straight."

"Oh, so it must be a woman."

"Bingo."

"In a word or two, please define the women in your life after I call out the category. Mother?"

"Tough love."

"First girl?"

"Golden-haired angel."

"Wife?"

"Black hustler bitch."

"Latest girlfriend?"

"Cheating Irish faerie."

"Current sex life?"

"Celibate."

"May I suggest a plan of action?"

"Absolutely."

"One. I'll refer you to a good psychotherapist for you to go to once you get back up north.

"Two. You're going to have two shiners to wake up to tomorrow. I'll send in a good aesthetician to treat your face daily. She's very good, and she'll take care of any scar tissue and other residue that crops up. She will make up some cool pads of Vitamin C and E mix for you to administer to your face and throat in between her visits. She takes care of the Hollywood's pretty boys all the time. Your brother knows her.

"Three. I won't put you on bed rest, but I'll get Joey to stick to tai chi, ballet barre work and Pilates for the next few days, until your face settles down. I'll give you something for tonight to make sure you get some sleep, but nothing after that. Just keep your mind on your gym program here, and do not, under any circumstances, dwell on the fairer sex.

"Four. Try not to cry. It's just too painful. You can cry all you want once you get on the shrink's couch back in Toronto.

"Five. The cook will keep you fed and hydrated. Listen to her. Eat and drink everything she pushes at you."

"Sounds like a plan, Doctor Rosen." Nigel smiled a little as he said, "I'll make sure to deliver my wholehearted, humble apology to Gerri for my bad behavior as soon as I can climb out of the Humiliation and Self-Loathing Department of this gym."

He continued while offering his hand to the Doc, "You're amazing. I'm very grateful for all your help. I've been struggling with this for thirty years, and you have narrowed it down to three devastating femme fatales in ten minutes."

"Anything else, judge?"

Nigel took in a breath and hesitantly spat out what had been really bothering him.

"The name's Nigel. It's Gerri who holds the gavel in this court. And, yes, there is something else. I'm a little embarrassed to discuss this with you, but you are a doctor and all. You see, I have been suffering from painful, humiliating erections that come into play every time I get into the ring with Gerri. Is it just me or do you think it's a love/hate chemistry between the two of us and we shouldn't continue our work in the ring together? Or what?"

"Don't be embarrassed. And yes, I can answer your question as to the chemistry between the two of you. It's all you, I'm afraid. The love part is because she is one hell of a good-looking woman, so there's nothing wrong there at all. You're healthy. Be happy that your sex equipment works so well. And the hate part of your self-diagnosed situation is probably because you are transferring some emotion from a woman in your past. Your new psychotherapy sessions up north will take care of that. As for Gerri, I can assure you she has absolutely zero interest in your manhood. She's the biggest dyke in Hollywood."

He continued, shaking his head, "Girls can be tricky, all right. I know from experience. I'm on my third wife. Now, about the nose. This is going to hurt."

"Go ahead, Doc. It can't be any worse than Gerri's medicine."

***

The kitchen smelled good. The long communal table was laden with juices, vegan protein powders, stacks of whole wheat pancakes, sausages, bacon, over-easy eggs, fried tomatoes, grits, newspapers, and snippets of small talk. The cook was manning the stove, Gerri was plowing into a plate of eggs and bacon, and Joey was trying to read the paper as the others drew him into the variety of conversations that were taking place.

They all stopped talking and reading as they watched a lone, unmanned white flag appear slowly out from the corner of the hallway. The flag waved from side to side. It appeared to be attached to a long, wooden broomstick. The operator was not to be seen. As the flag stopped waving, they were able to read the bold black sharpie print on the white paper flag. It read:

"I SURRENDER."

The room was silent for a moment and then burst into a roar of laughter that you could hear clear down to the beach as Nigel stepped into the room. He stepped forward with both hands up over his head as if to turn himself in. Both nostrils were packed with tampons, strings cut short but still dangling, and he sported two perfectly round shiners that left no doubt that someone had kicked his ass royally. He gave a little grin and shrugged his shoulders as if to admit his defeat.

"Sorry to interrupt your breakfast, but I have something to say," his plugged-up baritone announced. He paused to get everyone's attention and his smile disappeared.

He placed one hand over his heart and looked directly into Gerri's face, "Gerri, I am truly sorry for spewing all that hate and anger into your face yesterday. There is no excuse for my behavior, and I promise you it will never happen again. I don't know what's got into me lately, but it was so wrong of me to lay it all over you. Please forgive me."

"Nigel! Stop right there! Just shut up! Just shut the fuck up!" she said as she pushed back her chair to stand up. "Man, you had me at hello. I'm coming over there to shake your hand and tell you that I'm sorry for starting the whole mess. What I really fear right now is that your brother will never ever let either of us live this one down! He can be one royal pain in the ass, even worse than you!"

There was a lot of clapping and cheering going on in the big kitchen as both the teacher and the student earned an A+ for playing by the golden rule.

The cook, still stirring the grits on the stove while nodding sagely, said, "Yup, that's my boy."

From that day on, Nigel's painful erections were miraculously a thing of the past, and he and Gerri moved into a fruitful teacher-student relationship that was based on a mutual respect. His new, cut body was shaping up to perfection, and even the cook grudgingly approved with her lips pursed and head nodding up and down.

Nigel ended his six-week L.A. boot camp with the cook preparing a special graduation dinner for him. Brad had come into the gym early in the evening, and the whole staff was there. Doc, his nurse, and even the aesthetician came out for the occasion.

After Nigel had bear-hugged each and every one of them, with promises to Joey to keep in shape, he carried his bag full of the borrowed vintage tee-shirts and shorts along with a new pair of boxing boots that Joey had gifted him out to the car. He said, "Gerri, I will never be able to repay you for all you've done for me. I've already phoned ahead, and I'm starting my psychotherapy first thing next week. I'm gonna make you proud, girl. I love you. If I can ever do anything for you, anything at all, just call me. Whenever you need me, I'll be there."

As twilight took a backseat to a beautiful full moon, the brothers sat poolside in the private, hedged backyard. Using a big, long frond they picked out of the garden, they horsed around like brothers do, using the frond to measure each other's biceps in mock competition.

"I have one last thing to take care of tomorrow morning before I head out to LAX. Do you have a personal shopper or someone that can zip me over to a local mall tomorrow morning?"

"Yeah, no problem. Sorry, man, I just can't do the mall scene myself, but my housekeeper is due in early tomorrow morning. She'll be happy to take you over."

"Perfect. I'm happy to pay her for her time. It's just that I want to buy the cook a bottle of Channel No. 5 and some flowers and I can't do it over the phone, as I need to enclose a personal note with the delivery."
Nigel added, "It's the least I can do. I've already talked to Gerri about a scholarship program. She's agreed to run high-risk kids through a quiet little program, one kid at a time, and I'll pick up the tab."

"You are a class act, bro. I need to take some lessons from you."

"Not at all, bro. I know the score. Both Joey and Gerri would be in jail today if it wasn't for you stepping up to the plate."

"Yeah. I suppose, but meanwhile, you ain't seen nothin' yet. I'm going to beat your sorry ass in a race, five laps and no cheating," Brad said.

Nigel jumped out of his chair. "I call it! Jamaican-style all the way!" he said as he stripped down out of his borrowed bathing trunks and ran to the pool naked as a jaybird. "Last man in is a rotten egg!"

As Nigel treaded water in the deep end, he watched his younger brother saunter over to the pool's edge and break down on one knee into a free-balling, commando-style Mr. Universe pose.

"Oh. Oh. Wait. Wait. Really. There's something right there," Nigel said in a concerned voice.

"What?"

"Oh, there's a piece of skinny, white thread from out of the towel. It's hanging right down right there just down below your bellybutton. Oh, no, I'm wrong! Sorry! It's just your skinny little dick waving down at me."

Nigel had a split-second to move out of the way of Brad's expertly placed cannonball jump.

They ended their race with Nigel hanging on to the edge of the pool and panting, "I just let you win that one 'cause I feel sorry for you."

***

Chapter 8
Single Again

I looked at my watch for the umpteenth time that morning. It seemed to stand still at the countdown hour of fifty-two hours. I tried to busy myself with unpacking, to no avail. I laid out all my beautiful gifts that Nigel had bought me in Paris, but I simply did not have the appetite to enjoy them at all. If the truth be known, I was sick to my stomach with trepidation. My gut had told me out at the airport once we had landed that this was going to take place, and I simply couldn't face now, any more than I could face it then.

I sat in front of my computer, staring at the unanswered emails and tasks to no avail. The only reason I couldn't just call him wasn't because of my pride. Oh no, I knew right then and there that I wouldn't see him again. Call it a woman's intuition.

Day Two slipped into Day Three. There was no call from Nigel, not that I was expecting one. I knew. I couldn't even try to rationalize the matter. As the seventy-second hour passed, I got out my old notebook to map out a plan. I couldn't bear to use the beautiful red leather notebooks with my initials engraved in gold on the front cover that Nigel had bought me in Paris. Oh no, not at all. I was right back to where I started – back to before Nigel Royal and definitely before Paris.

***

"Thanks so much for all your help, especially with the topped-up health insurance for the year," I said to the travel agent sitting across from me. "So, I have one flight tomorrow night into Avignon, and then three days later, I fly from Avignon to Edinburgh, right?"

"That's right, Denise. Enjoy your time with your girlfriend in Avignon and your ancestral research up in Edinburgh. Call me when you're ready to leave Edinburgh and I'll take good care of you."

I walked into the bank and bought some euros and British pound notes. I notified VISA that I would be using my card in Europe and then walked back up the block to my apartment to cancel my cellphone's Toronto number to block roaming charges that were bound to start the moment the flight left Canadian airspace. I planned on picking up a Euro cell with a local number once I got settled. I called my girlfriend Maureen to see if her daughter was still looking for a small apartment in the city. My idea was that she could sublet mine, fully furnished, for a year.

My beautiful, small, jewel-box of an apartment had become like a prison over the past three days. I couldn't stand the thought of running into him. I just couldn't handle it.

The next morning, I met with Maureen's daughter, who had jumped at the chance to sublet my furnished apartment for the next ten to twelve months. She was working on her PhD at University of Toronto and needed just short of a year to wrap it up completely.

I carefully wrapped all of Nigel's gifts from Paris up in tissue paper and when I lifted up the pair of beautiful antique hand-tatted ivory gloves that he had bought me, I felt my stomach coming up faster than I could make it to the toilet to throw up all my fresh heartbreak. I cleaned myself up and took the few boxes of personal belongings downstairs to keep safe in my empty locker. I dropped into the super's office to tell them that my sublet would come in to complete any paperwork.

I packed a carry-on that included my laptop and paper file on my Scottish and Irish heritage. I slung my old leather knap sack over my shoulder and left for Lester B. Pearson Airport without giving it another thought.

I found myself sitting out in the airport lounge, pulling out my phone, and dialing his number. Realizing I had no service, I left the lounge looking for the bank of airport-supplied landlines to complete the call. To this day, I don't know why I did it. I knew better. The robot-operator informed me,

"The number you have reached has been disconnected, and there is no forwarding number connected to this file."

The overnight flight was half-empty in coach, and thankfully, I had the privacy that the two empty seats beside me gave. As the flight attendant kindly brought me the second full box of Kleenex for my tears, she quietly said, "I suppose this isn't just a case of a nervous flyer. Am I right? Have you got a sedative or something that you can take?"

"Thank you so much for all your kindness. I'll be just fine. I'm just coming down from a very intensive love affair that only lasted a week."

"Oh my God. You poor baby. Do you want to talk about it?"

"No. No, not at all. If I told you, you'd know what an idiot I am."

"Now, now, it takes two, you know. Listen, I'm going to go get you a few pillows and another blanket, and I want you to try and rest. Okay? But first, is someone meeting you in Avignon?"

I blew my nose and nodded my head yes. "Catharine will be there. Thank God for girlfriends."

"Amen, sister."

***

At the luggage belt, as Catharine's arms went around me, my tears started fresh and I cried, "Oh Catharine, I'm such an idiot."

She patted my back like one would pat the back of a child. "Now, now, enough, enough. I'm here. I've got you. And yes, you say you're an idiot, but you're my idiot and I love you. We're going to get you home and put you back together again, bigger and better than ever before. Do you hear me?"

At the end of the second day, after dinner, she poured us a glass of wine. "I need you to listen to me, and I need you to listen hard, Denni," Catharine said. She laid it on the line and insisted that I face my old nemesis, which was of course, myself. I was my own worst enemy, she told me, always running away from intimacy, always running away from a relationship once it turned serious.

"You're not a kid. Look at you. You're over forty, still wandering around the globe like a university grad on her parents' allowance, skipping out on relationships at the first sign of when it's the real deal."

"What do you know?" I wept. "You have Edouard. You don't know what being out there alone is like."

"Don't give me that bullshit, Denni," she continued. "You know the ropes. Being alone is the result of your own actions. Stop whining about being alone and do something about it. You must face the real problem and deal with it. Acceptance, not denial, is what allows us to heal. And you've got a lot of healing to do. Look at you! The last few years have been a nightmare for you. First the cancer, then the brain tumor, and your mother dying. And the court case against your sisters, that would kill anyone! And then your one sister dying. It's too much for anyone. And you're fragile right now. No wonder this Nigel guy and all the good sex was too much for you to handle. But we know all that, don't we? I don't mean to be so tough on you but it's time for you to grow up and get a life. A real life with a real relationship under your belt. You know very well that this Nigel was the perfect man for you and you tossed him aside at the first sign of emotional attachment. Are you crazy?"

She warned me, "Listen to me, your days of being a good-looking, independent hipster with nothing but wanderlust on your résumé are over. You're too old for that crap. Straighten up and go back home and settle down and write a book or get a job. I love you. I want you to be happy. And at the present, I see nothing but dark clouds on your horizon if you continue on this path. Now I'm going to give you a month or two up in Edinburgh to do your research, but after that, I expect better from you."

I dried my eyes. "Thank you, Catharine, for the wakeup call. I know. I know. You've told me this before, but somehow, I just can't catch on to being a couple with someone, even when it's someone as wonderful as Nigel. I love you too, and I'm grateful for your support. Yeah, you're right. The worst is behind me. And especially since I have my inheritance issue all settled. I'm going to clean up my act, become a famous author, and dedicate my first book to you and Edouard."

"My dear friend, I think I can sum up who you are by using the same phrase for both your best side and your worst side."

"What do you mean? How can that be? Even with a crazy person like me, there are opposite ends of the narrative, you know."

"No, no. Listen to me. This is the truth. You are annoyingly optimistic. Think about it. I know you can't change it, but from now on, keep it in mind, and pay attention. This sad case I see in front of me is not like you at all. I don't want you to get sick with emotional problems or mental health issues, you hear me?"

"Yes, I hear you loud and clear. I will try my best to be annoyingly optimistic at all times."

"*Hallelujah.* Make sure you send me some of the royalties, since you're going to be so rich and famous. Now let's make sure you've got this straight. You'll come back here for Christmas before you head back home, right?"

At that point, I didn't have the heart to tell her that I had sublet my apartment for the year and was in no hurry to go home and settle down, so I simply said, "That's the plan, girlfriend, but it may take me a little more time than that up in Scotland. Christmas is just around the corner. No worries, Catharine. We'll figure it out as we go along."

***

I rang the buzzer and a stout, gray-haired woman opened the door with, "Good to see you, lass. I was glad to get your call from the airport. Yes, indeed,

131

I can put you up in my bed and breakfast while you write your book, lass. Come in, come in. Don't let the rain in, lass."

I settled in quite nicely in Edinburgh. It was a relatively small city, especially in the autumn when most were indoors, out of the rain and sleet. My room at Mrs. McIntyre's was sufficient, although not luxurious in the least. It had a double bed, a wardrobe, and a small desk under the window so that I could write from my laptop. The adjoining bathroom had a small shower that I had to ease into sideways, but it was functional, warm enough, and a place to rest my head to get away from my sad thoughts about my life with Nigel that I so carelessly and stupidly had thrown away.

Mrs. McIntyre was a little offsetting, however. The conversations at the breakfast and the supplied dinner became a little too much like my old grandma advising me how to run my life, and I found myself spending all my days out and about in the small, gray city.

I loved to go to the old Edinburgh castle and sit on the steps, just like my maternal grandma, Annie Duffus Dunbar, used to do as a child. Her family lived in the tenements behind the castle, and my ancestors back into the seventeenth century had worked in the castle as well. I suppose you could say that the Dunbars, back then, were 'starting fresh' once again just like I was at the moment. My sympathetic thoughts told me that their humble lifestyle didn't change who they were; it was only real estate after all. I knew they had once reigned supreme from their own Dunbar Castle, and even Mary, Queen of Scots, had an apartment there. The passage of time and politics marched on, eventually squashing any remnants of privilege and prestige that the original Dunbars had enjoyed up to then. You never know!

Mrs. McIntyre wasn't exactly pleased that I wouldn't appear at the set dinner table for the meals on time, and I found myself avoiding her whenever I could. Like Catharine had reminded me, I wasn't some grad student with a curfew.

I spent my days taking classes at the Scottish Genealogy Society's library and family history center and doing my research of my maternal family, the Dunbars, at the National Records of Scotland Office. It was near a small pub where I began to take my lunch and dinner, rather than face Mrs. McIntyre, waiting for me to get home.

It wasn't long before I was a 'regular' at the pub, and I was part of the crowd that worked shifts at *The Scottish Sun* printing plant. There was always a pint waiting for me as I slid into the booths with the men just off their shift, with their ink-stained fingers and coats that smelled of beer and cigarettes. I accepted their friendship and curiosity without the blink of an eye.

They regarded me as an oddity though, a woman out on her own and all. Their wives were at home getting the supper on the table after their earlier shift working at the mill or at the supermarket. I was a Canuck, a writer with a funny accent, here in town to do research on her own roots before writing about others and their roots. They told me stories of their own. They would start with historical notes on their clans but would eventually come to the point of sharing their hopes and dreams for a better life for their kids. They always wanted to be in my book and would argue the point among themselves as to who would be the good guy and who would be the bad, all in the print of my masterpiece that they had no doubt would be a bestseller.

I was worlds away from Nigel, his tailored suits, and his Elmwood manicures, and I dulled my pain as I tipped back pint after pint with the boys like I was born to be there. It got to the point where the bartender, Patrick, wouldn't take my money. "Yer money's no good here, lass."

The minute I would swing through the big, old wooden doors, my favorite brew would be presented to me on an old tray with a clean, white kitchen towel matting and sopping up the overflowing head of the brew. The only way I could pay my way, it seemed, was to ensure that I tipped more than the actual price of the beer, and that money was graciously and quietly accepted with a semi-bow from the server, whether it was the bartender's wife or his adult daughter on the afternoon shift.

Over the eight weeks before Christmas, the combination of the rainy, cold weather, the heavy Guinness, and my sadness and pain of life in general took its toll, and I found myself listening to Mrs. McIntyre express her disappointment in me for coming in late without so much as a visit with her in front of her telly in the lounge. She may have won the battle, but she lost the war. After that, I was careful to wait until after 9:00 p.m. when she would shut the house down for the night. I would sneak up the creaking stairs, most of the time too drunk to change into my pajamas before falling into bed, just to wake up the next morning and start it all over again.

However, I did grant her the one request that was absolutely written in stone. Christmas-Eve dinner and Christmas-Day dinner were non-optional. I phoned Catharine and explained that I hadn't wrapped up my research yet, and that I had been invited to spend Christmas with Mrs. McIntyre and the other tenants.

I made the most of it and went out and bought Mrs. McIntyre a nice cashmere scarf and I bought the other tenants, boxes of shortbread and fancy nuts. I wrapped everything in fancy tissue and everyone was very pleased with my little effort. I brought in the mincemeat tarts from the local bakery and kept up my end of the conversation over both dinners as required. I must admit that over this short period of time, I was a good tenant, and she was a good landlady. We did have a giggle getting the ham out of the oven after we had both been sampling her brandy that she only brought out for special occasions, and I knew she had been nipping away at it since before lunch. I had my own stash up in my room, so by the time we all sat down for Christmas dinner, we were all mimicking each other's accents and telling funny stories of past Christmases.

I was wrapping up my research at the Scottish Genealogy Society that week after Christmas, so I was about to start making plans to go over to Ireland and actually visit my paternal ancestor's little farm, thatched roof and all, in the small hamlet called Skelpy, located a mile from the border between Ireland and Northern Ireland. It's funny how things work out. I never got to Ireland at all. And, unknown to me at the time, it was to be my last night in Edinburgh.

The boys were all back to work, and hence my table at the pub was once again full with the afternoon-shift workers, all back from a few days off. The drinks were flowing pretty good, and I don't remember if I ate the dinner that I had ordered or not. I do remember, however, hours later, Jimmy pulling my head back off the table and peering into my face, looking a little concerned. "No, lass, you're not in any shape to get home by yourself. You're coming home with me." I don't remember anything else.

I opened my eyes. The room was in morning light. I was lying on a mattress about six inches off the floor, that was centered in the middle of what looked to be a lounge, as they call it there in Edinburgh. My eyes were level with two white, hairy, bare legs, that I followed up to a pair of plaid undershorts.

"Who are you and where am I?"

"No. The question is who are you, lass? Me, well, I'm Jimmy's flat-mate. He had to go to work for the morning shift, and he asked me to make sure that you had metro money to get home. I have to leave shortly. Are you going to be okay? Can I get you a coffee, love?"

I closed my eyes and said, "So sorry, I'll be up and out of here right away. If you can just tell me which way to get home, I'll be grateful." My shame, coupled with my hangover, made looking at his face impossible. My hands moved down over the blanket to pat my body. It seemed that my clothes were still on, and I silently lifted one arm to receive his help to get up and off the low-lying mattress. He guided me to the small bathroom. As I splashed water on my face, I caught a glimpse of a person in the small mirror that was mounted over the sink. I didn't recognize her at all. I knew my stomach couldn't take even a small glass of water, so I smoothed down my hair with my hands the best I could and left the shelter of that small room with those four walls to face the harsh world outside its door. My coat, along with my knapsack, was hanging on a hook mounted on the wall beside the front door of the flat. My boots were lined up neatly on a mat by the door. I couldn't manage the boots at all, and Jimmy's flat-mate had me sit on a kitchen chair as he unzipped each boot and pulled them on for me.

I looked up as I entered the foyer of Mrs. McIntyre's bed and breakfast to see her with her arms folded over her ample bosom, which was layered with her small, dark-print day dress with a sparkling white apron covering the front of the ensemble. My suitcase rested beside her, locked and loaded for travel.

Mrs. McIntyre, with great officiousness, said, "At first I thought you were a nice lass. Then two weeks later, I thought you were a nice lass with a problem with the drink. Now you're staying out all night like a whore. You're not a nice lass at all, and I won't have a common whore staying in my house. It's time you went on your way, lass."

She opened the door and stood there, not seeming to care that she was letting the cold in. She firmly took me by my arm with one hand and tossed my suitcase outside with the other. I heard the door lock behind me as I stood there, unable to move. I was frozen in space and time, with the heavy burden of booze, guilt, pain, and loss overwhelming me. It was just beginning to rain, and I lifted my face to the heavens to feel the icy sting on my flushed cheeks.

I was still half drunk as I settled down into the coach's velour seat. I looked down at my ticket that I was still clutching in my hand. It appeared that I had bought a train ticket to London. As the train rolled out of Edinburgh, the sleet hit the window and my hot, salty tears ran freely. The soothing rock back and forth of the near-empty train over the first hour gave me enough courage to walk down to the food car, where I sat up at the counter sipping a coffee as the cook prepared my toasted egg sandwich. Although the kind cook didn't say as much, I knew I must have looked a sight. I hadn't even as much as combed my hair in over twenty-four hours, let alone brush my teeth. My clothes stank of pub beer and cigarettes, just like my drinking cronies' jackets back in Edinburgh.

The cook asked me where I was staying in London, and when I said I hadn't a clue, he was kind enough to write down the name of a hotel located centrally that wasn't too expensive. He said he used to work in their kitchen and that they served very good food. He also wrote down his name on the paper, and if I would be so kind, would I mention his name to the kitchen staff if I was able to do so.

"Oh, this is like the old joke, right? Mention my name and you'll get a good seat."

He laughed softly. "Yes, sort of." He continued on with his recommendation, which included that I should take the full-board plan that included breakfast and dinner.

I tried not to cry as I thanked him for his kindness. He sounded just like Catharine giving me her tough-love advice at exactly the right time. I was still too wired and too full of booze to sleep, so I pulled out a few British pound notes to keep ahead of the tab, and I helped myself to his pot of coffee. I pulled out a notebook and started to make a new plan as my new friend, Nadar, the train's cook, made up a little fruit cup for me to nosh on. An hour later, he was preparing a grilled cheese sandwich for me, and between me jotting down initial notes of my new life's plan, he talked of recipes and cooking techniques from back home in India like he'd known me his whole life.

It was a much-needed respite from life that I needed so badly, and I found myself sobering up enough to walk down the clattering, rattling car to try and freshen up in the small, rocking toilet before landing in London. I was pretty sure that no hotel, no matter what written endorsement I had in my pocket, would have given me a room judging by my current appearance. That five-hour train trip gave me enough time to swallow my pain and resolve to begin a new life, once again.

As it turned out, the mid-sized hotel in London, two blocks from Piccadilly, was the perfect hotel for me to recover in. I ate a full breakfast and big dinner, sans the wine, every day there in the big, old-fashioned dining room, without the landlady asking inquisitive questions as to why a nice lass like me wasn't married yet.

I knew that I couldn't face Catharine right now, so I guess you might say I lied by omission. I intimated over the phone that I was still up in Edinburgh. Well, why not? She didn't ask, and I didn't say. Oh, those little white lies! It seems so simple and reasonable at the time, but they do catch up with you sooner or later. I needed to get my act together before facing the real world. I would wait until I was settled somewhere before letting her know what was really going on. I wished her and Edouard a happy New Year, and I realized it would be my first New Year celebration in many, many years with just me, myself, and I, without a whisper of a drink in sight.

I spent my days walking the great city and visiting all the galleries I could find.

I spent the evenings in my room, having set up my laptop on the small desk, and I organized all my research that I had done over the mornings before the pub that would start around three in the afternoon.

I also fleshed out my notes of my new plan and faced the fact that I had to delve into my past before I could manage the future.

I thought back to the day that I had finally received a copy of Mom's will and what a surprise it had been. Up until then, I had thought that it was my sister, the executor, that wouldn't release any jewelry, photos, or *tchotchkes* to me over the last year and a half. Oh no, it wasn't that simple. Mom, in her meanness, and I admit, with her early-onset dementia, right down until the day she died, had documented in her will that I was to only get my portion of the money in the estate, and nothing else. Yes, she died not knowing how to love anyone, let alone herself. What a loss, for everyone concerned! But you never know when it comes to wills, or family for that matter.

This information, however, made forgiveness easier, as I realized that my sister had no choice but to follow Mom's wishes. I thought of what Catharine said to me as she dried my eyes earlier down at the *château*: *"Acceptance, not denial, is what allows us to heal."*

This priceless little gem of Catharine's allowed me to forgive myself first and to follow through with forgiveness of everyone else next. Every day of that week in London, I sent my forgiveness for all concerned up to the heavens, in the statement addressed to each individual. *"From this moment on, I send you love. I forgive you."* And, of course, I started by calling out my own name first and ending it with proclaiming to myself, standing there in my flannel pajamas, looking out onto the streets of London from my hotel room. *I am God's child.*

I instinctively let it all go, all of it, and all of them, and it felt damn good.

My main plan of writing my big, gutsy novel was still not within my reach. I guess I just wasn't ready yet. It sat on the backburner as I took care of myself and did my best to accept my painful past to go forward with a clean slate. *'Yes,'* I told myself repeatedly, *'acceptance is the key.'*

I bought all new clothes, a new coat, and a pair of beautiful leather boots, all the while thinking with each piece that it would be something that Nigel would have chosen. I stayed far, far away from the plethora of pubs that London had to offer. I was off booze completely. There was a small spa attached to the hotel, and I treated myself to a daily treatment – a haircut one day, a facial the next, a massage on the third day, and a mani/pedi to follow. By the time my two weeks in London were up, I felt like my old self once again, but just a little older and wiser.

Catharine was right; I wasn't a kid any longer. I warned myself that I'd better start taking better care. My sensitive Irish soul, so badly bashed over the past two years, couldn't take the lifestyle of a boozer any more than my fair Irish skin could take the hot, summer sun. If I wanted to keep my mental health intact, along with my girlish looks, it was going to take work from now on.

***

Since I had sublet my apartment in Toronto for the year, my new plan that I had hatched was that I would go down and live in Nice, in the south of France, for the remaining nine or ten months of my sojourn. I had stayed in Nice a few times over the years, and I always thought I could live there quite happily. I could do with some milder weather, and I planned on taking some French-language classes to pass the time away once I got settled in. It was a perfect opportunity for me to start my ever-elusive book that I had been researching for years and talking of writing for quite some time. Looking online, I found a monthly furnished rental apartment with a small balcony two blocks up from the beach, near the old town. It was a two-bedroom, and I realized that finally I could host Catharine and Edouard for a change, as I was always staying with them up at their *château*. I booked my new home right then and there.

I considered taking the Chunnel, as I quite liked traveling by trains, but then realized that I would pull into Paris on the French side of the trip. Oh no. Oh no. My fragile heart was not ready for Paris, even though I was definitely on the mend. I simply couldn't face the remembrance of all that exquisite sex and the all-too-new-and-intense intimacy that Nigel and I had shared in Paris. I knew my limits.

I booked a direct flight from London to Nice, and without further complications, I arrived in that beautiful little gem of a city in the south of France, right on the sparkling Mediterranean without a hitch. I unpacked my few worldly possessions, set up my laptop, and settled into my new digs like the sophisticated, savvy, almost-middle-aged writer that I always knew I was. I asked myself rather smugly, "What could possibly go wrong here?"

I got back into the swing of cooking once again, and I shopped daily down in old town for my onions, shallots, carrots, berries, vegies, and greens to prepare all my dinners which I had decided to eat in and enjoy my own company with a favorite French movie on TV or a good book. No more of that pub food, or the Scottish kidney pie, pan-fried bangers, and Christmas shortbreads at Mrs. McIntyre's for me.

I found an old copy of *Julie Child's Mastering the Art of French Cooking* in a second-hand book store, and I adapted many of the *crème* and butter-laden recipes into more modern, healthier dishes. I walked the Esplanade Anglais daily and would choose from the good variety of lunch spots along the way. I tried them all, the Negresco, the Blue Beach Restaurant, the Hotel Westminster, the Udo Plage, and the Neptune Plage, but I always ordered the same meal – the classic French tomato/basil/mozzarella appetizer with a large *Niçoise* salad to follow. I loved being back in a routine once again. I slept like a baby and woke up early, eager to start the day under the blue skies of the French Riviera.

***

"Bonjour, class. Mon nom est Lyonel Trouillot. N'cest pas Monsieur Trouillot. Non. Non. Non. Je suis Lyonel."

And so, the ragtag body of sixteen adults in Room 302 began their intensive twelve-week FSL program under the competent tutelage of Monsieur Lyonel Trouillot. There were four or five international business students like myself, but the bulk of the class was made up of newcomers to France. My heart went out to them, especially the students from the war-torn countries like Syria and Iraq. The women wore headscarves and it took a few days for them to be able to lift their eyes to meet Lyonel's kind questions head-on. The men struggled with the whole process, not being able to answer the question quickly enough to satisfy their own personal expectations. They were very hard on themselves. I believed that the French government sponsored these immigrants similar to the way our ESL classes in Canada were sponsored. Lyonel was a prince. He never turned the whole process into a social work program. Not at all. He forced the men to talk about their past careers. Most of them were engineers and had built bridges and watering systems throughout the Middle East. He used the business students to fill in the gaps, and we all bonded very quickly with the same goal of becoming fluent in the French language. When it was my turn to introduce myself, I told the class that I was a Canadian writer who had never been published in English, let alone in French. Lyonel claimed that from now on, I was the adjective queen and that I must be ready to fill in a flowery phrase on demand of anyone in the classroom. Everyone in the room laughed at Lyonel's orders, and I think about half of them really understood the little joke that the teacher had made. Yet, Lyonel had done his own homework, and it was obvious that he had read our written applications to be accepted into the program. He knew that I had spent a number of years teaching ESL to adults in Toronto and that I understood the theory behind teaching adults a second language. And he knew that I was ready to pitch in and help out however I could.

Our instructor had the personality to draw the individual students out to create a lively but somewhat stilted conversation between the trios he would randomly put together. He never asked for a volunteer to come forward. He never asked us to do anything. It was always a command, yet polite enough.

"Bruno, to the board, please. Write down everything Maria says." Or, "Denise, hand out the reading material for the day." Or, "Sasha, did you bring in that poetry for me? Meanwhile, the rest of you, look at the board. I have written down a universal saying. I need everyone in the class, starting with

Olga's row, to stand up individually and tell a story of how this saying has affected you personally at some point in your life. The universal saying that we are going to discuss is the Latin phrase, *Carpe diem*. And with this exercise being conducted in your choice of French, English or your first language, it is the last time today that I want to hear anything other than French, *comprendez-vous?*"

"*Oui*, Lyonel."

As we went up and down the rows, all standing up to introduce ourselves, the tall, dark, and handsome student that had taken the seat directly in front of me took his turn. He spoke a little French, but mostly English, in a low, confident voice.

"*Bonjour, Lyonel. Bonjour, class. Mon nom est Frank Miosi.* I'm an American, and I used to live in New York City. I used to be a police officer. I am currently a discharged army veteran from my last duty tour in Afghanistan. That's honorably discharged, just for the record." He laughed a little. "My family name is *Miosi*, which is Italian. My parents were immigrants, the same as most of us here today. They had to learn English the same as most of us here today are learning French." With that, he carried his lanky frame up to the board and wrote his name, *Frank Miosi,* with *New York City* under it.

"*Merci, Frank, très bien.* Good idea putting your name up on the board. As you may know, sixty percent of us are visual learners, so this ensures that the class will remember your name."

As Frank returned down our aisle and sat down in his seat, it was right then that my new, safe, interesting, and happy life began to unravel, ever so slightly.

My heart stopped and I instantly felt my gut tighten up as my olfactory receptors picked up his scent. No, it couldn't be. I leaned forward and breathed deeply. Oh, no, please, God. I reeled back, pushing against my chair. It was Yardley's Old Spice.

How could this be happening to me? I had traveled over five thousand miles to bury a memory, only to have it slap my face in one deadly fell swoop. Surely, there couldn't be another man on the planet that used that old-fashioned, out-of-date aftershave that Nigel wore.

That was when I began to recognize that Frank's back and long arms were just like Nigel's – long and lean. He had stretched his legs out in the aisle, and his size-thirteen crossed at the ankle, just like Nigel would have done. I looked around the room to see if there was another desk open so I could get away from him. 'No,' I decided, 'I would have to wait until lunch break when it wouldn't be so obvious.'

We all trooped out of the classroom to go down to the cafeteria at lunchtime. There were ten or twelve of us, and we all grabbed a long table. I took a seat near the end of the table, and Frank followed by, sitting directly across from me.

"So, you're writing a book." He smiled as if we were sharing some sort of conspiracy. "Am I going to be in it?"

I wanted to say, 'Never!' I wanted to say that he was my real-life nightmare and that I was trying to keep men like him out of my fantasy world altogether. But, of course, I didn't.

"Actually, I've met enough bad boys just like you over the years to fill three books, so no, you're not going to be in this one."

"Maybe next time."

"Trust me, Frank. Don't hold your breath."

We both laughed as we recognized that we shared the same sense of humor. He raised his bottle of water to tap mine, and we toasted the way old friends do. Oh, oh, oh. It all started innocently enough. I had let my guard down and found myself leaning forward and it wasn't so I could hear what he was saying in the noisy cafeteria. No, not at all. I couldn't stay away from his scent. 'Oh, Nigel. Nigel, where are you when I need you? Nigel, Nigel. What have we done? What am I going to do?' I was heartsick at the thought that I had twelve weeks ahead of me, sitting right behind a Nigel facsimile.

I straightened up a little in order to get away from the trouble that was sitting across from me. I focused on what the rest of the crowd was saying, but I was unable to add anything worthwhile to the conversation. I couldn't eat my lunch, so I wrapped it up carefully and put it in my knapsack to take home for a snack later in the day.

Over the days to come, I got to know my handsome Italian-American classmate little by little. It turned out Frank wasn't a sparkling conversationalist or especially charming with the ladies. He came to class well prepared, homework done every day, and was one of the best students in the class. He was knowledgeable, helpful, but certainly not the life of the party. He was a man's man, a decent man. He looked to be around forty-five years old. He always had a novel in his knapsack, and I figured that he would have been just as happy with his own company. He never spoke of his army days, and very rarely of his police work in New York City. Yes, he had his demons, all right. There was definitely a side to him that was moody, tough, dangerous, and of course, as sexy as hell. I chalked his dark moodiness up to his army days. Life in Afghanistan certainly wasn't a piece of cake by any stretch of the imagination.

By the time we had been in class for two weeks, I realized that I would have to focus on my studies to keep my mind off my Nigel smell-alike. I found that my French was improving by leaps and bounds. I really enjoyed being

141

back in the classroom again, and my instructor, Lyonel, took me aside one day before we broke for lunch.

"Denise, I want to tell you how much I appreciate your helpful attitude in class every day. It's not just your help with the grammar and conjugations; it seems to me that you have a special sensitivity to the needs of newcomers. I notice that you always steer the conversation toward their experiences. I suppose it's true; you Canadians are just so darn nice!"

"Thanks, Lyonel. I'm really enjoying your class. If there is anything that I can do to help, please count me in."

***

It was after that when Frank caught up with me after class.

"Denni, I'm heading down to the beach tonight for a beer. Would you like to join me? I usually go down to either the Le Lido Plage or the Opera Plage. Your choice. Both of them have excellent fresh mussels and frites. Can I pick you up on my way down?"

"Oh, oh, okay. Um, is it out of your way to pick me up? I can meet you there. I'm only five minutes from the Esplanade Anglais."

"Not at all. I know the city pretty well now. All ten blocks of it, that is. After living in the Big Apple, this is an easy five-minute walk either way. I probably don't live far from you."

"Well, it's a deal. Let's say, 7:30 p.m. Okay?"

I sat up to the bar, with Frank right beside me, close, so I could close my eyes and pretend that he was Nigel. Of course, it wasn't fair, and it wasn't nice of me to do it, but here I was, so desperate to be close to Nigel in any way that I would take advantage of a new friend and sell my sobriety for the small, selfish pleasure that Frank's kind offer had provided. I didn't have the classroom to hide behind now. I was out there on the front lines. There was no doubt about it that I was in trouble, and I was an asshole to boot. I certainly wasn't the nice Canadian that Lyonel had said I was. Just ask Mrs. McIntyre. She could set you straight.

Frank was right. The mussels were fresh and the frites were wrapped up in a paper cone, just like you would expect in a little beach restaurant on the Mediterranean.

"It's funny, but I know a place in New York City that serves mussels and frites just as good as these," Frank said.

"Oh yeah, me too! Let's see if we are talking about the same restaurant, and no cheating. We'll both write the name of our restaurant on a napkin so I can show you I'm a mind-reader."

142

We laughed as the bartender revealed the Balthazar that was written on both napkins. We chalked that one up as something else that we had in common as we continued ordering the beer up, one after another.

I brought out my red notebook to make notes on the muscles and frites, and Frank laughed at me for jotting down my tastes so diligently. "Do you always act like such a nerd?" he asked.

"Yeah. Kind of. It's just an old habit I picked up from a friend along the way."

The beer turned into shots and the next thing I knew was the bartender was shutting down the lights and politely asking us to come back another time.

***

Frank turned around in class the next morning and said quietly, "You okay? By the look on your face, we'd better stick to coffee next time. That's what happens when you try to drink me under the table. Have you always been this competitive?" He smiled slightly as he teased me.

I just gave him a look. The idiot. Of course, I was okay. The truth was, however, he was right. That was what really stung. I mean really, what was I trying to prove? But thinking it all over, I realized that Frank wasn't the only idiot in Lyonel's class that day.

Our fledgling friendship developed slowly. As if by some unspoken code between us, I never asked him about his family, and he never asked me about mine. It suited me perfectly. I was all about who I was today, living in the moment. The past bullshit should stay in the past, except for Frank's aftershave, of course.

Frank Miosi, as it turned out, was a very nice man to keep company with. He was well-read, sensitive, and had a good sense of humor. His nice manners spoke to his strict Italian upbringing by hard working immigrant parents. He taught me a couple of very valuable lessons in life. He taught me, no, wait a minute, he showed me the difference between an incompetent junior boozer and a full-fledged alcoholic.

I was just an incompetent boozer, with my bad behavior brought on by grieving the loss of someone. Burying my pain for the sake of a hangover was a price I was willing to pay. I knew it was short-term. I knew I was going to be okay. I'd just coast along and try to keep him out of trouble. After all, it wasn't the booze that did it for me; it was simply Frank's lanky form so much like Nigel's and especially with the combination of his scent when I would lean up against him.

Frank, on the other hand, was an alcoholic. I don't profess to know the origins of his disease, but I wouldn't be surprised if they were similar to my own. Loss. Loss of someone or something. Life in a tent, holding your rifle on your chest as you slept at night, if you slept at all, was no life for anyone to live. Poor guy!

We had been out nearly every night for almost three months, and one night, Frank was particularly moody. He motioned the bartender for another jug of draft and leaned over the booth to speak to me, directly into my face.

"You know, Denni, I can't figure you out. You run hot and cold, hot and cold, and I'm getting tired of your little routine."

He continued as I sat there quietly, dreading what was to come. "I've been around the block several times in my day, and I'm pretty sure you've been right behind me. Now I find myself not knowing whether to wait around for you or to give up altogether. I don't know if I'm ever going to be able to kiss you like a man, let alone bed you. I'm not satisfied with the small little tokens that you place on my cheek every once in a while. What gives with you? You seem to be happy enough to snuggle up to me or to hold my hand, but the moment I get too close, you pull back as if you don't even know me. Don't get me wrong. I know I'm way ahead of you. I decided quite a while ago that you were the girl for me, and sometimes I see that we're on the same page, and then other times I know I'm walking on a one-way street. I just want to be your man. We're not kids. Why can't you be straight with me?"

"Frank," I paused. "Frank, I'm sorry. I know. I know. It's complicated."

"Please. No bullshit. It's beneath you. Do you realize that we've seen each other every day for months now, and we have never had a serious conversation about who we really are? About who we are deep down in our guts? What is it? Are you into girls?"

"No. It's not girls."

"Is it me?" He grabbed my hand and made a little joke. "I mean really. I'm the original New York City Italian stallion. What girl wouldn't want me!?"

I looked at him and said, "There isn't a girl in the whole wide world that wouldn't want you, Frank. Including me. I think I can safely say our problem is simply a poor timing thing."

He sat back and looked at me, and he resigned himself to say quietly, "Fuck. How long has it been since you've seen him?"

"About six or seven months. What about you? Same deal?"

He laughed a little and said, "Here I am, blaming you for our ups and downs. I'm the worst. I was discharged from Afghanistan last year, but when I got home, I was suffering with PTSD pretty badly and just couldn't stand to be around my family. All of them. I just got up and left them all and came here to Nice. I haven't seen or talked to my wife or my family in almost a year."

"Kids?" I asked.

"No. You?"

"No. And no husband either. But I've been married twice before. But, back to us. Both of us currently have a truckload of unfinished business, it seems," I answered.

"You got that right, sister."

We sat there, across from each other, and after coming clean with my drinking buddy Frank, I felt freer from my heavy heart than I had since I had packed my bags in Toronto the year before.

I looked, really looked, at Frank, and I told myself to snap out of it! Here I was, out on a balmy night on the French Riviera with a handsome, sweet, sweet man that cared for me. And what's more, I cared for him. What the fuck! Why did I always think it had to be all or nothing? Why not just enjoy the moment without all the torture of being in love? I jumped out of the booth and ran around and snuggled under his arm. I lifted my face up to his startled one and introduced him to my lips and my tongue with a full-blown kiss that promised good things to come.

I have to admit though; I was being a little more honest with my good friend Frank, but I was lying to myself through and through. I found myself comparing that first kiss to the ones I had shared with Nigel in Paris as I slipped my hand under his tee-shirt to feel his long, strong, and lean back. "Would you like to come back to my apartment? I'll show you my etchings."

"Never mind your etchings. It's your body I'm interested in."

"Okay, okay. I think we can work that into the tour, Frankie."

"Call me Frank. Frankie is a little boy's name." He grabbed my hand and placed it on his crotch. "Now does that feel like a little boy?"

"You're right, Frank. But I'm going to have to see it to believe it."

We gathered up Frank's knapsack and my handbag and, arm in arm, stepped out into the fresh, salty air to begin the next phase of our friendship. For the first time in my life, I fully understood the term 'friends with benefits.'

He was very sweet and old-fashioned when we got back to my apartment. I suggested I take a quick shower before him, and I would meet him in bed, and whether it was because he was shy or just too eager to argue, he nodded and I took the fastest shower in my life. I didn't have the nerve or the inclination to put on any sexy nightie. I put on a plain teddy and a pair of cotton bikinis and I lay there in my bed, waiting for him to come out of the shower. He still had his towel around him as he swung his long legs under the sheets.

He lay there beside me, not touching me, propped up on one arm and smiling at me a little sheepishly.

"What the fuck! I don't know if I'm nervous or shy or half-drunk, but Denni, I've got butterflies in my gut."

I sat up and threw my leg over his towel to straddle him. His towel was still firmly wrapped around his hips and I put my hands on his chest and said, "What? The big Italian stallion from New York City is a little nervous? With little old me? Here, baby, help me pull off my top, and we'll work out the kinks as we go along."

He lifted my top off over my head and deftly flipped me over and tossed his towel on the floor. He lay there on top of me, and we both began to smile like friends that had done this a million times before.

He kissed me tenderly. "I've wanted you just like this ever since the first day I saw you in class."

"Me too, Frank. Me too." 'It isn't exactly a lie,' I told myself. I just made it sound like I was talking about him.

He was an attentive and sweet lover. He wanted to know what I wanted and what I needed. He told me how to please him. He made it so easy to love him. As I fell asleep in his arms, I knew that I had cleared a hurdle somehow to becoming a little less lovelorn, or so I thought at the time.

It wasn't quite dawn when I opened my eyes. Frank had moved in his sleep over to the edge of the bed, facing the other way, with his long legs dangling over the edge of the mattress. I was okay with everything until my eyes followed the length of his long, lean, sexy back.

I took deep breaths to stop my anxiety attack as I felt my chest bead up with sweat. It must have only been minutes, but it felt like a lifetime before I was well enough to turn over to get away from the pain. In all my years of playing around with men and plain old sex and even lovemaking, it was my first real lesson on how to fake it with a man. I certainly wasn't very good at faking it with myself, however. I told myself to toughen up and to appreciate what was in front of me and I closed my glass-half-empty eyes to get away from the whole situation. I swallowed my tears back as I cried inwardly, 'Nigel. Nigel. Where are you? I want it to be you, Nigel, just you.'

We both slept through the early morning and we were late for class.

Lyonel looked up as we entered the classroom at 10:40 a.m. He wheeled around and addressed the class. "Now class, it's time for new vocabulary. Who knows what 'walk of shame' means?"

Frank, like any good Italian stallion would, threw his hands up and laughed, "Guilty as charged!" He put his hand on the small of my back to claim his territory as the male species are prone to.

We walked down the long aisle, both of us joining in the laughter as the students, one by one, caught on to Lyonel's outing. My face was burning with embarrassment but I must admit Frank was a very sweet peacock showing his new girl off to his teacher, just like we were in Grade Nine, way back in the day.

It was the end of the twelve-week FSL program, and we decided that we would ask Lyonel out to dinner as a thank-you, even though we had signed up for the next level that started again on the following week.

Frank waited until the classroom emptied. "Lyonel, we would like to take you out for dinner, in appreciation of all your hard work here in the classroom. Our treat. Would this Friday work for you?"

At the last moment, I added in, "Please bring along your significant other, of course."

Lyonel was delighted with our invitation. He beamed, "That would be wonderful. You see, Friday night is usually date night in our house, so that's perfect!"

I continued, "Why don't you pick the venue? You know Nice much better than us. We usually just stick to the touristy spots, so please, surprise us with something new."

"Well, we do have a favorite spot. And the kitchen does have a great chef. Do you know where the Castel Plage is? Near the *Château* on the hill, at the east end of the Bay of Angels."

Frank said, "No, I've never been there, but we'll find it. How about if we all just meet there at 7:00 p.m.?"

Lyonel was still smiling from ear to ear. "Yes, yes, we'll get there a little early and get us a good seat. They usually have a live band there too, so it'll be fun."

I jumped in, "You're on. You can show me how to tango."

As we walked down the hill to have our usual drinks at the bar before going to my house for an early dinner, Frank said, "I thought so."

"Thought what?"

"That Lyonel's gay."

"No way. How do you know that? Did he hit on you?"

"No, idiot. He's much too cool for that. Besides, he was born with gaydar built right in. I'm not his type. Wanna bet?"

"Absolutely. Fifty cents. I say he's straight, and when we meet his darling wife, the proof will be in the pudding."

"You're on. American money though. None of that Canadian crap."

That Friday night, as Frank opened the door to the upscale restaurant right on the Bay of Angels, he looked very handsome and very sexy in a plain black tee-shirt with sleeves tight against his biceps and tucked into white jeans. He had ditched his regular sandals and had slipped his size-thirteen into a pair of soft leather loafers. He had slicked his thick, black straight hair back with a little gel, and I noticed that he was wearing it a little longer these days. He had a sexy, tough, Euro-footballer look about him. His thick gold chain was half-hidden under his tee, and it was all the bling he needed.

I wore my hair down loose around my shoulders and a tight, sleeveless, blue sheath with a deep V-neck and the high heels that Frank wolf-whistled at when he picked me up. Of course, I played the part of the Italian stallion's doting girlfriend and hung on to his arm and every word like he was the only man in the whole wide world. Our eyes scanned the crowd and before the maître d' could seat us, we spotted Lyonel's wave from a table on the open beachside of the beautiful, classy restaurant with the quartet warming up in the back corner.

Frank leaned over to me and whispered, "Fifty cents, honey. I'll take it out in trade when we get home."

"What are you talking about? She's the most gorgeous woman in the whole room."

"Transgender, baby, all the way."

"No way. How can you tell?"

"I can't tell at all. But I know Lyonel. He's complex. I've studied his every move over the past twelve weeks. I know men. I'm an army man, remember."

Lyonel and his trophy wife, Lucia, stood up to greet us, and the four of us exchanged the twelve cheek-kisses that Euro-couples tirelessly exchange with every greeting every day of their lives.

We all had the time of our lives. Lyonel and Lucia both were full of funny stories of growing up in Paris and discovering each other at the very tender age of eighteen when they were both presenting as young men. They had been together ever since. Lucia, in a very humble moment, took Lyonel's hand and raised it to her lips.

"My wonderful husband here has worked two jobs his whole life to pay for all my surgeries."

"Now, now, darling, are you saying you married me for my money?"

Lucia reached down and patted his crotch. "Honey, you know exactly why I married you."

We all laughed, and Frank looked at Lyonel. "Let's raise our glasses to our girls. Look at them. The most beautiful women in the room."

The two of them raised their glasses and said, "To our girls."

Lyonel and I sat the dance out as Lucia decided it was time for Frank to learn how to tango. I was so proud to be there, watching this sexy, handsome man be so charming and disarming as he proved himself to be the worst dancer on the floor. He finally got the hang of how to dip Lucia, who was almost as tall as him, and we were all laughing at his boyish enthusiasm. Even the other tables couldn't take their eyes off the beautiful couple that looked like they didn't have a care in the world. They were the perfect picture of living the dream.

For a moment there, I forgot my sadness. I had finally learned to live in the present. As the band broke into a Euro-style up-tempo tune, I reached over and grabbed Lyonel's hand to pull him up on the dance floor. Unlike Frank, he was an amazing dancer. I knew the two of us were showing off a little, but I couldn't help myself. I loved being in very capable arms on the dance floor, and here I was, dancing the merengue and then the samba like there was no tomorrow.

Back from the dance floor, I cozied up to Frank's chair. I put my arms around him and reached back behind him to grab a handful of his gorgeous longer black hair. "I love your new look. You are one helluva sexy man, Frankie."

"You do? Good to hear! I was looking too much like a serious cop or an army man, I'm afraid. Time for a change."

"Maybe I can help out with a change. What exactly are you interested in, lover boy?"

"Not so much a change. Just a helluva lot more of this," he said as he grabbed my ass from behind. "Meanwhile, stop touching my hair. You've given me one helluva hard-on," he whispered into my face. "Yeah. But on the other hand, stop looking at my hair. My party's down there," and he took my hand and placed it on his lap.

"Maybe for you, babe. But you have no idea what your hair does for me. I don't think I can wait for you until we get home. Maybe we can walk home along the beach. You know, just the two of us. And just to let you know, I don't have any panties on underneath this dress. Just in case you're wondering, that is."

I can safely say that that night was the best time Frank and I had together. Somehow, we had escaped from our individual problems for those few, short, precious hours. Perhaps it was because we were out with other people that made our own little injuries in life seem paltry. Our good time didn't seem to be alcohol-induced, as we both knew enough on this first date with Lyonel and his wife to stick to just the wine, stretching the bottles out through dinner and into the dancing hours. It wasn't the night to line up the shots on the bar like we normally did.

***

I lay there in my bed, with Frank sound asleep beside me. I knew better than to face his back; that seemed to be where I got into trouble, especially if his aftershave hadn't worn off.

I went over the whole evening in my mind, just relishing every single moment. After we got home, it was different between Frank and me. It was the first night that the sex between us seemed very slightly, almost, but not quite like real honest-to-goodness lovemaking. Could it be that our fuck-buddy relationship was capable of moving on to something other than just friends-with-benefits?

This new idea intrigued me, and I was wide awake. "No time like the present," I said to myself as I quietly slipped out of bed, put on my old flannel pajamas, and snuck out to my little kitchen to make a cup of decaf and to take a few notes down on the past, present, and future of the Frank Miosi and Denise Allen relationship.

I headed up my first page with my usual quote from Alex Colville that I used to spring-board off of.

I think of things as beginning rather than ending.

I have always been the eternal optimist, or as Catharine said, the annoying optimist, so of course I started with the possibility thinking part of the plan first. Yes, yes, yes. We could live in Nice fulltime. I could get a work visa to work as an ESL teacher, and with all his army and policing experience, perhaps he could apply for a work visa in the policing field. We could give up one of our apartments and be quite happy living out our current lifestyles. Or I would be willing to move to New York if he wanted to settle back down at home. Or we could move to Toronto. I knew that he could get work in Toronto, and I could simply continue with my own curriculum design contracts. We were both over the age of wanting a family, I thought, so we would be each other's family, enjoying life without the usual family issues to deal with. I could make him happy and make sure his dark moods and poor sleep patterns caused by his PTSD were kept to a minimum. 'Yes,' I told myself, 'of course I can. Look what happened to us in bed just a few hours ago.' I could possibly even fall in love with him. And I knew that he loved me. He certainly treated me that way, although he never actually said the three little words to me.

By the time I got to the 'cons' side of the new equation, I had to back up my plan a little. There seemed to be very little defense indeed to offset the many, many negatives that made up our relationship.

By this time, I knew that Frank needed more help than his current once-a-week trip to the psychiatrist. His PTSD would flare up, sometimes unexpectedly and always with a lot of drama. I would feel him tossing around in the middle of the night, and I'd wake him up fully to get him to shake off the bad dreams. The sheets would be soaked through. Sometimes I would have to help him into the shower and tell him just to stay there while I changed the sheets and put on some herbal tea for him to sip on. Other nights, I would coax him into a pair of shorts and a sweatshirt, and we would jog around the block a few times in the middle of the night, trying to relieve his body of all his pent-up anxiety.

I was always shocked by the amount of pain that was registered on his handsome face during these episodes. If he had an episode during our waking hours, he would abruptly kiss me goodbye and say he wanted to be by himself, or he needed to study by himself, or he just wanted to spend a day or two at his own apartment. He needed space, so I wouldn't see his pain and darkness that he struggled through on a regular basis. I was pretty sure that he didn't take his meds full-strength, as he chose instead to self-medicate with alcohol, and the two together were a deadly mixture.

He was such a good man. He couldn't stand the thought of pulling me down with him, but at the same time, we both realized that he depended on me more and more as time went by. He was very in tune with both our states of mind. One day, we were having a lively game of scrabble when he jumped up and tipped the board up and it flew off the table and the pieces scattered all over the floor.

"You are such a competitive, know-it-all cheater! Both in scrabble and life! You bitch!" he shouted. "Yo! Listen up! Do you think I'm an idiot? This is me! Me! Look at me! You're fucking me! You're fucking me, not him! You're nothing but a lying, cheating bitch!"

"Hey, hey, relax, babe," I tried to calm him.

"Don't touch me. Don't touch me!" His voice was full of panic. "I've got to go. I've got to go."

"Okay, honey. Let me walk you home. Yeah, we need a good walk."

"Stay here. Don't touch me. Just leave me alone."

I watched him from my balcony as he stormed up the street, trying to run away from the devil that was in his head. I was realizing how seriously this very smart and very capable man was being crippled with his mental health issues, and I had become part of the problem. I wasn't helping in the least. He knew I was just using him. We weren't good for each other, and we both knew it. It wasn't his choice to live his life wasting away on a beach on the French Riviera. It was killing him slowly and painfully. He never spoke of suicidal thoughts, but I realized that this was where it was all heading. First, he left his whole family, and now his disease was projecting onto me. He was so disappointed in himself. The poor man! How would all this end?

After his outburst, I slowly put on my trainers and went for a long run along the Anglais Promenade to calm my heartache for him. As my worry and sadness for my friend settled in, I realized that it was the first unselfish thought that I had had in a year. He was right; I was nothing but a lying, cheating bitch.

As to my own mental state, well, that was a separate issue altogether. Although I deeply cared for Frank, I was just using him as a crutch to get through another day without Nigel. I must say that my heartache had lessened somewhat, but my week in Paris the year before had killed any chance I would ever have for real happiness with another man. It was like I had taken chemo directly into my heart. If I couldn't fall in love with a man like Frank, there was no hope for me. As for the sex, funnily enough, we were both on the same page. We could take it or leave it. It probably had something to do with both of us boozing so much. Lots of times, we were simply too drunk to have sex. And I had always liked living alone, and he felt the need to be alone, so many nights we would stay apart, sleeping alone in our respective apartments, meeting up the next morning cheerfully to walk to school together. I was always so pleased, though, that we were always so considerate of each other and that we got along so well. We really enjoyed each other's company. We had become very good friends.

When we did have sex however, it was good for both of us, mind you, but neither of us were able to step into the intimacy of real lovemaking. We were too damaged, but both of us were smart enough to be grateful that we still had our basic sex urges that we could satisfy with and for each other without hesitation and with eagerness, fun, and affection. It wasn't what I would call lovemaking, but it certainly was an outlet for all the care and attention that we showered on each other. He would go to great lengths to pleasure me, and he was just so cute about always waiting for me to cum first. I couldn't have asked for a better friend and a better lover. He just wasn't the one. You know how it is – sad but true. Your heart wants what it wants. And there's not a damn thing you can do about it.

Since I was basically an honest person, living this pretense day in and day out, I understood that all of this was what was causing my anxiety attacks. I found that they came over me at the strangest times. A few times in class, I had to leave and just go sweat it out in the ladies' room. It incapacitated me entirely. I kept them from Frank. That was all he needed. I thought that I should check in with a doctor at some point, but right then and there, I was busy dealing with his much more serious issues.

I had thought through my anxiety attacks and kept track of when and where they would come upon me. I altered my lifestyle as best I could to avoid them. For instance, I moved my seat in the classroom. I couldn't take looking at Frank's back any longer. It was simply a stupid, non-productive thing for me to do. Sinking back into the past was a waste of time. And when Frank and I slept together, I never faced his back anymore. Why go there? Why do that to myself? Self-preservation was the name of the game. My own mental health issues simmered on the backburner, slowly, ever so slowly, gathering steam until one day, in the middle of a Saturday afternoon, all hell broke loose.

I had slept in late that Saturday morning. Frank had gone home the night before, after we had been out at a bar down on the beach, with the promise to give me my morning to myself. The plan was that he would come down late afternoon to pick me up to take me out for dinner.

I swung my feet over to the floor and immediately had a bad case of vertigo and landed up with my face planted on the floor. My head was swimming as I lay there, trying not to vomit. I didn't know if I had vertigo, the flu, or just a very bad hangover. The night before, I had been pounding the shots back, keeping up to Frank, being my old competitive self. I was such an idiot. 'Why does he put up with me?' I asked myself as I lay there, nauseous and sweating like a pig.

I made it out to the sofa and lay there. I couldn't remember feeling this sick before. Maybe I did have the flu. Sometime later, I managed a shower, and I got into a clean pair of my old flannel pajamas. I was still lying on the sofa when Frank arrived at 4:00 p.m. He took one look at me and canceled our dinner plans. He got some of my homemade chicken soup out of the freezer and babied it into me, spoonful by spoonful.

I had made it into the bathroom to try to freshen up a little and I noticed that Frank had unpacked his overnight bag and left his shaving kit on the bathroom vanity. The zipper was undone, and I saw the enemy. It was the opaque, cream-colored bottle of Yardley's Old Spice aftershave. This fucking little bottle of poison was what had caused me so much pain over the past six months. I went into a rage like one that you may see in Spain, if you take in the Running of the Bulls.

I grabbed the neck of the bottle of aftershave and marched it out to the living room where Frank was calmly reading the local newspaper from the safe confines of the sofa.

I could hear myself screaming, but I couldn't stop myself, "I am so fucking over this aftershave! Do not, do not, for the next one hundred years bring this fucking aftershave into my house ever again!"

As Frank slowly put his paper down and got up slowly to walk toward me, he stretched out his hand to take the offensive bottle out of my clenched fist.

"No! No! You are not touching this fucking poison! I'm through with it! I never want to smell it again as long as I live!" I screamed.

Frank had a very worried look on his face as he inched a little closer to me.

I raised my hand and threw the bottle as hard as I could and I heard it shatter into a thousand pieces as it hit the balcony's glass door. The room immediately filled with the smell of a 1958 barber shop.

I bent over in pain as my stomach retched to bring up the inner lining of my gut. By then, Frank's long arms had me scooped up and rushed me down the hall. He put me into bed, out of harm's way. He pinned me, and I finally calmed down. He got me a cold, damp facecloth for my face and tucked me under my duvet. He said, "Take these." And I took them. He sat on the edge of the bed and watched me.

When I woke up hours later, he was still there.

He got me up out of bed and helped me step into some fresh pajamas. I was so hungry, and he had already made us a light dinner. I could see that he had cleaned up my whole mess, but you could still smell the Old Spice. He had the good sense not to mention it.

As I quietly thanked him for taking such good care of me, he hugged me and said, "I'm just returning the favor, honey. But tonight, we're not going to talk about it. Just some mindless television and maybe we'll be lucky to find an English movie on the telly. Then we'll get a good night's sleep. Doctor's orders, you hear me?"

"Okay, boss. But please know that my humiliation is going to probably last for the next fifty years, so be prepared to see a different girl in the morning."

"I hope not. I like you just the way you are."

"You do?"

"Yeah, I like everything about you. I like the way you hold my hand. I like the way you need me. I like the way you please me," he half-sang, half-spoke the old Motown song. "Sorry, I don't know the second verse."

"I get the message. I like you too," I said as I tried to put on a good face for him.

But the truth was that I didn't feel right at all. It wasn't especially my stomach or my hangover. I felt anxious, but not like one of my attacks. It was more like a pending, big black cloud of disaster just waiting to attack my whole body. I was so glad to have Frank right beside me. For the first time since I can remember, even way, way back to when I was a kid, I felt afraid. But I didn't know what I felt afraid from. I couldn't even call up my guardian angel, the spirit that was my great-granddad, nor my dad. They weren't there for me.

Thank God for Frank. He gave me the whole sofa with a little blanket over me while he stretched his long frame out over the easy chair with his big feet propped up on the ottoman, all closely lined up with the sofa so that he could lean over and straighten my blanket or touch my arm. In the six months that I had known him, it was the most intimate few hours we had shared together. It wasn't only me; I knew that he felt it too.

***

After the movie, I was feeling so much calmer and I felt I was ready for bed. We both had a quick shower, and Frank made sure I was all tucked in. He kept on his own side of the bed to give me enough space in case I felt that I needed it. He'd had lots of experience with anxiety attacks before and he knew the drill inside and outside. Many men in his platoon suffered with these identical symptoms, and of course his own PTSD was similar in many ways. He lay there, eyes wide open, just waiting for all hell to break loose.

It must have been the middle of the night; the room was dark. I was facing Frank's back. I knew better. I should have rolled over immediately. But I couldn't move. I was facing my heartbreak and I felt my body tearing into shreds. That thirty seconds of savoring his skin, his toned, lean muscle, was all it took to finally break the camel's back. My heart shattered into a thousand pieces, exactly the same as the Yardley's Old Spice had earlier that afternoon.

Frank was jolted out of his sleep with my screaming. He automatically hit the floor like he would have done in the weeds, reaching out for his rifle, before realizing that it was me, in real time, spiraling into a full-blown breakdown. I was screaming, *"Nigel, Nigel, Nigel!"* over and over again. He called an ambulance and had me in the hospital in a matter of minutes.

***

I opened my eyes to see a woman in a white med coat standing over me, staring into my eyes.

"Where am I?"

"Well, good morning to you! My name is Nancy, and you are in the Hôpital de Cimiez, on the psychiatric floor. Don't worry. You're going to be just fine. We have taken the liberty of giving you some medication to keep you nice and calm until we can figure out how we can help you get well." She took my hand and patted it, smiling all the while, just like you see in the movies.

It took until the next day that they finally allowed Frank in to see me. It was kind of funny. He came through the door, carrying a beautiful bouquet of flowers. His face was a complicated mixture of relief and worry. He bent over me and kissed me tenderly on the forehead. He was quiet the whole time; I think he was choked up and didn't want to cry in front of me. I watched him silently arrange the flowers in a vase and fill it up with water from the sink in the room as he regained his composure. For a tough big-city cop and an ex-army guy with serious time spent in the weeds, he could be a real boob at times.

Finally, he pulled up a chair to my bedside and held my hand. All he said to me was, "Who the hell is Nigel?"

With that, we both started laughing so loudly the nurse came running in to see if we were okay.

The next three days, we were inseparable. We walked the halls, we ate the meals, and we sat through all the blood work, the x-rays, the CAT scan, and the MRI. He was there first thing in the morning until the nurses kicked him out in the evenings. We held hands and talked the whole time. I told him things I had never ever said out loud to anyone before, and he shared his whole life with me in return. He heard all about Nigel, and I heard all about his wife, Maria. He heard about my guardian angel, my great-grandfather, and I heard about his parents. He heard about my lack of sexual experiences throughout my twenties and thirties, and I heard about how he lost his virginity to his best friend's mother at the tender age of fifteen.

I explained my craziness that had erupted with my aversion to his bottle of Old Spice, and we both laughed the whole afternoon about it. He said that I scared the shit out of him, and he couldn't possibly even think to wear the old scent again as long as he lived. It was time to move on with the times and buy something like a new and breezy Ralph Lauren. After all, he wanted to be an original, not somebody's smell-alike.

When I listened to myself trying to explain my craziness, going on and on about Nigel's old-fashioned choice of aftershave, I realized that maybe I was a little obsessive-compulsive as well as still being in love with a man that didn't care enough about me to stick around for more than a week.

My doctor was very pleased with my progress but stressed that my good vibes were mainly due to all the happy pills that he had put me on to stabilize me. Frank assured him that as long as he had known me, I had been this annoyingly optimistic person and that he felt I was just getting back to my old self. Whatever it was, I was just so pleased to be feeling better.

The doctor was very interested in speaking with Frank as well, as Frank had told him that he had PTSD and was familiar with anxiety attacks from his time in the barracks in Afghanistan and his time on the mean streets of the big apple. In fact, Frank asked him if he would be interested in taking him on as a long-term patient, and the doctor agreed. He thought that Frank could possibly help out by taking part in a study that some psychiatrists in the city were working on, and there was room on the intake list for him if he would be willing to start almost immediately.

By Day Five, they were stepping down my pills, as the plan was to discharge me around Day Eight to attend a day clinic, if, in fact, I could get someone to live in with me until I got a final discharge in about thirty days from then. Frank said right upfront he couldn't help out, as he was way sicker than I was. I suggested that I call my old friend Catharine to see if she could come to my rescue, one more time.

On Day Eight, with Catharine fully moved into my apartment, I was discharged to her care, with orders to attend daily classes at the hospital for the next thirty days.

Catharine and Frank were both in my room as we packed up the numerous bags of books and clothes that Frank had been bringing in daily.

Catharine disappeared and it was just Frank and me. He pulled up the two chairs and took my hand. I knew what was coming, and I was ready to hear what he had to say.

"Denni, I love you more than life itself. That's why I can't see you anymore. If I want to get better, like you have, I have to break away and do it for myself. We're no good for each other. You see, I'm much sicker than you. My mental health problems require intensive care and long-term management for the rest of my life. My PTSD has evolved to suicidal tendencies, and you have made me realize that I don't want to go out that way. You've given me a sense of purpose. I'm going to fight back as hard as I can. I want to feel good every day, the way that you make me feel. You have given me so much joy and love over the past six months. You've brought me back to life. It's my plan to check in with our good staff here for intensive treatment. It's going to take a while, but my plan is to get well enough to go back home to my wife and family and to do my long-term health management program with my wife beside me. And hey, I'm not a hit-it-and-quit-it kind of guy, the same as you're not a friends-with-benefits kind of girl. You know that, and so do I. But meanwhile, I need you to do something for me."

"Anything, Frank, anything at all."

"Let me go so you can get what you really want. And that's Nigel. I want you to go home and find Nigel. I know he's waiting for you. You two sound like Romeo and Juliette somehow. And you, Denni, you're a keeper. You're a real wife just waiting to happen. Do whatever it takes. You deserve to be happy."

"Thank you, Frank. I know you're right. I love you, and I'll miss you so much. I'm so grateful for the time we've had together. I know that we're both on the right track now. We both have a new sense of purpose. When I write my novel, I'm going to put you and Maria in it as the happily married couple that I know you're going to be once again. I'll never forget you."

His tears were just as salty as mine as we silently hugged goodbye for the very last time.

***

The next month, with Catharine right beside me, I flourished. I was back to my old self. We spent the weekends up at the *château*, but a couple of the weekends Edouard came down, and I had the opportunity to treat them out to dinner with Lyonel and Lucia. It was written in stone, however, that I was in Nice for all the weekdays to make sure I didn't miss one day of my outpatient treatment at the hospital. If I live until I'm hundred years old, I'll never be able to repay Catharine for her care and devotion that she showered on me, day after day, until I was ready and able to fly home to be responsible for my own life back home in Toronto.

I crossed the Atlantic once again, and I was smiling on touchdown. I had accepted what had happened in my life to date, and I was ready to align my very own personality with my new sense of purpose. I had the power to move my life forward, and to hell with anyone that tried to get in my way! No more of Jimmy Ruffin's *What Becomes of the Brokenhearted* for this girl, no way.

From now on, I was going to be whistling to Pharrell William's *Happy*. Enough already! I was going to write my big, gutsy novel, come hell or high water!

***

Chapter 9

Under the Maple Tree

It was so good to be home. I only had one brief crying spell since I had opened the door. It had happened just after I had got in the door and breathed in my home. My eyes rested on a large package that had been delivered to me when I was away. It was perched on my bed, with international stamps all over it. It was shipped from the Four Seasons George-V Hotel nine months ago. The card was tucked into the pocket of the hotel's big, fluffy bathrobe along with the matching slippers. The card written with his fountain pen and purple ink read:

Missing you already. Love, N.

Other than that, I was feeling so much better after Catharine's month of pampering me. Over the past nine months, I had really missed my apartment and the neighborhood as well. Although Maureen's daughter had left my apartment in good order, I took the first week to paint it all a nice fresh bright white, and I bought some beautiful new bed linens and Turkish towels. I unpacked my locker and brought out all my beautiful gifts that Nigel had bought me in Paris. I had been a fool to tuck them all away when I left, but now I could enjoy them without falling apart every time I thought of him.

Two weeks later, as I glanced in the mirror on my way out that morning, I was so happy that I had had the month with Catharine in Nice. She had taken me shopping, and I had treated myself to some beautiful, casual summer dresses, girly-girl sandals, and all new sexy lingerie. She reminded me that I wasn't a spring chicken any longer, so why was I still dressing like a hippie from Kitsilano Beach in Vancouver? No more ripped jeans and tee-shirts for me. She convinced me to cut my hair a little shorter and have it professionally straightened. I treated myself to a fresh bikini wax at the spa and bought new face creams and makeup to top it all off.

Toronto was enjoying perfect summer weather, and I lifted my face up to the sun as I strolled down to my old favorite café on Spadina Avenue, my straightened, shorter hair clipped back with one of the vintage hair clips that Nigel had bought me at the fleas in Paris, newspaper in hand, along with one of Nigel's beautiful red leather notebooks with 'D.A.' embossed on the cover. I looked around at the near empty café, ordered a frozen coffee, and grabbed my old favorite booth. I was through the business section and fully invested in the style section, half-singing along to the café's music tape for that morning when I sensed someone staring at the back of my neck. I turned slowly as the hair on the back of my neck began to prickle.

It was Nigel.

I was instantly filled with rage, remembering how he had unceremoniously dumped me, without even the smallest of goodbyes. I stood up and, keeping my eyes on his, stormed over to his table, my hands now on my hips, just like my mother would have done.

"Where the fuck have you been?"

He stood up, very close to me, and whispered, "Never mind me, Irish faerie. Where the fuck have *YOU* been?"

By this time, I was very close to tears, but I couldn't tear my eyes away from his stony face. We just stood there, staring each other down, the hurt and anger washing over the both of us, wave after wave. I could see that his chest was heaving under his faded Bob Marley tee-shirt.

Fate entered the scene. It came in the form of Kelly Clarkson's hit from the summer before, *The Trouble with Love Is* and it filtered down innocently enough through the café's sound system. As we stood there, two silent, heartbroken souls, not being able to tear away from the train wreck, the chanteuse cried out her heartbreak that matched ours. I felt the famous singer's helplessness intimately. I looked into Nigel's dark brown eyes as she belted out her woe about being helpless in love; *you got no say at all.*

He gained his composure first and hissed quietly, "Listen up. Here is what is going down right here and right now. You are going to take my hand, we will pick up your handbag on the way out, and we will have a proper discussion outside. Without the bad language."

Remembering that I had started it all the year before with my demand for time on my own after our Paris trip, I bit my lip, lowered my eyes so he couldn't see my tears, and dutifully offered my hand.

His big hand and strong grip kept me in tow all the way up Spadina Road, across Heath Street, turning at the corner of Russell Hill Road. He didn't say a word, and I struggled to stay abreast to his long strides in my dainty sandals. I felt like a truant child being handled by a furious parent. Emotions aside, I was so pleased that I had worn a dress that morning, along with the new sandals. I knew I was looking good, but nothing compared to his new body that he was sporting. I looked sideways to catch his long arm, with the new bicep and triceps bulging out of his sleeveless tee-shirt.

Down past the front door, through the side gate, and into his backyard, he stopped in front of a lawn chair, under a big, shady maple.

"Sit!" He left me sitting there, and it was a good five minutes before he returned with a brown envelope in hand.

With those five minutes of reprieve under my belt, I looked him over as he pulled up a chair to face mine. Yes, his hair was a little grayer, and the dark brown eyes were the same, and his scar below his cheekbone was still evident, but I was puzzled with his nose. I always thought he had a beautiful, narrow, aristocratic nose. I didn't remember it looking like that at all. His overall face, though, showed a vulnerable, heart-open-on-sleeve look that had replaced the fury. I actually felt a little sorry for him as I continued looking him over. His body had changed big-time. He had really bulked up, and his biceps were twice as large as I remembered. It wasn't an overall weight gain, no, not at all; he was simply cut. He wore it well. His face was lean and his abs were tight. He must have got himself a very good personal trainer. He had the looks of a fitness model, even at his age. You know the type – big muscles on a lean frame. Only he wasn't all oiled up.

He handed me the brown envelope, and I noticed his hand was trembling slightly. "Tell me everything you know about these photos. And I mean everything."

I saw the photos of Kurt and myself and remembered the last time I saw him, in the café way over a year ago. Oh my God. I realized in an instant that I had spent the last year of my life blaming myself for running away from Nigel because of my own intimacy issues, and now it dawned on me that it wasn't my fault at all.

Nigel, in all his secrecy and jealousy, had had me followed for some reason, and he dumped me in a jealous fit. I was furious. I jumped up and stood in front of him, sitting there with his jealous, handsome face watching me intently. I ripped the photos up in small pieces and threw them in his face. I was trembling, and I stumbled back to sit back down in my chair, trying not to cry.

I spat out, "That was me, last summer, with an old colleague of mine, Kurt Byers. He's one of my best friends. We met at the café sometime last year when he got back from China. I was so happy to see him, as he had gone missing in China for over six months. He was a visiting U of T professor teaching in Beijing, and for some unknown reason, the Chinese picked him up and claimed he was a Chinese dissident. They put him in prison. Finally, the Canadians got wind of it and got him out of China and back home safely. Luckily, his wife, Gretchen, and the kids had come back to Canada the moment he disappeared.

"So, to make a long story short, they are all together once again and living back here in the city. I just saw them all together last week. Kurt is still recovering from his ordeal in prison, but well enough now to go back to work at U of T in the fall, and Gretchen and the kids are thriving as usual."

As I recollected the visit with Kurt, I added, "Oh, I know exactly when I saw him. It was one morning last summer, before we went to Marlbank. I remember now that I got to your house for our walk that evening, and I was wanting to tell you all about my visit with Kurt that morning because he had just got home from Chinese prison, and that was the night I think that you took it upon yourself to surprise me with your Hollywood brother. Or when the boys made me a smoothie. I don't know, but no wonder I forgot my story. And besides, you were the one with the secrets those days. Not me. And by the way, where did you ever get these photos?"

As I told the story behind the photos, I realized that Nigel's obvious jealousy was not my biggest problem. My real problem was the troubling realization that for some unknown reason, this man and his secret lifestyle had had me followed all the time he was so politely giving me my space. I felt very used. Or was this just another ugly version of jealousy being played out. I didn't even know this man sitting across from me with the bulging biceps and vintage Bob Marley muscle-tee. I only remembered a shy, humble, handsome intellectual in made-to-measure suits and size-thirteen Salvadore Ferragamos. Where did he go? How could I have missed this? And then I remembered long ago when we first met, his plea for privacy with his life-to-Vegas comparison. That was no excuse, I told myself, and I was not willing to give him an inch.

At the same time, I found myself staring into his handsome, distressed face and hoping against all odds that he would level with me so that I could trust him enough to let him back into my heart.

"What happened to you, Nigel? Tell me! What happened to that shy, sensitive intellectual that I fell in love with? You broke my heart. Yes, that's it. You're nothing but a heartbreaker."

He said softly, "I'm so sorry. I'm so sorry. Please, listen. After Paris, I went to my office to collect my mail. This envelope was on top of the in-basket. The photos knocked me down so badly that it was the end of my life as I knew it. I have been dying, slowly, of a broken heart ever since. I thought that you were seeing someone else on the side. I now know differently. I'm so very sorry, Denni."

"Whatever in the world happened to you in your past to make you not trust me? Or should I ask, *who* happened to you? When did this jealousy start? Did you feel like that when we were in Paris? Jealousy is one of the seven deadly sins, and man, you have paid the high price. Think about it. You had it all. You had a girl that loved you like nobody else could ever have loved you. And you pissed it away in one big jealous tantrum. And you broke my heart and you took away a year of my life."

I continued, staring at him intently, "I ran away for the last year because I thought it was my fault, that I had hurt you when I asked you for time off, but really, Nigel, if I had thought at that time that your absence was due to jealousy, I wouldn't have waited around for three days. I would have left town and you in a New York minute. I have a very low tolerance for jealousy."

"Please give me a chance. Whatever and whoever you need to know about. I'm here to tell you about my whole life, warts and all, and how I became the man sitting in front of you. I would never ever lie to you. The blatant obfuscation, which I am one hundred percent guilty of, is what I want to get off my chest, and right now. No revisionist history, I promise you from the bottom of my heart. Denni, I'm begging."

I dealt my final blow, trying to soften it as best I could. "It's not only the petty jealousy, Nigel. It's the sad realization that I'm having to swallow that you were having me followed throughout the whole time that I was slowly and shyly opening up to you. I feel used. I feel betrayed. Now I find out that we don't share the shyness. You were simply being secretive. At this very moment, it's the secrecy that is killing me. I feel like I don't even know you. No, no, wait a moment. Maybe it's all jealousy. That's the worst. It's like a cancer in a relationship. Claiming you're shy is just a sly cover-up for being secretive and jealous. What about what went down in Paris between the two of us? Remember when we locked the lock on the bridge? I gave you my heart and soul. And the sex – oh my God, the sex. Was that just a game you were playing? Was that all just a part of that sugar-daddy routine? I thought you loved me deeply, like I loved you. You just manipulated me. You turned me inside out and you took advantage of me."

"Whoa! Whoa!" He jumped out of his chair, anxiously pacing back and forth, with his hands raking through his hair. "Step back right now! Leave Paris out of this! No way! No way! Just leave it alone! I have beaten myself up for rushing you into intimacy before you were ready, every day for the last nine months."

He circled his chair several times and then sat down again and took a deep breath. He carefully modulated his voice, "Listen to me. Please. I wasn't in that alone, remember. You knew how invested I was while we were in Paris. You were my world. And you acted like I was your world in return. I'm not willing to accept all the blame for that, but please know I will never forgive myself for not being more patient with you and your intimacy issues. I just thought I could love you enough for both of us. I was deluded thinking that, but that's the message I was getting from you, that you felt the same way as me. Did you know that you used to reach out for me in your sleep? No, probably not. But I did. And that told me that you needed me just as much as I needed you. Your problem was that you simply didn't know how to let love in, and my problem was that I didn't truly recognize this big, fat disability that my girl had. Or maybe you still have it; all I know is that it was your problem and I wasn't able to compensate enough for it back then."

My face was burning from his insightful remark about me not knowing how to let love in, so I said in a quiet voice, "You're right on that score about me not knowing how to let love in. I'm sorry for all the hurt it caused you."

He leaned in a little and said softly, "And I'm sorry too. So sorry for my rant. But really, Denni, I wasn't complaining. In fact, when I told you that you used to reach out for me in your sleep, well, please know that it just made me love you even more. What the hell! The whole time we were in Paris, I don't think I slept more than thirty minutes at a time anyway. I forced myself to stay awake, just to watch you sleep beside me."

He sat back to regain his composure and said, "But now, back to my shyness. That's where you're wrong. I get the prize for being shy. The secretive part of me that has caused all of this misunderstanding, well, that's a whole different jar of wax. I was just trying to shield you from an ugly world that you know nothing about. Please believe me. I would never do anything to hurt you intentionally. Ever. I'm so sorry."

He stumbled along, telling me his story like all lonely, shy people do. "I'm still learning about all of my less-than-adequate qualities by attending psychotherapy sessions. She told me that I suffer from a chronic condition called psychological transference. After my first visit to the doctor, I realized how stupid I had been. I ended up at your apartment and speaking with the super. She told me that under the Privacy Act she couldn't reveal where you had moved to, even if she wanted to. You had moved out and left no forwarding address. Your phone had been disconnected, the same as mine. I am afraid that this is sounding more and more like Romeo and Juliette, the ill-fated lovers, as I plead my case here. I am willing to share everything with you, but may I suggest that we get inside, out of this heat? I'll make us up one of your favorite smoothies, and I will tell you the whole unabridged story that has led up to my need for secrecy and most of all, my own intimacy and trust issues. Please." He smiled slightly and added a cute little, "Trust me."

"Did you say trust me?" I said with both eyebrows up.

"I'm an idiot. Here I am making jokes when my life is on the line."

"Back to what you said about your therapy. Did you say that your psych problem is chronic? Does that mean that it can happen again? Because, Nigel, this time it almost killed me, let alone you. I simply don't want to and will not go through that again.

"I only see the shrink on a need-be basis now, but I will call her tomorrow and set up new appointments. You can come with me. Anything you need. Anything you want. I'll do it."

I stared him down. He had had me at hello, but I wasn't about to let him know that, not just yet. I swore to myself over and over again for the last nine months that I would never get into this position again, and here I was, heart melting with every word of his heartfelt and earnest story.

"Do you really understand what I need from you? Do you? Really, Nigel?" I grilled him.

"I'll do whatever it takes. I love you."

And I just laid it on the line as I delivered my final caveat, "Nigel, you can't just love me. I need you to love me all the way."

"I promise. Heart and soul. To the moon and back. I'll love you all the way, and any other way that you need me to, until the day I die."

We both sat back in our chairs, and we took a few quiet moments to really look at each other. I know my face matched his as we both drank in every little nuance, the hair, the laugh lines, and remembrance of the way we nodded toward every little word the other said, the small smiles at a silly little joke that wasn't worth mentioning that we had shared, the hands gesturing, and the body language. Over those five quiet moments that we allowed ourselves, I really think that was when the forgiveness on both sides fell into place.

He said softly, "I'm sorry for holding your hand so tight all the way home. I was just so afraid you'd run if I loosened my grip, and I couldn't take the chance."

He stood up and brushed the bits and pieces of the photographs off his shoulders and lap. We walked in silence into the cool of the house, and he purposely foot-pedaled the trashcan open and dropped the brown envelope with the bits and pieces of the photos down deep into the canister.

As I pulled up a stool to his big white-and-gray-marble kitchen island, I found myself smiling a little at his 'trust-me' joke. We always did share the same kind of weird humor. He deftly prepared my strawberry and banana smoothie the way I had always liked it with the two percent yogurt. He poured it into two glasses and we raised our glasses in a silent salute. Neither one of us had the courage to toast out loud, especially with all the stories that were hanging in the balance. And besides, I didn't know if I had the guts or the courage to tell him all about my sad little life in Nice, France, never mind Edinburgh. Oh God, never Edinburgh. I would die taking that story to my grave. On the other hand, why should he have to fess up when I wasn't willing to meet him halfway?

I gave him a little leeway and said, "So, Bob Marley, it's hard not to notice that you've been working out. Nice touch."

"Oh, yeah, Brad put me into boxing boot camp immediately after listening to my sobbing and crying over the phone for an hour after I opened the photos of you and your friend Kurt. Six weeks out on the coast in a dingy, little boxing gym. It was quite a workout. Actually, it was a very specialized program, a one-on-one with a retired pro boxer. She kicked my ass, day in and day out, until I got the message that I had to become a man and face myself in the mirror."

"She? You mean to say the pro boxer was a woman?"

"Yeah, a dead-ringer for Grace Jones. Six feet tall, and as mean as a junkyard dog. Her name is Gerri, and she gave me a brilliant piece of advice. Her delivery hurt like hell, but I'll never forget the message." He hesitated and, for effect, he slid his fingers up and down his somewhat off-center nose before quoting the boxer's advice.

"If you come for the king
You'd better not miss, asshole."

It took a minute for me to catch on, and then I howled with laughter for five minutes straight. Tears were streaming down my face, and I managed to say, "You mean, you mean, ha, ha, ha, ha, ha, she broke your nose?"

"She popped me with her right hook and laid me out flat on the mat before I knew what had hit me."

"No way!" I said, still screaming with laughter.

"Yes way! Actually, I was giving her lip, and I deserved it. As they say, never underestimate a woman," he added ruefully, but grinning from ear to ear. He lowered his voice and said in a subdued tone, shaking his head solemnly, "Good thing she has perfect aim; it would have been a shame to lose my teeth."

With that last zinger, I was beside myself. My mascara was running down my face faster than the Fraser River, and I couldn't have cared less. I hadn't felt this good since Paris, and I knew I was deeply in love with him all over again, regardless of his stories to come.

As I settled down, I shook my head in amazement, "In a million years, I would never have taken you for a pugilist."

He raised both hands in denial. "No. No. Don't get me wrong. I'm a far cry from an expert," he laughed and pointed to his nose. "Obviously. But Gerri, now that's a different story. She went pro twenty years ago. She's the real deal."

He just sat there across from me with his arms resting on the island, with love and happiness washing over his face as he finished his story about the six-week boxing boot camp out on the coast.

"But I really loved Joey, the trainer. I was such an emotional wreck, and he took such good care of me. Their program is based on a mind, body, and spirit philosophy, and if it doesn't kill you, it will cure you. That's for sure! I survived, and as soon as I got home, I booked in with a great psychotherapy expert to address all my issues that I had been carrying around for my whole life. As I mentioned earlier, it took the doc about thirty seconds to realize that I was suffering from a chronic disorder called psychological transference. But I digress, and I must come clean with my back story that has made me the man I am today."

And so, he began, with no humor, no lightness, and just the facts. It turned out he wasn't kidding about the unpleasantness earlier. The world that he told me about was indeed ugly. He had spent the last few years of his seemingly idyllic life under the Canadian Witness Protection Program, and every movement around 7 Russell Hill Road, his own included, had been under surveillance every moment of every day. That's why he was forced into an early retirement. He had had to drop his few friends and he lived in his loneliness with just Chi next door and his brother long-distance. He had been a sitting duck in his robes presiding over a packed courtroom, so he was unable to work. His career had crashed and burned. He was a statistic just waiting to happen.

He went on to tell me that when Intel had picked me up on their radar, I too was watched. When their chatter divulged that the man that I had met in the café was a Chinese dissident who had been in prison, they snapped the photos and delivered them to Nigel. Nigel, in his pain and grief, never asked Intel for a briefing on the photos; he simply put the photos in the envelope and buried it in his desk drawer. He told Intel instead that I was out of the picture completely, and he insisted that the powers to pull surveillance off my tail.

The only person that knew this side of Nigel's world was Chi Tran. Chi was in it from the beginning, years ago, with Canada's intelligence agency training him and coaching him as he learned the fine art of surveillance. Yes, Chi was, and continued to be, on the payroll of the Canadian government, Intel Division. He kept Nigel safe.

I shook my head in amazement. You just never know.

He continued to talk, and I continued to listen. I could feel his pain as he shared the stories of unhappy endings with the few women in his life. He told me of a first love, which was particularly poignant in the fact that he never learned her name. It was many years ago and had taken place in Stockholm, Sweden. The rebuff that he suffered as a result of an afternoon tryst sounded very harsh indeed, especially compared to the otherwise delightful, spontaneous lovemaking session that the two strangers had shared. He chalked it up to, once again, a racist incident.

I shook my head in disgust. "I can never understand that love-hate thing that some have against people of color. Thank God that we seem to have tamped it down to a semi-manageable level here in Canada. But wait a minute, if you don't mind, Nigel, you would have sensed that hatred in her long before you made love with her. Think about it. Please, if you don't mind, I'm curious. What transpired just before her insult?"

"Oh, well, I was just minding my manners. I was giving her some taxi fare to get home. I was in a hurry and I was about to miss my plane."

"Well, what did she say when you offered her the money?"

"Nothing! Oh, I forgot to mention beforehand. She was deaf. Stone-deaf. She didn't hear anything, let alone my offer of taxi fare."

"Ah ha. Yes." I sighed and shook my head. "You men!"

"What? What did I do? I was a gentleman from the get-go!"

"Nigel, look at it from her point of view. You just had sex with her and then you offered her money. And she didn't hear anything; she just saw the money. It may have looked like you thought she was a prostitute and you were paying her for her services."

Nigel just stood there, his mouth open and eyes wide. "Oh my God, Denni, no, no! Oh my God! That's exactly why she slapped my face into the middle of next week! Oh my God, no! No, no!"

"Yes. Yes, Nigel, yes."

"Denni, it's been thirty years and it never dawned on me to think of it from her point of view. And there's simply no way I can ever rectify this huge misunderstanding with her."

"Bingo. Sounds like a pattern is evolving here, Mr. Royal."

He was striding back and forth with this new insight, and I convinced him to leave the story of the deaf Swede and go on with his story.

It turned out the second encounter with a woman was even more disastrous than the first. Oh my God. The poor man. He had married a woman on the spur of a moment and barely lived to tell the tale. I wanted to find her and claw her eyes out after just hearing about it. He met her when she had been an articling student in his law office. Apparently, on their wedding day on a beach in Jamaica, he had stumbled across her in the arms of another man.

"Where is she now?"

"I really have no idea. When I got back to Canada and filed my annulment papers the very next day, my office got wind of the whole thing and promptly turfed her ass out the door. I imagine that she would have had a hard time convincing another firm to take her on to finish her articling year, so I don't know if she stayed around town or she hightailed it back to Kingston, Jamaica, where she was from. She didn't appear in court for the annulment, and I haven't seen or heard from her since. But of course, that is ancient history. I remember it all happened twenty-five years ago, as both Saul and my mother had died just the year before."

"I'm so sorry that you had to go through that, Nigel, but you know me. I'm the master of one-upmanship. I think my story of my second honeymoon has yours looking like a fairytale."

He slammed down his glass. "Whoa! Now wait a minute! You had a honeymoon? No, no, I mean to say you had two honeymoons? Now, would that be with two different grooms or are we talking just the one marriage with a second attempt of a honeymoon with the same husband thrown in."

"I hate to break it to you, but I have endured two honeymoons, with two separate husbands. I am a woman with a past, you see." I smiled a little at his surprise. "I, too, have my secrets. But I'm quite willing to match story for story. I mean, after all, we have tomorrow ahead of us, don't we? I'll tell you what. I would like to hold my stories for tomorrow, as you are still not off the hook and I have no intention of letting you off so easily, buster."

The afternoon passed, and we ordered in Chinese for an early supper. Before we moved into his beautiful, elegant, but rarely used dining room, he gave me the cook's tour of his large, done-up-to-a-tee home.

He explained that it was originally Saul's house and that he had arrived from Jamaica as a nine-year-old boy to live in the modest apartment behind the back stairs with his mama, who was Saul's housekeeper. Saul had left the house to him when he died back in 1980.

After his disastrous marriage in 1981, he reinvented himself, partly by renovating the whole house, using a topnotch designer and then moving back in, far away from his small one-bedroom condo downtown and all the memories of his wife Mercedes that continued to permeate the condo and especially the bedroom.

Over all the years of living in his inherited home, he had found it to be way too big and way too lonely. He tweaked the decorating as the years passed, but he found himself always holed up in Saul's old office, which was located at the front of the house, with a beautiful, large window looking out over the front gardens and beyond it, a sidewalk.

Nigel went on to explain to me that for some reason, Saul's old office, which he couldn't bring himself to redo, was the only place in the world where he still felt really close to the remarkable man that had looked out for him, right up until he died. I felt a little sorry for him when he said it was the only place he felt 'safe' or 'home.'

I was laughing when I said, "Oh, now who could this be?" as I picked up a framed photograph of an older man, a young boy, and a dog that was reaching up and out of the boy's arms, long tongue out, licking the boy's happy face.

"Oh yeah, that's a good one, isn't it? Saul bought me that dog as soon as I came to Canada. That's Saul, Little Daisy, and me. I was about nine at the time."

"Little Daisy?"

"Well, yes. Of course. Big Daisy was back in Jamaica; what else could I name the pup? You know, over all the years, I loved her like nobody's business, but really, she was always Saul's dog, no matter how many biscuits and table scraps I fed her. Actually, Saul died and the dog followed within two weeks of his funeral. Of course, she was Old Daisy by then; she lived to be over seventeen people-years."

"Yes, I hear you. Dogs choose for themselves. They just know somehow. I had a Great Dane for ten years. Her name was Duchess. We were family."

We moved upstairs to continue the house tour. The master bedroom was right out of Architectural Digest. My eye hit the painting on the wall above the low headboard and I simply stood still. It was an over-sized Wolf Kahn. It was one of my favorites but I had never seen it in this size. Pink, orange, yellow, and magenta trees just stood there, blazing out at me.

"Oh, do you like it?"

"It's literally breathtaking. I'm really speechless, and it takes a lot to get me to that point!"

"Yes, I love it too. He used to show, down at the Marianne Friedland Gallery in Yorkville, but it closed some years ago."

"Oh! I know where they went. That gallery is now in Naples, Florida. Last year, I saw a permanent collection of Wolf Kahn's work there. Where did you get this one?"

"I met him when he was in town some years ago, and I asked him if it would be possible to have a large print made from his original, which is quite a bit smaller, and we got to talking and made a deal for this signed print. Voila!"

The king-sized bed was dressed with a plain, narrow, dark magenta silk shantung headboard and beautiful white linens. A white, summer-weight eiderdown without a cover ran along the bottom of the bed. On top of the long nine-drawer dresser, there was a collection of Inuit stone carvings and two large, framed photographs.

The one black and white photo was taken in a formal portrait style of Saul, in his judge's robes. He looked to be around sixty years old. The photographer had caught his magnificent face – a combination of compassion, love, and wisdom. The other photograph was well done too, but the focus was definitely on Nigel, who, according to the hat and gown, was graduating. Saul, a good six inches shorter than Nigel, stood on one side of him, and his mother, a tall, black, handsome woman stood on the other side. Saul and Mavis' pride was jumping right out of the photo, and Nigel was wearing his big trademark grin from ear to ear. What a fantastic story the old photograph told!

On the far side of the bed, there were stacks and stacks of books, precariously piled on top of one another. "Now, believe it or not, that is a very sophisticated filing system there. One pile is a hit and another pile a miss, and then there's the re-reads over here."

It reminded me of my parents' bedroom years ago. "Wow, it looks like my mom and dad's bedside from years ago. They were both avid readers, and actually, it was my dad that doled out the many, many books to me when I was a young girl. He had me stuck on *Anne of Green Gables* and Nancy Drew for years before he allowed me into the classics like *Exodus, the Underground Railroad* and *The Apprenticeship of Duddy Kravitz.*"

"Duddy who?"

"You know, Duddy Kravitz. Mordecai Richler wrote it, along with his other really good one, *Barney's Version*. Actually, that's my favorite movie."

"Which?"

"Yeah. Barney's Version is my favorite movie. It's probably on Netflix. Perhaps we could watch it together in one of these days."

"Of course. But I'm sorry to hear that my bed reminds you of your parents. That in itself is serious couch material, you know. My shrink will have something to say about that."

I said, laughing, "Oh my God, don't even go there. Let's not throw my parents into our complicated mix. It's too much for any shrink!"

Both of us kept our distance, not trusting ourselves to get too close.

During the master-bedroom major renovation, Nigel had taken an adjoining bedroom and had his closet and ensuite made out of this extra space. The large, square, walk-in closet held more shoes in it than Imelda Marcus could ever dream of. The ensuite was spacious with double sinks, stand-alone tub and along the back wall, the glassed-in shower's multiple jets sparkled with all of Ginger's latest chrome fixtures. My eyes rested on his toiletries. There it was – the old-fashioned, opaque, cream-colored bottle of Yardley's Old Spice aftershave.

"That was my dad's scent."

"The Old Spice?"

"Yeah. How is it, all these years later, that it presents itself to me here, right here, in a strange man's bathroom?"

"First things first. I'm not strange. Secondly, it's how the universe works, Denni. It knows I need all the help I can get here." He grinned down at me, "And, in all honesty, it was Saul's one and only too, so I use it in memory of him."

I allowed myself to give him a bone. "I smelled it last year when you came into chambers to meet with me."

He teased, "You are getting dangerously close to being very sweet, Ms. Brunette. Are you prepared to follow through with this conversation?"

"Are you going to take all night to give me this cook's tour or what?"

He walked ahead of me and disappeared into the walk-in closet, and as he walked, he said, "Denni, would you excuse me just for a sec? I just want to grab a fresh shirt."

"What's wrong with Bob?"

He looked at me, smiling a little sheepishly. "This is my attempt to stand up to my word, you know. You said *love me all the way*. You see, my brother gave me this L.A. street-style shirt, but it's his style, not mine. I don't want to confuse the issue here. I'm just a plain, simple, white tee-shirt kind of guy."

"Yes, oh yes, Nigel, you are a plain and simple guy. And I'm a neurosurgeon."

The way he pulled Bob Marley over his head with one arm, standing two feet in front of me so that I could see the glisten of sweat all through his small circles of tightly coiled chest hair, told me he wasn't above playing every little trick in the book, just as I would have done myself in a similar situation. He stepped back into the walk-in closet and pulled out a drawer. He looked back at me, his big, new shoulders and pecs just begging to be touched, and although he didn't say a word, his big smile said, "Come and get it, baby."

I turned my head away from Armageddon before it was too late.

Good planning down the hall was everywhere. It was a cleverly designed large, long Jack 'n Jill bathroom where you could enter from the hallway or from either of the two guest bedrooms on each side. "Brilliant planning here, Nigel. It's nice that each bedroom has its own entrance. It looks like Ginger has been playing a role here."

"Oh no, Denni. You've got it all wrong. I laid every tile myself." He laughed, holding out his manicured hands for me to inspect his callouses.

Back downstairs, the living room was done up in modern style, but the designer had wisely left the traditional white millwork, limestone fireplace and plastered crown molded ceiling all in its original glory. There was a very good selection of big, brightly colored canvases mounted on the white walls.

"Oh, that one is so similar to mine. Is that a Simon Bull there?" I said as I pointed to a bright yellow, blue, and red painting.

"Yeah, I treated myself to it on a trip to London many years ago. I know he lives out in California now, but I met him at a gallery in London. Perhaps he was just back for a show, or maybe he still lived there at the time. I don't remember. But really, it's my Caribbean blood, I suppose, but I do love a big splash of color. We do have the same taste in so many things, don't we, honey?"

"Yeah. And that's a beautiful Maxfield Parrish."

"That's my favorite actually. Saul bought it when he was just starting out in his law practice back in the day, when the artist wasn't very well known. It's called *The Lantern Burners*. I insisted that the designers work the old-fashioned piece into their design when they were redoing the room. His yellow is so luminescent, isn't it?"

"This really big piece here is a great example of palette-knife work, isn't it!? Who is this?"

"Oh, this is another of Saul's paintings. He supported a lot of artists just coming up. This is Jean-Paul Riopelle, a Canadian, who worked out of Montreal in the early fifties. The mumble-jumble of it all reminds me a little of Jackson Pollock somehow."

We entered the small apartment where he and his mama had spent many years together.

I warily said, "Is this where my nemesis, the famous Matilda Mattis, lives?"

Nigel laughed with amusement. "No, she's happily retired, back in Jamaica, living on her Canadian pension. As it turned out, when she realized that a certain beautiful Irish faerie wasn't darkening the doorstep any longer, she took it upon herself to tell me that she expected as much and that I was better off without you. I decided then and there that enough was enough, and I suggested that she retire from her housekeeping duties with full pay to cover her over the next two years ahead. She jumped at the chance and I have enjoyed peace and quiet ever since. I just have a weekly cleaning service come in now and the apartment here is empty. You see, just another sad tale of me and the women in my life!" he said, still teasing me a little.

As he held the door that led back into the main house open, I brushed past him and his arm blocked me. I looked up to meet his eyes. We hadn't even come close to touching each other since his firm hand-holding exercise all the way down the street, and we found ourselves back to our shyness, which had taken over with his small overture. Neither of us had the courage to break the spell.

"Denni, I," his soft voice was interrupted by the doorbell.

"Literally saved by the bell," I bluffed as I raced toward the front door to greet the food-delivery person.

"I would like to make a toast," I said while he was pouring the red for me and the white for him.

"Go right ahead, Ms. Brunette."

"To new beginnings."

"To new beginnings," he offered back, with hope and love written all over his face.

"May I just revisit your story of the two husbands for a moment? Never in my life have I been so surprised. Since the moment I saw you stride into the Aroma Espresso Café, I had you pegged as a free spirit, a beautiful, elusive, unattainable woman that would never allow herself to be under the smother of a husband."

"Well, since we are laying all the cards on the table, Nigel, I must admit that my first thoughts of you during our first luncheon were totally the opposite. I feared that you had a wife at home, just waiting with cocktails and canapés served the moment you arrived home after your hard day in the courtroom."

"And here we are in the plain light of day, with nary a pair of rose-colored glasses in sight."

"But really, Nigel, I have a little matter to clear up. I feel very badly that I have never thanked you properly for the wonderful trip to Paris that you treated me to last year. Please, please, accept my apology for that oversight, and in my small attempt to make it up to you, I would like to take you out tomorrow night for dinner. Your choice of venue. The sky's the limit. Better late than never, they say."

"Brilliant idea, Ms. Brunette, and no apology necessary. After all, it was me who changed my telephone number. I will, however, leave the choice of restaurant entirely in your capable hands. Surprise me. You meet me here, say around 7:00?"

After many back-and-fourths on why my favorite dish was far superior to his, and sharing bites across the table, I explained to him that I had to go home to tend to some overdue phone calls and emails that I had been neglecting and to get a good night's rest to meet any other surprises that he may throw into the mix. I didn't say as much, but the truth was that I just didn't trust myself to keep my clothes on any more than he could keep his on. I didn't want this touchy clarification reunion to be mixed in with all that passion that we both knew was just simmering on the backburner. It was better that we started off with a clean slate going forward. Over the years, I had learned the hard way that makeup sex is not what it's cracked up to be.

And of course, there was the niggling little thought that was beginning to push forward from the backburner of my brain. And it wasn't a pleasant one. I needed time on my own to sort this out. It had been simmering over the past year, and after hearing Nigel's plea for understanding in the backyard, it was clear to me that we both suffered the same Achilles' heel – jealousy. I knew that jealousy can lead to downfall, and I had been on the receiving end of it enough times to pay attention. It could be a fatal weakness, and my coping skills were not up to par. His problem was that he was a jealous person, brought on by past relationships, and my problem was that I couldn't tolerate it, even in small doses. I instinctively would run away from the situation the minute it reared its ugly head.

We were a pair of troubled misfits that had inadvertently fallen in love with each other. Shit, shit, shit.

"I have to phone Catharine in France and Ann-Marie down on the farm and let them know that my absentee Mr. Wonderful is back in the picture," I confessed to him. I followed up with the story of all the tearful phone calls over the past nine months that went on between Ann-Marie and me and how we lamented the men in our lives, past, present, and future, and how she played her part as the supportive girlfriend throughout the months of my pain and sadness.

"Okay, so call your girlfriends, and please say hello to Ann-Marie and Walt for me. Meanwhile, I'll call Brad and Chi, who both have just about had it up to here with my sad tales of heartbreak as well."

We cleared off the dining room table, put the leftovers in the fridge, and kissed each other lightly on the doorstep. I quickly ran away from the sheer intimacy that had sprang up over the dinner table in full force. One step at a time.

***

"Hello, Ann-Marie? It's Denni, and I have good news."

"It's so good to hear from you," her voice was loud, so I had to hold my phone away from my ear. Now what can be such good news that you're calling me in primetime about. "Did you win the lottery or something?"

"No. No winning ticket. Better news than that. Mr. Wonderful is back in the picture."

"Oh my God! Thank the good Lord! I knew it. I just knew it. I hope you two love birds have smartened up now and realize that you should just get out there and get married right now. Don't even wait for next week. Do you hear me? Denni, are you listening to me? He's a good man, and you can't let him slip through your fingers, girlfriend."

Ann-Marie pulled her mouth away from her phone, and I heard her yell into the distance, "Walt, Walt, it's Denni. Nigel's back on the scene. Thank God for small mercies!"

"Ann-Marie, I promise I will keep you up to date on the romance, but don't hold your breath waiting for wedding bells," I said, laughing at her exuberance.

"Are you kidding me!? I'll stake my bet right now. Fifty cents says you're married within the month."

"Yeah, you think so, huh? You're on and I'll double the ante. I've got to go now. I have to plan out what I'm wearing for dinner tomorrow night with Nigel. Gotta make the right impression, you know."

I clicked off the phone, thanking God for good friends.

***

It was three hours earlier on the coast, and Nigel called his brother, hoping to catch him in.

"Hey, bro! Good to hear from you! What's up?"

"Turns out the world is a wonderful place after all. She's back. She's back in full force. The Gods have answered my prayers. My beautiful gray-eyed Irish faerie has once again graced me with her presence."

"Are you fucking kidding me!?" Howling with delight, he cried, "Too much! When's the wedding!?"

"Well, no, it's a little early to be talking about a wedding."

"What!? What did you just say!? Please God, tell me I didn't just hear you say that you haven't learned your lesson yet."

"What do you mean?"

"Bro," he continued in a softened tone, "we've all been burned, and you especially, but really, it's been twenty-five years! It's fucking time to just man up!" He pleaded, "You know I love you more than life itself, but I gotta ask you: how can such a smart dude be such a dumb fuck!?"

"Is this your way of giving me some brotherly advice?"

"Yeah, now we're on the same track. Listen, man, it's time for you to put your big-boy pants on. Get down on one knee and put a ring on her finger!"

"You mean right now?"

"Yes, I mean right now, yes! And, as a matter of fact, I do mean literally right now! Tiffany's will still be open up there in Toronto today, right? Or Cartier. Or Chopard. Or – no, no, no. In fact, here's what to do right now. Just call ahead and tell them that you are coming in to pick up their biggest emerald-cut yellow diamond that they have on the floor. Nothing less than five carats. Give them your VISA number over the phone. Tell them that you will have it sized later. Oh yeah, I just remembered something Stephie told me one time. About the ring size. A woman's shoe size is always the same as her ring size. Go figure, it must be some kind of a woman thing. But whoa, whoa! Don't overanalyze and get all hung up on that little tidbit, like I know you sometimes do. Just go right now like the man I know you are and take care of it. Now."

"Yah think?"

"For Christ's sake, man, yeah, I think!"

"Gotta go. I love you, bro." He signed off, his baritone rising with excitement stemming from his brother's blunt but sound advice.

***

I pushed the bell on his front door, just like I used to, a year ago. I had spent the morning at the hairdressers and treated myself to a mani/pedi on the way home. I wore a pale coral dinner-out dress that I had just bought at Holt's the week before, although at the time I admitted to myself I didn't have anywhere to go, and I also didn't have anyone to admire how it fit my curves just perfectly. It was way out of my budget, but I bought it anyway. I looked down at my high-heeled summer sandals. I smiled to myself at the ensemble, knowing fully well that Nigel would appreciate it.

I watched him as he opened the door. He took a moment to look me over, savoring the sight from head to toe. I couldn't help but smile at his enthusiasm. He was looking good himself. He was wearing a tan, cotton summer jacket over a white silk jersey tee-shirt, tucked tight down into pressed, Euro-style white jeans snug on his slim hips, bare feet slipped into Italian loafers – very cool, very sexy. He had lost that nerdy, intellectual, perfectly handsome look somehow. Now he looked a little bit more like a bad boy, a character, like a boy your mother said would break your heart or worse. But that was just his new nose speaking, of course.

"Before we get into the car, I thought we could have an aperitif in the backyard. I mean, it's summer and all. We may as well enjoy the evening."

177

"Of course, darling," I said and walked ahead of him, warily smoothing down the back of my dress. We walked down past the house and into the backyard.

There were two elegant, cushioned teak chairs facing each other, with a small table to the side. Cocktail napkins lined a plate with a few nibbles on it. A bottle of champagne was chilling in the bucket of ice. Two champagne flutes were sparkling, just begging to be filled up, all under the beautiful, green, leafy maple tree.

I sat down, tucking my bare legs away from his eyes. He slowly poured two glasses of the Dom Perignon and toasted to 'new beginnings' once again.

Nigel put me at ease by drawing my eye around the backyard, pointing out Chi's narrow greenhouse that faced the backside of the garage, telling me of Chi's green thumb that resulted in this beautiful, large, hedged, and private oasis.

He told me that as a youngster, before puberty hit and girls entered the picture, he and Saul had built a tree house in the old maple, right above us. He reached up, as if to show me where the ladder had been attached, and my eyes opened wide in surprise as his perfectly manicured hand corralled a small, square, Tiffany-blue box wrapped with a white satin bow from a protected V-shaped crux in one of the bottom limbs. Both my eyes and my mouth were open with surprise as he smoothly and quietly kneeled before me.

"Marry me. Please marry me. I promise to cherish you for the rest of my life. I love you. I will love you all the way, every day of our lives. Marry me. Denni, please marry me."

I stuttered in my surprise. "I, I, I love you too. I love you. I do love you. And I promise to cherish you right back for the rest of my life too. Yes, yes, yes, I will marry you. Yes, let's get married," I went on and on, babbling like an incoherent idiot.

He opened the blue box and slid a sparkling, emerald-cut, canary-yellow diamond that was cradled on a plain, modern, platinum base onto my ring finger. I was overwhelmed with the sheer beauty and grace of the magnificent piece of jewelry that fit my finger as if it were made for me.

We sealed the deal with a long, tender kiss and I noticed my hands were trembling.

I had booked us in with a table at the Four Seasons' main dining room, and to tell you the truth, I was in such a happy daze that I can't remember how we got there. I do remember, though, every second of every moment in between courses when Nigel stood up from our table that was situated in the middle of the dining room.

He clinked his glass politely to get everyone's attention, and he took my hand in his. He announced in his deep baritone voice, that had the slightest hint of nasal troubles, "Excuse me for interrupting your dinner. But I am bursting to tell you that I am the luckiest man in the world! She said yes!" He raised my hand high to coax me to stand up beside him so he could show off his wife-to be. The usually toned-down dining room erupted with cheers and laughter. Everyone stood up as he gently coaxed me up out of my seat to acknowledge the audience. He stood in one spot and gently pirouetted me around, as if to start a dance. He quickly grabbed me around the waist and bent me over backward in a deep tango dip. I instinctively raised one foot off the ground, straightened my knee, pointed my toes, and lifted my leg up high, just like they do in the movies. He planted a big, long kiss right on my lips before smoothly lifting me back up. He stood there beaming and gave a very slight bow to the audience. The applause was deafening as he tenderly sat me down in my chair. Oh, he was smooth, all right. I must admit he had all the moves. Sexy as all gets out, as Ann-Marie down on the farm might say.

Over dessert, I whispered in his attentive ear, "Did you know that I am the luckiest woman in the world?" as my tongue wet the backside of his earlobe.

He leaned ever so slightly forward to press his ear into my lips but stretched one arm out and away to reach for his napkin. He placed it over the bulge in his lap.

"You are a handful, Ms. Brunette."

"And you are one lucky man, Your Honor."

We ended the evening at the Four Seasons' bar, where the Maître d' insisted that our drinks were on the house.

Nigel called the car service, and we left his car parked in Yorkville, as the champagne, sheer joy and happiness, and the complimentary drinks at the bar had taken their toll on both of us.

I had the driver drop me off at home before he took Nigel down to 7 Russell Hill Road. Nigel had jumped out to open my lobby door, and it was all I could do to push him back outside, with the promise of coming down for breakfast the very next morning to map out our wedding plans. I had to get upstairs, take a shower, and clear my head. If the truth be told, I was totally drunkety-drunk, but not drunk enough to let Mr. Wonderful see me in that kind of shape, especially not while wearing that kind of bling on my ring finger.

I also knew that Catharine would be disappointed in my less-than-ladylike behavior, and I couldn't have that now, could I?

***

The next morning, we took our after-breakfast coffee into his living room to discuss our wedding plans, as I had promised that we would do the night before.

Nigel broached the topic of finances in a respectful tone. "If it's all okay with you, here's my plan for our day-to-day finances. You'll continue on with your current income in your current bank account and I'll do the same with mine. On Friday, though, I would like us to go down to my bank, and we'll set up a joint bank account. I'll take care of all the deposits, and this is for you to pay all the household expenses, our holidays, and also to give you an expense account for your own personal use. I have enough money for both of us and there's no need for you to be spending yours."

He continued on, "Since we'll be downtown at the bank on Friday, I'd like to pop in to introduce you to my lawyer. We'll need two new wills, of course, and he's just the guy to take care of everything. He'll also draw up our pre-nup agreement, which will ensure that you have full access to all accounts, if in fact, for example, I go missing or die before you. How're we doing so far?"

I nodded in agreement as he continued, "There are a couple of things, though, that I do insist upon, however."

"And what would they be?"

"I want you to tuck away your inheritance that you got from court last year. I don't want you spending your money. There's simply no need. I'll take good care of you and you can buy whatever you want to buy. The second thing is that I want you to keep your apartment up and running, so you will have a safe haven to retreat to if life with me gets a little too much for you to handle. It's going to take us some time to carve out a separate office and writing room upstairs for you, and meanwhile, you are all set up where you are. Hey, I've learned my lesson, and I know to give my little free spirit space when she needs it!" He laughed.

"Oh, so you really do know me. Thank you for that, Nigel. And yes, although I can tell you right here and right now, I'll never use it, but it's very thoughtful of you to work along with my gypsy ways."

"And we'll have everything you want to bring from your apartment here delivered whenever you're ready. You can hang your art and put your furniture wherever you like. Or buy new. It doesn't matter. I just want you to feel at home. This is our home now. However, don't get me wrong now! Your apartment may just turn out to be a safe haven for me on occasion!"

"Who – little old me? I'm a dream to cohabitate with. You'll see!"

"No, let's go back to your apartment for just a second here. Wait – please, let me share at how I've arrived at my conclusion. Through all of our evening walks last year, your poetry down at your farm, all of your stories, and all of our exquisite, sexy lovemaking in Paris, I've figured out who you really are, behind all the bravado and brunette fabulousness. And I get you. I really get you," he said in a low, soft voice.

I felt like an emperor with no clothes on. My soul was stripped bare. I couldn't move my eyes from his soft brown ones.

"Who am I?" I asked in a small, quiet voice.

"You are a storyteller, honey, plain and simple. You are a writer, a wordsmith with deep country roots right down into your poetic Irish soul, through and through. You are just on the verge of writing your first magnificent New York Times bestseller."

***

He had asked Chi to come in later that morning, to bring me on board with the Canadian Witness Protection Program that was in full effect, and to show me around the security system that kept a close watch on the front door, garage, and the street. I was learning quickly that behind the luxurious and well-manicured curb appeal of 7 Russell Hill Road, life was a lot more complicated than it appeared to be. I began to understand what he meant when he said he wanted a pre-nup to protect me *if he went missing,* or *if he died before me.*

"Nigel, I know and understand completely that trust is implicit in your world. Mine too. You have my word that I will never ever let you down. Ever. I surrender my heart to you. I love you so much, and I will be the best wife in the whole world. You'll see."

He just sat there, looking at me. He said quietly, "How did I get so lucky?"

"Now, what about our wedding? When, where, who, how?"

"I would rather just keep it small if that's okay with you, honey. On my side, just family, with Chi as my best man, and of course my godson, François. Brad is still shooting on the west coast, so I don't think he will be able to make it. What I'm saying is that I don't want the guest list to hold us up at all. How about if we pick a date within the month? Will that give you enough time to get a dress?"

"Perfect! Let's say for three weeks from now. On my side, I just want to invite Ann-Marie and Walt. I'm pretty sure Ann-Marie will stand up for me. I'd love if Catharine and Edouard could make it, but it's a long way for them to come on such short notice. Kurt and Gretchen, and a few of my local girlfriends. That's all. We can always have a party later on in the fall. If Chi is going to be your best man, perhaps I can cajole Walt into walking this blushing bride up the aisle."

He nodded in agreement. "Location? Any ideas?"

"Would it be okay with you if we got married right here at home, under the big old maple tree in the backyard? We could just have it catered right here, or maybe all of us go down to the Four Seasons for a dinner and dancing after the ceremony. Whatever you want. Maybe Chi could help us organize the backyard; the gardens are so beautiful back there."

And so, it was all set. Nigel was to ask his old friend, Rabbi Klieman, to officiate. He explained to me that he wasn't actually a Jew, but Saul had taken him to synagogue with Rabbi Klieman over all the years enough to pass muster with the current interdenominational trend of holding hands with all faiths. My job was to tell Ann-Marie that she had won the bet.

***

After lunch, we spent the afternoon sketching out a first draft of my new office, which was to evolve from an existing guestroom upstairs, located at the front of the house. Nigel insisted on renovating his big closet, with a new bank of built-in drawers and several more shoe racks that I assured him were going to be more than adequate to house my meager wardrobe. And he asked, "Do you mind that we would have to share the ensuite bathroom?"

It was dusk by the time we rummaged around in the fridge and laid out a humble spread of leftovers. I can't remember enjoying a meal more – just the two of us pulled up to the kitchen island, cold beer, and slices of ham and cheese on thin, black pumpernickel bread. I cut up an apple to fill out a half bowl of fruit salad that Nigel had left from breakfast, and we ate out of the single bowl, two spoons slurping back and forth.

As he sat there, grinning at me for insisting on having the last spoonful, I was reminded of that first little supper we had shared in Paris, in our bathrobes and me with a towel tied up over my wet hair. At that time, I knew that I had never been happier, but this simple meal of leftovers, sitting up to his kitchen island, was running a close second.

As he put some coffee on, I brought up the subject of our mental health. I said, "Nigel, there's something that we haven't really organized yet, and it's on my mind."

"Shoot, baby. What's up?"

I said softly, "Darling, we've paid the price for our mental health issues, and we've both suffered a lot of self-induced pain and trauma over the past year. Despite our current happiness, I think we need to talk about a plan of action for times when or if we have an emotional relapse of some sort. As you know, your condition is chronic. It's something that's always going to be with you. And in the past, my reaction was always to run away from issues. So, we both need to develop a good strong plan of action to be prepared to deal with issues together, just in case your condition comes into play again, which may trigger my poor response. We've been lucky so far in that we haven't suffered more than we already have, but emotional duress is a killer, you know. Anyone can have a stroke or a heart attack in the blink of an eye due to stress."

"Oh, you're right. I see. I see. I hadn't thought of it that way. What do you suggest?"

"Well, like you suggested in the backyard, perhaps we should have a few sessions of couples' counseling with your shrink, just to let her know that we are going to deal with life and all that it brings us, good and bad, together. As a married couple."

"Good idea. I'll call her and set up an appointment for us," he smiled, "as a married couple."

"Yeah. *As a married couple* has a good ring about, doesn't it!?"

We both shouted out at the same time, "Rings!" We had forgotten about wedding rings. We decided right then and there on small, plain bands, engraved on the inside with our names and the date of the wedding. We would go together to Tiffany's to pick them out.

We had returned to the living room to jot down a few more notes on our wedding. I was stretched out on the sofa, with a pillow propped up under my shoulders, and he was sitting across from me in his favorite Eames recliner, taking the notes. We sketched out a guest list, and I included my four French friends, Catharine and Edouard and Lyonel and Lucia. He would book and pay for all the rooms at the Four Seasons, including Ann-Marie and Walt and any other out-of-town guests, and we both agreed to defer the honeymoon until later in the fall.

The conversation all of a sudden fell away to silence, and we faced the elephant in the room. Our trip to Paris the year before, with all its raw emotion that was so new to both of us and that had ended with such pain and misery was in front of us all over again. Back then, we had both tried to mask our truth with chalking it up to fantastic sex, and now the time had come to test the waters, so to speak. Saying we had forgiven each other was one thing, but with our histories of trust issues, right now and right then, was a high hurdle for both of us. Did we have the guts to lay ourselves bare once again? Did we have the brains to accept the love that was on the platter, right in front of us?

He slowly put his notepad down, stood up, and quietly floated toward me. He kneeled down, and we were face-to-face, eyes locked.

The room was absolutely still. All I could hear in my head, and pounding down through my chest, was Norah Jones' sexy, sultry voice, begging her lover to turn her on. I looked into his dark brown eyes, and keeping time to the song's beat with my pounding heart, I sang the words in a whisper into his face:

Like a flower waiting to bloom
Waiting for you to turn me on
Just sittin' here waiting for you
To turn me on.

"You're beautiful, inside and outside, and I love you," he whispered. "Baby, don't move. I'm going to pleasure you, just the way we pleasured each other in Paris. Just lie still and let my love wash all over you. I want to taste you and unfold you slowly and make you feel good with my mouth and my tongue. I want you to know that this isn't just sex, baby; it's love. It's all for you, just you. I loved you in Paris, and I love you now. I'll love you forever."

He undid my blouse slowly, button by button, and pulled my summer skirt down over my bare legs and past my bare feet. I heard the skirt plop onto the carpet below. I couldn't move. I was absolutely paralyzed with wanting him. All the months and months and months of dreaming of his touch, please God let this be really happening.

He raised my shoulder to free my shirt. I felt my bra falling away. My hands curled into his hair as his mouth covered my nipples. By the time he had removed my panty and had buried his face into my fresh bikini wax, the insides of my thighs were trembling. I could hear my voice, and it sounded like it was coming from some far off, out-of-body experience, like in a dream, only a really, really, good dream.

"I'm all yours. I'm letting you in. The love part and the sex part. I love you all the way. I'm giving you my heart right here, right now," I whispered fiercely. "Make me feel like you did in Paris," I implored.

***

I phoned Catharine to bring her up to date. "Hi, Catharine. Denni here. I know this is very, very short notice, but I want you and Edouard to come to Canada to be with me on my wedding day."

She shrieked over the phone, "Oh my God! Oh my God! Are you kidding me? What did you say? And, yes, yes, we will be there! Just tell me when. Really, Denni, you're not joking, are you?"

"Yes, Mr. Wonderful and Ms. Hard-to-get-along-with are tying the knot in two and a half weeks."

"Of course! Of course, we'll be there! But right now, fill me in on the details."

"Just a small wedding in Nigel's beautiful backyard, a few friends and family. Nigel is paying for all the out-of-town guests to stay at the Four Seasons, so your hotel bill is taken care of, and I want to pay for your airfare as well."

"I won't hear of you paying for anything, Denni. But we will be there. Can I do anything for you meanwhile?"

"Well, yes. There is something. And it's a little tricky, but I'm sure you can handle it."

"Anything, my bride-to-be, anything."

"Well, remember Lyonel and Lucia from Nice?"

"Yes, of course. We still see them. They were just here for the weekend and they taught us how to tango. They are such a great couple."

"Well, here's my idea. I want them to come to the wedding, but I know they can't afford the trip. I want to e-transfer you the money for their airfare so that you can book their flights along with yours so they won't have to pay. Of course, like all the guests, the hotel accommodations are paid for by Nigel. So, I'm going to e-transfer you the money tonight so they simply cannot say no."

"*Oui. Oui.* I hear you. I think we can manage that, okay. Leave it with me, and meanwhile, book the four of us in for two rooms at the Four Seasons. But can you afford this, Denni?"

"Yes. Not to worry. I'm marrying a man of means, it seems. Or, at the very least, a very generous one. Nigel is adamant about paying for everything and everyone, but I'm insisting on paying these four airfares myself. I still have my inheritance, and he won't hear of me using it for anything. You've always been so good to me, Catharine, and I hope that you can understand that this is a very, very small token of my love and respect for you and for all your help over the past year."

"Oh, so it's that way. A man of means, you say. Yeah, I think you've kissed enough frogs, Denni, and I'm so happy that you've found your prince. But seriously, think about it." She laughed, "We're both so lucky to have rich husbands, and you're right, Lyonel and Lucia deserve a break once in a while. They will be thrilled to hear your good news. Count the four of us in. God willing, we'll all dance the tango at your wedding in two and a half weeks."

She added at the last minute, "Oh, before you go, Ms. Fancy-pants, what are you wearing to your page-six event of the year?"

"I'm wearing a pair of vintage-ivory, hand-tatted, three-quarter-length gloves that he bought me in Paris last year, along with my four-carat emerald-cut, canary-yellow diamond over the glove on the ring finger."

I could sense her smiling as she queried, "Nothing else?"

"Nope."

"You bohemian Canucks! It sounds like you have forgotten everything I taught you in Nice about how to dress like a lady, but the gloves do sound perfect. And the ring! To die for! I know as well as you do that old-style etiquette says that the ring must not be worn over the top of the gloves, but I think we can make an exception here. A four-carat emerald-cut, canary-yellow diamond takes precedence. That does it. I'd better get over there to give you a few more lessons on how to dress that is appropriate for your new station in life, even though I have a suspicion you will only need a suitcase full of sexy La Perla for the honeymoon."

"Goodbye, girlfriend. *Je t'aime.* Please give Edouard a kiss for me."

***

The next few weeks flew by, and Chi transformed the already-beautiful backyard into a fantasy garden. He and Nigel had arranged for a chuppa to be installed right in the branches of the old maple, in keeping with the traditional Jewish custom. Nigel explained it was all for Saul's memory, and the chuppa, along with all the men wearing kippas, would also be respectful of the Rabbi that was willing to marry us.

***

I stood there in my old, well-worn flannel pjs, giving Ann-Marie a little lip back as she chastised me for my raggedy-looking pajamas.

"No man wants to see his girl in flannel pjs, Denni. As sure as God made little green apples. Now come on, you know the rules."

"All right, all ready, I agree! Yes, boss! I'll throw them out tomorrow morning as we leave the suite! But just to let you know, don't worry, I've been out shopping for La Perla like there's no tomorrow."

"What's La Perla?" she asked.

The two of us were having the traditional girls-only bride's party on the eve of my wedding. Nigel had booked a beautiful suite for Ann-Marie and Walt, but it ended up that for the night before the big day, the girls would take the suite, and Walt dutifully packed his bag and moved into the house where the boys would have a little bachelors' party on their own.

I've never seen Ann-Marie more wound up. Although she and Walt had arrived in town two days beforehand and we had sampled all that the city had to offer, she was still like a kid under the Christmas tree.

As part of her matron-of-honor duties, she had insisted that she choose the music for me to walk up the garden path with, and for Nigel to sing back to me once he had taken my hand. She played and replayed the two songs over and over, making sure that I knew the words well enough to sing along as I walked up the aisle. She had instructed Walt to practice Nigel's song with him and had asked Chi to take care of the 'karaoke box' and speakers in the garden. I must admit the two old country classics were the icing on the cake. After all, what's wrong with a little karaoke thrown into the mix? Yes, we were going to sing our wedding vows to each other.

I was to sing along with Ann Murray's hit from the seventies', *Could I Have This Dance?* and Nigel would sing along with Roy Clarke's song, *Come Live With Me.*

For just a moment, I flashed back to what was happening to me one year earlier in terms of favorite tunes. My main man was David Ruffin all the way, every day. *My Whole World Ended the Moment You Left Me* and *I Wish it Would Rain* were daily staples of my crying-in-my-beer music.

Ann-Marie insisted that we both try on our dresses once again.

"Ann-Marie, now – this is just getting a little old. This is the last time I'm putting on the damn dress for you. Do you hear me?" I said with hands on hips and a smile on my face.

"No really, Denni. You have no idea. My new dress is Walt's favorite shade of blue. Whenever I wear that color, he just can't keep his hands off me. There will be a helluva raucous coming from this big bed tomorrow night. Let me tell you!"

We both howled with laughter and once again, I unzipped the garment bag to pull out my wedding dress.

I must admit my dress was a stunner, but it had nothing on the accessories. As Coco Channel once set out the tried-and-tested correct way of dressing, *"La simplicité est la clé de l'élégance."*

I lifted the hat box lid and carefully took out the bridal headpiece. My dressmaker had joined two of my art deco hair clips together and added a small bit of tulle around the piece to give it a little more presence. She finished it off with a bit of fine netting that I was to wear layered over my eyes as a statement of a bride's modesty from days gone by. It complimented the ivory silk dress perfectly. My mother's old triple-strand of pearls that she had bought in the forties for her own wedding matched the ivory dress perfectly. The dress looked like it was strapless at first glance, but there was a sheer organdy wrap that went around my shoulders and was sewn and gathered into the three-inch, stand-alone, dainty lace cuffs that were to be worn at mid-arm. The back of the wrap stood up to frame my neck and shoulders and floated in freedom to just above my waist, almost like a veil. My gloves from Paris were carefully folded in the hat box. I would wear my big, blingy, yellow-diamond engagement ring over them during the ceremony.

"Tell me one more time about the gloves, Denni. Please. Just one more time."

And so, for the third time in as many days, I told Ann-Marie the story that the gloves were a gift from Nigel during our trip to Paris the year before. On that particular shopping day, I was admiring them in the front-window display of a paper shop that we had wandered into in search of some notebooks for Nigel. They were simply part of the exquisite, vintage 1920s window display at the time. Later in the week, unknown to me, Nigel had telephoned the shop and had them wrapped up for me as a surprise.

Ann-Marie and I danced around the room, all primped and polished from our day at the Elmwood Spa. Flaunting my engagement ring on her newly-manicured finger, she pranced around in her seventies' pink, sponge hair curlers and her best, perfectly pressed, below-the-knee-length nightgown with the puff sleeves. I stood there laughing at her antics, in my old flannels that had seen me rock-bottom heartsick and through thick and thin over the past nine months of wandering around Europe with no anchor, just trying to forget Nigel Royal.

***

As our limo pulled up in front of 7 Russell Hill Road, Walt was standing there, handsome in his tan summer suit, waiting to escort Ann-Marie and me to the garden. Chi had taken care of the long red carpet, the music, and the flowers. He had chosen simple white roses for the men's lapels and also for Ann-Marie and my bouquets. It was a classic, understated, but elegant choice. Nigel had asked him to arrange for a videographer, who was waiting there to video the two of us getting out of the limo, along with François, who would queue up the music for our walks up the aisle.

Ann-Marie had been right all along. Walt couldn't take his eyes off her in that blue dress. We walked up past the front door and queued up on the side lawn, with Ann-Marie slapping Walt's hands down every few steps. We were on the red carpet, but still out of sight of the groom, best man, and the Rabbi. They were standing under the big maple, where the Rabbi had used a little poetic license in tying the borrowed, pieced-together chuppa to the leafy branches that once held Nigel's tree house.

Ann-Marie would walk the aisle first to Mendelsong's *Wedding March*, until I appeared, where I would begin, adding in my two cents' worth with Anne Murray's *Could I Have This Dance, karaoke style.* Timing was everything. I fussed and fidgeted, but Ann-Marie assured me that she had timed it out a dozen times beforehand.

By then, Walt had tucked my gloved hand under his arm. François confidently clicked the remote control for the music, and Ann-Marie entered the backyard in perfect timing to the *Wedding March* and it gave me the confidence I needed to follow suit. I stepped out of the privacy and shade of the side yard into the afternoon sun to see our guests who were all standing in honor of the bride. There were Catharine and Edouard, Lyonel and Lucia, Kurt and Gretchen, Maureen and Ian, Opal and Colin, Phylis, Renee, and Donna. Fran and Verna were standing on each side of Brad and Madison, along with Farahnaz and Siavash, and Parto beside her husband, Farshod. There was a very tall, stunning black woman, with three other people that were Nigel's guests from L.A. that I hadn't met yet. 'Quite a global mix,' I thought to myself. It was hard to differentiate the religions represented, as all the men had kippas on, but Vietnam, Israel, Iran, Hollywood, Jamaica, France, Canada, city folks and country folks, black, white, Asian, gay and straight, educated and not, all were there, smiling out at me. They all came together to wish a Canadian country girl and a Jamaican country boy the very best as they travelled through the rest of their lives together.

I turned my head to look forward toward the big old maple. There he stood – the love of my life. He was wearing a very pale tan suit, white shirt, white tie, white rose in the lapel, and the biggest smile I had ever seen. My eyes never left his face for the rest of the ceremony. I took a deep breath, listened to the background music of Anne Murray's classic, and sang my heart out:

I'll always remember, the song they were playing
The first time we danced, and I knew
As we swayed to the music, and held to each other
I fell in love with you
Could I have this dance, for the rest of my life?
Could you be my partner, every night?
When we're together, it feels so right
Could I have this dance for the rest of my life?

Rabbi Kleiman led the cheers, whistles, and clapping for my efforts as I reached the old maple. Ann-Marie took my bouquet from me. She whispered, "Good girl," as if I was performing in a Grade-Four Christmas concert.

I stood there in front of him, and he took both my hands in his, raising my one gloved hand to his lips as the music started up once again. His big baritone voice filled the garden. I'll never forget. He moved slightly side to side to the music in a simple one-step, and I followed. He sang out in his pure baritone, and love was all around us. He never missed a word and he never took his eyes away from mine as he sang his very own version of Ray Clarke's old song:

Come live with me and won't you be my love?
Share my bread and wine
Be wife to me, be life to me, be mine
Oh, come live with me and be my love
Let our dreams combine
Be great to me, be fate to me, be mine
With these hands I'll build a roof to shield your head
Yes, and with these hands
I'll carve the wood for our baby's bed
Oh, come live with me and be my love
So I can love you all the time
Be part of me, girl, be the heart of me, be mine.

He smiled a little as he sang *I'll build a roof* as if he was admitting that that particular skillset may be a little bit of a stretch, and I raised my eyebrows a little at his line and smiled out to the audience to let them in on his little joke. My handsome *chanteur* was stepping out of his shyness big-time to please his bride.

His voice became a little softer, and his finish was flawless as he ended on a humble askance with the last three lines of the song:

Oh, come live with me and won't you be my love?
Hey, hey, share my bread and wine
Be part of me, oh, be the heart of me, baby, please be mine.

As he ended his performance, there was just a slight moment of complete stunned silence. All of us were spellbound with Nigel's rendition of the old love song, and his big grin took over his whole face as our guests applauded him like he was Andrea Bocelli.

Nigel's dark brown eyes, still fixated to mine, squeezed my hands gently and gave me a little insider's wink as Rabbi Klieman boomed out, "This is the best wedding I have ever officiated. I think I'm out of a job, as these two lovebirds have just married themselves! I have never heard such beautiful vows in all my days! I suppose I should just make it all official however, with the standard phrases, only so I can say *you may kiss the bride* afterward. But first, I would like to thank you for taking part in our Jewish traditions here by wearing your kippas to show respect and awareness of God above." He pointed up as he continued, "Our chuppa above us symbolizes the home that the couple will build together. Will you all please leave your chairs and come up and stand with the bride and groom under their roof, as their family, embracing our love for each other and our journey together. Everyone, please hold hands to complete a full circle so we can join in with a prayer for our family that has departed before us, and for these two lovebirds in front of us."

Chi and François immediately organized everyone around us with much jostling and laughter under the chuppa, and as Nigel and I stood facing each other, each of us holding both hands, we tipped forward and shared a soft kiss. Someone from the crowd yelled, "*Get a room*," and Nigel threw back his head in laughter. He took me in his arms and dipped me back as he had done in the restaurant three short weeks ago. We were both laughing by the time he found my lips, and our teeth hit before we could get the kiss down pat. The Rabbi threw up his hands and shook his head back and forth, laughing along with everyone else.

Nigel and I repeated the Rabbi's traditional vows, and we exchanged our plain and narrow gold wedding rings with our friends and family circled tightly around us.

I looked up into my husband's handsome face as he gave a prayer of remembrance and thanks for the long-departed parents of the bride and groom. He started the prayer by stating their names – Lillian Duffus Dunbar and Harold Leitch, Mavis Royal and Saul Himmel.

He paid homage to Saul, telling us of the wise words that Saul had given him one day long ago when he was explaining that someday Nigel would be hunting for a partner in life, a wife. He said that when he did find his special girl, he was to 'love recklessly and love with abandon' for the rest of his days.

He also spoke of my great-grandfather, George Leitch, who had cherished and loved me unconditionally so long ago on the old family farm in Brown Hill and continued to do so, day after day, as he acted as my guardian angel that was still watching over me.

After that, everyone started clapping as my husband gave me a soft kiss on the lips. I turned around to be buried in the ample bosom of the sexy blue dress amidst many, many Mazel tovs joyously given and received under our chuppa in the beautiful backyard, with Nigel's big old maple tree standing guard over us all.

***

The champagne flowed. Several caterers offered us champagne, drinks, and fancy canapés that would tide us over until we got back to the Four Seasons for the 7:00 p.m. dinner and dancing. Chi had done a magnificent job of arranging everything. There was a small mat with a microphone, although it wasn't really needed for such a small gathering, and Chi acted as a casual emcee, asking everyone to step up and tell the story on how they met the bride or the groom. He introduced himself first and said that Nigel was his best friend. He told us that Nigel had hired him over thirty years ago to take care of his parents, Saul and Mavis, along with a dog named 'Old Daisy,' and he had never looked back. He added simply, "We are family."

He continued to introduce his son, explaining that he was also Nigel's godson, François, who was a lawyer today, all because of Nigel's love and generosity since the day he was born. He then introduced Nigel's brother, Brad, and told of all the years of secret airport pickups in the blacked-out Benz. He explained that Nigel had met Brad many years ago through business and that they had been together ever since through thick and thin. Madison, Nigel's nephew, was next, with Chi saying it wasn't so long ago he was changing his diapers and that Madison was his second son.

Madison called out, "Uncle Chi, for God's sake, too much information! I'm eighteen years old! But you're right in one department; we're family for sure!"

Chi also told the story of being hosted by Ann-Marie and Walt during our road trip down to Marlbank and of the magic of my old farm. He told us that Ann-Marie and Walt were warm, welcoming Canadians that were just like the Canadians he met when he arrived in northern Québec, fresh from the roll call of the Vietnamese boat people back in the seventies.

Nigel stepped up after Chi, and he said, "How'd I get so lucky? How'd I get so damn lucky? I'm so grateful you all are here with Denni and me to celebrate our marriage today. Like my wife always says, *pinch me.* Thank you from the bottom of my heart for being here. I hope you all got settled in at the hotel. I'm looking forward to our dinner tonight at seven in their main dining room, and the dancing afterward. And just to let you know, I'm a lousy dancer, so I need all you ladies to get up on the floor with me tonight to show me how it's done. We'll all have breakfast in the bridal suite together tomorrow

192

morning. And thank you, Chi, for being my best man. You really are, in fact, the best man. For over thirty years, you've always been there for me, and my parents before me. I don't tell you often enough how much I love you and how much I appreciate all you do for me."

He continued his speech by telling us the story of how he met his brother about twenty-five years ago when he was a young lawyer and Brad was a young actor working on location in Toronto. He said that they met and instantly became good friends. It wasn't long before they were like family and always called themselves brothers. He added, "Not as in a 'brother' from the hood; they both meant 'brother' as in family." In a very poignant moment, Nigel told us that after all his years, first as a black kid growing up in a Jewish neighborhood and then being a black lawyer in Toronto, he had only met two people in his whole life that were truly colorblind. His wife was one, and his brother was the other.

At this point, everyone was silent and Brad jumped out of his seat and cried out, "What!? You're black?"

As the expert Hollywood timing had everyone laughing, I watched my husband as he changed from his earnest, rather shy, and heartfelt self into a grinning, confident, handsome man with a funny story to tell.

"I'd like to share the story of how I met my wife," and he proceeded to tell our guests of when he first laid eyes on me and how I had head-butted him in the middle of the café just over a year ago. He told of going home and dreaming about Ms. Brunette, the unknown Irish faerie that had stolen his heart while breaking his jaw.

Everyone was laughing as he continued his story with his long arms flapping, describing the courtroom scene, how he dropped all his papers at the front of the court and was on his hands and knees in his robes, scrambling to pick up the papers. He told of hiding behind the witness box at floor level and peering out like a six-year-old would do, looking out from behind the box to see if Ms. Brunette's gray-eyed gaze could spot him. He finished that story by saying softly that it was his first foray into the world of love, and he had no idea what could possibly feel worse than this, but he was about to find out when he met the famous Gerri Green from Gerri's Gym in Los Angeles about four months later.

He continued to say that Gerri's lesson was even tougher than the mild little head-butt from Ms. Brunette.

He told the story of when his Ms. Brunette had disappeared. His brother had taken him under his wing and, trying to mend his broken heart, had booked him in for a six-week boxing boot camp at Gerri's Gym in Los Angeles. He told our wedding guests that he had been giving Gerri lip in the ring like a real idiot, which was all to do, of course, with the absent-due-to-a-misunderstanding Ms. Brunette. He motioned to Gerri to come up to the front to demonstrate on what went down on that fateful day in Gerri's Gym in L.A.

Gerri was such a good sport as she took her place beside Nigel. Her high heels made her taller than Nigel, so she laughingly kicked them off and started dancing and prancing around him like professional boxers do, with her big, beautiful shoulder muscles flexing in the sleeveless, scooped-neck, short summer dress she was wearing. She threw out little jabs as Nigel fake-blocked her moves while he threw a little comedic Muhammad Ali action into the scene. We were all laughing as he espoused Ali's famous line, "Float like a butterfly. Sting like a bee." Nigel was coaching Gerri and his audience along with his best nerdy, intellectual, nervous stance, "Now Gerri, when I fall down voluntarily, that is, I want you to put your foot on my gut and to tell our guests what advice you gave me. But pretending only, Ger, and don't hurt me! And don't knock off my kippa!"

Gerri was Hollywood right to the core. She continued dancing around him, back and forth, and when she faked a lightning-speed jab to his nose, Nigel fell straight back, lying on the grass with arms outstretched and legs splayed open.

She placed her bare foot on his gut, turned to the audience, and said loud and clear, "If you come for the king, you better not miss, asshole."

The howls of laughter that followed had Nigel's face all flushed and animated. He jumped up, holding his nerdy stance, adjusting his kippa by carefully reinserting the bobby pins one by one into his curls.

Nigel kissed Gerri's hand and said to us, "There are three other people here today that came with Gerri, and I am eternally grateful for their love and support that they gave me when I was such a lovelorn emotional wreck at the time. Thank you to Caroline, Gerri's wife, and then there's Joey who kept me safe and physically healthy, and the cook who took me under her wing and spoiled me with her good cooking."

The cook half-stood up from her seat and yelled out in her big voice, "That's my boy!" and everybody clapped to acknowledge Nigel's thank-you to the three of them.

Everyone said the Gerri-Nigel match was the best comedy they had ever seen and from then on, it was all jokes coming from the mike.

My three Jewish girlfriends, Phylis, Renee, and Donna all got up together to laugh about our patched-together chuppa hanging from the maple tree. They wanted to know if they could take it away with them to demonstrate to new couples on how not to hang a chuppa from a maple tree.

Fran and Verna, my girlfriends from my high school days, told of us thirteen-year-olds hiking up our skirts as soon as we were out of sight from our mothers, putting on lipstick and eye makeup in the girls' bathroom before the high-school dances. Verna added, "While our girlfriend Fran grew up as a good Catholic girl." She raised her eyebrows and threw up her hands and said, "Whatever that means." She said that she had grown up in the Anglican Church, like Denni, and that it was her first time under a chuppa.

Kurt was joined by Parto and Farahnaz to tell of our years and years of working together at the school, where we all taught a government-sponsored TESL program when we were all very single and lonely, as they looked over at their spouses.

Maureen, Catharine, and Edouard told of meeting me way back in the day in Vancouver and how happy they were that their globe-trotting girlfriend had finally met her match.

But out of all my guests, my heart belonged to the next couple at the mike. The pleasant-looking, middle-aged Frenchman and his trophy wife made their way up to the mike. "*Bonjour*, everyone. My name is Lyonel, and this is my wife, Lucia. We met Denni last year in Nice, France. That's where we live. Denni introduced us to Catharine and Edouard at that time as well."

Lucia added as she held Lyonel's hand, "My English is not as good as Lyonel's, so please excuse my mistakes."

Nigel called out in perfect French, "You are just perfect the way you are, exactly the way you are."

She beamed and continued in English with her delightful French accent. She put her delicate, manicured hand over her heart and murmured, "*Nous sommes très appy to be ear, to meet you, and to wisit your très beau ville. C'est la premiere vacance au Canada and c'est notre greatest pleasure to meet the love of Denni's life, Nigel... um... et... et... um... et bien sûr, all of you too.*"

I was so proud of her, and Nigel immediately planted kisses on both of her cheeks, along with Lyonel's, in true French style. She played the femme fatale to the limit and demurely took her husband's hand to take their seats among the cheering and clapping for her brave second-language speech.

Brad and Madison stood before the mike, and I knew I would have to answer to my girlfriends as soon as the party broke up. I had never mentioned to anyone that Nigel had a famous brother over the last year, so they had had no idea whatsoever of our guest list that I had described as being just family and a handful friends.

How times had changed for all of us, and for the better!

Brad said, with his arm around Madison's shoulders, "Hi, everyone. I'm dying to introduce this wonderful young man standing here beside me. May I present my son, Madison? And I want to say thank you, Denni, from the bottom of our hearts, for coming into Nigel's life. From the moment I met you, way back last year, I knew that you were the girl for Nigel. But there is one bone of contention that I would like to settle, regarding my good-looking, charming, and brainy brother. As we all know, Nigel is one of Canada's most brilliant minds and has served his country wholeheartedly over all the years, but really, today, for the first time, I doubt his abilities in one certain department. When he was up there in front of us, singing his vows to his girl and showing off big-time under the chuppa, we all heard him sing the words *with these hands I'll build a roof.* For God's sake, that man has never held a hammer in his whole life! He gets a weekly manicure! Look at him. He's got the hands of a princess! And really, if he did build the roof, just take a good look at that sad and sorry-looking chuppa. It's about to come down at any minute!"

There was a lot of clapping, and someone yelled out, "Let's see the manicure!" And Nigel stood up and displayed his hands for everyone to see as Brad continued, "But I must admit, he can go toe-to-toe with Levi Stubbs or Andrea Bocelli any day of the week. Good job, bro. I love you." He put his hand over his heart and looked at me. "Denni, we love you too. Welcome to the family."

Madison motioned to Chi and François to come up to the front to join him and his dad. Madison said, "Okay, this is a little better. We're not all here today, but now Dad, me, Uncle Chi, and my cousin François are all speaking for Mom and my brothers and sisters too, you know, the whole family."

The four handsome men stood there, arms around each other's shoulders, all looking down at me and shouting in unison, "Welcome to the family!"

Ann-Marie shouted out, "I've never seen Denni this quiet in my whole life! Get up there, girl. We want to hear from you."

With everyone clapping, Nigel gracefully took my hand and led me to the mike. He just stood there, holding my hand, looking down at me, grinning from ear to ear, and he said humbly, "Ladies and gentlemen, may I present my wife?"

I reached up to kiss him. "Thank you, Levi Stubbs." I faced my family and friends, all gathered together with the big, old maple throwing shade over the big, beautiful backyard. "This is the first time I can remember not really being able to say anything. Anything at all. I'm too busy just feeling. I just want to soak it all in. All the love here today among us all. Family, old friends, and new friends. The love is all around us. It's almost palpable. I can feel it deep down. Can you feel it? I want that for all of you too. I love you. We love you. And thank you for all your love over all the years and all your love to come."

Chi was right on cue as usual, and he had lined up all my favorite Motown tunes that boomed over the backyard as Nigel grabbed me around the waist and started dancing me all over the grass and bending me back to kiss my neck like a crazy teenager on a first date.

The caterers came into play with more drinks and canapés as Walt and Chi moved the chairs to the side of the garden so everyone could mingle.

Chi had arranged for the car service to take us all down to the hotel at five p.m. so that the guests could freshen up in their rooms before dinner at seven p.m. Nigel had spared no expense, and he had generously blocked off enough rooms all on one floor to accommodate all of us. Brad, like a lot of Hollywood people, liked to use the Four Seasons, as it was a trusted, discrete hotel that did not tolerate paparazzi in the least.

Nigel had asked the Four Seasons to sit our dinner party in a semi-private enclave, just off the dance floor, to ensure that his brother could enjoy their private family function away from the public for the evening.

We had arranged a set menu, starting with a big variety of appetizers served country-style. The big, tiered trays were placed along the table for everyone to help themselves, as we all got to know each other. The service was seamless, and by the time dessert was finished, we had all changed seats several times in order to get to know everyone a little better before the dancing.

The dining room featured a bluesy torch singer with a great backup band, and we were all up on the dance floor, trading dance partners like we had all known one another our whole lives. Brad chose to stay at the table, which afforded him privacy, and he was never without someone to talk to, but Madison asked every girl there to dance; I was so proud of his social skills. Nigel danced with every girl and I danced with every man.

Both Lyonel and Lucia taught, or tried to teach, everyone the meringue and the tango. The Muslims danced with the Jews, the singles danced with the marrieds, and Madison, Chi, François, and Nigel spoke French the whole night to accommodate Catharine, Edouard, Lyonel, and Lucia, more out of respect than out of need.

Renee was saying to Gerri, "This is Canada. Get up there and dance a nice, slow, sexy dance with your wife. Just be yourself!"

Joey had the cook up on the dance floor, and she was all about showing him the right way to do things. Walt was eager to learn how to say 'I love you' in French, and he couldn't keep his hands off of Ann-Marie, who, after a couple of glasses of champagne, leaned back and said, "What the hell! I may as well join the party." She found herself returning the roaming hands, which startled the hell out of Walt.

He asked himself, 'What the hell has gotten into her? She's hotter than a heifer in heat! This feels really good. I'm going to go to night school and learn how to speak French all the time.'

I was struck with an unusual thought as I watched Nigel float the cook around the dance floor. She almost looked like his mom up there. The cook was beaming like she was thinking the same thing, and Nigel had a soft, tender look on his face as he held her back gently. It was like I was seeing an apparition. 'I hope Nigel is feeling this like I am,' I thought to myself.

Nigel spent our dances whispering in my ear how much he loved me. I responded with, "I can't hear you, darling. Come a little closer and tell me again."

In the privacy of their suite later, much later, Walt got out of the big king-sized bed to put on his old, faded, well-worn undershirt that he liked to sleep in. He quietly padded back to bed, undershirt on top and bare-assed on the bottom, and slipped back under the covers. He spooned his girl and whispered, "*Je t'aime. Je t'aime.* I love you so much. I could just holler." He smiled as she responded with the soft snore of a party girl gone bust.

My husband's last words were not as up-country-expressive as Walt's, but they said volumes. "I love you. I love you all the way. Good night, Mrs. Royal."

"Good night, and I love you too, Levi Stubbs."

***

The next morning, Chi and François showed up for the breakfast with copies of the edited wedding video.

During our breakfast with all our guests in the big bridal suite, we played the video on the big flat-screen. Chi and François' hard work over the whole week before the wedding, tweaking and testing the three cameras, one located on a branch of the maple tree and another from the back of the house and one from the side garden fence plus the videographer who filmed all the speeches perfectly, paid off.

We were bawling out loud, with intermittent howls of laughter, as the love and sentiment of the special occasion poured out of the screen. Ann-Marie had a big smile on her face as Walt's big hand on her ass was spliced in throughout the film.

The very best was the clip of our friends and family holding hands underneath the chuppa when Nigel was raising my gloved hand to his lips.

I had nothing to say to our guests at the time, but trust me, I knew exactly how good I looked walking and singing for my man all the way up that long red carpet.

And with that video, the Gerri-Nigel match would live on forever and ever.

That little, exquisite love-fest video was our most treasured object that Nigel and I would play and replay again and again for years and years to come.

***

Chapter 10
Addendum: Musings in the Kitchen

Nigel stood at the door of his wife's office quietly, with his heart written all over his face. He drank her in slowly, savoring her from head to toe.

Her hair, the usual sexy, can't-keep-my-hands-out-of-it mess, half up and half down, with a clip of some sort holding the concoction all together, had a pencil piercing the top knot. She was wearing, hmm, he had never seen this before. What exactly was it? Oh, oh. A pair of old-fashioned flannel pajamas, similar to the ones he wore as a kid during his first few winters in Canada. Her new attire was a first for his La Perla princess. She was in her bare feet, with eyes on the screen, fingers nimbly working away on the keyboard. She stopped typing and turned around to meet his eyes.

"Hi, babe. Do you need something?"

"Yeah, you," he suggested.

She gave him a deadpan look. "Now really, Nigel, can't you see I'm working?"

He knew he wasn't going to win this one. "What's up, my darling?"

"I've got an idea for my novel. I've got to get it down on paper before I get distracted," and she added emphatically, "by my husband."

"Well, we don't want to interrupt the great novelist, do we? Can I get you anything?"

"Yeah, thanks, babe. Can you make me up a pitcher of iced tea?" I added, "You know, just the way I like it."

He walked over and leaned in close. He put his arms around her shoulders and nuzzled into her neck. "Yeah, I happen to know exactly how you like it."

Amidst her protesting, swatting, and half-laughing, he backed up across the room toward the door, dancing to the sixties' Motown songs that she always played in her office. "See, sugar, there's someone else that feels the same way I do."

"What are you talking about?"

"Your tunes, sugar, your tunes. *Mighty Good Lovin'* by The Miracles. They know the score." He continued his dance and asked her, "By the way, where on Earth did you get this anti-Perla getup?"

"Nordstrom's. What's it to you?"

He grinned at her childlike defense.

She went on, her face beginning to flush with her decidedly defensive response, "I mean, after all, if I am going to become a New York Times' bestseller author like you claim, I have to dress for comfort as I churn out the chapters all alone in my fancy new office that I slave away in. This is my turf, and this is how I work. End of discussion."

He burst out laughing and strode back into the room and pulled her up out of her chair. "You are so cute when you're mad. I love you. I love you, my very own fiery Mary, Queen of Scots."

By this time, a little chagrined with her bratty retort, she lifted her face for a quick, perfunctory kiss. "Are you dissing my illustrious ancestor?"

"I'd never do that!"

"You better not. However, just to let you know, Mr. Perfectly-dressed-for-every-occasion, my new flannel pjs are office-wear only, and will never ever darken the doorstep of our bedroom."

"Good to know," he whispered into her hair as he pulled the pencil out from the mess.

"You see what happens! I give you an inch, and you take a mile!" she exasperated as her hair took on a life of its own. She was trying her best to hold her smile back from him.

He pulled the door softly behind him and said to himself in wonderment, "*Hallelujah*, she is finally starting the book. Thank the good Lord for small mercies, as Ann-Marie would say."

As the kettle boiled to make the iced tea from scratch, just the way she liked it, he perched on the barstool and looked around him. Ever since she had moved in, the whole house had come alive somehow. He had carried all her old French copper pots and pans down from her apartment, and Chi had installed a proper black wrought-iron pot rack up and over the island for them, for easy access to their many cooking sessions. There were cookbooks on all the kitchen shelves and an ongoing grocery list on the fridge door. Yes, at times it looked a little topsy-turvy, but he had to remind himself that he was just an old judge that had lived alone his whole life, who liked things well documented and well organized. It wasn't that she wasn't organized. Hell, no, not at all. But every time she came into the room, he simply couldn't think straight. He decided it was simply her faerie dust that permeated everything around her.

He smiled thinking about just this morning when he came downstairs early. He had made himself a coffee and was sitting there in his favorite old Eames recliner when he noticed a small corner of blue peeking from under the sofa cushion. He got up and walked over for a closer inspection. He pulled. A dainty blue lace bra dangled from the tips of his fingers. Shaking his head, he had to admit that he was to blame for this one. The night before, he had ripped it off her in his haste to feel her nipples in his mouth after they had come in all sweaty from their walk. Oh my God, she was a handful. And he was one helluva lucky man.

His phone brought him out of his reverie. "Hi, Chi, what's up?"

"Hi, boss, just thinking here, I'd like to introduce Denni to your out-of-sight flight bags sometime soon, if that's okay with you. Hey, we have another person to think about now, so we have to make sure Denni understands our exit plan if the Canadian Witness Protection Program says we have to lay low or leave town."

"Oh! Yeah! I'd kind of forgotten about that. You know the old saying, 'Time flies when you're having a good time.' What do you think? Say, around 8:30 tonight once we get back from our walk? Does that work for you?"

"Absolutely. So, we'll meet up here, right?"

"Perfect. Thanks, Chi." He added playfully, "You da man."

"No! No! *YOU* da man!" Chi responded, laughing at his happily married boss who was trying his hardest to put aside the delicate balance of living under the radar so that he could enjoy his new station in life as a doting husband.

***

Chapter 11

On the Lam

Nigel grabbed my hand to slow down in the middle of our nightly huff-puff around the neighborhood.

"What's up, babe?"

"Chi asked if we could pop into his place tonight. He wants to show you what he has been working on as a part of his assignment."

"Oh. Oh, you mean that assignment."

"Yeah. Right after our walk. Okay with you?"

"Drats."

"Oh, oh. Are you too busy with your book and all?" Nigel asked in a concerned voice.

"Naw, I was just hoping for a re-run of what happened in the living room after last night's walk," I said.

"Don't you worry, baby. I'll collect a rain check as soon as the briefing is over." He was grinning from ear to ear as he loped ahead of me and I sped up to catch him.

Chi opened his door to greet us, and I was impressed as all get out when I stepped from the foyer into the living room. It was a large, square room with long, rectangular windows on both sides of the room and a cathedral-type ceiling above. Two beautiful Turkish rugs in dark oranges and reds covered the hardwood floors. There was a cream leather extra-long sofa, with two Danish modern armchairs facing a large, low, teak coffee table, with full-to-the-rafters bookshelves on the opposite side. A mid-century modern Danish dining room set was positioned at the other end.

"This must be your darling, Nuyen!" I exclaimed as I looked at the impressive oil painting's beautiful subject.

"That's my girl, alright!" he said lightly as he offered to show me the rest of the apartment.

"Oh, Nigel tells me you've started the book. How's it coming along, Denni? I have a little present for you. Now, now, don't get too excited. It cost me a whole seven bucks." He pulled a bright orange USB out of his pocket and put it in my hand. "Please, please, please, back up every day. Every single day, Denni. You never know when you need a copy."

I was a little taken aback by his caring gesture and said, "Why thank you, Chi. And yes, indeed, Nigel tells me the same thing. I will take care of it."

His kitchen, very sleek and very modern, was galley-style, with a small, round breakfast table and two chairs at the end of the long, narrow room. The back wall was all glass. It overlooked the two-story atrium greenhouse. I looked down over the railing to see the perfectly laid-out layers of gardens, some planters in soil, and a hydroponic section as well. I was impressed. Behind a solid pocket door that blended right in with the wall, a small, circular stairwell led from the kitchen down to the ground floor.

"May I get you something to drink?"

"No thanks, Chi. Not at all. But I do want to make a date with you so that you can show me around your greenhouse. This is my dream come true! You must love it! But right now, I understand that you want to show me something?"

"Yes, one moment please," he said as we moved back into the living room. He moved a chair away from in front the bookshelves. He clicked a remote.

One section of the bookshelves silently began to move toward us, then filed smoothly in front of the other section, and an opening appeared.

"Ladies first." Nigel smiled as we all stepped forward.

It looked like a command center. There were eight screens on the long work counter with a large, built-in cabinet at one end and a traditional-looking file cabinet at the other end. One screen showed the street, another showed our front door, and another the backyard, etc.

Chi opened the file drawer and took out a brown envelope. He handed it to me to open. The two Canadian passports bore our photos but under the names of Susan Brier and Noah Rosenberg. All of a sudden, I realized that this wasn't a little game of sorts. The gravity of the situation hit me with a wallop.

Chi had opened the cabinet door and placed two flight bags on the work counter. They were matching Louis Vuitton club bags, one in red leather and the other in black.

"These are your two emergency-only flight bags. Please take a look inside, yes, both of you."

Nigel handed me the red one. We both unzipped. We both pulled out a small toiletry case filled with toothbrush, paste, face cream, and shampoo, etc. Two black long-sleeve cotton tees, in our respective sizes, two pairs of black jeans, and two dark navy no-label wind jackets and ball caps, with non-descript, no-name phones lying on the bottom of each case.

As I picked up the cell, eyebrows raised in question, Chi explained, "These are what we call burner phones. You usually use them a few times and then get rid of them," he explained, "in deep water like the Pacific." He joked to break the seriousness of the information.

"We don't mean to alarm you, Denni, but it's Chi's job to keep an eye on us. These phones are programmed to keep track of the two of us. We need your help to complete the coding."

"I do have a question."

"What is it? Anything at all, Denni. What do you want to know?"

"Which one of you is 007?" My little joke wiped the worry off their faces, and Chi began to explain how I could help program the burner phones.

There were three locations programmed on the phones. Location 'A' was always Lester B. Pearson Airport, Location 'B,' was yet to be determined, and Location 'C' was always Toronto Police Headquarters.

"Here's where you come in, Denni. In the case of an emergency, and for our safety, we have to go uncover for a while. We need a very, very secure place to meet up, or to hide out, until the heat is off. A safe house. Anywhere in the world, but somewhere that no one else knows about. Can you think of anywhere, and anyone in the world, that you can trust our lives with, that either of us could arrive without questions asked? It seems that after being under surveillance for over five years, I'm kind of a sitting duck. Now, this may take you some time; we don't have to know right this minute, but please give it some thought."

"Oh, I don't have to keep you waiting. I know right now. I looked around and behind me. Can I tell you where and who?"

"Really," Chi said in a disbelieving tone. "Really. Where Nigel could go immediately on his own and there would be no questions asked."

"Yes, Chi, really. Trust me," I said, feeling a little annoyed at his tone. "Why don't we all sit down somewhere, and I'll tell you all about my two old extremely-trustworthy friends who happened to be family-friends with the late, great Pierre Elliott Trudeau way back in the day. They just happen to live in their big old ancestral fifteenth-century *château*, up in the mountains of Southwest France. That doesn't even have decent cellphone service. They were at our wedding. It's Catharine and Edouard De la Cour."

Nigel laughed out loud in delight. "I think she may be on to something, Chi. Let's hear her out." There was pride and respect written all over his smiling face.

I looked into Chi's embarrassed face and I added softly, "Chi, I can't tell you how much I appreciate you and all you do for Nigel, and now you've got me to worry about. Please know that it's not my intention to buck the system in any way. I'm on your team; whatever you tell me to do, I'll do it. However, when I can help, count me in." I leaned over and gave his arm a little squeeze.

Once we were settled back in the living room, Chi brought out a tray of mugs, a steaming pot of green tea, another pot of chai tea, a few biscuits, and real linen napkins. I was impressed.

I started my story with how and when I met Edouard and Catharine for the first time.

"The timeline must have been the mid-eighties, I guess, and I was living in Vancouver. I was working for Seaboard Lumber in an administrative capacity, and Edouard was working within the world of international banking, although if I remember correctly, he had passed the bar exam out at UBC as well. We had met through mutual friends, and Edouard and I really hit it off. It wasn't long before I was a regular third wheel with Edouard and the love of his life, Catharine, although they were quite a bit older than me. I was invited to their wedding, and that's how I know that Pierre Elliott Trudeau attended, with many other illustrious and well-known guests. I had no idea at the time that both Edouard and Catharine came from old money and aristocratic French families, but I gathered that there must be connections tied into the mix somewhere along the line."

I continued with my story, "We all moved on, and the next time I met them was years later, at my girlfriend's horse farm in Caledon, back in Ontario, quite by happenstance. Maureen was having a barbeque, and she invited her neighbors over. It was a total surprise for all of us when it turned out that the neighbors, Edouard and Catharine, were old friends of mine.

"About three or four years ago, when I was living in Naples, Florida, Maureen emailed me, saying that she was in France, visiting Edouard and Catharine, who had moved back home to France a few years prior. They all wanted me to come over and join in the party. I promptly hopped on the next plane, rented a car in Avignon, and headed to the mountains to see my old friends. I was very, very surprised when my rental car's navigation system urged me to turn up through the huge, black, wrought-iron gates. The *château* was breathtaking, along with the acres and acres of gardens, lawns, and streams that led to their adjoining farm and vineyards."

I continued on with the part where Nigel came into the story. "Not counting our wedding, the last time I saw Catharine, however, was not on such a happy occasion. She actually saved my life. It was just last year, and I was living in Nice, France. To make a long, sad story short, I had a complete nervous breakdown because I was missing you, Nigel. The psych ward found Catharine's name in my cellphone. She came to my rescue. She stayed with me in Nice for some time. She patched me up and got me back home to Canada."

I wrapped my story up with, "And then, to top it all off, with me in my fragile condition, a couple of weeks after I returned home, I went down to the Aroma Espresso Café and that's when we saw each other and had our famous big fight right in the middle of that all-too-public place."

The two men just sat there with their mouths open wide.

Nigel threw his head back, with both hands clenched into his hair. "Oh my God, my poor baby, my poor baby, I'm so sorry!"

Chi by this time was staring at his employer, with disappointment all over his face. "Nigel, Nigel, man, whatever happened here!?"

I walked over in front of Nigel, sat down on his lap, and put my arms around his neck. "I must admit that it does take two to tango. I'm not entirely the innocent party here; I was just a woman in love." I summarized the whole story with, "So, am I to understand that our government will consider the *château* as Location 'B?' And that they will ensure that Catharine and Edouard are compensated for their time and effort for each and every day that we stay there, if in fact we ever do?"

"Absolutely," Chi and Nigel chimed in.

And that was how the team decided on Location 'B.'

***

Later in the week, as we were reading our papers and sipping a morning coffee down at the café, I looked up from the style section to see my handsome husband watching me, his face solemn and thoughtful.

"Baby, I'm just thinking out loud here, but let me run this by you. I haven't been able to sleep ever since I found out about you being so sick in Nice, and all because of me. Do you think it would be okay if I phoned your good friend Catharine just to thank her for being there for you?"

"Actually, Nigel, I think that would be perfect! It would give you a chance to say hello after they were so kind to travel all the way here for our wedding. But first, let me assure you that she knows all about you. Well, not the Witness Protection Program, but she doesn't blame you for our breakup in the least. And that's because she knows me very, very well. She knows what makes me tick, and when I arrived on her doorstep eight months prior to my breakdown, she sat me down and told me to stop running away from intimacy before it really ruined my life." I sat back, smiling at his relief of finding a way to kiss it and make it all better.

I was a little concerned, however, about my husband. After the night at Chi's apartment, and Nigel's distress listening to the story of my breakdown, he took me to our big bed, and there was a definite change in our lovemaking. He treated me like I was a fragile invalid, and he held on to me for dear life the whole night long. And I didn't like it a bit. At the time, I thought to myself, 'Maybe, just maybe, it's just a one-off.'

Three days later, I was totally sick of this new turn of events in our otherwise robust sex life. I took matters into my own hands. It was late, just before bed, and I heard Nigel in the shower. I peeled my clothes off, marched into the ensuite, and joined him in the big shower.

"Oh, to what do I owe the pleasure, ma'am?" he laughed, delighted with my entrance.

As we soaped each other all over, I delivered the harsh wakeup call as best I could. "Nigel, I need to say this and I need you to hear me out," I complained. "Over the last few days, you have been making love to me like I am some fragile, Dresden china doll. Trust me, I won't break. I need you to stop this nonsense. Now. Right now." I stamped my foot down for effect. "I'm your girl, and you're my man." I softened my voice a little, stepped closer, and put my hands up on his chest. "Baby, I want you to love me like you mean it. You know, like you did in Paris in the shower that time."

He smiled down at me as if he was indulging a small child that was having a temper tantrum. He calmly lifted me up under my ass and pressed me up against the wall. As he was thrusting inside of me, he whispered into my ear, "You want it rough, baby? Is that what you want? Here's rough. Do you like it? Do you want more? I can do this all night long if I know that's what you want. Tell me when you've had enough. I'm your man and we're not leaving this shower until you cry, "Uncle.""

***

I can honestly say that we were the most deliriously happily married couple on the whole planet. Nigel was an early riser, and I would wake to feel his arms circle me with his lips on the back of my neck. Our morning sex was always quiet, slow, and easy, just the way he liked it. I would lie in bed afterward, all sleepy and happy, listening to him half-whistling and half-singing in the shower, getting ready to start his day before I would doze off for an extra hour. Our weekday mornings were spent apart, with Nigel up early to work on his book in Saul's office or going downtown to his court office or to the gym. I would make a quick breakfast for myself later and head up to my office. That was my carved-out and written-in-stone writing time. Once in my flannel pajamas, time would just fly by. My writing flourished, and I had a few projects on the go. I had settled on a publisher, and I finally could call myself an author. Nigel and I would meet up down in the kitchen at noon, ready for the day ahead of us.

"Nigel, do you realize we are becoming hermits? I love being with you all the time, but I think it's time we started entertaining so my friends don't think I've run off to some foreign land once again. We have such a happy life, and have such a beautiful home, so we should take care of our friendships as well."

So, we made a point of having friends in for dinner once a week, usually on a Sunday, and it wasn't long before we were accepting invitations in return. Some days, we would go over to Kensington Market or down to St. Lawrence Market to buy some new kind of cheese or fish or certain ingredients for a special dinner we were making. I seemed to be always raiding Chi's greenhouse for the fresh vegies that he encouraged whole-heartedly.

One afternoon, Nigel said, "I have a surprise for you this afternoon, Mrs. Royal."

"Give me a hint. When and where?"

"Right now. Upstairs. Right upstairs. In the attic."

"This is beginning to sound a little Hitchcockian. Should I be afraid?"

"It is somewhat of a mystery, even to me. Come on. Let's go."

I held the flashlight until he found the light switch. The eves were filled with all of Saul's furniture that Nigel simply hadn't had the heart to get rid of when he renovated the big house before moving back in, in the late eighties.

"If you'd like to use any of this furniture, I'll get Chi to help me bring it down. There are a few nice mid-century pieces that you may like to mix in downstairs. The rest we can donate. And I know you love nice linens and china, and those two armoires are full of Mrs. Himmel's china, silver, and table linens. Oh, I think there's a chest of linens too. I remember as a kid, Mama was always washing and ironing all the fancy linens. I used to help her polish the silver."

That evening, as I ran back and forth to the laundry room to put in another load of the beautiful table linens, Nigel helped me clean the sterling. He told me many little tidbits and stories from his childhood and we laughed over his mama's stern admonishing of what would happen to him if she couldn't see her face in every spoon polished.

The next afternoon, I announced to Nigel that we were dressing for dinner that evening and that I was about to prepare a big gourmet meal for the occasion. I suggested that he wear a jacket and tie.

"What's the occasion, Mrs. Royal?"

"We're celebrating our new linens, along with the twelve place settings of sterling that we've inherited from Mrs. Himmel."

"Whatever you say, honey. If you're cooking, I'm doing the washing up. Deal?"

***

I smiled as I caught a glimpse of myself in the big hallway mirror. I looked like a happy, somewhat pretty, forty-something wife who had dressed up for her husband. I was wearing a longer, ankle-length full skirt that was made up of meters and meters of fine turquoise silk that was gathered into a wide waistband and topped with a white cotton shirt. I wore the shirt with sleeves rolled up, unbuttoned down to the skirt's wide cummerbund, and of course, sans bra. I had put on my old pink ballet slippers so I wouldn't be clattering around as I served all the courses.

The dining room was in darkness, except for the candlelight, and I switched the jazz station over to *music for lovers*. After the chocolate mousse dessert, I brought in a cheeseboard to finish the meal Euro-style. "Honey," I said, "can you change chairs for me? Here, please. Sit here. This chair is exactly what you need for this final course. You have to forfeit your armchair for this side chair so that I can serve you this cheeseboard properly."

"Whatever you want, sugar. I have a feeling there is yet another scattering of faerie dust to descend over me."

I straddled him and lifted the full turquoise skirt to fall over his knees. I began to ply him, a little bite and then a little sip as I licked the wine from his mouth in between servings. I kept it slow and easy, just the way I knew he liked it.

"Brie?" he queried.

"Could be the right country, but definitely the wrong cheese," I hinted.

"Ah, French Camembert."

"Good boy," I smiled.

I whispered into his mouth, "Guess where I went the other day."

"I'm way, way beyond guessing. Tell me, baby, where did you go the other day?"

"I went to that sex shop down in Yorkville called Lovecraft."

"And tell me, what did you buy?"

"I bought some new panties. And they don't have a crotch."

"How did I get so lucky!? How did I get so damn lucky!?" he whispered as his hands left my ass from beneath the layers of skirt to unzip his trousers.

With the heels of my ballet slippers firmly on the ground, I proceeded to demi-plié. I pumped him until he cried out with pleasure, and all this with his impeccable Windsor knot still in perfect order.

I'm sure Mrs. Himmel would have been rolling in her grave if she could have witnessed me, during the aftermath, gently wiping my husband and myself with her exquisite linen napkins.

***

From that day forward, I spent time every afternoon dressing the dining room table for dinner. There was no sense in saving the sterling and the good china for a special occasion. I used it all every day for breakfast, lunch, and dinner. Pinch me. Just pinch me.

I convinced Nigel to send his ancestry.ca kit in, just so we could follow his heritage along, the same as I had done a few years earlier. It was a year ago now that I had spent those months up in Edinburgh, completing my research of that part of my family roots. Nigel had developed a keen interest in my little project, and on many nights, we would get out my long and complex 'family tree' to connect all the dots.

He especially loved the story of one of my ancestral grandmothers who was born in Edinburgh. I had found her in the City Census Records, in the mid-1700s, listed as a fifteen-year-old girl, working as kitchen help in Edinburgh Castle. I followed her through forty years of the census, where I found her to be listed as still working in Edinburgh Castle, at age fifty-five, but not in the kitchen. The tough Scot, mother of five, had risen through the ranks and was documented in Scotland's census as being one of Edinburgh Castle's dressmakers.

"That's where I get my love of all the fabrics, the silks, the velvets, the linens," I would enthuse, and he would sidle up even closer to me, telling me how beautiful I was.

I told him the story of my very rich and very powerful family that owned Dunbar Castle and where Mary, Queen of Scots, who was one of my ancestors back in the 1500s, had an apartment. I really exaggerated all their wealth and told him, "Oh, take a look at the magnificence of it all. Look at my photos of my very own Dunbar Castle."

When I brought out the photos of the burned-down eleventh-century pile of rock and rubble, with trees growing out of the burned-out chimneys, he laughed so hard that he fell off his chair. He put his arms around me and teased me, "So that's where you get your fire. Mary, Queen of Scots, you say!"

"Don't mess with me."

Fall turned the leaves, and I was forging ahead with my second novel. Nigel was just too happy to cater to me and my work hours, up in my tastefully appointed office, all the while dressed, of course, in my flannel pjs. Through it all, I must admit, I think Nigel was secretly relieved that I stuck with my resolution to keep the flannels within the confines of my office. La Perla still reigned in the bedroom.

He was a little behind me in writing his memoirs though, and occasionally I would hear him on the phone, trying to placate the eager publisher while he was asking for yet another extension.

We were so into our own little bubble; we rarely left the neighborhood. We read each other's books and had some great discussions on how I was right and he was wrong on certain premises. I had no interest in delving into his shelves and shelves of law books housed in Saul's office, but I had brought in my books from my old apartment, and he had a good selection of his own that we both picked from. I was delighted when he said his favorite book of all times was actually one of mine as well. Two Solitudes, written back in 1945 by Hugh MacLennan, told a generational story of both French and English Canadians living in Quebec. Where Nigel honed in on the law side of things between the French and the English, I honed in on the cultural differences caused by the Catholic Church and the state-butting heads. Both of us had lost our copies long ago, and I made a mental note to try to find a copy on *E-bay* or somewhere to surprise him one day.

He must have been thinking on the same track, as one morning, FedEx delivered a small parcel for Nigel. I signed for it and left it in Saul's office. That night, over dinner, he brought the parcel out for me to open. It was a copy of Stefan Zweig's *Mary Queen of Scots* that he thought I may like to read, since after all, the infamous ruler of Scotland, Mary Stuart, was family and all.

I remember pouring my heart out to him one night over dinner about reading The Blue Castle, by L. M. Montgomery, back in the day when I was a girl. The old book was about a girl living around 1915 in a very small town up in northern Ontario, in Muskoka, I believed. Exactly like me, a country girl, or sort of, I reminded him. I suppose I was a little too invested in the story, as I passionately described the plight of the poor, orphaned-early, innocent country girl meeting up with a bad boy with a mysterious past and going to live with him in his lean-to shack in the middle of the Muskoka bush, all to her family's horror. By the time I came up for breath, I looked up to see that he was sporting a huge grin. I got the impression that he was making fun of me. I wanted to wipe that large dose of hubris right off his smug face, and I set him up perfectly.

"Are you mocking L.M. Montgomery, one of Canada's greatest literary talents?"

"No, not at all. I was just…"

"Exactly whom, then, were you mocking?"

Ha! The big-time lawyer had fallen into the novice prosecutor's little trap. I stood up from our dinner table, took our two wine glasses from the table, and marched them into the kitchen. I ceremoniously dumped them down the kitchen sink. I stormed off to my office to make sure that he didn't have the chance to explain himself further.

Later, he pleaded with me to come out on our walk that night. He walked it alone, as I furiously busied myself with laundry that really didn't need to be done. To hell with him! I'd show him that he'd miss his water when his well ran dry!

As it turned out, he was crafty enough to get into our bed first, and I certainly wasn't going to give him the satisfaction of me giving up my side of the bed. In no way was I going to be the one sleeping in the guestroom. I remember waking up in the middle of the night, only to find that in my sleep I had turned, and I lay facing him.

He was lying there, awake, just watching me quietly. There was so much love in his eyes that whatever I was so mad about earlier dissipated into thin air. I moved in a little closer and offered the first of several small, tentative, makeup kisses.

"I have only loved you more than I do right now at one other time," he whispered.

"What other time?" I whispered back.

"That day when we were sitting on the ramparts of your old farmhouse down in Marlbank, after you had read out your Robert Frost poem to me. We were just by ourselves, looking over the back fields, and I called you my Irish faerie."

"You loved me back then? Now really, Nigel, you hardly knew me."

"You're right there, honey. And now I know you a whole lot better. But at the time, it was your sweetness that got to me. Once in a while, your poetic Irish soul peeks through your Mary, Queen of Scots, exterior. It's like you're peeled down to your core, and it's really you in front of me. I love you for this ephemeral sweetness more than anything. And that day down on the farm, you were so earnest and so invested from way down in your heart. It was your purest energy. But wait. Wait a minute. I do remember that it was then that I saw your imperfection."

"Imperfection? What do you mean imperfection?"

"Your eyes. Your large, perfectly round eyes. Did you know that the left iris is ringed, with more gray-green flecks than the right? Yes, the right is definitely blue-gray while the left filters through to green."

"You are such a nerd. Too nerdy for your own good. I suppose you have jotted that down in your famous little notebooks, haven't you? If you must know, my paternal grandma had one green eye and one hazel eye. And she was perfect, so I'm just going to forget you ever said that. It's ridiculous. I'm perfect and you know it."

He laughed softly and said, "No, no, honey, let's be totally honest here. You are simply a capricious and spoiled little girl, and I enjoy spoiling you morning, noon, and night. For instance, just last week, when you were stamping your feet in the shower, demanding that I service you the way a stallion services a mare down on the farm. You are a handful, my darling, and I'm just the man to keep you in line."

He continued with an afterthought, "Actually, I must admit, though, that it was you who taught me how to be the man to keep you in line."

"What do you mean?"

"What I mean to say is that when we first made love in Paris, everything including you and the lovemaking – it was all so new to me, on top of me being so shy. I had never felt a woman's inner thighs tremble like yours did when I was kissing your tummy during that very first time for us. I was so in awe of you. You were magnificent. I forgot my shyness for the moment and you made me feel like a real man. And yes, I admit, a few seconds ago, I was teasing you a little about your sexy needs in our big shower, but honey, I never dreamed in my whole life of the sex life that we have, and it's all because of you. To tell you the truth, you simply thrill me just by being you. You thrill me through and through."

I smiled a little and said, "I *thrill* you?"

"Yes, you thrill me."

"Oh!" I said softly as I moved in a little closer.

He continued, "Since we're talking honestly, there is one time every day that I look forward to so much that I find myself daydreaming about it constantly."

"When's that?"

He whispered, "Well, this particular time each day is so selfish of me. I hesitate to tell you. I'm afraid the Gods will punish me and it will all disappear."

"Oh, you mean when you have the mornings to yourself? Why didn't you say earlier? I can occupy myself for the afternoons."

"No, not at all. It all takes place before you wake up. I look over at you and I need you so much. You're all sleepy and warm and it's that sweetness I'm talking about. I feel so selfish and it's simply a basic sex urge, baby. It's all about me. I don't care if you aren't fully awake. All I know is that I have a terrific erection and I just need to have you, right then and right there. And your skin smells so good. It's that same sweetness that I see short, fleeting glimpses of when you are concentrating on a recipe or reading one of your many books."

He pulled back a little and smiled into my face. "For instance, I know that your favorite book takes place in the early 1920s, where a young, virginal girl is about to get laid by a mysterious man who lives in the bush. Not that I think that's amusing or anything. Just sayin'."

"You are a very bad boy," I said into his mouth as I inched a little closer toward him.

"I'm willing to do penance."

"So, tell me what you think your appropriate punishment should be, and I will consider it."

"Okay, okay, fair enough. I humbly ask you to consider this. First, I'm going to wet your soft, bikini-waxed vaginal lips with my mouth, and then I'm going to fill you up, slow and tight. I'm going to rock your world all night long, baby, just the way you like it. The neighbors are going to hear your girlish pleasure all the way over to Heath Street."

"Sentencing to start immediately, with no chance of early patrol."

***

We spent many evenings sifting through all my old cookbooks that we had lugged down the street from my old apartment, picking recipes to follow for an upcoming meal or to make for company on the following Sunday. We would try to match the recipes to what was ready for us to pick in Chi's greenhouse. We were happy to make dinner for just the two of us at home, where Nigel, forever the consummate professional, would carefully wrap a clean, white restaurant-kitchen-staff cotton towel around his slim waist as I stood there in my bare feet, flour dusting down my tee-shirt, with my big, emerald-cut yellow diamond firmly on my ring finger.

We ran the gamut from the sensible plant-based winter Buddha bowls to using thick cream and egg yolks that was called for in *Mastering the Art of French Cooking*, Volume Two, Page Nine, for Julia Child's *Potage A La Florentine*.

We would stand side by side over the big white and gray marble kitchen island, me dashing and picking from cupboard to cupboard, and him methodically jotting down his notes in the secondhand gift that I gave him. It was a Julia Child's cooking notebook that I had picked up but never used, and he loved it. We made that famous cook proud, with our nitpickery that described the small nuance that the pinch of cardamom made in the classic French tart that we had baked the day before.

I smiled as I re-read his note on the cardamom that he had written down at the time: *It is only meant to be a hint. An aside. An innuendo. If it is the real thing, it should be plenty.*

We would debate the pear-almond tarts or the *crème brûlée*, or any of the classics, completely engrossed in the culinary tasks in front of us. He would set the oven's timer in orderly fashion, just like a judge would work while he keeps order in the courtroom. This judge had left his judicial robes behind him and had switched over to a simple kitchen apron in its place.

Although I teased him constantly about his nerdiness, I loved him fiercely for it and found myself deferring to his suggestions without the long, drawn-out back-and-forth that I would have posed a short three months ago.

I broke our concentration with a fresh idea, "Let's phone Ann-Marie and Walt and convince them to come up for a couple of days so we can take them downtown to see the beleaguered Toronto Maple Leafs in live action," as I continued to sprinkle the flour out over the marble island top to roll out the dough.

"Oh, honey, I'm not sure about having them stay in the guestroom. Do you think it's comfortable enough for them? Do you think we should just book them into the Four Seasons like we did for the wedding?"

"Nigel, listen to yourself. You are just being shy about sharing your home with someone. We both know how that goes. Trust me. We all need to be together so you'll have a good time. Just forget about them for the moment. I know you. Just be yourself. Please just enjoy yourself and don't worry. And I know Walt and Ann-Marie. They don't need the fancy Four Seasons. They're both happy with a roast in the oven and cold beer in the fridge. We'll play cards after dinner. And besides, that's how we live, isn't it? I don't want to be showing off with a fancy hotel room. Ann-Marie would see right through me."

"Yeah. You're right. I'm just not used to overnight guests, except for Brad and the kids, but I do love it when we have friends in for dinner. Okay, I'll pick up tickets for the hockey game. Where do you want to go for dinner after the game?"

"Let's take them to old Chinatown. You know, Dundas Street's style. We'll have Chinese. That's something they probably don't get too much down in Marlbank. And maybe the next day we could take them to the old Eaton Center for a little shop and then book in at the Elmwood for lunch and we'll all have the couples' massage treatment. That would definitely be something different for them. Would that be okay with you? Oh, by the way, this little plan is my treat. Yours, or Walt's, or Ann-Marie's money is no good here, understand?"

Nigel was smiling as he stepped away from the island, arms down by his side, with fingers outstretched and said, "Yes, boss. I understand completely. Walt and Ann-Marie are sleeping in our guestroom. You've got it under control. You're paying for everything, but I'm to get the hockey tickets, right?"

"Oh no, wait. Change of plans. Let's include Chi. We'll get him to choose his favorite Vietnamese restaurant. They love Chi, of course, and it will be fun." I put my arms around his neck. "That's why I love you so much. You spoil me, and yes, I know I can be a bit of a brat at times. I do promise that while we have the houseguests here, I will keep my lovemaking sounds down to a dull roar."

"Don't you dare," he said as he placed his well-floured hands on my ass.

I didn't catch on quick enough, and as I jumped back to run to the full-length mirror in the hallway, he was laughing as he watched my hand-printed ass sprint away. He was always one step ahead of me.

***

I realized one day that I hadn't been up to collect my mail at my old apartment for weeks. I hadn't even thought of it. I grabbed my old keys out of the kitchen drawer and found Nigel in Saul's old office.

"Wanna come with me? Just running up to my old apartment to check for mail."

"Sure, give me a minute. Meet you at the door."

While Nigel stopped in the lobby to speak to one of my old neighbors, I walked into the mailroom. I retrieved my mail and opened an envelope from the management company. It was a notice that my lease was ready for renewal. I tucked it away in my pocket and knew that it was time to let it go. I realized that my real home was with my husband at 7 Russell Hill Road. What had taken me so long?

The second piece of mail had a return address on it that really gave me pause. My time for being secretive had run out. The letter was from Frank Miosi, from Queens, New York, USA.

217

I thought back to the day that Nigel and I had our big fight in the café that led to my demand that he loved me all the way. Nigel had followed through with his promise without a hitch, but me, oh no, I was still holding back just like I had with all my relationships with men for as long as I remembered.

I had never come exactly clean with Nigel about my breakdown in Nice, France. I had told him that Catharine had done all the heavy lifting with getting me back on my feet, but really, it was mostly Frank, my handsome, tormented, good, good friend, the PTSD-suffering vet and ex-cop from Queens, New York, who saw me through to the bitter end in the psych ward.

At least I had the sense of decency to feel a little anxious. I was a piece of work. Not coming clean to Nigel before now made this more difficult than it had to be. Shit, shit, shit. I opened the letter and steeled myself against the words that I knew I had to share with my husband.

Dear Denni,

I hope my letter finds you well and happy to be home once again. I got your address from Catharine.

I'm writing to tell you that I owe my whole new, healthy life to you, and I want to thank you sincerely for all your true friendship that you shared with me after we met in FSL class. Your kindness and your good listening skills when I was really sick with my PTSD actually kept me alive, though I know now that I was simply the walking dead. That was just a shell of me, and I'm sorry that you had to see me like that. I apologize for all the booze and drugs and hurt that I caused you.

After you crashed and burned, and Catharine came onto the scene, I realized that I was nothing but a tortoise, you know, a hard-outer shell with soft innards. I checked myself into the psych ward fulltime, and within a couple of months of excellent psychiatric treatment, coupled with being clean and sober, I was well enough to go back home to Queens to Maria. My sickness had put my wife through hell and back, yet she was there with open arms as soon as I was well enough to contact her.

I'm so happy to tell you that we're expecting our first baby in the spring. I'm back at work, but I'm not on the beat. I have a desk job at my old precinct, and I'm loving it. Of course, I have a great shrink that I see every week.

In closing, I know that perhaps you don't want to hear this, Denni, but I've learned that clear communication is necessary between friends and family. If you haven't already found Nigel, and if you can possibly bring yourself to do it, get out there and find him. Just start looking for him, hunt him down, and don't give up until you find him. Love him like there's no tomorrow. You deserve it. He'd be the luckiest man alive, in Canada that is. I've got the USA covered!

Love, Frank

PS: Hello, Denni? This is Maria, Frank's wife. Thank you, and thanks to Catharine too, for taking care of and getting my husband back to me in one piece. I will say a prayer for your happiness every day until I die. Not that I'm dying! I'm having our baby!

Love, Maria

We walked back, holding hands. I was silent and Nigel was whistling as usual. He got to the door, and while unlocking it, he looked at me and said quietly, "What's up, baby?"

"My lease is due. I'm not going to renew it."

With a huge yahoo, he lifted me up and carried me over the threshold, all the while teasing me that I had gained weight.

"Welcome home, Mrs. Royal!" he whispered in my ear.

Over dinner, I said, "Nigel, I got mail today from an old friend in Nice, France. I want you to read the letter, and then I'm going to fill in the blanks on what really happened to me after we came home from Paris."

I handed him the letter. "Please, you read it out to me so I can hear his voice talking."

"*His* voice?"

"Yes, his name is Frank. And he was the person that got me admitted to the psych ward, not Catharine. I know I wouldn't be alive today if it wasn't for Frank Miosi. Out loud, please, read it out loud. Actually, it's such good news that I want to hear it out loud."

Nigel read the letter out loud and then folded it back onto its crease-lines and pushed it back over to my side of the table.

"Now it's your turn to read, but just the words between the lines, if you know what I mean. Tell me the whole story, the real story," Nigel said quietly, showing no emotion whatsoever on his face. "I've been waiting for this conversation ever since I met you. We are exactly alike. We deserve each other. All the secrets, the half-truths, the sweeping-it-under-the-carpet. All because of deep-down trust issues. On both sides. I now feel the brunt of your secrecy. Like I've been used, just the same as you did when I showed you the photos of you and your friend Kurt. I understand completely that you haven't exactly lied to me; you just decided to be secretive about yet another part of

219

your life. I'm just facing the fact that I'm married to you and I really don't know anything about large chunks of your life."

He leaned over the table a little and said, "Just remember, Denise, as a judge, I've heard it all. To quote Dr. Martin Luther King Jr., *'There comes a time when silence is betrayal.'* Do you understand me? I know very well when a piece of key evidence shows up out of the blue that tweaks a situation to one side or the other. And this letter takes the cake. It gets you off the hook handily, I must say, with even a note from the missus included. Not that the actual deed itself even deserves an explanation. It doesn't. You were a single, grown, independent woman. It's not the act that will kill you. Oh no, not you, darling. It's your own shame and trying to bury the body that will get you in the end. Do you understand what I'm trying to say here? Please know before you start your story that I'm not easy. I can't be had. When you finish, no matter what you tell me, I'll know the truth."

As he looked at my serious, sorry face, he relented a little. He smiled and said softly, "Please tell me, Mrs. Royal, you're not married to this Mr. Frank Miosi, are you?"

That was the moment I started acting like the wife that my husband deserved. When I had heard him say that it was my shame and trying to bury the body that would kill me, a light went on. He was exactly right. I simply grew up. I faced the music and spilled my guts. For a whole year, I couldn't even think of Edinburgh, my shame had been so overwhelming. I hadn't told a soul of what happened, until this very moment.

So, that night, sitting at our dining room table amongst Mrs. Himmel's pristine Irish linens and good china, I became a responsible human being by starting my story with the gritty details of my eight weeks of boozing and carousing in Edinburgh. I spared no details of how I woke up in Jimmy Somebody's bed and I didn't even know how I got there. I told him of my terror as my hands patted the blankets down to see if my clothes were still on. I told Nigel that my long-term bed-and-breakfast landlady, Mrs. McIntyre thought at first that I was a nice lass. Then she thought I was a lass who was in trouble with the drink. It ended up with her thinking I was nothing but a common whore. I described how Mrs. McIntyre had packed my bags and booted my ass out of her door. I also told him that I was still half-drunk as I got on the first train that was leaving Scotland. My ticket read that I was headed for London and I didn't have the slightest inkling as to where I was going next.

"So that means you don't want to tour Edinburgh on our belated honeymoon, Mrs. Royal?"

"Very funny. Do you want to hear my story or not?"

I was still talking hours later, long after we had switched from the red for me and the white for him to decaf for both of us.

I told him that I arrived in London, walked the city day in and day out, sobered up, forgave myself, let me family go, and decided that I would go on to Nice to start fresh once again. Yes, I would settle down, take some French classes, and start to write a book. Then, on the first day in FSL class, I sat behind a quiet, nice, handsome man who seemed to be around forty-five years old. His name was Frank. Frank Miosi.

"What is FSL class?"

"French as a second language. Like our ESL here in Canada."

"Got it. So, you met Frank. Maria's husband," Nigel smiled.

"Let's save the comments until the end, shall we? You're going to feel like an idiot when I tell you why I sat behind him."

"Okay, so I bite, honey. Why did you sit behind Frank?"

"Because he was lanky. Like you. His arm span was exactly the same as yours. His lean back underneath his tee-shirt looked exactly like yours. He stretched his long legs out in the aisle, and he had size-thirteen shoes just like you. I would just sit there and pretend that it was you. If I leaned forward, sometimes I could smell his Yardley's Old Spice." I shook my head and offered a question, more to myself than Nigel, "How is it that in the whole wide world, I had to run into the two only men that still wear Yardley's Old Spice?"

Nigel smiled a little and said, "Just lucky, I guess. But please, may I ask, was he a black man?"

I looked at him and hesitated before I answered. 'Oh no, no,' I thought. I never would have guessed that Nigel would have a chip on his shoulder about being a man of color.

"I think that that question is a little beneath you, Nigel. I know, it's way beneath me, and under usual circumstances, I wouldn't answer you. But these are strange circumstances that I find myself in, so, in answer to your question, no, Frank is not a black man. He is an Italian-American, as far as I know."

"Forgive me, Denni. And you're right; the question is beneath both of us. But you did say he was just like me. Believe me, I wasn't asking for myself. You see, I asked you that simply to confirm something about you that I have known since I first met you."

"And what's that?" I bridled. "That I'm some sort of a latent bigot or something?"

"Quite the opposite. I think you're colorblind. In my whole life, I have only known one other person that's colorblind. That's my brother, Brad. I simply asked the question to clarify one of your finest attributes."

"Oh, oh, sorry for my insulting response. Thank you. And yes, I know I'm colorblind. I get it from my dad. Lucky me. He was the only other person I have ever known to be like that. Now I remember that's what you said about Brad and me at our wedding."

"So," I continued, "that being said about your similarities and all, as Frank and I got to know each other by going out to the café with a few other students every day after class, I knew very well that he was a far cry from you. He was a war vet and had been medically discharged from his last tour in Afghanistan, suffering with full-blown PTSD and a big drug and/or alcohol dependency. Poor guy! His pain was too much for him back home in the USA, so he just ran away and left his wife, family, and friends behind, and he ended up in Nice of all places. It wasn't long before we were drinking buddies. We were quite a pair. He drank to forget his wife, and I drank right along with him to remember you. My sobriety had only lasted about a month, I'd say, and there I was, with Frank, sitting up to a bar, any bar, every night, lining them up and tossing them back, right along with anyone else that happened to be in that particular bar on that particular night. Some days, we couldn't make it to class. Other days, we would straighten up and buckle down, but it didn't last long. Some nights, we would end up passed-out at my place, and other nights, we would end up at his.

"That last night, I remember I woke up. It must have been the middle of the night; the room was dark. After being sick all morning, Frank had come in at lunchtime to feed me and to help me get into clean clothes. He had stayed over to make sure that I was going to be okay."

"Okay, so what happened? Were you okay?" Nigel asked, looking all concerned.

I answered, "Well, not really. That night, I was lying there, facing Frank's back. It was long and lean, like yours. But it was his back, and not yours. That simple realization was what caused the final full-blown breakdown. It actually broke my heart. That's all I remember. I woke up in the psych ward."

Nigel's face mirrored my pain as I continued my sad tale, "Apparently, according to Frank, he was in a deep sleep and all of a sudden, he thought he was back in the barracks. Screaming was all around him, and he hit the floor, reaching out for his rifle. It wasn't a PTSD attack at all; it was his real life. When he realized that the sounds were coming from me, he recognized that I was having a full-blown breakdown. I was screaming *Nigel, Nigel* over and over again. Frank called an ambulance and had me in the hospital in a matter of minutes. It was a few days later, after some serious meds had calmed me down, that he was allowed to see me. It was kind of funny. All he said to me was 'Who the hell is Nigel?'"

"Oh my God. You poor baby. My baby. I'm so sorry for all your pain and sadness. And all because of me."

"Now, now. Don't let your ego think that it was all because of me missing you. Not at all. Actually, it was that deadly combination of alcohol on top of the unfinished business with you. I'm pretty tough on my own, but booze will kill you before you know what hit you."

He nodded in agreement. "Oh yeah, I've seen that happen before. When you listen to the same story told over and over again, you realize that alcohol, sex, and drama cannot cure old wounds."

"Now you tell me!" I continued to wrap up my story about Frank, "So, after a week in the hospital, I regained my strength and Frank explained to the hospital that I couldn't be released to him, as he too was a psych patient suffering with PTSD and alcoholism. Oh yeah, we were a great pair. The wounded and the really wounded. I called Catharine, and she came down immediately and stayed with me at my apartment for a month to get me back on track. But back to Frank. Once Catharine arrived, he came into the hospital and said a final goodbye to me, telling me that we were not good for each other and that he simply could not see me again if either one of us, or both of us, ever wanted to get well. I know that he kept in touch with Catharine over that last month to check in to see how I was doing, but I never saw him again, and actually, Catharine has never mentioned the whole mess to me since. That's why this letter is such good news. I'm so happy that he made it through his dark days too."

"Actually, I am too. Really. Frank sounds like a great man that deserves any happiness that his world can offer him. Are you going to write him back?"

"Yes and no."

"Explain."

"Yes, I'm going to send him and his wife Maria a congratulatory card with a short note in it to tell them how happy I am for them and their news of the baby, to thank Frank for his friendship in Nice, and also to tell him that I found you and we're very, very happily married. And no, I'm not going to give them a forwarding address."

"That sounds like a good plan, Mrs. Royal."

I continued on with my last story from Nice, and although Nigel had met Lyonel and Lucia at our wedding, I told Nigel their love story of how they met when they were both eighteen-year-old boys. Lyonel had spent his whole adult life working two jobs to pay for Lucia's surgeries, and being out with them the one night made Frank and I both realize how small our struggles really were.

Nigel continued to sympathize and nod along to all the outpourings of my childhood that followed my Nice story, stepping back through my long history of my dad dying so young, and dealing with my cold, distant mother who didn't know how to let love in, along with her dementia that all ended with the court case resolving her last will and testament where I met him in court just over a year and a half ago. I tacked on the remembrance of my sister dying before either of us had a chance to resolve our differences.

My husband was a prince throughout this whole long, sad storytelling ordeal, and he said quietly, "Actually, Denni, at some other time, I need to tell you about my own early childhood, before I came to Canada. As we know, our upbringing sticks with us – all the good, the bad, and all the ugly as well. And mine is mostly ugly, the kind of ugly that you wouldn't know anything about. I've never really discussed it with anyone, other than my shrink, but she had told me that it's part of what caused my breakdown and my bad behavior toward Gerri in L.A. last year, when I called her names that I didn't even know I knew, names from a sad culture of men who laid their pain on their women who in turn only know to survive the best way they can. As you know, patterns of behavior can be set early in life. And the scary part is that my mental health issue is, as you reminded me a few months ago, a chronic one."

"Oh, now, now, don't worry about your mental health. You are doing just fine. More than just fine. Look how happy we are. And about your childhood, it can't be any worse that some of my stories."

"Trust me, baby. I came from a different culture altogether. As a child living in rural Jamaica in the sixties, I saw things that no child should see. Our kitchen had a dirt floor, and our bathroom was a shanty outback. I saw men routinely beat their wives, and the women beat their children in return. I was hungry most days when I went to school, because men would come to our house and steal whatever grocery money my poor sister had, or beat her so badly that she would give it to them. In fact, my sister was beaten to death by a man called Roy, who I remember kicking my dog until she couldn't walk. I was a little boy who didn't know any different. I thought that all men were like that. And I only knew black men. My idol was Muhammad Ali, but I had no idea that all men didn't beat up their women or didn't provide for their families. I never knew a white man until I met Saul Himmel. Lucky for me, when I came to Canada at age nine, Saul spent his whole life de-programming me and molding me into an educated black gentleman that lived in Saul's respectable Jewish world. He couldn't hurt a fly if his life depended on it. But that kind of early trauma that I went through never leaves you. So, we'll save it for another day. It's too ugly and I don't want you to hear about it right now. It's the same as my work in the courts. It's ugly. You're much too sensitive to stories and it will upset you. You are my precious angel that I just want to shelter from certain parts of real life. Don't get me wrong. I want to return all your openness and honesty to you, but later."

I put my arms around him and kissed his solemn face. "First and foremost, I love you. All of you, the little boy in your grin and the sophisticated man that you've become. And trust me, I'm as tough as nails, and I'll be right beside you to fight your demons all the way, baby. However, that being said, I've learned through my therapist about me and how my past has affected me, just like you. I know that I try too hard and that I can be a pain in the ass with all my competitiveness, but that's because deep down I feel unworthy and that I fear that I don't deserve you and that you're going to leave me. Does that sound familiar to you?"

"Oh, baby, you've hit the nail right on the head. That's my greatest fear too. I know if you ever saw me like Gerri saw me when I had the breakdown, you would be gone in a minute."

"I think we've just saved ourselves five hundred bucks."

"How's that?"

"It's the cost of a forty-five-minute visit with your shrink."

He smiled and grabbed my hand. "Now, tell me about your multiple marriages. Tell me all about how you were never wrong."

I got through the stories of my two failed marriages – the first marriage to a charming party boy that liked booze and other women more than he liked me and the second marriage to a dirty cop that took out an insurance policy on my life and tried to collect on it. Nigel's eyes widened when I told him that both of my marriages had very little to do with sex. I explained that although I was married when I was twenty-two years old, I just didn't mature sexually until I was about thirty. My first husband had many girlfriends on the side, but I could safely say we had, on average, sex once every six months over the five-year marriage.

"Are you kidding me? You? With your healthy appetite for sex?"

"Yeah. I know. Weird, huh? And then, with Husband Number Two, we were only married for a couple of days, but we had dated off and on for about three years. I never lived with him before we married; I always had my own place. He always worked midnights as an undercover cop on the Vice Squad. He was quite a bit older than me and had been on the force for over twenty-five years. So, we slept with each other on holidays, so that relationship was even lonelier than the first one."

"Wait a minute. Wait a minute. Go back. How long were you married? Did you say a couple of days?"

"Yes. We were married on a Tuesday, down at City Hall, and I remember well that I left for the honeymoon on Thursday. I went on the honeymoon to

France myself. Once I got back home, I ran for my life, and I lived a very quiet life by myself, as I knew he was still following me. I finally went to the SIU, and he lost his gun privileges and was demoted, so he retired. I went to Africa for a while and finally calmed down enough to come back home to get my life back. So that kind of wraps that one up, doesn't it? Oh, Nigel, I understand completely about your very short-lived marriage or annulment or whatever you call it. Been there, done that."

"A cop. Well, that in itself requires special handling. And a veteran cop, especially in the dirty world of vice. He would carry a hell of a lot of baggage home with him every night."

"Exactly."

"You know, I've always thought that you would have made a perfect mother. Didn't you want any, or did it just not happen for you? What happened there?"

"A little both of each, I suppose. I've always had very irregular periods, sometimes six months in between, and you put that together with not-a-very-active sex life, and that's the results you get. So, the years go by and you strengthen your independence and accept that your blessings are of a different nature. What about you? The same?"

"The same. Except for the periods." He was smiling as he continued, "But never mind that. Back to your multiple marriages without enough sex for a minute. So now you take all your latent sexy needs and wants all out on poor little me?"

"At this very moment, sir, the complaints department is closed for the night."

He reached for my hand across the table. "No complaints here, Mrs. Royal. I look at you asleep every morning beside me in bed, with your messy hair, arms spread out all over my side, mouth open while dreaming up the next chapter of your book and I thank God that we found each other. What took us so long?"

So, the evening of my stories continued.

"Wait a minute. Hold up. Back to Africa," Nigel said. "Did you say you went to Africa? Why on Earth would a single woman want to go to Africa all by herself? That's not the safest part of the world."

"Oh, there's a perfectly good reason. Do you remember the book and the big movie in the eighties with Robert Redford and Meryl Streep called *Out of Africa*?"

"Vaguely. She had a farm or something in Kenya. Oh! I'm beginning to see the connection. Oh! Yes! She was also a strong-willed single woman who tackled lions all by herself as I remember. And the farm! Now I see! And she was a writer, right? It was her autobiography, right? You must have identified with her, darling."

"Well, yes, indeed. I did identify with her. So, I went to Kenya to see her farm. Karen Blixen was her name and it's a true story, Nigel, and I felt every word of it as I traipsed around her farm, day after day for the summer. But I never realized until right now that we were both writers. Oh yes, I remember, she used to tell Robert Redford's character many stories as well, just like I tell you. Wow!"

"But I'm a hell of a lot better-looking than Robert Redford, wouldn't you agree?"

And we continued on. Nigel would cajole me back into a lighter side of the situation when the story got bogged down with pathos. At other times, he would join me with tears and blowing his nasal-impaired sinuses throughout my stories of disappointment and painful letdowns by people that I had trusted and loved.

I saved my health issues till last. I should have told him about my brain tumor and non-Hodgkin's lymphoma before I married him, just from a legal standpoint, but I hadn't. Better late than never.

"I'm sorry that I didn't tell you before we got married. But the truth is I never think of either event now. That was all a few years ago and I'm very healthy now."

"Oh, baby, I knew there had been something. I just thought you would tell me when you were ready. Your long scar than runs down the top of hairline and down your spine. Was that where they took out the brain tumor? But besides that, now really, think about it. Did you think I wouldn't notice it?" he laughed softly.

"Oh, really? You can see it? I thought it had probably faded away by now. And yeah, they did a spinal fusion in the upper spine at the same time."

"Why do you think I always kiss the back of your neck?"

"Really, Nigel?"

"Just one question, more out of curiosity than anything. Was the cancer in the brain?"

"No, the brain tumor was benign. The non-Hodgkin's tumor, which was malignant, was in my gut. And it's long gone. But I had a brother who died at age forty-two from non-Hodgkin's lymphoma, the same kind of cancer that I had, so it alarmed me to a point."

"Do they know what caused your lymphoma?"

"Oh yeah, the doctors at Sunnybrook told me lymphoma is a sneaky one, but sometimes it's caused by coming into contact with chemicals in one's childhood. And on the farm, we had many chemicals back in the day, you know, spraying the fields and all. However, personally, I have a different opinion on my case. You know what they say about gut problems. I'm pretty sure my tumor stemmed from emotional problems. My gut tumor popped up when my sisters kicked me out of the family. They wanted control of Mom's money and her will, etcetera, after her early dementia took over her world. Lucky for me, I have a guardian angel on my shoulder who looks after me. My angel is my great-granddad. I used to live with him on the farm when I was a child. But that's another whole different story for another day. And it's a happy one at that."

"You mean you lived in Marlbank as a child?"

"Oh no, not at all. I lived there with my first husband. When I was born, my mom, dad, brother, and great-granddad had a farm just north of Toronto in a little hamlet called Brown Hill. Someday, I'll take you there if you like. It's a very special place to me. It's just a bush now, but I feel my dad's and my great-granddad's spirits are there with me somehow. I know it sounds crazy, but it's very real to me. You know."

"Yes, I do know. Intimately. Honey, it's like that for me with Saul, too. Like they say, '*In spirit, there is no lack.*'"

"Exactly! How is it that we end up agreeing on every little thing in life!?"

"Everything except onions, babe. That's us. Two peas in a pod."

"But back to my great-granddad for a minute, do you believe in ghosts?"

"No, but I'm pretty sure you do," he said, smiling. "And I'm very willing to learn about anything that keeps you safe from harm. So, tell me all about your great-granddad. Is his name Casper?"

"Very funny. You'll see. I'll show you. And you will beg me on your knees for forgiveness for your non-believing attitude."

He hesitated a little and then said soberly, "Actually, baby, now that we're talking about all this, I too have a scar, and not the one on my face."

"Oh my God, Nigel! Where? What happened? Why didn't you tell me? Tell me right now."

"I may have to show it to you so you'll know where to kiss it better. See, it's right here, honey." He stood up and started to unzip his fly. "It's right here on my third leg."

I was trying not to smile. "Story hour adjourned. You impertinent boy!" I said as I stood up. "I won't have my true, earnest stories upstaged by a sex-crazed satirist. And especially one that's not going to get lucky tonight."

All the way up the stairs, he held on to my ass while singing the lyrics to Robin Thicke's Blurred Lines, *"I know you want it. I know you want it. I know you want it. But you're a good girl-l-l-l-l-l."*

It turned out that I was right. We didn't have what you would call sex that night. It was sheer lovemaking from heart to heart. Nigel loved me all over and he didn't want anything for himself. He simply wanted to pleasure me. I just lay there, soaking up every tender touch.

It was just like last year when we were in Paris, and we had had that amazing, intimate, silent lovemaking session on our second night together. But back then, after the glow had faded, that powerful closeness had left me overwhelmed and anxious, not at all ready for the deep end of our relationship. Thinking back now, I think that was the exact night that had caused me to ask Nigel for some time out once we got back home. I guess I just wasn't ready. I must have been nuts. And now, over a year later, I just couldn't get enough.

***

He was on top of me and his hands were wrapped up in my hair. "Oh, baby, I'm so ready. Can you meet me there? Can you cum for me, baby? Do you need more time? I can wait for you. You're my girl and I love you."

I reached up and guided his mouth down to mine. "And you're my man. And I'm ready. I'm ready right now."

I watched him sleep, his face all soft. He was blissfully unaware of the Gerri-inflicted snoring that his poor nose suffered through night after night. It was time to get the damn thing fixed up and straightened out. Not by Gerri. By a good ENT doctor over at Sunnybrook. I smiled to myself and thought, 'Look at me. I'm thinking like a real wife now. Next thing you know, I'll be buying us matching cardigans.'

***

It was about 7:30 one night in late September. We had cleaned up the dinner dishes and we settled down in front of the fireplace. We were flipping through Netflix for a movie that we both could agree on when Nigel threw his long legs over the sofa and ran up the stairs, saying, "Don't start without me! It's not your turn to choose the movie! No cheating allowed, Ms. Brunette!"

Smiling to myself, I clicked on my choice, and I could hear his deep baritone answering his phone, "Yo, what's up? Oh. Oh. Yes. Got it."

I looked up to see him coming down the stairs. He had a very sober face. He walked directly over to me, sat down beside me, and put both hands on my shoulders. He spoke softly into my face, "Honey, I'm sorry, but it's time to go. Chi got the word that we may be in danger. He's waiting in the garage, and he has already packed our flight bags. We have about twenty minutes to pack a few extra things in a carry-on."

I ran upstairs while he went downstairs to bring up two pieces of carry-on and to pick up our passports and I.D. that were always kept in a drawer in Saul's office. Slipping into my office, I pulled my orange USB out of its port and dashed down the hall to start pulling from my wardrobe. I put a sweater on over my long-sleeve tee-shirt and jeans that I was wearing, and I laced up a pair of black Nike trainers. I grabbed my new Hermes scarf that Nigel had just given me, a few favorite pieces of my La Perla, and my ivory, antique, tatted gloves that I had worn on our wedding day. I folded his new French terrycloth robe, along with my matching one, and I grabbed his old moccasins that he liked to wear around the house, thinking ahead that he wouldn't be warm enough in the big old *château* with the cold stone floors. I was packing and neatly folding a few essentials on the bed when Nigel arrived with two bags, our real passports, even though we knew we would not be using them, as well as other I.D. and our copy of our wedding video in one hand.

We worked quietly together, understanding that we would buy whatever we needed later.

"Take a couple of sweaters, babe, and just one jacket, and I'll take just one skirt. We'll be staying in for dinner while we're at the *château*, and the aristocrats just don't dress for dinner these days. You know how it is with the old money crowd."

"Yeah, they're probably nothing but fancy farm folks. Upscale Marlbank. I can't wait to see their wine cellar, though."

While we were both in the bathroom and I was packing the beautiful art deco hairclips that he had bought me at the Fleas in Paris, I caught his eye watching me through the mirror. He looked sad. "Don't forget your USB, honey."

I confirmed with a silent nod and turned to him for our last embrace in our big, beautiful bathroom. I had to admit it was a toss-up of who loved the other the most.

"This is not the end of our life here, Nigel. We'll be back."

"One last thing," he said, looking down at me. "If you must take your jewelry, please promise me that you will wear your diamond turned around so it's hidden. We cannot attract any attention."

"No, you're right. I'll be happy just to wear my wedding ring." I took the big yellow diamond off and put it in his hand. "Will you put this in the safe before we leave?"

As we slipped through the hallway door that led directly into the garage, I took a look back and smiled to myself. Every light in the house was on, the

T.V. was blaring, and the dishwasher was busily scrubbing my old copper pots and pans.

Chi loaded us into the big Benz, with the windows all blacked out. He asked us to lie down in the backseat until we hit the highway. He turned the key. The garage door opened, and we were off. Nigel's arms were around me as we lay there, and I couldn't help myself. I began laughing quietly, and when Nigel felt me shaking, he said, "Don't worry, honey, don't worry. Are you okay, baby?"

I whispered into his shoulder, "Nigel, no, no, I'm shaking with laughter! You couldn't make this up!"

And Nigel Royal, the target of a deadly international money-laundering hit squad threw his head back and joined me with his big baritone reverberating around the big, fast-moving, blacked-out Benz.

Two men, all wired up with earphones and God only knows what else, opened our doors as Chi pulled up at the airport. Nigel and I both kissed Chi goodbye from over the backseat, and I heard Nigel say, "I love you, man," as my feet hit the pavement. I looked back from the airport door, and he had disappeared. I didn't know it at the time, but while I was asking God to protect him, he was praying for our safety too.

Our two new *men-in-black* attendants whisked us through special handling, and we were sitting in a private, guarded, and secure room, coffee in hand, waiting for the Toronto-Avignon flight that would take off in one hour.

"Well, Susan, Suze, or Suzi-Que, or whatever your name is, I hope to hell they booked us first-class," Nigel said with a little laugh, and that was what started our second round of giggling.

"No, but really, Nigel, I mean Noah, I have to tell you how impressed I am with this whole process. Is all of this just because of Chi?"

"Oh, no, honey. Our Canadian Intel is a huge protective net, let me tell you. They are very, very slick. We don't have anything to worry about. They will wrap all of this up very quickly."

He paused and looked at me a little sheepishly. "I might as well tell you about the other little twist in all of this."

"Oh please, what now!? You mean there's more?"

"Yeah. The CIA is involved. You know, the American Intel."

"Are you kidding me? What have they got to do with it?"

"It's a crazy story, but my brother out in L.A. may have just saved my life. He phoned me three weeks ago and confessed that has had me under surveillance for the last ten years, unknown to me, of course. He has always been so protective of me, with my position on the right side of the law and all. He knows firsthand how the other side works. He said his guys had picked up a Chinese dissident or something over a year ago, but that there was nothing since. The joke, if there was one, was on him though. I told him that I had been in the Canadian Witness Protection Program for the last five years and that I was one step ahead of him. Long story short, he was very, very happy to know that Chi and the government had been on top of everything, taking good care of me."

"Oh, the Chinese dissident; that must have been Kurt!"

"Yes. One and the same. And then, a month ago, Brad's Intel guys picked up some serious chatter that something was about to go down, so that's when he phoned me to let me that the CIA were now on the case, and they in turn would be working with the Canucks."

By the time we had settled down in our sleeper cabin for the overnight flight, my husband had assured me for the hundredth time that everything was going to be okay. I had no doubt, as I snuggled down into Noah Rosenberg's arms.

"Keep the snoring down, and just don't drool on me. That's all," were the last teasing words in Canadian airspace that I heard him whisper in my ear.

* * *

We had just disembarked, and I watched as a man strode toward us as if he knew who we were. "Good morning, Ms. Brier, Mr. Rosenberg. Welcome to France. My name is Ray Robinson. Thanks, Tom," he said to our attentive flight attendant. "I'll take it from here." He took my carry-on and ushered us down the ramp and into a small, empty office.

"I work for the Canadian government as a special envoy, so I have been briefed fully on your itinerary. We're going to circumvent the usual procedure here at the airport, so as soon as I can brief you, I'll take you to your hotel, and you'll be free to enjoy your time here in Avignon for two days, before you leave to drive to your chosen Location B. Location B knows that you are coming, so you do not have to worry about that. And they have already been fully compensated by the Canadian government for putting you up. After that, you will leave for London. This briefing will take about ten minutes. May I get you a beverage meanwhile?"

"No, thank you. We're just fine, but did you say London?" Noah asked as he was smiling at me.

"Yes, London. We will have a temporary home all set up for you within the next two weeks. It's strict policy, of course, that we couldn't have given you the location of your new home until you had arrived safely in France, where you will spend your first week or so at Location two. We have taken the liberty to check you in for your next two nights at the Hotel de l'Horloge, which is in the old town here in Avignon. You'll be quite comfortable there, and I know you'll enjoy your time in our lovely town. You are free to travel around France, and go ahead and rent a car, but you are not allowed, of course, for everyone's safety and privacy, to visit your family that I understand lives in the south, not far from here. If your family, or anyone else for that matter, tries to reach you, hang up immediately. Your brother and your associate Chi Tran have already been contacted that you have arrived in France. Do we understand each other so far?"

"So far so good. Thank you for all your help," Noah said.

"I have everything you are going to need in this carry-on," he said as he put the case up on the table and began to unzip it.

"This is like Christmas morning!" Noah exclaimed in order to assure the diplomat that we were all on the same page.

"Yes, it's a nice little package, but it's one hell of an ordeal you have to go through to get!" the diplomat offered. "You'll find that your bank accounts have been topped up, and you will have automatic weekly deposits to take care of all your expenses. The Canadians don't scrimp on things like that. And oh, Ms. Brier, the card there, with the London phone number, you can reach your London assistant there. She will help you both get settled into your new home. Mr. Rosenberg, the other card with the French number on it is how you can contact me. I will be able to advise you when your London home is ready for you, so please call me at any time, for any reason."

The case had two of everything – two money belts, cash made up of British pounds and euros, drivers' licenses for Susan Brier and Noah Rosenberg, with a complete London address with bank cards and a tag with pin numbers attached, two cellphones with London exchanges, two laptops fully loaded, with email in both our new names along with UK IP addresses, and two business cards with his name and phone number.

"Do you have any questions before I take you to your hotel?"

"None." Noah stretched out his hand, and I followed his lead. The Canadian government representative stood there with one hand on the doorknob and hesitated. He turned around and faced us both, up close. His pleasant, confident demeanor had vanished. His face was stone–cold. His narrowed eyes focused on Nigel. He leaned into Nigel's face. "You are a small cog in a very big wheel. Don't you forget for one moment that you are on the down-low, until I say you're not," he warned.

Nigel responded with a combination of age-old boy puffery trying to protect his girl from a bully, while at the same time, acting like the consummate professional he was. He stood up tall to make himself a little larger than the government worker and, not backing down, took my hand in his. His eyes were glued to the government official and he responded in a loud, confident voice, "Yes, sir."

The special envoy turned to me and stared for a full thirty seconds into my face, taking his time to ensure that I was understanding the gravity of the situation. "Act accordingly. Don't bring attention to yourselves in any way."

"Yes." I was so glad that I had left my showy ring at home in the safe behind the old A. J. Casson in Saul's office.

Before I knew it, we were whisked from Avignon's Airport to the small city's core, within the old Roman wall that circled 'old town.' We checked into our cozy room at the Hotel de l'Horloge, steps away from the medieval Palais des Papes. I couldn't wait to show Noah around, as I had enjoyed a few summers in Avignon years ago and was eager to share my old experiences and build new ones with the love of my life.

***

"Baby, take a look at this," he called out from our hotel room's bathroom doorway.

"Oh," I said, looking at the smallish, high tub with the one-head shower behind a half-wall of glass. "Yeah, Euro-style, all right. On the small side, definitely for one person at a time."

He had his arm around me, with both of us squeezed into the doorway, and he looked down at me. "Looks like you won't be stamping your feet and demanding a big show in this shower, Suzie-Que," he said with a big grin on his face.

"You're incorrigible," I miffed, and as I turned around to go back to unpacking, I felt his big, beautiful hand slap me on my ass as I turned away.

We were deciding where to have our first meal in France. After all, it was mid-morning in our new time zone. I had actually stayed in this very hotel a few years back when I flew over from Naples, Florida, to visit Maureen, Catharine, and Edouard up-country. I knew they had a nice breakfast room, so we went down to partake. We were both starving and had a little bit of everything on the buffet – sausage, scrambled egg, European cold cuts, oatmeal, black steaming coffee, fresh and ripe figs, and the works.

I woke up to a darkened room, with my husband still asleep right beside me. We hadn't even turned the bed down, and we both still had all our clothes on. 'That's a first,' I mused to myself. Checking my watch and noting it was 10:30 p.m. Avignon time, I shook him gently. "Babe, I'm so hungry. Can we go out to get something to eat?"

The night concierge of our small hotel listened to our jetlag woes and told us that Avignon was a small town and all restaurants were closed up at that hour.

"However," he continued in perfect English, "there is the American Bar just a five-minute walk around the corner and down Rue de la Republique. They usually stay open a little later, but it's not fancy. It's just really a beer joint with very good wings. Will that do? I can phone down ahead to let them know to put some wings on for you. His name is Joe, and he'll take good care of you."

We walked up the steps and into the bar, dressed in our black jeans and dark-navy no-label jackets. It was a big square-room bar in the middle with a lone bartender. The place was relatively empty, with only a couple of couples and a few singles perched up at the bar.

"Looks a little like the Marlbank Hotel, don't you think?" Noah said, arm protectively around my shoulders.

The man wearing the football jersey behind the bar yelled over to us.

"Yo!" he yelled out over the Motown music that was blaring from an old-fashioned jukebox. "Are you Susan and Noah, the hungry Canucks? You came to the right place. Grab a booth and I'll be right over."

And he was absolutely right. There weren't Buffalo wings this side of said city that could've been better. As we made our way through the pitcher of draft beer and basket of wings, the tired old bar had thinned out, and it was just the two of us sitting in our booth. The American bartender named Joe had fed the jukebox the whole time. Percy Sledge plopped into play, filling the dingy, empty bar with *When a Man Loves a Woman.* My husband, without a word, pulled me up on to the dance floor.

Joe watched us through the bar mirror's reflected view as we slid out from behind the booth to dance. He dimmed the lights and cranked up Percy to top volume. "Somebody's gonna get lucky tonight, and sadly, it ain't me."

My man took me in his arms on the dance floor and held me close. I slipped my hand up and underneath the back of his sweater, and I felt his smooth, tight lumbers and we were thigh to thigh as he guided me into the slow dance. His feet moved back and forth in an uncomplicated one-step that allowed us the tight fit that the song called for. He looked down and smiled at me, and his sexy, deep baritone spilled his guts, word for word, right along with Percy, directly into the depths of my heart and soul.

When a man loves a woman
Can't keep his mind on nothing else
He'll trade the world

For the good thing he's found
If she's bad, he can't see it
She can do no wrong
Turn his back on his best friend
If he put her down
When a man loves a woman
Spend his very last dime
Trying to hold on to what he needs
He'd give up all his comfort
Sleep out in the rain
If she said that's the way it ought to be.

He bent down to kiss me between verses, but it ended up that the kiss took precedence, as neither one of us wanted to break the heat. As Percy wrapped it up for us, I thanked God for the woman, whoever she was, that had taught my husband to kiss like that.

Our lovemaking that first night in the walled city was slow and tender, just the way my husband, Nigel Royal a.k.a. Noah Rosenberg, liked it.

***

The next day, we wandered around Avignon and shopped for some new, under-the-radar clothing that would suffice for country living up at the *château*. We needed rubber boots, toques, jeans and sweatshirts, so we went into the Gap.

"Yeah, I get it. This is like dressing down in L.A. It's not really my style, but I can do this, Suzie-Que."

"Just think of the farm, babe, and we'll be just fine," I said as I tried on the shorter version of the hunter army-green rubber boots.

"Oh my God!" Noah exclaimed, looking at my boots. "There's a limit though, don't you think?"

"No, no, no. You too. Try them on. You'll see. We need rubber boots. They are a staple at the *château*. They call them barn boots. Get with it, Noah. This is what the kids back in Canada wear too. And it's the fall now, so there's plenty of mud to go around up at the *château*. Trust me. We can just leave them there once we head out for London."

"I understand that the days of the country squire are long gone; I just don't want to look like the country squirrel."

"Just remember one thing, buster. You're my country squirrel."

***

Noah let out a long, low whistle as we slowed down at the gates. I drove our rented car down the long, winding crushed gravel drive that led up to the *château*. As he was lowering his passenger side window, he said in awe, "This is right out of a French impressionist painting, Denni, I mean Suzie. Look! Look at the turrets! Oh my God!"

I drove slowly around the last bend, and the drive split into the circle. The huge stone fountain spurted water from the center lawn. I could see Edouard and Catharine standing out in front of the massive ten front doors, and their beautiful Great White Pyrenees, Patou, was sitting there right beside them, all three of them ready to greet their on-the-lam visitors.

Noah had opened the passenger door, stepped out, and had his arm up in a friendly wave. It all happened so fast; none of us could even call the dog to try to reign him in. The Great Pyrenees, weighing just over hundred pounds, flew across the drive and made a magnificent jump of joy right into Noah's chest.

The dog pinned him down right on the crushed gravel drive, licking his face, like a dog would lick his master that had just returned from the war. Edouard and Catharine were screaming at the dog and running toward us. I just stood there, laughing hysterically. In the takedown, one of Noah's loafers had been knocked off completely, and as the happy, whimpering dog backed off him, he grabbed the toe of Noah's sock and danced away with it as if to dare the owner to come and get it. Edouard changed direction and chased the dog across the lawn, shouting at the top of his lungs. Catharine ran over and bent down to see if Noah was okay, while he was still roaring with laughter. Noah got up, one foot clad and the other bare, and slapped his knees, signaling to the dog to come back. Patou trotted back immediately and dropped Noah's sock at his feet. Noah bent over the big white face with tongue panting and tail wagging and hugged him like he had known him his whole life. The dog never left Nigel's side for the rest of our visit.

"It's a cool day, so we're going to have lunch in the lounge, in front of the fireplace today, if that's okay with you. Catharine is going to be showing off later on, and we'll have the fancy china out in the dining room for dinner tonight. But meanwhile, let's get you settled in. We'll put your bags up in your suite first so you can freshen up before lunch. When you're ready, would you like a tour of the main rooms so that you can get your bearings? We don't allow the dog upstairs, so he will have to wait patiently for us and behave if he wants to get a little tidbit under the table at lunchtime. He knows the drill, and we just can't have any more bad behavior from him."

It took us a good twenty minutes to make it up the grand staircase to our suite. Nigel just couldn't stop asking questions about every ancient tapestry on the stone walls, every hand-knotted Persian carpet from the Ottoman Empire that we passed over, and every imperious ancestor staring down at us from their gilded frames that hung in the hallway's plastered walls.

Edouard laughed as he explained to his impressed guest, "We try to follow what the rich people are doing right now. And those rich people are abandoning rich-people rugs these days, so we have picked up some of these carpets for next to nothing at estate sales. And some are reproductions, not expensive in the least. Catharine is very talented in her role as interior decorator, so she's one hundred percent responsible for the overall effect here. Since you're a man of justice, and skilled at seeing right through people, Noah, I feel compelled to confess to you that we're actually just how Denni has always pegged us. We are just farm folks living in fancy digs."

Our suite was way beyond what you could ever imagine. The ceilings were fifteen feet high, hand-painted with hunting scenes of a past era. Massive, original French armoires flanked each side of the king-sized bed, which was dressed in European hundred percent linen, not cotton, with deep embroidery on the pillowcases. There was a big, white, fluffy eiderdown rolled up on the end of the bed. You could actually walk into the massive limestone fireplace, and Catharine had put dozens and dozens of candles on the mantle. The ensuite bathroom was built into the original turret, so it was completely round, with a stand-alone claw-foot tub and modern glass shower that curved with the wall. The walls were the original rough-hewn stone, and the floor's traditional smooth marble tile had been restored to perfection. Catharine had hung white, fluffy robes on modern stainless-steel hooks, and there must have been a dozen towels folded underneath a basket of soaps to choose from. The two long, narrow windows opened to the front lawns. You could hear the fountain tinkling its water onto the pavers below its massive round rim. The prize in the bedroom was a giant writing desk, and Catharine had laid out magazines and writing paper supplies along its leather-tooled top. It sat between two large, tall windows that were flanked with traditional shutters that looked out over the back lawn, sloping gently down to the pond in the distance. The view was partially obscured by tall pines just outside the window sill, but between the windows and the pond in the distance, the vast lawns were covered with a beautiful blanket of red and yellow leaves freshly fallen from the carefully hulled hardwood forest.

I had stayed in this particular suite before, so it wasn't exactly new to me, but I was still overwhelmed by the perfection of Catharine's brilliant restoration of the room. Nigel was entirely speechless. He walked back and forth, touching everything. Finally, he laughed and said to Edouard and Catharine, "Please excuse my bad manners. I'm just overwhelmed by the beauty of it all. I can't even speak. Catharine, I'm afraid I'm going to drive you crazy over the next few days. I'll have a million little nit-picky questions on every inch of your design here. It's magnificent. Thank you, thank you from the bottom of my heart for giving me this visual feast. It's a gift I'll never be able to repay."

Catharine said quietly, "It's funny, but that's exactly how we felt when we watched you two get married under your old chuppa in your backyard. It was so beautiful and touching. We couldn't even tell you what it meant to us. And now, you feel the same. I guess we're all a little crazy." She laughed at her sentimentality.

"Enough already, you two sentimental fools. I'm starving. Let's have lunch," Edouard added, and we all trooped downstairs to a big lunch in front of the roaring fireplace. The dog, Patou, lay on Noah's feet, and every time Edouard nudged him away, the dog simply circled around once or twice and settled down back exactly where he wanted to be. And that was close to his new best friend.

The four of us had wonderful full two days. We toured the vineyard and played badminton on the front lawn, dressed in our barn boots and our sweatshirts. We played table tennis in the library and danced to Edouard's old collection of French music in the lounge after dinner, with the big fire roaring to take the chill of the big stone-walled room. Catharine and I cooked the meals as Edouard and Noah talked law in the library, with Edouard's impressive collection of law books that his father and his father before him had gathered. Edouard had earned his law degree in Vancouver, Canada, and had worked in international banking, so he understood completely Noah's whole story of being involved in the money-laundering racket on the right side of the law and paying the consequences of having to live under a witness protection program. We ended each evening with a nightcap and a game or two of cards. Noah had never played mahjong before, so we all took full advantage of him and he played right along with us, playing the part of the nerdy, bumbling intellectual that I loved so dearly. Every five minutes, he would jump up and stoke the fire with the long, ancient pokers, just like a kid on his first camping trip.

Noah was so taken with the whole *château*; he was like a curious boy that could hardly contain himself. Edouard smiled as we finished a round of cards and announced to the table to excuse him, but he must go downstairs to 'feed his mistress.'

Noah looked up in surprise, not understanding what Edouard was talking about. He jumped up as Edouard motioned him to follow, and Catharine and I smiled at his enthusiasm. He was following Edouard around exactly like the dog was following him around.

Edouard's 'mistress' was a couple of ancient wood-burning furnaces in the basement that demanded to be fed every six hours to keep the vast property warm, even with a constant feeding of all the fireplaces in the individual rooms as well.

I heard his big laugh as they came back into the room, arms full of wood to feed the fire.

"Denni, you should see the two big, old wood-burning furnaces downstairs. They operate with dozens and dozens of chains that are attached to the floor registers. It's amazing!"

"Yeah, and a lot of hard work feeding them every six hours," Edouard moaned.

It was our second night sleeping in our big suite when I awoke to some sort of noise. I came out of my sleep and reached out for Noah. He was gone. The moonlight was streaming in through the windows, and I sat up to see him standing there, in front of the windows, in the moonlight.

"Honey," he whispered. "Come here. Come see."

I threw back the big eiderdown, and he held his robe open and motioned me inside. I snuggled against his bare chest in my scanty nightie inside his robe, and he turned us around to look out the window. The moon had lit the back park like a fairytale. An autumn frost had fallen, and between the reds and golds of the leaves poking from under the silver frost on the lawn, it was breathtakingly beautiful. I leaned back against Noah to catch the heat of his chest, and his arms tightened around me.

"You see all those hardwood trees in the forest down over the park as they call their backyard," I explained to him. "Catharine told me last year that each tree is numbered so they know which trees to cut to maintain the forest properly. It's amazing. And a lot of serious work."

He whispered into my ear from behind, "Wait. Just wait. Listen."

I listened. It added to the magic of the moment like I'd never known before.

"Who-o-o. Who-o-o," the owl called to us from the pines, right in front of us, and I whispered, "Oh, baby."

"Oh, honey."

We just stood there, completely entranced by the surreal, magnificent world that mother nature had laid out in front of us.

Nigel whispered, "Now I know how you feel about your storybook, the Blue Castle where the girl and her man lived in the woods. This is the most romantic scene I have ever experienced in my whole life. Is that how you feel about your old books, honey?"

"Yeah. I always thought it was because I'm a country girl at heart, but now you tell me that you feel it too. It's something to do with nature, I think. It's God's work. I love you. I love you all the way."

"I love you all the way too. Let's never forget this very moment."

"Yeah. And now you're never going to tease me again as long as we live about my stories, right?"

"Right. You're always right, honey."

"Good. I'm glad that we've got that straight."

Back in bed, we couldn't help ourselves. It wasn't but a few minutes until the eiderdown was tossed off the bed, and the embers from the fireplace were enough to keep us warm all through the intermittent who-o-o, who-o-o, who-o-os that were hooted at us through the open-shuttered windows of the old *château*. Our lovemaking went on and on throughout the night.

I woke to my husband saying in my ear, "Honey, we've got ten minutes before breakfast at nine. We can't be late. I'll take the first shower, but we've got to rush now."

I smiled and said, "Yeah, babe. I'm right behind you. Tell me, was I just dreaming or did we have the best night ever?"

"Don't give me any of your sexy talk right now or we're in big trouble. Get your ass in gear. You hear me?"

***

Catharine and I had finished cleaning up the breakfast dishes, and as we walked into the big library, Noah turned from the map that was laid out on the big desk, and with a very excited look about his face, said, "Honey, I'm taking you on a hike. With a picnic lunch and everything. We're going down to the Ardèche."

There it was. It was that little-boy look on his face that I simply couldn't resist. I smiled and nixed my planned sarcastic retort before I spoke. He could no more take me on a hike down to the Ardèche than a two-year-old could. He was a city-slicker through and through. How would his $800 Salvatore Ferragamos fare on a hike like that? I waited for him to explain.

As if he were reading my mind, he assured me. "No, no, wait a sec. Don't discount the idea altogether. I'm wearing my barn boots, and Edouard has given me a map. He even gave me his Swiss Army knife in case we have to whittle a walking stick or something."

"Oh, honey," I joked, "are you going to take a rifle, too, to shoot the wild boars down there? Nah, no need. We'll take Patou. He'll protect us."

Edouard jumped into the conversation, "Oh, no, seriously. Patou can't go. It's deer-hunting season for the next two weeks, and he might wander off to the estate next to us, where they hunt. He'll have to stay up here in the house while you're gone."

I realized that the two men were not kidding, so I got on board as Edouard laid out the map for us. He explained that we would hike down the old Roman road which was actually now just half-buried cobblestones that were faintly visible along the trail. We would reach the Ardèche River, which is a right-bank tributary of the Rhone. Its big cliffs, also called du Pont d'Arc, are quite a tourist attraction. The river also forms the Ardèche River Canyon, which is the largest natural canyon in Europe. We wouldn't get that far, as it was a little too far downstream. We were warned by both Edouard and Catharine not to go into the river under any circumstances. The river had a dangerous pull, and we would be underwater before we knew what hit us.

Catharine made us a beautiful picnic lunch of cheese, cold cuts, and croissants and tucked in a half bottle of wine into the old leather knapsack that Noah slung over his shoulder as if he did this every day of his life. He patted his pocket to make sure he had Edouard's Swiss Army knife and his compass. He was just so damn cute. I didn't have the heart to tease him.

As it turned out, we had a magnificent hike down to the river. Noah was in full control, and halfway down, he suggested we stop for a rest so that he could source a few branches to make into walking sticks. I honestly didn't think that Noah had ever even held a knife in his citified, manicured hands before, but he persevered and whittled two perfectly adequate walking sticks without losing any fingers. I told him I would keep mine forever. Every little while, he would take out the map and the compass to make sure that we were heading east. It reminded me of the movie Out of Africa, where the Robert Redford character gave the Meryl Streep character a compass, but I didn't say anything to him. After all, this was my husband's shining moment, and I didn't want to spoil it in any way by getting into some deep discussion about some old movie as we often did at home. I just loved the little boy in him so much. I found myself holding his hand and circumventing all conversation to his way of thinking. I was playing the Maid Marion to his Robin Hood, or something like that.

We reached the Ardèche, and we were both in awe of the mighty river. We imagined the Romans rolling through France and pillaging their way through all the villages and the few old castles along the way.

I said playfully from our seat at the edge of the river, "I might not be able to whittle a walking stick like you can, but there is something right here that I bet I can beat you at."

"Oh, she's back. My competitive little Irish faerie. I was wondering where you went. You've been so sweet all morning long. After last night, I'll even let you win any little game you present today. I'm still on cloud nine. Now what little game have you got up your sleeve to get me into a big kerfluffle?"

He knew me all too well. I smiled as sweetly as I could as I gathered up a few smooth, round stones. "I'm going to beat your pants off in skipping stones across the river. Whoever has the most skips wins."

He raised his eyebrows, leaned back, and pursed his lips. "What's the prize?"

"Hmm. I haven't decided yet. But I'll go easy on you. Something like, umm, you'll have to piggy-back me all the way back to the *château*. Something like that."

"A piggy-back ride, you say. Deal. Yeah, count me in, wonder woman."

I should have been alarmed with his smooth-talking, confident retort. I couldn't read any of that little boy on his face at the time. I felt uneasy. Maybe I had underestimated him in some way.

I watched him as he decided to pick his own stones from the pebbled beach. He loaded both pockets of his jacket and called out, "Get over here to count the skips. No cheating. None of your magic faerie dust. You're going down, sister. You have no idea who you're dealing with."

I watched in amazement as stone after stone skipped multiple skips over the fast-moving water. He went through two full pockets of stones and never missed one.

I stood there beside him as he dusted off his city-pampered hands. "What's wrong, sugar? Cat got your tongue?"

I turned around, my back to him. I took a good, solid stance, spreading my legs apart a little to get a good balance. I stretched out my arms and said in a humbled tone, "Get on."

I felt his long arms surround my shoulders, and he hung them down in front of my chest, not knowing really where to hang on. He was riding high; his chest was even with the top of my head. I almost buckled under his weight, but I managed to stay upright. His knees were clamped around my waist. He had jackknifed his long legs up and back so he wouldn't be dragging them along in the dirt. He leaned into and over me and yelled out loud in his best cowboy voice, "Giddy up, little pony. Giddy up!"

I put my head down, as I was of the opinion it would be easier on me to trot rather than to plod. My system worked well for about thirty yards, even under the duress of having to listen to his howls of laughter coming from above my head. Finally, I felt my legs buckle, and my rider sprang off in time to see me waive first to the right, then to the left, and to finally hit a sandy patch of turf, my one shoulder breaking the fall.

He was still laughing uncontrollably as he kneeled down beside me, trying to pull me up. I pulled him down on top of me, and we just lay there laughing at the top of our lungs like idiots. Complete idiots!

We finally settled down enough to find a nice little spot at the river's edge for our lunch. We were both hungry by this time and settled back after wolfing everything down, taking turns to drink our wine right out of the bottle. It was a cool fall day, but the sun came out for a little while, and we lay back with no words, just feeling its rays on our faces.

"You know, honey, that was really my first big, crazy, out-of-control laugh since I went into the witness protection program years ago. It's been a long time having that heavy cloud over my head. Even when I'm not thinking about it, I am, if you know what I mean. It ruined my whole life for three years, until I met you. Although I refused to leave 7 Russell Hill Road, I had to give up my few friends, and I was watched twenty-four-seven no matter what I did, when I did it, or who I did it with. It took its toll. I became a lonely, bitter old man. And now, here I am, on a riverbank, wearing barn boots, having the time of my life. I forgot for a few, short minutes that my life is not my own. I thank God every day that I have you beside me. I couldn't do it without you. If I hadn't met you, I know I would be dead by now."

"Oh, baby, don't talk like that. You're scaring me. You're my hero. I can't stand the thought of you being so unhappy. I'll tell you what. Once we get up to London, we'll both check in with a psychotherapist and have a few sessions. You know, like couple's therapy or something to get us through this. But we'll be home before you know it. Just hang in there. Don't be getting sick on me, honey. It would break my heart to see you unhappy."

"You're the best medicine for me. But I just want to keep you safe. And you're right. We won't be in London for long. The government will clean up this mess in short order and then we can go home and enjoy our freedom."

"Okay, okay, honey. Hey, meanwhile, I have a question for you."

"Shoot."

"Where did you learn to skip a stone like that?"

"I've got lots of little tricks up my sleeve to put my cocky little Irish faerie in her place. And I'm not about to divulge any secrets to you. I know you'll just use them against me. Like you do when we're playing cards. I see right through you, doll. And don't you forget it."

"You've got me all wrong. I'm not some little trickster. I'm your devoted wife who's going to be right beside you through thick and thin for the next hundred years. Right?"

"Right, honey. You're always right. Now let's get the hell out of Dodge before it gets late and we lose our way back home, like Hansel and Gretel."

***

We had decided to leave the river and go inland through the cedars to find the sun in the sandy soil of open clearings that we could see in the distance as we looked to the left of us. We could just circle back easy enough when it was time to head home. Or so we thought.

"Oh, maybe the map goes this way," he said as he turned the map upside-down. "Oh, I know, let's see where the sun is – oh, it's not sunny."

We stood there, him smiling down at me, neither one of us willing to admit that we were lost. The quiet was breathtakingly beautiful, the cedars gave off their special scent, and all was well in the world in that moment, lost or not.

In one millisecond, I heard a 'zing,' like a bee, near Noah's left shoulder. As I started turning my head to see where the bee went, Noah's right arm came up around my shoulders, and he threw me, literally threw me into the ground. My face hit a flat rock in the soft dirt, and I pushed my head away from the dirt to breathe. He was lying on top of me.

His breath was on my face. He whispered, "Don't move, honey. Listen to me. I'm sorry. I'm so sorry for everything. They got me. I've been shot in the shoulder. I'm so sorry. Remember our plan. When your coast is clear, head back as fast as you can to Location 'B.' Don't wait for me to say when. Just go. Go. Be safe. I love you." His breath was labored, and he was panting. "I'm going to decoy out to the middle of the clearing. You take the cedars. Do you understand?"

"Yes. I love you."

He groaned as he got up on his knees. From my position on the ground, I watched his muddy barn boots lope away from me. I raised my head and saw him struggling to keep his wounded arm close to his side. He was bent over but he put distance between himself and me, and he raised his good arm in surrender, shouting out in French, "My name is Noah Rosenberg, and I'm a guest at the *château*! You've got the wrong man! I surrender! Don't shoot!"

In fear, my heart raced and I slid back a little, hoping for extra cover from an outcropping of dirt in front of me. I tried to reason with myself through my initial adrenaline rush. 'No! No! I can't leave him now. And I wouldn't. I would rather die with him than to run away like a coward for my own safety.'

Another sickening wave of fear gripped me, and I retched and spat out the bile that came up from my stomach. I peeked out once again, my eyes riveted on my husband.

I saw him stop and turn toward the cedars across and away from me. He slowly kneeled down on his knees, with his one hand still raised in surrender and his injured arm tucked down and pressed against his side. I could see that the shoulder of his nylon jacket had been shredded by the bullet. My heart broke at the sight of him surrendering on his knees. I had no choice. I pulled myself up to walk out into the clearing to accept my fate alongside of my husband.

I put both hands up high and held my head up high as I shouted out in my best authoritative voice, *"Je m'appelle Susan Brier. Je suis une visiteuse à la château!"*

I focused on my husband, and I strode across the clearing toward him, my one eye closed completely from the searing pain emanating from my cheekbone.

I was about fifty meters into my surrender, full of faux-bravado, as I started squinting and blinking my one good eye, thinking that I was seeing things. Two men, one very large and one smaller, bespectacled one, came out of the cedars, and walked toward Noah, who was still on his knees, with his one arm up in the air. They both had their rifles up over their heads as if they were surrendering to Noah, instead of the other way around. What the fuck was going on here!?

"Nous sommes chauseur de chevreuil! Nous sommes désolé! Nous sommes désolé!" they shouted across the clearing as they made their way across to the clearing toward Noah. Noah, upon hearing their declaration, crumpled to the ground.

What did he say!? Did I just hear that my husband was shot by a fucking deer hunter!? And that the same fucking deer hunter was sorry! The logical side of my brain told me to be happy that it wasn't a hitman; it was only a deer hunter.

However, in an illogical, fury-filled reaction, I stomped across the clearing, and my focus shifted away from my husband to zero-in on the deer hunters. I was clearly out of my mind as I made my way closer to the two of them, who by now were looking at me in puzzlement. Their dull, stupid faces were perplexed. I imagined that they were thinking, 'Now, wait a minute, who the hell is she?'

The fucking idiots! They had shot my husband! They were going down! I stomped toward them with murder in my eyes. I promptly and disdainfully ignored the smaller, older one with the glasses. He was undoubtedly nothing but a coward, as he slowly backed up and away from me, obviously terrified by the look in my eyes. I concentrated on the larger, younger one. He still had that puzzled look about his stupid face. As I advanced, he met my eyes and slowly lowered his gun to the ground, away from him. I assessed my position and realized that he was a little more than 6'3" tall. I got up to about three feet from this person.

My second rush of adrenaline kicked in, and the Irish wild banshee in me let go. It was my intent that he would die in a violent manner. I leapt. I flew up into his face, spreading my nails out to claw out his eyes. I remember hearing a wild banshee war-cry all around my ears as my fingers met his two-day-old stubble.

The human teeter-totter that was his huge 6'3" frame wavered slightly before giving in to the weight of its rider. He fell backward as I held on with my hands around his neck. He toppled backward, with me riding the wave. We landed with a jarring thud into the soft dirt in the middle of the clearing. Stunned, we both lay there, me on top, my hands still around his neck and his arms holding onto me just under my ass. His legs were spread-eagled. His feet were at least twelve inches out and past my feet, which were dangling midair, just above his knees.

For the first second or two, I felt somewhat satisfied. I had taken him down in one fell swoop. I loosened my grip from his neck just a little.

That was just before Goliath gave out one hell of a roar. He sprang up into action, with me still clinging on to the front of him, like a sad little fly stuck on flypaper. He marched over to where Noah was still half sitting and half lying with his wounded shoulder. The deer hunter plucked me from himself, like one would pluck a flea, and dumped me unceremoniously down in the dirt beside my husband.

I opened my eyes after hitting the ground to see my husband peering into my face, although I must say he didn't look too alarmed. He gingerly lay down beside me, and as the two of us lay there on our backs, facing the blue sky and the cedars all around us, I heard a big, old crow cawing about the scene being played out beneath him.

Noah said quietly, "Honey, they're not the bad guys. They're just deer hunters."

I responded with sarcasm, "What was your first clue, Columbo?"

With that, we laughed so hard, with tears streaming down our face, that finally, the father-son duo of deer hunters came over, sat down, and laughed until they cried right along with us. The younger, larger deer hunter stripped off his coat and shirt down to his white undershirt. He peeled it off, brought out his hunting knife, fashioned a sling for Noah's shoulder, and very carefully wrapped the shoulder and arm musculature as my husband gritted his teeth against the pain. His face was white as the deer hunter stabilized his arm tight around his waist to immobilize him for the bumpy ride to town in their three-wheel electric vehicle.

Their vehicle that was designed to carry two hunters in the front, with the carcass of a deer on the small flatbed, did double duty that day. We silently motored through the cedars, up the old, cobbled-stoned Roman road, and straight into town to the doctor's office. Goliath and my husband rode up front, and the old man with the round, frameless spectacles, with one hand still holding on to his rifle and the other holding on to the collar of his dog, rode with me in open-air on the flatbed. My ass felt every cobbled stone of the old Roman road all the way to town, and I knew that I would be black and blue and sore as hell by dinnertime that night.

The deer hunter had called ahead, and word spread quickly throughout the village. The doctor and two nurses were standing outside, along with a host of others to meet the wounded. Edouard and Catharine pulled up as we did. By that time, Noah was in extreme pain and the right side of my face felt like it was on fire.

The doctor quickly cut off the sling, as Noah kept insisting that he take care of me first. After a local anesthetic, he was relieved to find that the bullet had exited clean out the other side of his triceps. It could have been much worse. He was put on lots of pain meds and bed-rest with a nurse to watch for fever and infection at four-hour intervals throughout the couple of days, and daily fresh bandages after that.

As for me, the cleanup required a local anesthetic as well, to get the dirt and debris out of my cheekbone. Nothing seemed to be broken, just badly scraped and bruised. I too was put on the same pain meds and bed-rest to watch for fever and concussion at four-hour intervals, with the same daily fresh-bandage routine.

We couldn't have asked for better treatment. I suppose that staying at the *château* was all part of the mix. Of course, Noah had asked Edouard to explain to the doctor's office and the French-speaking nurses that they would be well compensated upfront for their service and house calls. As Noah was getting last-minute instructions from the doctor, I asked to speak with the two deer hunters, and, with Edouard as my interpreter, I explained that we had gotten lost and inadvertently trespassed onto their property. I apologized for my bizarre behavior during the attack and asked them if we could please take them out for lunch by the end of the week once we got feeling a little better. My apology and suggestion that we kiss and make up was met with, "D'accord! D'accord! D'accord!" We certainly didn't need the locals to be suing us for trespassing or anything like that and I'm sure they felt the same way about us suing them.

It took a good few of days of bed-rest and meals on trays in our suite before Noah could stand up and feel well enough to venture downstairs. It felt so good to be back at having our meals with Edouard and Catharine, who were such excellent hosts throughout the whole ordeal. I was so glad that we had had those two wonderful nights of playing cards and dancing in front of the roaring fire before the accident.

Noah was facing months of physiotherapy ahead up in London to get his damaged tricep back into shape, so we made do with hanging out in the library, where the boys would spend hours discussing cases and swapping stories from their careers in justice. The dog never left Noah's side. He slept at the foot of the stairs and cried all night long until the night nurse would finally allow him to sneak upstairs with her, where he was happy to lie down at our bedroom door quietly.

Catharine kept me busy up in the attic, as she opened up trunk after trunk of the old World War Two Red Cross nurse uniforms so that I could dress up and play nurse with my immobilized patient. This was the first time in our relationship that Noah simply wasn't up to making love, and I thought that the whole 'playing doctor' shtick might be a good intro back into the swing of things if, in fact, I could manage to lower my head to try to give him a kiss. We were quite a pair; he couldn't role over on his side, so we couldn't even spoon, as the side of my face that was still so raw was not on his corresponding good side. So, we slept nose-to-nose, him snoring into my face and me intermittently tossing and turning to get away from his noise, while at the same time trying to avoid touching my face.

Dawn broke on Day Four of our recovery and I opened my eyes to see Noah smiling at me. He looked better somehow, even with the four-day growth of beard.

"Good morning, sleepyhead. I'm starving. Do you think we could go downstairs and rustle up some early breakfast?"

"Oh, baby, you're back! It's so good to see you looking a little better."

"Yeah, and look what else is working." He grabbed my hand and guided me down to feel his big erection.

"Oh my God. Don't move, baby. I'm going to inch over very carefully and see if we can manage a faceless, armless, but still-fabulous rendezvous right now. Don't touch my face, and I won't touch your arm. Okay, baby?"

"Anything, babe, anything. Just don't hurt me."

"Yeah, exactly. That's what I'm saying to you. Don't you come anywhere near my face."

"And don't you come anywhere near my arm. Are we clear?"

"Yes, yes, we're clear. Now careful, careful. I'm going to inch my hips over to match up with your hips. Maybe you can use your good arm to guide yourself into me. Okay, honey?"

"Come on, come on. Stop talking and just get over here. Just be gentle with me. None of your usual flailing about and squealing at the top of your lungs."

"For a man with a big, throbbing hard-on, you have a lot to say. You are totally at my mercy right now, so if I were you, I would stop dispensing with the advice and just concentrate on satisfying me before I decide if, in fact, I'm going to satisfy you. If. And to use your words, are we clear?"

"Clear as a bell. Now shut the fuck up and get over here so I can make love to you before you get all crazy on me and they hear you down in the village."

"Okay, honey. You're my man and I just want to please you."

***

As Edouard, Catharine, Noah, and I entered the restaurant for the lunch that I had promised the deer hunters, I realized that I was the target-of-the-day for the deer hunters' particular sense of humor. Big signs of 'danger ahead,' 'watch out for protective lioness,' 'beware of mother bear,' and 'don't shoot' were pasted up everywhere, both in English and French. They guided me to the head of the table and crowned me with a homemade crown and a sash that read: *"Jeanne d'Arc."* It seemed to me that the whole village had turned out for the event, and everyone had a great time at my expense. I sucked it up. I took solace in the fact that my sash represented a great woman of courage. 'Good old Joan. Yeah. And also,' I mused, 'my ancestor, Mary, Queen of Scots would be proud of me.' Both of those women saved the day on many occasions with their wile and wit, but I imagined that they had to take teasing along the way too, just like what was playing out in front of me. At least I lived to tell the tale!

My charming husband stood up with his wine glass in hand and clinked his glass a few times to get the attention of the party. The room quieted, and everyone stood up, glasses in hands. Catharine, on the other side of me, pressed her hand down on my shoulder, indicating that I should stay seated.

Speaking in his impeccable French, he asked, "Will you please raise your glass with me in honor of my wife? She is the most formidable and courageous woman I have ever met in my whole life. To my wife, Susan Brier."

The walls of the old restaurant echoed my name again and again, right along with many *Jeanne d'Arcs.*

His eyes were wide in disbelief. He looked at both of us, peering into our faces. "What the hell happened to you?" he barked at Noah.

"Good morning, Ray. Thank you for being here to see us off to London. We appreciate your time."

"You were ordered to lie low. Now I see that you've been involved in some sort of mess. By the looks of your jacket, and your arm in a sling, I'd say that you've taken a bullet. Am I correct?"

"Yes, but it's not as it seems. No danger at all. A careless deer hunter up country at the *château*," Noah explained calmly.

"I knew it. I knew it the minute I saw the two of you holding hands while disembarking from the plane. Way, way too much in love with each other to have enough common sense to follow my orders. Did you have anything to do with this, Susan?" he snapped.

"Just a minute here, Ray. Calm down. No sense insulting my wife. We're both just fine, and we're both looking forward to getting settled in London. Are we all set on your end?"

During the flight, we Googled our new London address, and we were pleased to see that we would be living in the upscale neighborhood of Notting Hill. Although we missed 7 Russell Hill Road every day, we were looking forward to getting settled in once again with a daily routine of physiotherapy for Noah's shoulder and arm and to wait out our exile in peace and quiet. That being said, we were hoping it wouldn't be a long sojourn.

Noah had loved our time at the *château* so much that he had insisted on wearing his shot-up jacket on the plane to London and had packed his rubber barn boots in his suitcase to keep as a souvenir of his foray into the world of country living and all its perils.

***

The frail, white-haired man stood on his top front step with bowler hat in one hand and pipe in the other. He stood there in the damp late afternoon, looking over his domain with satisfaction. The old, retired banker had certainly done well for himself and ended up here in Notting Hill with his bride of fifty-five years right beside him.

The said bride came out of their elegant townhouse, carefully locked the front door, and stood beside him, making sure that her Channel bag was closed and clipped down tightly. He tapped his pipe on the wrought iron and put it away in the pocket of his topcoat that signaled to his dutiful wife that he was now ready to proceed.

Just as they were about to descend the stairs, they watched as the airport limo pulled to a sudden stop in front of the adjacent, elegant, limestone-clad, four-story townhouse across the street. The driver dropped off his two passengers with their two suitcases and two travel bags before quickly speeding away.

The old, retired banker observed that the two arrivals looked all around them. 'A little furtively,' he thought to himself. The middle-aged Negro had given him a short, formal nod of the head when their eyes met. He studied the tall, slim man with somewhat graying, unkempt Afro hair sticking out every which way, while his black brows defined a lean, alert face. He had a hooked scar on his left cheek and had one arm in a sling. His partner looked no better. She was a white woman, holding on to the two travel bags – one red and one black. Her long, dark hair was a disaster, flying around every which way. She looked like she had fared the worst of a street brawl, with a large, dark bruise with overlying dried bits of a leftover, half-healed scab over one cheekbone. As the two of them made their way up the stairs of the townhouse across the street, in their matching dark blue wind jackets, the elderly gentleman concluded that the two of them didn't look like they belonged in his neighborhood at all. He tucked his wife's Channel bag and her arm protectively under his.

"There goes the neighborhood, Bernice. Mark my words. There goes the neighborhood."

"Oh my! Oh my, Harford! It looks like a dog with sharp teeth took hold of the top of his one sleeve! Blimey!" she added in hushed agreement.

As they gingerly made their way down their steps, on their way out for afternoon tea at Claridge's, she said to her husband on an upward beat, "Nice-looking luggage though, Harford, if I do say so."

***

Over the next month, I found out quickly that my husband definitely did not share my gypsy blood at all. We had settled into our beautiful new home in the heart of one of the greatest cities in the world, but Noah's heart just wasn't into it.

We took in all the sights, and he surprised me by getting great seats for the televised variety show, The Graham Norton Show. It turned out to be such a good time, with all the guests, comedy, and music. We really both enjoyed a David Hockney Exhibition during this time as well. We scouted out a few good jazz bars, tried out a few of the restaurants, and shopped and browsed constantly, but it seemed that nothing we did was of any great lasting interest to either of us.

As the weeks passed, I knew my husband was struggling and that he did his best to try to keep me happy by planning so many diversions. It wasn't just that his physiotherapy for his left arm was slow in taking effect; he simply wasn't himself.

***

I opened my eyes to the dark. I rolled over to reach for Nigel, to find that I had been sleeping alone. It wasn't like him to get up in the middle of the night, so I grabbed my robe and padded out into the hall. I could see a light filtering through from downstairs, but as my hand reached the bannister, my ears picked up a sound.

I stopped, honing in on the noise that seemed to be coming from the kitchen. My heart sank as I recognized deep, heart-wrenching sobs of someone who was definitely in distress. I was halfway down the stairs before I realized that he would be embarrassed with me seeing him like this. "Shit. Should I go to him? No, it would embarrass him. Yes, I should go. No, stay put," I argued back and forth with myself.

I lay there, feigning sleep, as he quietly slipped back into bed an hour later. There was no spooning that night. He was facing the other way and was sleeping on the outer edge of his side of our bed. I rolled over to his side, still pretending to be asleep, and dropped my arm around his waist to silently comfort him.

***

"I hope we're home for Hanukkah and Christmas," he said quietly as we sipped on an after-breakfast coffee at the kitchen table, with all the daily newspapers in front of us.

"I hear you, babe. I must say, though, the holidays don't really matter to me one way or the other, but it will be good to get back to being ourselves. And I agree with you, the fun of being Noah Rosenberg and Susan Brier wore off a little while ago, didn't it?"

"It's not the holidays, as you say. It's just that I don't even know who I am anymore. I'm just sick and tired of hiding. Don't forget I've been in the witness protection program for years now. And ever since I met you, I just want to be a normal, happily married husband leading a normal life at 7 Russell Hill Road, where we belong."

"So, here's what we can do meanwhile. We could start making a plan for when we do get home. Do you want to go back to work in the courts? If you stay at home, will you still be on full salary? Are you going to stay retired? Are you going to write another book? How about taking a few painting lessons? You have an avid interest in art. But please know, babe, whatever your plan, count me in."

"I know, I know. I should be grateful for all I have. Especially having you in my life. I'm just not myself these days. I don't know how you can put up with me. I've lost my sense of humor somehow. To tell you the truth, it's more than just the hiding out, honey. I'm always worrying that my psychological transference disorder will reoccur and I'll lay all my deep-rooted anxieties on you like I did with Gerri. I just couldn't bear it. I'd rather kill myself than have that happen."

I threw my newspaper down with a thwack and laid it on the line. "I think you misunderstood me, Nigel Royal. When I said that I agree to want to get back to normal, I did not agree in any shape or form for you to be feeling sorry for yourself. I won't hear any more of your pity party."

I grabbed his hand over the table and said, "Honey, you should know by now that you can't mess with me like that. I love you. And we're in this together, come hell or high water. Remember, it wasn't that long ago when you got shot and you pushed me into the dirt and lay on top of me to save me. And I followed by running after you. For better and for worse, right?"

I continued, "Now's here's what we are going to do. Listen up. First things first. I'm going to forget what you said about killing yourself, but before I do, I am going to report that to our shrink at our next visit. We both know that you're out of line, and I intend to get you back on track with the help of our doctor right here in London. I mean, after all, we both like her, and so far so good in that department. Right? Let's go all the way and get you some good drugs to help us through this little patch."

We both smiled a little and he said, "Yeah. You're right. I'll phone her right now and make an appointment for as soon as possible. I definitely need some happy pills. It may just be the stress of the wound to my triceps that has got me down. It's hard for me to handle all the treatments for the bullet wound because it's just not progressing as fast as I want it to. But actually, getting shot was a tremendous psychological stress on me, and that's hounding me as well. You're so much tougher than me. It doesn't seem to bother you that you chose to die with me rather than run away and hide. But my stress from the bullet seems to be more so than anything I've ever been through. Including losing you to France for that year before we were married, I think. I do know that stress can trigger an episode, so that's what I'm really worried about. I'm sorry, honey. And you're right. We're in this together. And don't you worry. A stray bullet isn't going to take us down. No, not at all. We're going to die at age hundred from an episode of multiple orgasms."

I jumped up and put my arms around his neck. "Now you're talking! Count me in for that one, honey!"

As I nuzzled his neck, I said softly, "Okay, okay, I've got an idea. I've just decided that I'm taking you out for a big night on the town. After all, we've done so much shopping here in London, and you really haven't had an opportunity to wear that nice suit that you had made. And, of course, I'll wear my new red dress that you bought me."

"Okay. Yes. That sounds like a plan. Where are you taking us?"

"Dinner and the opera."

"Oh! We're really going out! Nothing but the best for Noah Rosenberg and his wife, Susan Brier!"

"You're damn right. Nothing but the best."

***

A month later, as we were enjoying our night out at the opera, I could feel Noah's cell vibrate from the inside pocket of his new Saville Row bespoke suit. He lowered himself as he crawled over all the other patrons of the arts to leave the theater to answer the call. After all, it was our cellphone that Ray had given us. Noah kept it on him at all times, but to date, it had only rung once, and that was when Ray notified us to go to the Avignon Airport to move on to our next location.

A few minutes later, Noah was waving to me from the darkened aisle. His face was lit up like a Christmas tree. My heart was pounding. I excused myself again and again as I squeezed past the irate opera buffs to grab my husband's hand and to joyously run out of the theater.

"Really, honey, really? We're going home?"

"Yes, my darling. We're going home."

"What are we doing just standing here? Let's get back and start packing."

We stayed up all night packing. I hadn't realized how much shopping we had actually done. Noah, of course, was way ahead of me. He had gone out one day and had bought three large suitcases, just to be prepared. All of a sudden, all of our nice, new clothes that we had idly bought just to pass an afternoon were so beautiful. We had a little fashion show as we packed, and

Noah zipped up my new dresses, one after the other, as I paraded in front of him.

"There! That's it!" I exclaimed as I pointed at him from where I was standing in the closet doorway, holding on to my new Liberty shirts.

"What?" he said as he stood there in his new, dark blue silk pajamas.

"My little boy is back. It's written all over your face with your big grin! Do you know how cute you are?"

He reached over, grabbed me, and growled, "I'll show you cute. Take a look down here. Now that's cute."

We caught the next flight out – at 9:30 a.m. London time. We both said we had never known a sweeter touchdown in Toronto. As the porters managed all the luggage, the doors opened and we saw the sign before we saw Chi and François. It read:

Welcome Home, Royal Family.

***

Chi unlocked the door for us, and he and François left us there after a promise that we would arrive at 6:00 p.m. at Chi's apartment for a big celebration dinner and a good visit to catch up of what had transpired on our trip.

As we stepped into the house, there was a very nostalgic smell. We looked at each other and smiled. The big, freshly cut tree, totally devoid of all decorations, took precedence in the front window of the living room. Thank God for Chi. It was three days until Christmas, and he had thought of everything. The whole house looked lovely. Chi had brought in fresh flowers everywhere, and he'd also stocked up the fridge for us. It was like we had never left .I was happy enough just to unpack, but Nigel just couldn't settle down enough to even empty a suitcase. He just kept roaming from room to room, enjoying every little nuance along the way.

I ran downstairs to check up on him and found him in Saul's office, sitting in his old chair, with his feet up on the old desk. He grabbed me and pulled me down into his lap.

I murmured, "Something on your mind, Mr. Nigel Royal?"

"Just you, Mrs. Denise Royal, just you," he said as he slipped my big, flashy yellow diamond back on my finger.

I woke up in our darkened bedroom to Nigel's whistling coming from our big shower. I joined him. My handsome, sexy husband that I knew and loved was back. Oh my God, he was back in full force.

We scrambled into our clothes so we wouldn't be late for our dinner at Chi's apartment.

Chi opened the door and took one look at us. He laughed and shook his head. "What is it with you two? You look like a couple of teenagers that have been making out all afternoon. It's so damn good to have you home. Come in. Come in. I want to hear all about your trip. François is running late, but he'll be here soon, so we'll hold dinner until he gets here."

Ten minutes later, François arrived, so Nigel began his first story by taking off his shirt to show his bullet wound.

"Save your sympathy, boys," I said dryly. "I have a feeling that this story is going to end with you laughing your heads off at my expense. Your old pal here is quite a storyteller."

It was the first time that Nigel had got to tell anyone about me attacking the 6'3" deer hunter, and I must admit I was laughing right along with Chi and François. Chi was in hysterics, with Nigel's long arms and legs flailing around, making his point at how my nails had landed on target on the poor, startled deer hunter's face and how the deer hunter had plucked me off his large body like one would pick a fly off a string of flypaper. Nigel had, of course, embellished the story, adding in a wild banshee war cry that he claimed I sounded. At that point, I couldn't really argue or deny anything. I was laughing too hard at my charming, funny, handsome husband.

After dinner, Chi brought out the files that he had kept for us during our absence. He had downloaded our emails from our computers daily, printed each email out, paid our household bills as they came in, and had answered our phone messages where necessary to cancel appointments and upcoming dates. He insisted on not filling us in on what went down to free Nigel from his witness protection program by saying that it was all a bunch of technical stuff that could wait for another day. Today was a day for celebration – no shop talk allowed.

I looked on as Nigel gave Chi the Noah Rosenberg and Susan Brier passports, phones, etc. along with the Harrod's cashmere sweaters and scarves that we had bought for Chi and François. We all toasted to our original identities being restored, without a hitch and without a scratch, save Nigel's gunshot wound, of course.

"Boys, may I make a toast?"

We all lifted our glasses and I said, "It's Sunday night. We sit here, the four of us, finally able to make simple, ordinary plans together for not only the week ahead of us but for the rest of our lives. We are finally free. Nigel, here we sit, a middle-aged married couple living in a quiet, upscale neighborhood in the best country in the world, our Canada, having dinner with the best friend in the whole world, and our amazing godson. It doesn't get any better than this. It's all because of you three remarkable men. I salute you and I love you more than you'll ever know. Thank you for bringing me into your world. Here's to family."

As we opened yet another bottle of wine, I made my boys a promise that I was going to cook them the best Christmas turkey dinner and all the trimmings including potato latkes that they'd ever tasted in their lives. There were many *Merry Christmas, Happy Hanukkah, and Happy New Year* toasts surrounding Chi's dining room table that night at 7 Russell Hill Road.

***

Our utopia lasted exactly for twenty-four hours.

The following evening, Nigel checked for new email messages. Upon reading the two-page correspondence from a barrister and solicitor's office in Stockholm, Sweden, life, as we knew it, changed dramatically.

***

Chapter 12
Nigella Hansson

I heard Nigel bellowing from Saul's office. "Denni, Denni, take a look at this! Honey, are you there!? Come! Please! Hurry! For God's sake, take a look at this!"

'Now what could possibly be so important that he has to yell from four rooms over?' I mused to myself.

I had never seen that look on his face before – animated and distraught, all at the same time. He couldn't speak. He just pointed to his screen.

The email, dated December 23, 2005, read:

Dear Mr. Royal,

I am the solicitor for Ms. Nigella Hansson, and she has authorized me to forward the following three attachments. If you do not wish to correspond with Ms. Hansson, please notify me immediately so that I can close this file. Thank you for your attention to this matter at your earliest convenience.

The first attachment read:

Dear Mr. Royal,

My name is Nigella Hansson, and I live in Stockholm, Sweden. I am thirty years old, and I work as a barrister and solicitor in the field of international law.

I have recently discovered that we, meaning you and I specifically, share the same gene pool. In fact, after much research and investigation, it appears that you are my biological father, according to information that you filed under ancestry.ca late last year and that I filed under ancestry.se two years ago. I was very surprised and so delighted with my find!

My mother (now deceased) had apparently met you during a brief encounter in Stockholm thirty-one years ago. Her name was Martina Kaufman Hansson, and she was one of the most remarkable women I have ever known in my entire life. She was an excellent mother to me. She never married and I was her whole life.

She was born Martina Kaufman. Her Polish mother, who was a Holocaust survivor, died shortly after giving birth to her daughter in 1946, while living in a Displaced Person's Camp in Germany, right after World War Two. The Red Cross took over and sent the orphaned baby (my mother) to Sweden with a new Swedish passport, adding the last name of Hansson, in hopes that a Swedish family name would encourage adoption of the deaf baby girl. She lived in the Stockholm Orphanage for Displaced Children until she was age fourteen when this particular barnhem was closed down in 1960. She was transferred to another barnhem and then aged out of the care system at the age of eighteen.

When you met her, at age twenty-eight, her survival skills included sign language and pantomime. She worked in hotel kitchens mostly but had difficulty holding a job down due to her hearing impairment. She chose not to speak, as she never had any formal training on how to sound out words.

The day you met her, you were kind enough to write your name 'Nigel' and 'Canada' on a piece of hotel notepaper. She kept it for many years before she gave it to me. She told me the story of your all-too-short, tender love affair that resulted in her pregnancy. She told me that you held her hand to the radio speaker and that you danced with her around the room to Ray Charles. She named me in honor of you. I was her love child. I have attached a screenshot of your handwritten name and country that you gave her so long ago.

Of course, I Googled you the moment I found you through the ancestry.ca alert. I found out that you wrapped up your distinguished law career with an early retirement from the position of Supreme Court Justice of Canada.

I am a little shy and hesitant to mention this, but although I look a great deal like my mother, I really think I look a little like you too. Please peruse my photo (attached) so you can judge for yourself. It's something about our eyes, and of course our curly hair. I wonder, due to your dark skin tones and our afro hair, are you of African descent? Or perhaps Asian or native descent?

I can be found on LinkedIn and also under my law firm's directory. If, in fact, you are interested in meeting me, please know that I am very much interested in meeting you. I look forward to your early response.

Yours, Nigella

I clicked on the other two attachments. The penned 'Nigel' and 'Canada' were definitely a match to his current penmanship, and the beautiful, blond, light-skinned woman staring out from the screen had a striking resemblance to Nigel.

I stood there after studying the attachments, as stunned as he was. He stood up and took me in his arms.

"How did I get so lucky!? Please God, tell me how I got so damn lucky!"

"Merry Christmas, darling."

***

We discussed the situation the whole night long. We placed the call to Stockholm in the middle of the night, which would make it the morning of Christmas Eve in Sweden.

A charming Swedish voice answered our ring, changing mid-sentence from Swedish to English, "*God Jul, glad hanukkah,* how may I direct your call?"

"Hello, may I speak with Nigella Hansson?" Nigel's deep baritone was carefully modulated.

"This is she. May I ask who is calling?" the voice that was speaking English with the charming Swedish accent inquired.

"Yes, yes, of course. It's Nigel, calling from Canada."

"Oh, it's you! Happy Christmas and Happy Hanukkah! Thank you for your prompt response to my email! I hope that it wasn't too much of a shock for you!" Nigella laughed softly. "Now I'm all flustered, but please, do you have any questions for me?"

"Yes, yes. I do have one question, and only one, Nigella."

"Yes?"

"May I please send you an air ticket to come visit me here in Toronto? I simply can't wait to meet you."

"Absolutely! I feel the same way too! But there is one small detail to be considered with any travel plans, Nigel."

"And what would that small detail be, Nigella?"

"It's not what, Nigel; it's whom. Her name is Martina, and she is my five-year-old daughter."

Nigel drew in a long breath, and with hope and joy very much evident in his words, he said, "Are you saying that I'm a father as well as a granddad?"

"That's exactly what I'm saying."

"Oh! Oh! Oh! Nigella, you have made me one happy man! I can safely say this is the best Christmas and best Hanukkah I've ever had! Will you please email me yours and Martina's travel information along with your chosen departure date? And the open-end tickets will be waiting for you to pick up at the airport counter in Stockholm. Does that work for you?"

Two hours later, Nigel had received all the information he needed from his daughter. He immediately emailed instructions to his assistant that read:

Sophia,

Please rush this one.

Two first-class, open-end tickets, Stockholm – Toronto – Stockholm, to be made out for one adult and one child. All their details below.

Please email copy of the two tix and itinerary to adult passenger, and cc me as well.

Passengers will p/u tix upon check-in at Stockholm Airport. And of course, please throw in all the usual bells and whistles.

Thanks, N.

***

Two weeks later to the day, Chi, Nigel, and I stood in the 'arrivals' area of Lester B. Pearson. The moment the flashing arrival sign was posted under *arrivals*, Chi promptly raised the new sign so all disembarking passengers could see. It simply read: *WELCOME – HANSSON PARTY.*

I saw her approach actually, before she was aware of us, as she arranged her face into the appropriate response for airport greetings. She was holding her small daughter's hand, and her arm was flapping up and down to the little girl's skipping and hopping. The younger beauty of the two spotted our HANSSON sign and pointedly excitely. I watched as the mother bent down a little to follow the small pointing finger. She closed her eyes and seemed to take a deep breath before standing up tall and walking toward us full of confidence and grace. The porter with a full load of luggage struggled to keep up. There was no doubt about it; they were a pair of real showstoppers – perfect mom-and-daughter duo.

I looked up at Nigel. He was transfixed. He managed a wave that Nigella saw. He lowered himself down to his five-year-old granddaughter's level and waited for her response to his big smile.

The smaller of the duo shook off her mother's hand and ran up and stopped dead in front of Nigel's crouching figure. They were nose-to-nose. Her blond, curly afro ringlets that fell to her shoulders were dancing back and forth with her every jump and wriggle.

"Are you my granddad?"

Nigel said in a soft voice, "Yes, my golden angel, I'm your granddad."

"Mommy! Mommy! I told you it was him! He's my granddad!"

He scooped her up in his arms, stood up, and floated forward to meet his daughter for the first time in their lives.

It was very obvious that they were family. Nigella was tall and lanky, with lighter skin than Nigel's, but she had those Jamaican-Chinese dark brown eyes of her father, even though her hair was long and blond and she was wearing it straightened, poker-straight, that added to her super-model look.

Nigel simply couldn't take his eyes off the two of them but was motioning with his hand for me to join in the collective family hug.

I was enveloped in the love fest, and Nigella said, "You must be Denni. Thank you, thank you, for taking such good care of my dad. Martina, this is uh, uh –"

And I finished her sentence, "Hello, my beautiful baby, I'm your grandma."

By then, Nigel was getting Chi into the circle, who had been paying the porter and taking control of the luggage, and we all just stood there with our arms around each other, basking in the remarkable odds of it all and not wanting the moment to end.

After we had managed to get all the luggage into the back of the big Benz, we pulled out of the airport, ready to begin our two-week family-style holiday. I sat up front with Chi, and Nigel was sandwiched between his two girls in the backseat.

"Granddad, you have very curly hair," she said as her little fingers gently unraveled each graying spiral one by one.

"Martina, mind your manners!" her mother warned, and Nigel roared with laughter.

7 Russell Hill Road would never be the same.

***

I woke to a tapping at the bedroom door. The morning sun was still low, and the bedroom was dim. I felt beside me for Nigel; he was gone.

The tapper's voice was anxious. "Denni, where's Martina? She's not in her bed!"

"Oh, honey, so sorry, so sorry. Don't worry. She's probably with Nigel. He was up all last night, checking to see if the two of you were okay every five minutes. He couldn't wait for this morning. Did you check the kitchen?"

"Yes, I've looked everywhere, and she isn't used to not being with me. She's only five. She'll be frightened."

"Okay, okay. First, come here. Come to the window. I know where they may be."

I was right. There they were. Nigel was still in his pajama bottoms, with his winter jacket on and snow up to his knees. He was holding Martina high up in his arms, underneath the old bare maple. She had on her long flannel nightie, and her ski jacket was gaping open. Her thin, long legs dangled freely below her and her fluffy, white bunny slippers peddled the air as she tightened her grip on the old maple, wriggling to get loose of Nigel's hold. He wasn't facing us, so it was impossible to hear their conversation, but his head was thrown back as if he was offering his laughter to the Almighty God above him.

Nigella put her arm around my shoulder, and I slipped my arm around her waist. We just stood there, soaking it all in.

"I know him. I know exactly what he's doing out there, standing like an idiot in snow up to his knees."

"Oh. Now what would that be, Denni? What's my dad doing?" she asked as she smiled, watching her dad and her daughter.

"He's visually mapping out the tree house he will be building for Martina as soon as the spring weather comes along. By tonight, at the very latest, he will be in Saul's office, sketching it all out on paper."

"Are you kidding me?"

"Not in the least. Saul built him one in that very same maple tree when he was nine or ten. As sure as God made little green apples, he will build the perfect replica of it for Martina."

"Denni," she said quietly, "English is my second language, so please tell me what little green apples have to do with anything."

I was a little startled by her question, and I looked up into her face. She was grinning from ear to ear, simply teasing me about my folksy colloquialism, just like Nigel would have done.

"Well, try this one on for size, missy. *The apple doesn't fall far from the tree.* Don't give me that English-is-my-second-language crap. You think I just fell off the turnip truck?"

She hugged me tight, laughed, and said, "Oh, you Canadians are so much fun. Does my dad know how lucky he is to have you in his life?"

"Yes, I tell him every day."

She looked back out the window. "But really, Denni, this is double trouble we're in for. Martina can be quite a handful, and it looks like her granddad is going to be her perfect foil."

"Yeah, I know. I understand. But I'm looking at this whole thing in an entirely different light. I'm just so happy to have you here, right beside me.

Finally, someone in the house to talk about fashion, makeup, and hair-straightening techniques!"

Nigella was nodding her head in agreement as she asked politely, "Would it be okay with you if we go downstairs and start a pot of hot chocolate? It looks like our two kids might need some warming up."

"You got that right, girlfriend. Let's just stay in our robes. We don't dress for breakfast."

"Really? Would that be okay? You and Dad have such a beautiful home here, and you both look like movie stars. Look at you in your silk robe. That looks very fancy to me. Back home, I seemed to live in my old flannel pajamas."

"Oh, my God. A girl after my own heart. We've got some shopping to do. I know where they have the best flannel pjs ever."

As we were about to leave our bedroom, she stopped and looked right into my face. She said earnestly, "Denni, just one last thing before we go down."

Taken aback with her solemn look, I said, "What is it?"

"I don't know what a turnip truck is," and she threw back her head and howled with laughter.

"That does it. You are just nothing but a saucy girl, and I'm not going to share my favorite pajama store with you. Ever."

As we went down to the kitchen, I thought of her 'movie-star' remark. She had no idea. I wondered how Nigel would arrange for his daughter and granddaughter to meet his brother, the real-deal movie star in his growing family. I smiled to myself as I used my fingers to count the family's heritage. Let's see. There was Jamaican, Canadian, a French Jew, Vietnamese, Cambodian, the Americans, and now the Swedes, and of course, Nigella's mom, Martina, who was born a Polish Jew in a German refugee camp. I thanked God right then and there that this wasn't only Nigel's family. It was mine too. After years of being alone, I had a family again. And I thought of my dad, who was the absolute king of Canadian-style diversity. He was up there smiling down at us all, with his wit picking up on every little joke and tease within the loving banter going down at 7 Russell Hill Road.

***

The two-week holiday passed so quickly, and we all savored every single moment of it, not that we did anything too fancy, and we were all in bed every night by eleven. I ran into Canadian Tire one day and bought us all new skates. It had been years since Chi, Nigel, or I had been skating, so I thought we had all better start afresh. We all went down to the outdoor rink at City Hall, including Chi, and I thought Nigel would burst with pride as his little golden angel would try to teach him her latest figure-skating twirls, hands up in the air like a ballerina. Martina did not approve of his size-thirteen hockey skates; they just didn't make the little princess' grade at all, but she was pleased as punch with her own little white figure skates.

Nigella had taken to Chi ever since she met him at the airport and insisted on inviting him in for dinner, which, she explained to us, was going to be Swedish, and that we were not allowed in the kitchen at all.

That was the first night that I heard all about the beautiful, middle-aged Vietnamese cashier that worked at Loblaws. Nigel told the story that over the years, the two bachelors at 7 Russell Hill Road had always made a weekly visit to Loblaws to stock up on groceries. Over the past six months, Chi always insisted on going through this one particular lane, even if the lane had a line-up ten people deep. He had a boyish crush on the pretty cashier that always seemed very happy to see him.

"What's her name, Chi?" Nigella asked.

"I don't know," Chi said shyly.

Nigella looked at me, and I looked back at her. Nigella shook her head a little, smiled, took his hand, and said, "Well, by this time tomorrow night, you will know her name. We are going over there tomorrow, and you, my friend, are going to ask her. You are going to introduce us all to her, and then you are going to give her your card and ask her to call you if she would be interested in coming over for a coffee on the weekend."

Chi knew that he had met his match. "You think?"

Nigel chuckled and said, "Yes, Chi, it's time to jump in the ring. I'll be right beside you, and you'll be the smooth operator that will sweep her right off her feet."

"What if she's married?"

"Trust me, Chi, I've watched the way she looks at you. She's not married. She's totally hot for you. She's just patiently waiting for you to make a move. Since I met my beautiful Irish faerie, I know about such matters."

"Well, okay then. I trust your judgment. But Nigella, you'll have to help me out a little."

Nigella said, "Chi, my friend, you are about to find out that when love is in the air, you don't have to worry about a thing. Just go with the flow and let all the happiness just wash over you."

The very next morning, we all packed into the big Benz to drive around the block on our trip to Loblaws. As it all turned out, it was Nigella's careful and skillfully executed plan that got the ball rolling, but it was definitely Chi's shining hour.

Nigella was first in the target's grocery line, with Martina placed firmly in the cart along with a few groceries. Chi was right behind her, holding onto a bag of coffee in one hand and some dish soap in the other. I was next, and Nigel was squeezed up right behind me, not wanting to miss out on the action.

Nigella, with her Swedish accent, said to the very pretty, dainty, middle-aged cashier, "Oh, I'm sorry, I don't have my groceries all ready for you to check through. My daughter is in the way. So sorry, I'm new to your store. You see, I'm just staying with family here; I'm visiting from Sweden. My name is Nigella, by the way."

"Well, I'm pleased to meet you, Nigella. My name is Diep. You have a very beautiful daughter. Her hair is magnificent. What's her name?"

"This is Martina." She turned to Martina, "Please say hello to Diep, Martina."

"Hello, Diep. I like your name. I'm on holidays. I'm staying with my granddad and my grandma," said Martina, pointing down the line to Nigel and me.

"Oh, my goodness, we are holding up the line here," Nigella said, and she turned to Chi. "Chi, you probably already know Diep. This is the store that you always come to, right? Would you mind lifting Martina out of the cart and I'll get busy unloading the groceries."

Chi nodded to Nigella and then stepped in a little closer to the counter. As he offered his hand over the counter, he smiled directly into Diep's eyes. "Hello, Diep. Chi Tran. Pleased to meet you. I think in our culture, your name means lover of nature, right?"

"Yes. And I do recognize you and your friend, the one that the baby calls granddad," she said, batting her eyelashes at Chi, who was calm, cool, and collected as if he did this every day of his life.

"Actually, I have a confession to make to you, Diep," Chi said with a charming little laugh. "Every week, I come here with my friend Nigel," he said, waving down to the said friend. "I always wait in line to check out with you. I've been wondering if you would like to come over to the house while our girls are in town, to have some Vietnamese pastries and coffee with all of us, maybe on the weekend if you're free."

At that moment, another cashier appeared, standing quietly behind Diep.

Diep, playing her part in the little *tête-à-tête* so well, was nodding her head, saying, "Oh, actually, perfect timing. I'm just going on break, so my colleague here will cash you out. I'll meet you at the down escalator in five minutes, and I'll walk to your car with you so I can give you my number. Does that work for you?"

She gracefully backed out of the cash-desk cubicle as Chi lifted Martina out of the cart. All of us had smiles for miles, all the way up and down the checkout line. It was all just so damn cute.

Two days later, on Sunday afternoon, after Diep had sung in the choir at her local church, Chi picked her up at her apartment on Raglan Avenue, which was about four blocks from 7 Russell Hill Road.

By the time Martina, Nigella, Nigel, and I arrived at his apartment over the garage, Chi had the coffee perking, and the delicious smell of something baking in the oven wafted through his sparkling home. He had set the beautiful teak dining room table with bone china and the same linen napkins that I remembered from my first visit to his apartment last year. At Martina's place setting, he had placed a Popsicle stick kit, glue included, so that Nigel could help her build the small birdhouse while the adults enjoyed the visit. The only thing different was that the big oil painting of his first wife, Nuyen, was nowhere to be seen.

As Chi gave Nigella and Martina the cook's tour, Diep told Nigel and me that she had been living in the neighborhood in her apartment for the past two years, ever since selling her house after her husband and adult son were killed by a drunk driver on their way home for work one night. They were both printing-press machine operators that worked the midnight shift out in Etobicoke at the Toronto Star Plant. She actually told the sad story very calmly and said that her part-time job at Loblaws had been a real lifesaver. It gave her something to do and something to look forward to.

Diep adeptly changed the topic. "I'm so impressed with Chi's greenhouse operation. It's a lot of work but totally worth it in the long run. It's nice to know that the local food banks can count on him, month in and month out."

With that, Chi called over from across the living room, "Denni, did you notice I had taken down Nuyen's painting?"

"Oh, yes, now that you mention it," I said.

"Yes, François has been after me for years now to let him have it for his condo, and I thought it was about time."

I looked at Diep, and she was nodding. She said quietly to me, "Yes, a time for all seasons. When I sold my house, I didn't keep too much. I have one plastic tub of old things I keep in my locker now, and that's about it."

"Hey, we're all in the same boat. Last year, I wrapped up my mother's will and all the paraphernalia that surrounds times like that, and when I married Nigel, I moved into his house with one suitcase."

Nigel interjected, "Yes, one suitcase. And one moving van full of books, treasures, *tchotchkes*, and old copper pots and pans."

Diep was laughing, and she gave me a high-five. "Good girl. I don't suppose you have many complaints when you're using those old copper pots and pans to put the dinner on the table."

"You got it, sister!"

***

Later that night, as we sat in the living room while Martina watched *Frozen*, Nigella said, "But Denni, Chi and Diep just acted like an old married couple. And this was their first date! They'll be getting married soon!"

Nigel and I both thought the same thing.

In the evenings, after we all went for our walk around the block, and after Martina was tucked into bed for the umpteenth time after her bath, the three of us would just sit around and tell stories for hours on end. It turned out that Nigel played to his adoring audience like he was born to be on Broadway. He was on queue with every question that Nigella had for him and he kept us all laughing the whole time.

Where on Earth had my shy, nerdy, intellectual introvert gone? I must admit I quite liked this side of my husband just as much as the other quieter one.

I put in my two cents' worth, of course, just to keep the record straight, especially when the two of them were laughing at me, instead of him.

Nigel told the story of how we met in the café, how I had head-butt his chin and drew blood in the process, and how he had stormed out of there with his ego crushed but totally in love with the nameless Irish faerie with big gray eyes and messy, good-smelling hair. He went on to say he almost fainted in court when he saw me sitting there in the plaintiff's chair and was too painfully shy to even look at me during the whole court case. As he was telling us that for our first luncheon date that he had tried on six different shirts, ties, and suits and still couldn't decide, I chirped in and admitted that I had tried on as many dresses for the same occasion.

Nigella, with her wit and her expert prosecuting throughout her young career, knew exactly how to squeeze out every little nuance out of every story and played the Dean to his Jerry as if they had known each other their whole lives.

Nigel's best story, I thought, was the one of how Gerri, the female pro boxer, had knocked him out cold and broke his nose. When he told it, he always danced around a little, throwing out his jabs left and right as he imitated his coach. The punch line, "If you come for the king, you'd better not miss, asshole," was delivered with his big foot up on the edge of the chair to mimic Gerri's foot on his gut.

Of course, his favorite story, and I must admit he told it so well, was the one of me attacking the 6'3" deer hunter, taking him down with one fell swoop. He pulled off his sweater to show her his scar where the bullet had entered and left his triceps. It always ended up with me looking like some kind of crazed lunatic somehow.

Our wedding video was on hand, and Nigella referred to it often throughout our time together.

There were stories that Nigel and I didn't talk about. They were the stories about our broken-heart days – those dark days in between Paris and our marriage ceremony. I quietly mentioned our Paris trip as an acknowledgment to my husband being such a romantic and wanting to start our new relationship off on the right foot, but actually, neither Nigel nor I had the stomach to go there into that black hole that was to follow Paris, even for a second. That was nothing to joke about.

Nigella didn't offer us too many stories of her own. Both Nigel and I knew not to ask. We were all too familiar with the lonely, sad, single life. We figured when the time was right, she would fill in the blanks as she saw fit.

What she did offer was the touching story of how Martina came to be born. She told us that when Nigella was in her early twenties, her mother urged Nigella to get married and have a child. She told Nigella the whole story of her love tryst with Nigel. Her mother had described her long-ago lover as being a smart, kind, very handsome, light-skinned black man who was tall and slim, with afro hair, a thin, narrow nose, beautiful full lips, and a big scar on his cheek. She had given Nigella the piece of paper where Nigel had written his name and his country.

Nigella had made up her mind right then and there that she wouldn't wait for the gods to deliver a husband out of the blue. She hadn't had any luck with men up to that point, and she felt that she had better take matters into her own capable hands. By then, at the tender age of twenty-three, she had graduated and had started her career as a barrister and solicitor with a very good law firm. She made plans immediately, as a single woman, to go to a sperm bank to find a donor that matched what she knew of Nigel's looks.

It took her a year to become pregnant and she never looked back. She had the baby when she was twenty-five years old, on the fast track with her career, and her mother lived a joyous life with the two of them, taking care of the baby during the day while Nigella worked as a junior lawyer at her law firm, until the doting grandma and babysitter passed away with cancer when Martina was three years old.

Nigella's ancestry.se gene match to Nigel's ancestry.ca match was simply a coincidence when everyone in Nigella's office was joining up with the popular gene databank and she had sent her kit in along with the rest of her colleagues.

Nigella finished her story by saying that God had granted her three miracles – her mother, her child, and now her Canadian parents.

A few of the nights Chi joined us, and we would play cards, having girls play against the boys. Chi added several new stories from earlier years when Nigel and Chi were friends that gave us girls new teasing ammunition for the days to come, and Nigella and I trounced the boys hand after hand.

When I asked Chi to bring Diep along, he explained to all of us that it was his plan to develop their budding relationship carefully, to keep it between just the two of them until it was the right time to introduce her to his son, François. He was concerned that with Diep losing her son, the very same age as François, it may alter the course of the new love affair one way or the other, and he wanted to be sure they were strong enough to handle all the ups and downs that would come their way. He had already told François that he had fallen in love with Diep, and his son was very eager to welcome her into the family, but Chi, in his sensitive and caring manner, decided that he would bide his time until he knew his girl was ready.

During the two-week holiday, I made sure that I kept Martina busy with either baking cookies or outside making snowmen in the yard so the two lawyers in the family, the dad, and his daughter had some time to talk shop without any interruptions.

One day, the UPS truck pulled up with a delivery for us. It was something from Sweden that Europeans know something about. We unwrapped two magnificent Swedish winter-weight down duvets – one king-size and one queen-size. Nigella had ordered them for us just before she left for Canada. Nigella explained that there was simply nothing she could buy to match the gift of family, but it was a small token of love and appreciation for their Canadian holiday.

We were all up at Yorkdale Mall, and Nigel asked me to take his card and to buy Nigella everything that she expressed the least little interest in – whatever she wanted. He took Martina to the afternoon movies to give us girls some serious shopping time. As we walked through Nordstrom's and Holt's, Nigella stopped and wanted to treat Nigel and me to matching cashmere sweaters when it dawned on both of us how crazy this all was. We didn't need or want a thing, and neither did she. And besides, as I told her, "You've seen our closets, they are full of beautiful clothes and accessories, most of which we never wear."

She nodded in agreement and surprise. "Exactly!" She added that her own style was definitely young and Euro. She modeled part-time and got a very good discount on her clothing. And she wasn't really too enthused with buying things here because, after all, she was European, and she could buy Armani and Dolce & Gabbana much cheaper at home.

"I'll speak with Dad to make sure his feelings aren't hurt. But thank you, Denni, for respecting my viewpoint on this. I love you."

We met up with Nigel and Martina and after his surprise of seeing us empty-handed, Nigella explained to him that she expected him to respect her shopping habits as much as she respected his. "Dad, I love you. I simply don't need you treating me to unimportant stuff just for the sake of buying me something. You're my family and we have to come to terms with just being ourselves. Okay?"

He nodded thoughtfully and said, "Yes, yes. It's quite obvious to me now that you don't want me buying you a bunch of unnecessary clothes. Have I got this straight now?" He hugged her tight. "Oh my God, I'm the luckiest man on Earth."

He added, "I have a great idea. I've been wanting to buy Denni and myself those great Canada Goose down jackets with the fur around the hood for our nightly walks around the block. Why don't we all go down to their store and we'll all try them on. We can all choose our own colors. They have them in Martina's size as well. Now that's something that you can really use back home, and it's a nice souvenir of Canada too."

"Okay, Dad. That's a great idea. I'd like that."

And so, we all wore our new jackets around the block that night and Nigel was on cloud nine.

It was far into the two-week holiday when Nigel and I were alone out on our nightly walk.

"Baby, I've had something on my mind for almost two weeks, and I need to ask you for your opinion."

"Well, shoot, big boy. What's up?"

"I want to know how you feel about something. But first, I need you to know the back story."

"What's the back story then?"

"Remember last year, when we got back together, you laid it all on the line to me in the backyard on that hot summer day. You told me that I had to love you all the way. Remember?"

"Yes, of course I do, darling."

"Well, I have lived my life like that every day since then. It's all or nothing. It seems that it has overflowed into the rest of my family over the past two weeks, and I can't imagine going back to life without Nigella and Martina being a daily part of it. I want to ask them to move to Canada and to live with us. We can add on an apartment for them on the back of the house, or whatever it takes, but I just need to have them close to us. How do you feel about possibly giving up our empty-nester's lifestyle? Or we could get them settled in a place of their own if you don't think it would work out with having us all under one roof. I could help her get settled into a law firm here very easily as well."

I didn't have to think about it for one second. "Yes, the answer is yes. It would be my greatest honor to be the in-house stepparent and grandma to your girls. Count me in, darling, whatever you need. I'm here. I will leave it up to you to discuss everything with Nigella first. But please know, whatever you two decide and however it turns out, I'm with you all the way through thick and thin."

He stopped on the quiet, dark street, and held me close. After we shared the first of a few long, deep kisses, I reminded him of nearly getting run-over after our first real kiss in the middle of the quiet street a year and a half ago.

"Well, tonight, you are not going to be running away from me like you used to, you little tease. In about ten minutes, I'm going to march you upstairs to our big bed and remind you of how good I can make you feel. I don't care if your noise wakes the baby or not. You're all mine tonight, and I don't give a damn who hears what goes on between me and my very sexy wife."

A few more kisses took place. I had my hand up the back of his winter coat, feeling his warm, smooth back. I smiled as he unzipped my jacket and reached around to snap my bra open. We stood in the shadows, between the street lights on Forest Hill Road, like a couple of teenagers. His one hand was down the back of my sweats, squeezing my ass, while his other hand was reaching for my nipples.

"One last thing, lover boy. You will have to run into the hardware store one day very soon and buy a lock for our bedroom door. I mean, after all, we can't have the girls barging into our bedroom in the middle of the afternoon while I'm having my way with you."

"Yes, boss. Whatever you say."

"Hey," I said to him, "I thought the cold caused boys some shrinkage. What the hell's going on down here?"

We jogged home to find Nigella waiting up for us.

"Hi, you two love birds. Would it be possible to have a word with both of you before you head upstairs?"

Nigel responded with, "Of course, honey, what's on your mind?"

I added that I'd make us all a decaf to go along with the leftover Christmas cake that Nigella seemed to love.

The three of us sat at the kitchen island as Nigella told us that she had made up her mind to immigrate permanently to Canada. She said that she couldn't imagine living without us now, and it was the only way forward, especially for Martina. She asked us if we would mind helping her get a job in a law firm downtown and an apartment near us in the neighborhood so that we could see each other on a regular, if not daily, basis. She went on to say that she had savings put aside, so she would be able to pay her own way and that she didn't need any financial help from us.

By this time, Nigel had reached over and was holding her hand. "Absolutely. This is your home. We are your parents. We love you. And we love the baby. But you are not to touch your savings, honey. We have enough money for the four of us. I will make some calls downtown regarding your career. Denni will do the research into all the schools in the neighborhood to find the best one for Martina. We'll all make sure that she settles into her new environment."

I added, "I have only one question for you, Nigella. That is: are you a mind-reader? We have already discussed how we could add on a suite on the back of the house for our girls in hopes that you would stay with us permanently. We both love you so much."

Nigel added, "And, this is probably a good time to bring a related matter up. Speaking for myself, I know that Martina has me wrapped around her little finger, and I understand that you will have to school me in parenting skills so I don't make a mess of everything. I mean, look at the two of us here. Really. Neither Denni nor I have raised children, and, lucky for all of us, Denni is a natural. Me, on the other hand, well, I'm just a disaster, just waiting to happen."

Nigel stopped talking and just sat there as the light just went on. He quietly said, "Excuse me, girls, for changing the topic a little, but hear me out. It's funny. I just realized that I have, right at this very moment, answered a question I had way back in 1987. What took me so long? Trust me, this is the best story. I mean, it's the very best epochal story over our whole holiday. Can I tell you? Can I? Are you ready?"

I teased him a little, "Epochal, you say! My oh my! And I thought I was the drama-queen of the family."

"We're all ears, Dad."

He jumped up and paced around the kitchen island, arms gesturing as he began his story. "Here we are – a Canadian farm girl, a Jamaican immigrant, and a self-made Swedish single mom, all coming from humble beginnings but sitting together in Saul's big house as family. And all because of his love and generosity toward Mama and me so many years ago when we were his family, especially after his wife died so early on. It's the perfect time to tell you two girls about how far-reaching Saul's generosity still goes on, right up to the present moment. Nigella, your granddad, Saul Himmel, as you know, was born a Jew in France, who came to Canada before the war. He immigrated to Canada and worked himself up to becoming a Supreme Court Justice of Canada. What both of you don't know about Saul is that he married into money, and I mean big money. His wife came from a very wealthy family, and she was an only child. Saul and she never had any children. Saul came into a large inheritance when she died. I never knew how wealthy he really was until he died and I inherited this house and the bulk of his estate. Years before that though, when I came to live with my mother at age nine, Saul had quietly bought Mama a very healthy life insurance policy, with me as the beneficiary. So, when they both died in 1987, I came into a couple of chunks of serious money which I invested, and I still have. I've never needed to use it, as I have always made my own money with my career. I never had a family to share it with. Brad always had more than enough. I just had François' education to pay for, and that was it. Now I know what to do with my inheritance."

He continued, "I'll call my lawyer in the morning and have him divide my parents' money up equally between their son, their daughter-in-law, their granddaughter, and their great-granddaughter. It's a perfect plan. It's like Saul is sitting right here beside me telling me exactly what to do, just like he used to years ago."

I just sat there in silence. I was dumbfounded. I knew that Nigel was financially comfortable enough because of his big, fancy career and high-paying job. And I knew that he had inherited the big house from Saul. But I had no idea that he was actually wealthy. Nigella didn't say a word either; she just sat there with a shocked look on her face.

"Girls! Girls! I didn't mean to throw a wet blanket on the party. You two look like I've just lost the family farm in a crapshoot. It's only money. I love you. Lighten up a little!"

I snapped out of my stupor and jumped up. "You're absolutely right, darling. I'll be right back; just running to the basement to get a bottle of Champagne. Nigella, honey, get down three champagne flutes from the top shelf. We're all *nouveau riche* and that's just a cause for celebration!"

"Now that's my girl!" Nigel said as his grin stretched from ear to ear. "Yeah, time to celebrate. We'll toast Saul and Mama first."

Over the course of the next hour, Nigel laid out many options for all of us to live together under one roof at 7 Russell Hill Road. Nigella insisted that we didn't add a huge addition on the back, but she did agree to stay on with us, at least for the first year, until she got settled in a new job at a law office.

We had to agree with her that the plan that she drafted out was the best. She wanted to keep the sleeping arrangements as they were currently. She said that was how real families lived – all together. And she loved sharing the bathroom with Martina, with us just down the hall from the two of them.

She also suggested that we start from scratch and tear down the old back staircase that we never used, tear down or renovate the empty apartment at the back of the house completely, and replace both areas with a nice, big four-season sunroom, a family room that would mean that the whole back of the house would be all windows, and it would give us all a little space to share another television for the whole family and a place for Martina's toys. She suggested that she could use a corner for a desk for her. A bedroom and bathroom at one end for overnight guests and a galley kitchen and wet bar at the other would be a good use of the space. That way, we wouldn't be stuck with another empty apartment like the one downstairs once she moved into her own home. It also would open up access to our beautiful backyard instead of walking down around the side of the house. Nigella wrapped up her vision by suggesting that we use her share of Saul and Mavis' money to pay for the renovation.

Nigel was also on a roll. He explained, "Leave the finances to me, girls. I've been thinking for a while of selling my old condo that I still have downtown. It's time to move on, just like when Denni gave up her apartment. I'll use that money for the renovation."

As Nigel ran into his office to bring out a notepad, I shouted out to him, "Excuse me, Nigel. Can you also bring out your new sketches that you have been working on in Saul's office?"

He poked his head back into the kitchen. "Really? It's just a tree house that I thought I would build in the old maple for Martina."

I looked at Nigella, and we both started laughing.

"You told me he would do that."

"Yeah, I've got his number, all right. That's your dad."

When Nigel was out of earshot, Nigella confided in me.

"Denni, I had no idea that Dad was rich. If I had known that, I would have been much, much clearer about using my own money for everything. I would never have allowed him to even pay for my airfare here. I just feel so embarrassed now about asking him to help me get a job and everything. I hope and pray he doesn't doubt my motivation for coming to Canada."

"Honey, I'm his wife, and I didn't know either. I married him blind, the same as you came to Canada blind. And you know what? He married me blind too. And he loved you the minute he received your very first email. He never ever asked me anything about my finances. And I'm pretty sure he hasn't asked you either. So, we're all in the same boat. It's obvious. Neither he nor I are real money people, you know. It just doesn't matter to us. It's not our focus in life. He gives me a very generous allowance for myself and to run the house, and he won't put up with me using my mom's inheritance for anything at all. Please don't feel bad about it. It would break his heart. We will have to be the gracious ladies like I know we are. That's how we'll handle this. Now listen to me. Just shut up and drink your champagne like rich people do in situations like this. It's a helluva nice problem to have."

She raised her glass and said, "To my father."

And I responded with, "To my husband."

The very next morning, Nigel called the architect to set an early date to come over to discuss our plans, and then he dashed out to look at drafting tables and equipment so he could set up a full design shop in a corner of Saul's office.

***

The next night, once again, Nigella presented us with news, but this time, it was not so pleasant. In fact, it was the worst kind of news a family can get.

By the end of our nightly walk around the block, I had stepped up the pace, and I stood on the front doorstep, laughing at Nigel coming up the walkway behind me. All of a sudden, the door swung open, and Nigella grabbed me and motioned quietly for both of us to get inside. She locked the door behind us.

Concern was written all over Nigel's face as he implored, "Where's Martina?"

"Dad, Dad, it's okay. She's okay. She's upstairs in bed."

He dashed upstairs, took a look in Martina's room, and dashed back down.

"Okay, honey, what's up?"

"Dad, you had two visitors. I told them you weren't home, but to come back at 10:00 p.m. and they said they would. They wouldn't give me a name, but one said his auntie was *a Mrs. Mattis*. I had a feeling that it wasn't a friendly call."

By this time, Nigel had his phone to his ear. "Chi, it's show time. We're all okay, but we had two visitors. Check the front door and streets' cameras between 8:00 and 8:30 p.m. When you come, wear a jacket over full gear. They're coming back at 10:00 p.m."

By the time I got my coat off, Chi had arrived and the four of us huddled in the kitchen. Chi took over as Nigel ran upstairs once again to check on Martina.

Nigella said, "Okay, I'll start from the very beginning, Chi. Don't worry. I didn't let them into the house, and they posed no immediate threat."

She told the story of hearing the doorbell and opening the door to two men younger than her, with Caribbean accents, asking to speak with Nigel Royal. She sized them up and had a hunch that they were up to no good. She had smiled wide to disarm them and told them that Nigel wasn't home, but he would be home at 10:00 p.m. and if they would mind very much coming back. Nigella assumed the two of them were fairly young, inexperienced, and unprofessional, as one looked her up and down and wolf-whistled her while the other called her *sister.*

Chi peered into Nigel's face, which was ashen. He said, "Nigel, get a grip. I've got this. They said Mrs. Mattis, remember? Girls, for your information, Mrs. Mattis was our housekeeper for a few years, and she lives in Kingston, Jamaica, now. This has nothing to do with the witness protection program. And it has nothing to do with a plan to kidnap Martina or you, Nigella, or you, Denni. Mrs. Mattis wouldn't have any idea that you even exist. This is probably just a little shakedown for money from Mrs. Mattis' family, as Nigel's generous pension ended a couple of months ago. We've got 'em on camera. Downtown has filled us in on them already. They're driving a rental which they picked up at the airport yesterday. They came in from Jamaica. They're not known by police here in Toronto."

"Do you know their names, Chi?" Nigella asked.

"Yeah. Stupid and Stupider."

"It's too early to know if they're armed, right, Chi?" I asked.

"Yeah. But look at it this way; if they're stupid enough to pull up in a rental car, then they don't have the savvy to know where to pick up a gun on the street. If they actually knew someone here in Toronto, that third party would have laughed them out of town using a rental car for a shakedown. Don't worry, girls. I believe we are dealing with a couple of idiots on their travels looking for their golden goose."

"Should I put my vest on Chi?" Nigel said quietly.

"No. If they've been watching gangster movies on TV, they may want to give you a pat down and we don't need you wearing anything except a tee-shirt. Nigel, you and I are going to clip in a couple of cameras in the hall fixture and in Saul's office, and the second we know that they're carrying heat, they won't know what hit them. I'm wired in, and our plainclothes will be too. Blackmailers don't shoot until they've got their money. They probably just have a photo or two of Mrs. Mattis on their phones. All three of you will be well covered. Downtown is sending up a full takedown team immediately."

Chi continued, "Now, here's what we're going to do. Listen up, everybody."

Within fifteen minutes, we had two plainclothes policemen in the house, two stationed in the backyard and two unmarked police cars on the street, and instructions going out to assemble a S.W.A.T team on a neighboring street. Chi and Nigel worked quickly to install miniscule cameras in the light fixtures at the front door and in his office. Chi knew his stuff.

My post was to stay put in Martina's room and not to move until someone came to get me. Nigella was to stay in the kitchen, casually having a coffee while surfing on her laptop, and to call out in a friendly manner as Nigel answered the door to invite the two men into the house, with Chi hidden away in the pantry, right beside her. Chi was wired up, the same as the policemen, so he could hear what was going down in real time, but it was agreed that the two unmarked cars, also wired up, would do the takedown once the two visitors passed back through the front door after the transaction. Nigel was to be relaxed, friendly, and to ask the two visitors how Mrs. Mattis was doing.

As I was going upstairs to my post, I heard our two undercovers ask Chi if he was ready. Chi spread open one side of his bulky jacket, and I saw a black bulletproof vest and with a gun holster peeking out from the side of his chest.

"I'm ready. Bring the bastards on."

My ear was to the bedroom door as I heard the doorbell chime at 10:00 p.m. exactly.

Nigel's big baritone boomed, and I could hear a little chuckle in his voice that had acquired a Jamaican accent as he welcomed the two men. "Hey, mon, to what do I owe the pleasure? How's Mrs. Mattis doing? How's the good life back home, mon? Come in. Come in. Don't let the cold in, as Mrs. Mattis used to say. My God, she ruled the roost while she was here. I hope she's okay, bro. I'm just in my office, having a coffee. Can I get you one? Can I take your coats? Oh – no and no. Well, okay. Here, this way. For Christ's sake, mon, come in."

***

Nigel listened carefully and thoughtfully as one man advised Nigel that his auntie had given him a photo of her face with a black eye that was documented at the Toronto Airport as she left his employ in Toronto to go back home to Jamaica.

"Oh, oh. Oh my God! You wouldn't happen to have a copy of the photo on you, would you, boys?"

The visitor brought out his phone, and sure enough, a picture of Mrs. Mattis with a black eye and scraped cheek graced the screen.

"Hmmm. Hmmm," Nigel offered.

"Yeah, Auntie is okay now, but we felt we should take the trip up here to show you that we've got our eye on you. And you – a brother! Fuck, mon! It cost us a bundle just to get up here. What the fuck, mon? You think we've got all day, having to leave our beautiful beaches to come all the way up here in the dead of winter, mon? We're out of pocket here, mon."

"Sorry, boys, sorry. I'm sorry for your troubles. It's over now for Mrs. Mattis. She's safe and sound back home, as you say. And she's doing okay?"

"Yeah, mon. Enough of your phony *sorry*. Now Auntie is saying it's about time that you paid up for your past, and she sent the two of us to talk to you about it."

"I see. I see. Do you know exactly what she had in mind? Does she want her old job back? Is that it?"

"Are you a fucking idiot, mon? No, mon, she doesn't want her old job back. She wants money."

Nigel sat tight as he slowly considered the deal on the table. "Oh. Oh."

He sighed and shook his head. "I don't carry a lot of money on me, boys. But I could probably scrape up enough to cover your expenses for now, until I can get down to the bank tomorrow. How much are we talking here?"

The two visitors looked at each other and turned their heads away, all the while nodding as if they were considering Nigel's suggestion.

They came back to Nigel with the best they could do. "Listen, mon. We're out $5,000 Canadian; that's $500,000 Jamaican. Cash. And that's just us. Auntie has her own amount."

"Oh my God! Boys, boys, settle down here! I, uh, I, uh… I don't know about all this," he stammered. "Yes, yes, I can see where your expenses would be $5,000 Canadian, but what about Mrs. Mattis? What's that going to cost me?"

"One step at a time, mon. Have you got cash – the $5,000 on you, right now?"

"Oh. Oh. No. What the fuck! No, I haven't got that kind of money here at home, but listen, boys, listen. I give you my word; I'll go to the bank first thing in the morning."

"You think we were born yesterday? Fuck you. What have you got right now?"

Nigel pulled out a drawer of Saul's desk and took out a rectangular metal box. He placed it on the desk and carefully took out all the bills. He began to count it out slowly, bill by bill, in a voice loud enough for the two young hustlers to hear, right along with Chi and the team.

He looked up after the counting and said, "Yeah, there's $2,200 here. Listen, mon. Take this until tomorrow – please. I promise to have the rest of the $5,000 right here by noon tomorrow. Or you come to the bank with me. Then we can get on with Mrs. Mattis' amount after that. Please, boys, I need your help here."

He held the $2,200 out to the two visitors. They stood up, and the talker of the two took the money, fanned it out, rolled it up, and stuck in down deep in his jeans' front pocket.

Nigella looked up casually from her laptop as the two visitors, accompanied by Nigel, walked toward the front door. She stood up with a big, cheesy smile on her face and said, "Bye, guys. Take care," as she walked down the back hall, out of sight.

Nigel, with his hand on the doorknob, took his time confirming the deal.

The two of them could barely conceal their excitement brought on by their success and they said in unison, "Yeah, mon."

Yeah, mon, indeed! It was confirmed by Nigel that the two men would be back at 12:00 noon tomorrow to pick up the remaining $2,800 and they would fill him in on Mrs. Mattis' part of the deal at that time.

Nigel kept talking as he opened the door slowly. By the time the two visitors had turned their heads away from Nigel's constant stream of assurances to step through the threshold, they were met with the solid mass of the S.W.A.T team, kneeling in wait, with their guns drawn. As the two grifters turned around in panic to go back inside the house, Nigel had stepped aside and Chi stood there, legs apart, with his gun cocked and loaded, aiming directly into their chests.

"Fuck, mon!" was all they said.

***

Nigella and I got busy in the kitchen, making the coffee and scrambling through the freezer and the pantry to get out enough cookies, pie, and snacks for the takedown team. The smell of hot apple pie from the microwave floating through the kitchen was reassuring, to say the least.

I shook my head as I fanned out a handful of chocolate chip cookies in amongst the peanut butter ones as I thought about my writing career. I worked so diligently on crafting my stories day after day, and then this piece of nonfiction popped up out of nowhere! You couldn't write this stuff!

By the time the S.W.A.T team came in, as well as the unmarked car officers along with the plainclothes guys, we had a houseful. They all had their paperwork to do, and they needed statements from all of us, but mainly, it was a gathering of comrades that had been through the war, so to speak. The adrenaline had begun to taper off, and they were all grateful for the time around

281

our big kitchen island just to decompress, with the relief that came from a perfectly ordered takedown relating to nothing more serious than an unprofessional hustle.

Nigel, with his arm around Chi, said to the crowd, "I'd like to make the first toast. Can we all raise our coffee cups up to my best friend and fearless leader? Here's to Chi Tran. I love you, man."

"Just doin' my job, boss."

As Chi moved away to get out from under Nigel's big kiss that he had planted on his cheek, everyone laughed at Chi's response. While he wiped off the kiss with the back of his hand, he succinctly summed up Nigel's words of praise in the language of the day, "Fuck, mon!"

***

"Okay, girls, you go up ahead of me. I'll just finish loading the dishwasher. Tonight, I'm tucking all three of my girls in. So jump into bed and I'll be up in a minute."

***

"Nigella honey, is it okay if I snuggle in with you until Nigel comes up?"

"I wouldn't have it any other way."

Nigel had pulled up the big, overstuffed chair tight to the bedside to be close to us, and as I woke in the middle of the night, I watched him. My heart went out to this sensitive, brilliant, and loving man who just couldn't get away from stress and worry, no matter how much Chi and I looked out for him. I had had no idea whatsoever that he was constantly dogged by the idea of one of his girls being kidnapped, especially since Nigella and Martina had come into our lives. What can you do?

He was snoring softly, head tilted back and to one side in the big easy chair. I had dozed off earlier, and he and his newly found daughter had talked way into the night and had fallen asleep mid-sentence.

I got up and quietly put a blanket over him and then tiptoed back over to the other side of Nigella's bed. I snuggled under her covers, thanking God over and over again for my family, asking Him to keep us all safe.

The next thing I heard was Martina whispering in my ear, "Grandma, are you awake yet? Granddad and I made you and Mommy breakfast in bed."

***

Martina was all excited. Chi had invited her out to go to the mall to buy her mom a little surprise present for bringing her on the holiday. He had also arranged a little something for the adults in the house to do while Martina was out. A police woman, who was a psychologist that specialized in victim responses, came to the house to speak with Nigel, Nigella, and myself. As I sat there, all of us around the big kitchen island, with this savvy, insightful, and chatty professional outlining all the reactions that we could all expect to go through over the next little while, I realized that I was going to be okay. Nigella was on top of it as well and even saw a little humor in the unfortunate plight of the two inexperienced hustlers. My husband, on the other hand, was taking the whole 'home invasion' episode very badly. He blamed himself for every little move and step along the way that had put his girls in danger.

***

We all met Chi out front as he backed the big Benz out to drive us all down to Tiffany's on Bloor Street. The Toronto to Stockholm flight didn't leave until almost midnight, so we packed the night before to give us time the next morning to enjoy our last little excursion on our last morning together.

"Thanks so much to all of you for helping me out here. I know it's a little early to be arranging for a ring for her just yet, but Nigella, I really wanted your help here before you leave town. I owe you everything. I'll always be grateful that you pushed the envelope to make a man out of me. And you, Nigel. It's kind of funny that we two very old friends, who have been confirmed bachelors, both fell in love with our girls instantly."

Nigel said, smiling at me, "All I know is that when Denni saw that ring come out of the box, I was able to tone down the begging and pleading somewhat. But you see, I had Brad's help. He was the one that pushed me to put a ring on my beautiful Irish faerie's finger. I had no idea. Let's face it; we're all lucky. Just don't wait too long to give it her, Chi. As Brad says, girls like things like that."

As Chi introduced himself to the salesperson in Tiffany's, he showed him my four-carat emerald-cut yellow diamond that was purchased from the same store the year before. The salesperson discretely asked Chi what his ballpark budget was, while the rest of us busied ourselves with the displays. He listened very carefully to all of us, who were chiming in to describe the bride-to-be's personality and lifestyle.

Nigella, with her charming accent, added a twist to the whole conversation. She asked for all the information on Canadian diamonds and explained that she was a Swede working in international law and that she had worked on a global case last year against a syndicate that was passing off South African stones as Canadian stones.

The Tiffany expert was quick enough after that to give us all the background on all the stones that he showed us. He offered us loops to inspect the facets for ourselves and educated us to the four Cs of diamonds sold in Canada.

Chi listened carefully to all that was being offered, and after we had all enjoyed the tea that was served to us in fine china tea cups, he said, "I know exactly what stone and what setting I want for my bride. I need it sized down to a size-six-and-a-half, and I would like to pick it up next week, Friday morning at the latest."

"Of course, Mr. Tran. Now, let's put all the pieces together for you here on a mat, and you can show your family the components of your bride's beautiful engagement ring."

***

"Denni, we're in the middle of the airport. I expected better from you. Now wipe those tears away. I have enough to handle with Dad not letting Martina out of his arms the whole afternoon. We'll be back in ten weeks' time for goodness' sake." She lightened her tone and said, "Get a grip, girlfriend. Now you see, you've even got me talking like a folksy Canadian."

I looked at her, coffee cup in hand and leaning over me. She sat there, with her new Canada goose jacket over the arm of the chair. She was wearing a pair of sweats, well-worn Ugg boots, and one of Nigel's big cashmere sweaters that hung down over her lean frame. Her hair, after two weeks, was back to being curly, falling to her shoulders in ringlets just like Martina's.

"You're right, Nigella. After all, I have to go home to listen to Nigel crying into his pillow all night long. I've got to straighten up," I offered back to her.

I smiled at little, but I didn't share my thoughts with her. The truth was that Nigel and I had been planning over the last couple of days what, how, and when we were going to enjoy our newfound freedom of sex-on-demand, at any time and in any room, on any whim, to start as soon as we could make it home from the airport.

That all being said, as I stood there beside my step-daughter, in the first-class lounge at Lester B. Pearson Airport, I was reminded of how my life had changed, and for the better. Pinch me. I remembered my past all too well. Not that long ago, I had stood in the customs' line up to re-enter my beloved Canada, old worn knapsack on my back, wearing a pair of beat-up huarache sandals on my feet, with the face of a sad, drawn, pasty-white single woman that was not a kid anymore but who was about to start her life up, yet again.

I smiled across at Nigel, with Martina still in his arms. She was in her flannel nightie and had her favorite bunny slippers on her feet. He had called ahead and got special clearance to board with her so that he could tuck her into their sleeper cabin. I would wait here in the lounge with Chi until he said his last goodbyes to his girls. He was a remarkable man. I loved him so deeply.

As Chi and I waited there, I took advantage of the few minutes of privacy between us. "Chi, about the other night. I can never repay you."

He grabbed my hand and interrupted me, "Hush. We're family. We don't have to worry about repaying. Nigel and I are both so blessed to have you with us. We're a team, and we all do exactly what we have to do at the time. I'm just so lucky you are a smart, tough cookie who plays her part so well. I love you and I'm honored to be your friend and family. Now, enough said!"

He smiled and continued, "To change the subject, Denni, I want to let you know that I'm following Nigel's lead."

"How's that, Chi?"

"I remember when he first met you. He confided in me why he stayed his distance and never invited you in after your nightly walks around the block. He said he couldn't trust himself, and it had been a long, long time since he had been with anyone. He didn't want to rush the two of you into sex just out of sheer need. He had fallen in love with you the very first time he set eyes on you, and he wanted to wait for you to catch up to him. He thought you were a little skittish regarding intimacy. So, he booked your trip to Paris for your first night together. So that's what I'm doing with Diep. We're flying out for a three-day weekend to New York City next Friday, right after I pick up the ring. I'll take it with me to give it to her there."

"Please allow me to drive you out and pick you up at the airport. It's the least I can do. As Nigel would say, how did we all get so lucky? How did we all get so damn lucky?" I added, "Wow, Chi, you da man. Diep is even willing to miss her church choir routine on Sunday morning for a long weekend of nothing but sex with you?"

"You're damn right. I am da man. And I intend on showing her exactly how I am da man for the whole seventy-two hours I have her all to myself in the big apple."

"Hmm, just thinking ahead here. You may want to get over to Home Depot once you get back from your love fest to pick up some soundproofing for the east wall of your apartment. She's probably a screamer, and Nigel and I don't want to be up the whole night long listening to you two making whoopie."

As we made our way back to the big blacked-out Benz in the airport parking lot, Nigel asked, "Chi, do you mind if I ride in the back with Denni?"

"No worries, man. Go for it," Chi said. He slid behind the wheel, buckled up, and as we rounded the on-ramp at top speed, we hit the highway eastbound at one hell of a clip. Chi tuned in and amped up some old-school badass Tina Turner. He was sporting a huge grin on his face and knew enough not to look back to check on his passengers. The surround-sound was thundering all around us in the backseat as I snuggled up close to Nigel. I was belted into the middle seat to be close to my man. I opened up his top few buttons so I could smooch him and smell his chest. Tina belted out all her standards. She started off the set, singing with her whole heart and soul. *Simply the Best* was followed with *Better Be Good to Me*, and every song sounded better than the last.

"Baby, I love you all the way," Nigel whispered in my ear, "but I can't wait for you." He unzipped his fly, took my hand, and shoved it into his heat.

I whispered back, "What makes it so big and so hard all the time?"

"An Irish faerie. She has the magic touch."

"Does she know any other magic tricks besides just holding on to this big old thing?"

"Yeah. If she kisses me with her tongue touching my tongue, while her hand is still on it, she can make me cum instantly."

"Oh! Really?"

"Trust me, baby. Here, let me show you. Just kiss me. Yeah. Like that."

It was the craziest, most fun, most exciting backseat make-out session that I had ever known.

Nigel came up for air and gasped, "Now I know what Etta James was talking about."

"What's Etta James got to do with this?"

"*Footprints on the Ceiling*. You know, that rough and rowdy song of hers."

"No. Don't know your song. But I do know rough and rowdy. And I like it."

"Never mind, never mind. Help me with your jeans," he laughed. "I can't get them down past your ass. I want to kiss you. I want to taste you. Help me. Help me now," he laughed as he braced the back of the front seat with one long, bare leg that he had freed from his pant leg. His other leg was jackknifed up behind him, against the side door, the lone pant leg down around his ankle.

"No, no," I advised. "It's better if I'm on top. Just move over a little."

"What's gotten into you?"

"You, baby, all you. You make me crazy."

"Okay, okay," he whispered. "Try to spread your legs a little. Oh, baby, I've just got to reach you. I need you like never before."

My belly was heaving with laughter as I lifted my head to see his long legs flailing around. I struggled to sit up, to catch my breath, and he pulled me down under him to try another angle.

"This isn't so funny anymore. God, I need you. Right now," he whispered from down somewhere under my arm.

Thirty minutes later, I felt the car slowing as it turned off the highway. I snapped our belts off and kicked my jeans down further off my last leg. Nigel had his hands full of my breasts, and as I heard our garage door open, Chi turned out all the lights, left the radio blaring, and shouted out to us as he was jumping out of the car, all in one smooth second, "Hey, man, lock up. Later."

I whispered as if my life depended on it, "Baby, move over. Move over quickly to the middle of the seat."

By now, Nigel was laughing out loud. "Easy, sugar, easy. We're only a hundred feet from our big bed."

"It's okay for you to say. This can't wait. I want to ride you right here and right now. Come on, move over so I can get my other leg around you."

I needed him too much by then to be laughing, but Nigel seemed to think this was the funniest situation he'd been in in a long time. "Honey, I see your bra on the floor. It's under your dirty boots. Look at my shirt. You've ripped all the buttons clean off. I've got a big love bite on my neck. I can feel the hard seatbelt under my bare, boney ass. I promise you. I'll make the few extra steps upstairs worth your while."

"No way. I need you now. Right now. You just sit there. Don't move, baby. I'll ride you."

I felt his big hands cup my ass as I straddled him. My fingers were closed tight, full of his beautiful, kinky spirals of African hair. His beautiful lips were on my neck. Oh my God, it was fantastic.

***

I must admit that after all that crazy, hot, pent-up backseat action, we were both pretty quiet as we took a quick shower together in our quiet, empty house. We climbed into bed and sighed as we felt our clean, white linens. Without a word, Nigel reached down to the foot of the bed to pull our new Swedish down duvet up over our shoulders.

He spooned me and said softly, "Now, honey, listen. Listen to me. I'm too old for all this craziness. I'm putting my foot down. Don't come near me until at least Friday. Every muscle in my body is aching. My ass will never be the same."

"Yes, Your Honor. But following proper court decorum, I would like to, at the very least, plead my case even if it's just for the record."

He sighed and said tiredly, "Proceed."

"My own hands-on experience tells a different story altogether. That was no pesky Irish faerie working her magic in the backseat of the car, Your Honour. No, sir-eee. That, in all his primal majesty, was just a big old Jamaican bullfrog expressing his needs with his deep baritone mating call. Trust me."

I pushed in a little so that he could feel what he was going to be missing out on and said softly, "But really, babe, maybe you just need a massage. You know, if I started with your shoulders, it may work out all your kinks."

"Don't you dare touch me."

"Okay, okay, I can take a hint. I suppose we can leave it until tomorrow."

"Read my lips. I'm free a week from now."

As I turned back into our spoon, I closed my eyes, and the last thing I remember was feeling his lips on my long scar that ran from my hairline down my spine and my husband saying, "You thrill me, Mrs. Royal. You simply thrill me."

***

Chapter 13
7 Russell Hill Road

I sat there in the quiet, empty kitchen, relishing the complete silence. I sipped my coffee and thought back to earlier that morning in bed.

I had felt Nigel nuzzling my neck and whispering from behind me, "Is it too early for you, baby?"

I responded by asking, "Is it Friday on your calendar yet? Isn't that the date you set last night?"

"You don't have to do anything. Don't even open your eyes. God, I need you so much. Feel me. I'm aching for you."

"Back to what you said last night. You did say not to touch you until next Friday, right?"

"Yeah, but I'm an idiot. You were right and I was wrong."

"Now you're talking my language. I'm always right. Right?"

"Right. You're always right."

"Well, okay, let me see now… Do you think you could pull down my panty, even if I just lay here with my eyes closed?"

"Absolutely. Even with my hands tied behind my back. I'll use my teeth to pull them down over your beautiful ass."

"That won't be necessary. And once you get them off, then you can fill me up tight to make me feel good, right?"

"Honey, enough already. I'm looking for a little faerie dust here. Right here, right now. I'll be damn sure to take care of the rest."

I smiled as I felt his big, eager hands tug my panty down. I snapped my knees back together, and he whispered, "You're such a tease. You want me to beg? I'll beg. But just know that I'm about to rip these damn panties to shreds right off your ass if you don't stop squeezing your knees together."

I laughed, rolled over, and pressed up against him. "You're so grouchy this morning. Now is this better? This feels really good now, doesn't it?"

"You're damn right. It feels really good."

Later, I had listened to his beautiful baritone singing his usual repertoire in his shower as I sprawled over to his side of the bed. I smelled the sheets, searching for his scent. I thanked God like I did every morning for my blessings and closed my eyes to the bleak January sun straining through the window.

***

I took another sip of my coffee as I re-read his note:

Good morning, honey,
    Picking up my drafting table and supplies, back in time for lunch. The architect is coming by at three p.m. Love, N.
    P.S. So good to have you all to myself this morning without the girls here.

We were amazing! xxx

I glanced at the kitchen clock. It was exactly ten hours since we had put the girls on the plane, and the renovation at 7 Russell Hill Road was already in full swing.

***

It was February, and I lay there in Chi and Diep's guestroom, bone-tired but unable to sleep. I told myself I was being stupid, missing Nigel so much, especially when he was right next door, having the bachelor party with Chi and François. But it was my duty as Diep's matron of honor to stay overnight with her the night before the wedding, as tradition insists upon.

We had all gone out for a pre-wedding dinner downtown, and the five of us had had such a good time. Nigel, Chi, and François were really whooping it up, and Diep and I were right behind them.

We were all so happy that they weren't waiting around; they were to be married tomorrow at Diep's lovely interdenominational church without further ado. Nigel was the best man, I was the matron of honor, and François would walk Diep down the aisle of the beautiful, small chapel with the stained-glass windows looking down on our small but perfect wedding party. Diep, over the years, had forged many friendships within her church, and once Chi had made his move, he too attended the church with her every Sunday. The guest list was fairly small, made up of a few of Diep's friends from Loblaws and the rest from the congregation of their church. François was treating them to a luxurious couples-only resort in Mexico for their honeymoon.

Morning came, and I insisted on making Diep a big breakfast. I told her she would need her strength because Chi was going to keep her up all night with mind-blowing sex.

Diep laughed and retorted, "No, Denni, it's the other way around. I just can't get enough of my man! Do you know that we belong to the twice-a-day club?"

I helped her dress her like Ann-Marie helped me the day of my wedding, and she was a beautiful bride. Our limo pulled up right on time at the church to see François standing on the steps, waiting for us. The wedding was at 11:00 a.m., with a lovely lunch afterward put on by the church ladies, downstairs in the community room. It was just beautiful. Everyone had a wonderful time, and Chi, Nigel, and François were all so charming and funny with their stories up at the mike as they entertained the guests.

We all stood on the church steps showering them with rice and good wishes as the limo waited to take them to spend their wedding night at the Four Seasons downtown, before an early flight out to Mexico the next morning.

I had put a roast in for an early dinner, and as François, Nigel, and I kicked back at home for the afternoon, François said, "Uncle Nigel, I'm so sorry that I missed your daughter when she was here. It seems that every time I thought I could pop in something came up at the office. You know how it gets down there; it's crazy busy."

"Well, son, you really missed something there. Those two sweethearts are absolutely the very best. You would have loved them. But not to worry, they'll be back in a couple of months, right after the reno wraps up. And be prepared to be impressed."

"Yeah. Dad has been telling me all about both of them. He says he has Nigella all picked out for me to marry. I don't know if I could get my head around an arranged marriage though," he said, laughing.

"Don't discount the idea entirely, son. Just wait till you meet her. You'll see."

"Now you're scaring me, Uncle Nigel. I'm quite happy being a bachelor, you know, a man about town."

"That's what we all say, until love walks in the door. It's like that young singer Kelly Clarkson says in one of her songs about when love comes knocking on your door: *you've got no say at all.* All I'm saying is consider yourself warned, Don Juan."

***

About six weeks later, I carefully unzipped the large plastic construction wall that separated the whole back of the house from the new addition before ducking into the tidy workspace. The team seemed to be in transition, cleaning up and hanging up their tools. It was one of the days, late in the renovation process where everyone was present – Nigel, the architect, designer, contractor, electrician, plumber, and a variety of helpers.

Nigel was wearing his checked shirt untucked over a pair of blue jeans, just like the Alan and Bill, the architect and the general contractor. Of course, he was dressed perfectly for the occasion as usual. Both Alan and Bill had tried to tell him that he was overdoing it with the whole security system, but Nigel wouldn't hear it. He finally told them of the home invasion and his initial thoughts that it was a kidnapping, and Alan and Bill developed a new understanding of their client's needs and wants. Nigel reviewed the new system time and time again, reassuring himself that his girls would be safe. We would have the safest house in Canada. I was sure of it!

I caught his eye. He had his hard hat on and I just couldn't get enough of him. I was relieved to see that his face, at the moment, was animated and happy. Over the last few days though, I had caught him staring off into space, stone-faced, just not his usual self. It somehow seemed to happen when the construction guys were there. It somehow almost felt like he was jealous of me when they were all there. Or it was something I just couldn't put my finger on. And he wasn't eating like he usually did – no appetite really. Two nights, he wanted to go up to bed fairly early, even before our walk. He had never done this before. It seemed like he was exhausted from stress or worry or something. He was asleep by the time I jumped into bed. Or was he just pretending?

When we started the project, Nigel agreed with me that we would provide lunch for the workers, as that would keep them on all tasks and organized. Every day I would have a big pot of homemade soup ready for them, along with chicken, ham, beef, and vegies of all description to tuck into a pita or build a sandwich with a variety of rolls and always a big Caesar salad. It was nothing fancy, but the crew really appreciated it. They were all so respectful, taking their shoes off and washing up in the powder room just off the laundry room near the new addition. Nigel wasn't his usual charming self with them over the lunches though, which surprised me. I had a hunch, and to play it safe, just in case he was jealous, I didn't eat with them. I stayed out in the kitchen, bringing in seconds and making the coffee.

I lifted my lunch bell up high and rang to get everyone's attention. "Soup's on!"

***

That evening, just after dinner, my world came crashing down with the innocent sound of the door chime.

"Oh, hi, Alan! You're back? Did you forget something?"

"Hi, Denni. Sorry to disturb you and Nigel, but I meant to drop off these layouts that the designer gave me for you and Nigel. It's the leather furniture, tables, and kitchen-island chair layouts. Would you mind if I brought them in and put them back in the new addition?"

"No, not at all! In fact, we're dying to see everything. It's all good!"

As Alan and I stood there in the doorway, Nigel came into the hallway and stood quietly, looking at us. He had a terrible look on his face as if he was in an agony or something.

"Hey, man, you okay?" Alan said, and he stepped into the hallway as if he was ready to catch Nigel in case he fell over.

"Honey, what's wrong?" I said, alarmed at his face. He looked like he was facing the devil.

Nigel came apart and roared, "You lying bitch! It's him, isn't it!? It's him! I knew it! You bitch! You cheating bitch!" His body was frozen in the spot, and his arms were straight down as if he was in some kind of hell. I could barely recognize his face.

"Nigel! Nigel! Take it easy, man! What's wrong? You can't speak like that to your wife! Take a seat, please. Take a seat!"

Nigel screamed, "Get out of my house, you fucking coward! Get out! Get out! You're fucking my wife! You're fucking my wife right in front of me!"

I was in high-alert mode and said to Alan, "I don't know what's wrong, but you go, and I'll calm him down and call the doctor. Just go. Please go!"

Alan was extremely distressed and said to me, as if Nigel couldn't hear him, "No, I think we should call an ambulance. Something isn't right here. I think he's having a mental breakdown or something."

I pushed him out the door. "Go. Just go. I'm okay. I'll take care of it."

I turned and looked directly at Nigel. He didn't look like himself, but he had calmed down somewhat.

"I knew it. I knew it. From the moment you laid eyes on him. You're fucking him, aren't you? Right in our home. How could you? You fucking bitch! You cheating bitch!"

I shouted, "Nigel! Nigel! Can you hear me?! Stop. Sit down. Sit down right now. It's me, your wife! I love you! It's me. Can't you see?"

He looked at me and, surprisingly, went into the living room and sat down almost in a daze, but I did notice the rigidity in his body had left him, and his hands were trembling.

I wanted to go to him and put my arms around him to calm him down, but I was afraid he might hit me, or worse, strangle me or something. I kept my distance but kept talking in a loud voice to keep his attention.

His new face just hurled out ugliness, word after word and phrase after phrase. I felt that my presence was just aggravating him all the more. In a short moment of clarity, I thought to myself, 'No wonder Gerri broke his nose.'

"Nigel, listen. Listen to me. I'm getting annoyed with all this ugly talk. Stop right now or I'm leaving."

He became more enraged.

I nervously made the executive decision to calmly walk into the kitchen, grab the car keys, and get away so he could calm down. And maybe to save my life. My hands were shaking as I peeled out of the drive. What to do. What to do? What should I do? What could I do? Should I call Chi? No. That would embarrass Nigel to no end. What to do?'

I ended up at Yorkdale Mall, and I ran in, just trying to get away from the nightmare at 7 Russell Hill Road. 'What to do? What should I do? Was he having a psychotic breakdown? Or was he just jealous?' I couldn't cry; I was in panic mode, and I powerwalked the mall for I don't know how long. By then, I was so anxious just to see that he was okay that I decided I would leave the mall and go to Chi's house to see if he could go over and check on things.

It was dark as I clicked the lock open to get into my car, and it was then that I noticed our big Benz was sitting right beside me. I fell apart as I felt Chi's arms wrapped around me. I tried to quiet my wails to no avail. I couldn't even talk. All I could say was, "Nigel."

"I know, Denni. I know. Hush. Hush. Hush. Everything's going to be okay."

He buckled me into the passenger seat of the Benz, and I calmed down enough to ask, "How did you know I was here?"

"Nigel came running into my apartment; he was like a madman. He said that you had left him. He told me to find you and make sure that you were okay. He said that he would leave the house, but first just to bring you back to my apartment so you would be okay. He said he didn't deserve you and he made me promise that I would take care of you."

"But how did you know where to find me?"

"Denni. All women go to the mall when they're mad at their husbands. Don't you know that?"

"Chi, I think he's having a breakdown. You know he has that disorder called psychological transference, and it's chronic. It can come back at any time. He had a breakdown out in L.A. and that was his first attack. I think he's having another one now. It may be the stress of that takedown night, or even the reno. He hasn't been himself for a couple of days now. He hasn't been in to see his shrink since London, and he's been so well up to now."

"Okay, Denni, okay. Here's what we're going to do. We're leaving your car here, and I'll pick it up later. We're going to take you back to my apartment where you will stay with Diep, and I'll go over to see him. Okay? I don't think it's a good thing for you to see him; it may upset him more. But I can call the doctor or take him into a mental health clinic at Sunnybrook Hospital after I get you settled. Okay? Please don't cry. Everything is going to be okay."

I nodded and blew my hose into the Kleenex that he offered me. Chi said, "Now I'm going to call him just to let him know I've got you here safe and sound, okay? But don't say anything. I don't want to upset him, okay?"

I said in a small voice, "Okay, Chi. Thank you so much."

He held his phone up to his ear. "Hmm, no answer. Hmm, I'll try later. Don't worry."

We got back to Chi's apartment, went up the stairs, and Diep put on the kettle to make a cup of tea for me and he left to go see Nigel. My tea wasn't even steeped, and Chi ran back into the kitchen.

"What!? You're back so soon? What happened?"

"He's gone! I looked through the whole house. He's gone!"

"How could he go!? We have both cars. Are you sure?"

Chi looked worried and I know he didn't want to say it, but time was of the essence, so he calmly said to me, "Okay, here's what we are going to do. We are going to phone the hospitals to see if he's been admitted there, and we're going to phone the police if that doesn't work. Okay?"

I was overwhelmed by it all, and I started sobbing into my arms on the table.

"Chi. Chi. Remember in Marlbank when Stéphane died by suicide? Do you think Nigel has harmed himself? You were there with him and Stéphane. Do you think he could do that to himself? He told me about thoughts of killing himself in France and London."

Chi lifted my shoulders off the table and spoke loudly into my face, "Denni, get a grip. You are the toughest woman I have ever met in my life, and this is no time to change! Dry those eyes and get your phone out. Now! Right now! You take the downtown hospitals and I'll take Sunnybrook and North York. Now get busy. Do you hear me? I'm counting on you."

Diep added with her arm around my shoulders, "He's going to be okay, Denni. Please don't cry."

Ten minutes later, the three of us were back in the Benz, racing to Sunnybrook. Nigel had been admitted with a heart attack. He had called 911 himself, and the ambulance was on site two minutes after he placed the call. We were to meet the doctor in the ICU. He was still alive.

***

"Yes, you can see him, Mrs. Royal, but not for long. This is ICU, so you'll have to gown up before you go in. We've got him all doped up, so he may not even recognize you. We're going to keep him on serious meds until we know what route to take with him. We don't know at this point exactly how much damage there is to the heart. He's very lucky to be alive. Good thing he had the where-with-all to call 911 himself. He's a tough one. You might want to think about staying over with him once we get him his own bed, and out of ICU. I understand he has top-notch coverage, so we'll get him in a private room as soon as we can. There's going to be a lot of tests and in-and-out for him over the next couple of days though. Anything of importance you can tell me? Any current stress at home? Drugs? Alcohol? Girlfriends on the side?" He smiled as he offered this last little question.

"No to all the above. But he hasn't been himself for a couple of days. No appetite and going to bed early. We are having major renovations done at the house and he's a perfectionist, so it's been busy, but overall, it's a happy time for him. His thirty-year-old daughter is moving back home from Sweden next month, which is also good news for him. But he suffers from chronic psychological transference and doesn't deal with stress well. I think that he had some sort of breakdown earlier this evening. He was like a crazy man, and maybe this is what may have caused the heart attack. His last breakdown was about two years ago, before we were married. Oh, but when I think about now, we went through a false-alarm kidnapping with our granddaughter this winter as well. He found that very stressful, of course. I can give you the names of his doctors tomorrow. He drinks a glass of wine with dinner. He is not on any drugs of any sort, and he goes to the gym and walks every day."

"That sounds good, Mrs. Royal. Don't worry. We've got him all doped up to keep him nice and calm. Can I meet you here tomorrow morning when we're doing rounds? I'll bring you up to date as best we can on the heart attack. But first, please see the nurse and sign, or not, his DNR form."

"Of course, anything you need. But what's a DNR form?"

"Do not resuscitate."

"Oh. Oh my God. Of course. Thank you, Dr. Gilbert. God bless you. I'm so grateful that he's here at Sunnybrook. It's the best, and so are you."

"You got that right, Mrs. Royal. Now get in there and see your husband and tell him you love him. That's what he really needs to hear."

He was as high as a kite. I'd never seen anyone that doped up before. It was kind of a relief for me because I didn't want to lose my composure and break down in front of him. He had enough to worry about. I leaned over, careful not to disturb all his hookups and equipment, and I kissed him on his mouth, below the oxygen flowing into his nostrils. He gave me a little grin.

"Hi, darling. I'm happy to see you all tucked in here for the night. I love you. The doctors here at Sunnybrook are taking very good care of you. I love you. You're going to be having lots of tests tonight, so I'm going to go home and come back in the morning, first thing. I love you. I'm going to bring you in your toiletries and some pajamas and your robe. Baby, I love you and I want you to get better. You're my world, my whole world. Now close those eyes and get some rest. We'll talk tomorrow morning, but please know that I love you and I'll miss you in our big bed tonight. Sweet dreams. I love you."

He closed his eyes, and I kind of doubted whether he would remember me being there.

I sat and decompressed with Chi and Diep, and we all decided we would all stay for an hour so I could go in a few more times just to say an extra goodnight, just in case he was awake.

I phoned Alan and brought him up to date. I told him of Nigel's chronic disorder that would explain his attack on me. Alan was a prince and said that, in fact, he had heard of that disorder before. He added that he thought Nigel worrying about a future kidnapping may have triggered his breakdown as well.

I told him that it would be full steam ahead with the project and that Chi or I would be there as usual tomorrow to have lunch ready for the crew. I asked him to tell Bill, the general contractor, to tell the whole crew that Nigel had had a heart attack and that he was on the mend and in good hands at Sunnybrook. I asked him not to say anything about Nigel's breakdown, and he agreed wholeheartedly.

I wouldn't call Nigella and Brad until I had further news. No sense adding to anyone's stress before we really knew what we were dealing with.

I thanked God for Nigel's life and promised Him I would be the best wife in the whole world for the rest of my days.

***

The days flew by and Nigel's recovery was sure and steady. I was very aware of all the doting, young, pretty nurses, male and female, that were in and out of my handsome and charismatic husband's private room every five minutes, making sure that all his little asks were taken care of. I paid attention to all this and decided to dress up in a dress or a skirt and high heels every day when I visited him. Make up on, hair down and shining, and underneath it all was barely-there lacey lingerie and my standard fishnet stockings for each and every morning and evening visit.

"Oh, I thought I just brought your fresh laundry in the other day. And now there's a whole bag of it here! Oh, what is there, three or four pajama bottoms here?"

"Sorry, honey. I know it's extra work for you. But really, it's all your fault anyway."

"What do you mean all my fault? Am I somehow wearing your pjs around this room?"

"You know what I mean," he said with a big, sheepish grin on his face.

I sauntered over to his bed, hands on hips, and leaned over him. "No, tell me what you mean, big boy."

He lowered his voice. "Your jealousy turns me on, and I masturbate to you. I don't want the nurses to know, so I use my pajamas to mop up rather than the sheets."

My face flushed at the idea that he had tuned into my jealousy and had read me like a book. I decided to own it. I played with his hair as my eyes met his, with his oxygen tube dangling from his nostrils between the two of us.

I said quietly, "Your little blame game deserves more explanation than just that, you bad boy. You just sit tight, Mr. Royal. I'll be right back to deal with you and your antics."

I marched out of the room before he could tease me any further, and I went directly to the nurses' station. I gave a little laugh and spoke quietly to the young nurse, "Would you be so kind to let the staff know that my husband and I need twenty minutes of privacy in his room? Would that be possible?"

"Of course, Mrs. Royal. Whatever you need. In fact, take your time. I'll be in with his pills in forty-five minutes from now," she said as she lowered her head to hide her wide smile from me.

He lay there, grinning, sheets kicked off, as I stood at the bottom of his bed. "You're not the only one that knows how to striptease," I claimed with false bravado as I unbuttoned my shirt to the sway of the up-tempo jazz playing from his iPod. By the time I had made it over to the side of the bed, I had wriggled out of my skirt and tossed it across the room. It left me exposed in my one-piece lacey camisole with the garter-straps holding up my stockings, all the while balancing my shy little moves in my high heels. He made a lunge to grab me, and I danced away from him, laughing. I turned away from him, toward the window. I bent over with locked knees to pick up my skirt off the floor, and all I heard over Winston Marsalis playing in the background was his deep growl, "Get over here. Now."

***

A few weeks later, before going to bed, I stepped in the new family room to put the final touch on the room. I just stood there, admiring everything for the umpteenth time that evening. It was finally done. It was absolutely stunning – a ten-foot ceiling, lined with light honey-colored cedar boards and pot lights, four sets of black steel French doors that led out to the logia where the outdoor kitchen was already installed, with furniture in place, just waiting for warmer weather.

Transom windows above all the French doors opened and closed by remote, in order to allow for fresh air to flow through the room while keeping the doors closed.

The one long inside wall had been the original brick outside wall of the house when it had been built years ago, so Alan worked it into the design. It was sandblasted and left exposed, accommodating the long, black steel modern fireplace with a rustic oak beam mantle installed above it.

Two big, beautiful saddle-colored leather sofas, extra-long and extra-deep, huge flat-screen, marble-topped kitchen island complete with swivel-padded leather barstools, and two new Eames chairs with matching ottomans in another area for reading coordinated in nicely. I had my old friend, Manny, who was an upholsterer, wrap a round table with a three-inch apron in a dark aubergine-coloured leather for Nigel's poker parties with the boys. The big brass nail heads all around the apron took the precious look away from the piece. It was definitely a nod to the masculinity that would sit around it. It was designed to age with wear and tear, not fearful in the least of wet beer cans and spilled drinks on it. I wanted it to show its history of all the laughing and joking that would go down around it. Alan had found the perfect leather armchairs on castors that completed the set.

We also had a large, round dining room table commissioned that was positioned in front of the windows, near the kitchen island. It sat comfortably and was made slightly lower than the average dining table, that helped bring down the impressive piece to a friendly, family-style dining experience. It had a modern, clean, three-inch apron, and the whole table was clad in a large sheet of hammered, burnished copper. The patina would age beautifully. The tulip table base was made out of heavy, industrial cast iron, the same as the poker table. The artisan had done a beautiful job, and like the poker table, it was almost a work of art but very user-friendly and inviting. Like the rustic oak mantle and the leather poker table, the dining room table gave the whole room a sense of warmth and history. All the pieces toned down the newness of the space. There was also a children-sized table and chairs for Martina, her own pint-sized drafting board and swivel stool, just like her granddad's, only smaller, along with wide open spaces for floor play on the bleached oak hardwood.

At the far end of the room, there was a hallway that led into the guestroom and en-suite, but we hadn't brought in the bedroom furniture yet. Instead, we had furnished it as an office for Nigella. She would need her own space just for herself, so the designer brought in a beautiful modern desk and chair, a sleek new computer, bookshelves, and a pull-out sofa just in case we needed it. We would change it back into a bedroom once Nigella moved into her own home at a later date.

I admired the three eight-foot tall *ficas benjaminas* that were stationed in front of the windows, and three more were stationed out on the logia, only in a hardier version, to give the room a depth like looking into a forest of sorts. The whole tree installation was a visual trick to blur the lines between inside and out and were just a small part of Chi's landscaping plan for the backyard. I remember looking over his landscaping drawings and plans for the first time. He had printed out in bold letters on the front of the first page his *modus operandi*: *Is it a garden, or is it nature?*

We hadn't chosen any area rugs yet, and the only piece of art that I had hung so far was going to be a nice surprise for Nigel. It was a huge six-foot long and four-foot high enlargement of the little, old picture from 1970 that always sat on Saul's desk. It was the one of Saul, Daisy, and Nigel sitting on the front steps of 7 Russell Hill Road, with the dog licking the boy's face as the boy was leaning back, laughing. The new size brought it into a life-sized viewing experience. The pixels in the old photograph didn't let me down, and with a little retouching, the picture was magnificent. I wanted to leave the rest of the art for Nigel to choose what he wanted, except for the one piece that I was carrying in my arms, hugging it close to my chest.

I had to get a little stool to place my second piece of art up on the high oak mantle to one side that counter-balanced the big Nigel-as-a-kid photo that was mounted right onto the brick wall. This was my very own Denise-as-a-baby photo. My dad had taken this photo when I was about nine months old, and he had given it to me just before he died so many years ago. I had kept it in an old box along with a few others all those years, but whenever I pulled it out in remembrance, the solemn picture spoke volumes to me.

The photographer down on Vaughn Road, where I had had Nigel's photo enlarged, had worked his restoration magic on my small, dog-eared black and white photo. I propped up the 24" x 36" weathered, barn-board frame carefully on the oak mantle before stepping back to check the placement.

I wondered if my father ever had any idea of the impact of this image that he had snapped with his little Brownie camera that he bought himself when he came home from the navy. He had captured my great-grandfather carefully balancing me on his lap. My small, chubby, nine-month-old hands were gripping my great-grandfather's big, rough fingers while he carefully tucked his elbows in tight, propping me up on his knees in order to keep me sitting up straight for the photo.

The background of the photo told the story of the old homestead. My great-grandfather was perched on an old, spindled kitchen chair, on a stoop outside of the back kitchen. The unpainted wooden railing lined the few wooden steps on each side of the dark screen door. The bricked arch above the door was the only relief on the rough and patched stucco that had been applied over the wooden farmhouse many years prior. Dad had taken the photo that showed the small back stoop and the back-screen door, but he had avoided the worn dirt path that led out to the chicken coop and the barn. He did capture, however, the left side of the farmhouse and the clothesline, with great-granddad's second pair of farm overalls pinned to it, flapping in the summer breeze. The wooden pinned clothesline continued with a few plaid shirts and men's boxers until the sagging line was cut off abruptly by the border of the photograph.

It was the foreground, however, that held your interest. It wasn't the preciousness of the rough, old farmer dressed in his undershirt with the worn and ragged neckline underneath his overalls, holding a baby, naked as the day she was born, except for a cloth diaper held together with big safety pins. No, not at all.

It was the old man's solemn, protective look emanating from his soulful, translucent, Celtic eyes that really got you. His sparse white hair was lifted a little in the breeze that day. His bushy white eyebrows framed his large eyes on the top, and his prized white handlebar moustache, for which he had won first prize at the county fair many years before, framed them from below.

As I stood there, pulling out and away from my captivation, I wondered if others would feel the impact of the photo. It certainly worked for me. No matter how many times Nigel had teased me about believing in ghosts, I knew in my heart that my guardian angel, or whatever you would call him, was looking out for me. He had moved from the clearing at the farm down to 7 Russell Hill Road just to be close to me and to watch over me here in the big city, right from the mantle in my big, new family room.

My heart was full, and tears rolled down over my cheeks in gratitude. I was home. I was really home, and my great-granddad, George, was right here beside me.

***

There was one big bag that I had stashed away downstairs so that Nigel wouldn't see it, as I didn't want his homecoming surprise to be spoiled.

The surprise that I had arranged for Nigel had a name. His name was Patou, and he was arriving tomorrow afternoon on the flight from Avignon, France. He was an offspring of Edouard and Catharine's purebred Great Pyrenees, Patou, and he was old enough now to come to Canada to join his new Canadian family. I thought a puppy would be the perfect gift for Nigel, as I remembered how much he loved the older Patou in France last year. The pup would be good exercise for Nigel and would give him something new to focus on. As the pup grew to his full hundred-pound size, it would also be an excellent deterrent to kidnappers and grifters alike.

On a less-serious note concerning the new member of the family, now that the girls would be living here fulltime, I knew that Martina would love the pup too. And for me, well, I just couldn't wait to have those four paws and wagging tail making a mess of my clean floors. It was a win-win all the way around.

The plan was that Chi and I would pick up Nigel the next morning. I knew I wouldn't be able to sleep tonight. I was so happy to get him home once again. Although he would have a nurse come in every afternoon for the first few weeks, Nigel and I were both confident we could handle his new lifestyle without too much problem. Not too much of the new lifestyle was different from before, except for all the meds. We had been warned that the drugs made the patient tire easily, and he would need lots of rest and he should stay away from stressful situations. And regular psychotherapy was back on the books as well. His heart had been damaged permanently from the heart attack, so the pharma care was permanent too. The drugs would keep him alive.

***

"Do you approve, Dr. Gilbert? Or is Nigel just kidding me? Sex is okay as long as we're not overdoing it?"

"Yes, Mrs. Royal. In fact, your husband is a lucky man indeed to have such a vibrant sex life at his age and stage in life. It would be a shame to end all that now. It will be good for him, but take it easy on the old guy. No crazy stuff." He laughed as Nigel grinned, standing with his arm around me.

302

Nigel responded, "No more multiple orgasms, doc?"

"Nigel!" My face was beet-red as I exclaimed, "Oh! My God, you are incorrigible!"

You could hear Dr. Gilbert's laugh all the way down the hall. "Nigel, I must say you could probably teach me a few things in that department!" He continued, "But really, you two are the real deal, you know. Do you know how lucky you are? Just go home and be happy. I'm right here if you need anything. And I know my office has coordinated all your meds for both your heart and your mental health for you, so you're all set."

***

We got Nigel home and settled in the big, new family room. He and I were both propped up on the big leather sofa, with him at one end and me at the other, with our feet touching each other's in the middle.

I kissed him as I got up off the new tan leather sofa and Nigel growled good-naturedly, "Hey, beautiful, where are you going? You know what the doc said; I need lots of sex. We've got to christen this sofa, you know."

"I'll be right behind you in the new kitchen. I'm going to make us a nice black tea with lemon, just the way I like it. And besides, I have something to discuss with you."

We sat there at the island, sipping the tea, and he said quietly, "Okay, okay, tell me what's on your mind."

"Yes, okay, honey. You see, it's the two of us. Ever since we got married, we have failed miserably in dealing with your chronic mental health issue. We said way back then that we would go together to see the doctor, and we only went once. We're both to blame for this naïve and lax attitude, and we should have known better. I know we saw the doctor a few times in London, and then before we could get the prescription for the drugs filled, we got the call that the coast was clear to come home. Once again, we just swept your symptoms under the rug and came home. And then we went through that whole crazy home invasion mess. And now, it seems to me that you're still worrying about a possible kidnapping with the girls arriving soon, with all your extra surveillance and cameras you had installed on the property. We should have been on this from the get-go as soon as we were married. It can be deadly, honey, and we almost lost you this time."

"I'm so sorry, honey, but I won't hear of you taking the blame. I'm so sorry."

"This isn't about being sorry, darling. This is about for better and for worse, remember? How about if we make a deal right here and right now?"

"Whatever you say, honey."

"Okay. We both agree that we'll be vigilant about your current pharma regime, both for your heart and your mental health. The doctors went over every single pill with both of us, and they've got us covered for both areas. Right? So, on top of the pills, I'm suggesting that we both go together once a month, come hell or high water, to your shrink so that we can get on with our happy life in a safer manner. Deal?"

"Deal. I love you all the way, Denni."

"Back at 'cha, Mr. Wonderful."

It seemed the two of us couldn't bear to be apart from the other. I had brought in all his favorite books and stacked them all up on the big square coffee table, and we had a couple of beautiful throws on the sofa to snuggle under. We had the big, new sixty-inch TV screen on most times, and I lightened up the mood with YouTube's Carpool Karaoke with James Corden. We spent hours and hours watching James and all his guest singing and laughing through their lyrics. With Nigel's good voice and aptitude for music, he was a natural and followed along with the best of them.

We had installed a new BOSE music system, with speakers throughout the room, and as much as he wanted to tinker and play with everything, every half hour he was closing his eyes to rest.

The days passed and Nigel was so pleased when I asked him to give me a crash course in his favorite music genre, jazz, and I must admit that I grew to appreciate it as we listened to all the greats that he had collected over the years.

I didn't care how long his recovery took; I had him home once again, and I couldn't let him out of my sight for a moment. Lucky for me, he felt the same way.

"Now, honey, I'm putting my foot down. So, there's no need to bring it up again. I'm not going to look at any other art for our new room. You know how I feel about it. The two photos that you had restored and enlarged are the only art pieces that our new room should ever have in it. Nothing else will do. There isn't a Picasso-painted that can compare to these two photos."

"But, Nigel, I want to have your input in the room."

"You're in the room. That's all I want. You're not seeing the big picture here, Denni."

"Well, tell me, Mr. Know-it-all, what's the big picture?"

He pointed over to the two photos. "It's all right there, right in front of our eyes. Two great men. The two great men that shaped the two of us and continue to inspire us to this day. You can't beat that no matter how many Wolf Kahns or Simon Bulls you hang. In fact, I know this word may sound a little overboard, but our two photos are what you might call, umm, umm, exquisite."

"Exquisite, you say! Oh my! You say that the two old white guys are exquisite!" I said, laughing at his emotional descriptor. "You have a beautiful A.J. Casson hanging in Saul's office; now that's what I'd call exquisite."

"Okay, Mrs. Royal, purveyor of the arts. What adjective would you use to describe them?"

"Well, since we're describing feelings here, I don't have to use a word. A symbol will do quite nicely." I brought my hands together and curled my fingers around to form a heart.

"You're right. You're always right. Now, please. Get over here and kiss me so I know that we agree that the two old white guys as you call them are all we're hanging on the wall."

We received a letter from Sunnybrook, thanking us for the donation. They wanted us to confirm that the inscription to be added onto the list of donors on their big, bronze donor plaque in the Cardiology Wing was exactly as Nigel had requested: *Denise and Nigel Royal.*

I broached the subject with Nigel about how to repay Chi for all his care and help over the last month, not only with the heart attack but with finishing up the reno project as well.

"Honey, that's the whole problem. It's not just over the last month. Chi has been with me through everything over all the years. Look at the years of watching over me when we were in the Canadian Witness Protection System. And he literally kept me alive for the year before we were married, while you were living in France. I've never been able to thank him properly."

"Would he like a new car?"

"Oh, no. Chi would be so disappointed. He likes to drive the Benz, and although it does belong to me, we both think of it as his car. The Porsche is ours and the Benz is his. But actually, now that I'm thinking about it, I didn't even pay for that truck. Brad bought it when he renovated the basement apartment for me. He needed a big, secure, blacked-out vehicle so that Chi could pick him and the kids up at the airport without attracting any attention, so that's the real reason why I have the monster in the garage."

"It's not really my style of car either, but I am really fond of the backseat."

Nigel grinned from ear to ear and shook his head. "Baby, that was a crazy night. Did you ever find your underwear? What ever gets into you?"

"Me! No, no, no! I don't think so, big boy. You're not pinning that one on me, so let's get back to the topic at hand, shall we? Back to Chi now, I have another idea. What do you think about treating him and Diep to a trip back home to Vietnam? I know the two of them have never been back over all the years. Do you think that would work?"

"Bingo! Denni, you're brilliant! I think if we gave it to them as a belated wedding present, they would accept it."

"Perfect. And just to let you know, I love Chi just as much as you do. And for Diep, well, she's just the icing on Chi's cake, isn't she? He's a very happy man."

***

Chi & Diep were picking up the pup at the airport late afternoon, so I told Nigel that I was having a surprise delivered to him around 6:00 p.m. and it was the best present a guy could ever receive in his whole life. I think Nigel thought it was something for the new room, like a rug or a painting or something. Oh no, he was in for a surprise, all right.

Chi called softly from the garage door, and I shouted back, "Come on in! We're back here!"

I had my eyes glued to Nigel's face as he watched Chi and Diep walk through the old living room and down into the family room. Nigel was blinking as if he couldn't believe his eyes. The little round ball of fluff that was Patou strained at his leash, slipping and sliding on the hardwood as Chi walked him along. Once Chi let him off the leash, Patou was up in Nigel's arms on the sofa in two seconds flat. It was like he knew why he had moved to Canada. Nigel was roaring with laughter as the pup licked his face, and Chi, Diep, and I were crying like babies at the two of them.

Nigel said, "Honey, where did you get him? Is he really mine? I just love him. Has he got a name? He's really mine?"

"I got him from Edouard and Catharine's latest litter. He just flew in from France. Their old Patou that loved you so much when we were there is his father. He's a Great Pyrenees dog. That's why I thought we should call him Patou too. It means Pyrenean Mountain Dog in France, and they were once known as the royal dog of France. They were working dogs, protecting sheep, livestock, and people. They're trustworthy, affectionate, gentle, and good with children."

"How'd I get so lucky!? How'd I get so damn lucky!?"

Diep and I brought up all the dog paraphernalia from the basement, and we put the food and water bowls in the new family-room kitchen and the doggie bed right beside the French doors, as Chi suggested, so the dog would develop the guard dog side of his nature. The new family room was Patou's room. It was my intention to keep the little fur ball in one part of the house, with easy access to the backyard. He wasn't going to be allowed upstairs at all, and I knew that Nigel would be too much of a softie with the dog, so I only had two weeks to train him completely before Martina and Nigella arrived. I had my work cut out for me.

Nigel, Patou, and I spent the next few weeks mainly on one of the new sofas in the big family room. We spent these days talking about nothing as well as everything. We read, we snoozed, we ate, and we shopped online. We watched television and listened to the jazz greats and all that Motown had to offer. We were back to having our lengthy conversations and debates of just about everything and anything. Of course, Nigel was studiously jotting down his notes all day every day, and we couldn't have been happier. We let the dog in and out a hundred times a day, and slowly but surely, Nigel could walk up to the corner and back without stopping to rest.

Chi offered to come in every morning and take the dog for a walk around the block to train him on the leash. We interviewed several dog walkers in the neighborhood, and Patou simply wouldn't leave one of the interviewee's side, so we decided on Mary, who lived two blocks away from us. The deal was that she would walk him daily, along with her other dogs, and gradually train him to stay over with her on the occasional weekend to train him for doggie overnight care, if and when we were going to be away.

We had a forty-eight-hour overnight guest during that time. Brad flew in under the radar as usual, and Nigel, Chi, Brad, and François, who took two days off work, played cards, breaking in the new card table. They shot the shit from morning till night. Nigel dozed off on the sofa in between hands dealt, with the pup lying there on his chest. Brad brought it to everyone's attention that Nigel only felt tired when he was losing and that he was sick of it. I did note that for all his whining and complaining, he got all of them to turn the one sofa around to face the table so that Nigel was included in the party as he went back and forth to the sofa for his rests. Chi called Brad 'pretty boy' the whole time, and the three Canadians ganged up on the American and insisted that the Canadian money on the table was on par with the American dollar. The air was blue with 'fuck this,' 'fuck that,' and 'fuck everything.'

At one point, Nigel said, "Boys, boys, watch your language. We are in the presence of great men here," as he pointed over to Saul and George, who seemed to be looking down at them from our two prized photos.

The perpetrator said a quick, "Sorry, George. Sorry, Saul. Oh, fuck, man, now I've fucked up my hand. Fuck you, Uncle Nigie, and get ready. You're fucking going down."

Nigel tilted his head back, crowing with delight as he laid out his straight flush on the table to the disbelief of the other three players.

I happily pampered all my boys with trays of good, hot food and beer in between letting the pup in and out every five minutes, trying to train him to pee outside and not on the new family-room floor, and certainly not upside the large terracotta planters that held Chi's prize ficas.

Nigel's nurse came every afternoon to check up on the patient and was pleased to note that his vitals were all good. She took one look at Patou and said that was the best medicine anyone could have and she had no doubt Nigel would be jogging his three kilometers every night again in the near future. She had some good advice for me as well, out of Nigel's earshot.

"Mrs. Royal, don't mind me here, but I'm just saying this for your own good. Both you and Mr. Royal have been through a lot, and your husband has aged dramatically. And the meds are tough on him as well. And he needs rest, lots of rest, to heal the damage to his heart. Not only has he lost a little too much weight and muscle tone, but his face and hair are showing signs of stress that will lead to aging as well. He may be fully gray or even white within six months. That's not a good look for a handsome, vibrant man like him, in my opinion. I don't want that to happen to you. Take care of yourself. You're not exactly a spring chicken either. I'm sorry for speaking out of turn here, but you are a beautiful, handsome couple that needs a little extra TLC, if you know what I mean."

I laughed, "You sound just like my friend Catharine. She lives too far away from me to lay it on the line like you just did, but I needed to hear this. And don't worry. We are both committed to the new pharma routine and we eat organic here. I'll just make sure we get more vitamins through our fruits and vegies. I'll throw in a few extra carbs for him too. I'll get us both in for some facials and massages at The Elmwood as well."

I hugged her at the door and said, "We're so happy to have you on board!"

***

Once again, Chi and I found ourselves standing at the airport, waiting for Nigella and Martina to arrive. This time, Diep was with us. Nigel was disappointed to have to stay home but I was afraid that standing for too long, especially if the flight was delayed, would be too much for him. He agreed that he had the rest of his life to spend with the girls, so what was another two hours anyway? He really was a good patient. I was so in love with him.

***

Martina was nose-to-nose with Nigel as she sat on his lap with her one hand clutching Patou's collar so he couldn't wriggle away. With her perfect little Swedish accent, she asked him, "Granddad, do you feel sick? Mommy told me that you had a heart attack. I'm going to take care of you forever and ever. Do you want some ice cream right now, Granddad?"

As I set out the bowls for the ice cream, Martina was all about scooping the ice cream by herself. "Grandma, we can't forget the sprinkles that you have here in Canada. Granddad likes the sprinkles, you know."

I explained to Nigella and Martina that we were having a big Sunday afternoon party for the crew that built the new addition for us. It was Martina's job to share her toys and games with the other children, but she was adamant about not sharing the dog with anyone.

***

A few weeks prior to the girls' arrival, Nigel and I had talked the idea of the party over with Alan and Bill, the general contractor, and Bill said he would be happy to invite the whole crew and their families over to celebrate the new family room. He warned us that most of the crew was in their thirties, and they all had young families and also some new babies among them. He totaled them all up and said to expect about forty adults and about thirty children – toddlers and babies.

At that same meeting with Alan, Bill, Nigel, and myself, all with our feet up in the family room, Nigel added, "Please make sure that everyone is invited, and I mean everyone. All the wives and girlfriends, boyfriends, whatever. We're pretty inclusive here; our wedding here in the backyard had as many gay people as straight in attendance. And one of our friends has a transgendered wife, so I stress that everyone is welcome. All ages and stages. We'll have help here to take care of the babies. We have a five-year-old granddaughter ourselves."

"Never mind the babies, Nigel," Bill added in, laughing. "Just take care of the bar."

Nigel told the two men a few of his famous stories, like the one of Gerri breaking his nose and the one of me attacking the 6'3" deer hunter, where it looked like David and Goliath being played out in front of him lying on the ground with a bullet in his arm. It was almost he was trying to make up for his churlish behavior right before his heart attack. Alan and Bill just couldn't get enough. Tears were running down Bill's face as Nigel described how the deer hunter had flicked me off his big body like a little flea. Of course, I played right along as a straight man to Nigel's delight.

The beauty of his stories was, however, not the actual story itself. It was that this man presented himself as the sensitive, nerdy, intellectual fuck-up bumbling through his complicated life, always ending up on the short end of the stick that always made the story so comical. It was his humility that made all the stories so funny and so endearing to the listener.

***

The day arrived for the big party. Our dog-walker, Mary, had taken Patou for the day, the caterers had a special menu all set up for the kids, and we had a children's party planner supply the staff to make the party balloons and to paint their faces that all kids seemed to love. As it turned out, most of the adults had their faces painted too, so it was a noisy, fun-filled day for everyone. We had stocked the bathroom off the family room with diapers of all sizes, and the adults took full advantage of the staff to help with the children.

It was just the beginning of the party, and there was just a handful of kids, mostly holding on to their parents' hands, despite Martina urging them to play with her games. One little boy, about six-years-old, in the middle of a lull in the conversation said loudly to Martina, "You talk funny."

Martina, with her little Swedish accent, still struggling with her second language, didn't lose a beat. "It's not me; it's you. Do you want to ride my bike or not?"

"No, it's pink."

The party was going full-blast; everyone was having such a good time. Nigel had sixties' Motown surround-sounding around the room, all emanating from his new BOSE system. The kids were all running around, acting like kids, once their parents had let them loose. Nigella was so charming with all the women. Of course, they were more or less her age, and I could hear her big laugh, just like Nigel's, over the crowd and the music. The husbands stayed away from her, perhaps out of intimidation or perhaps because it was the big boss' daughter, but probably knowing that their wives and girlfriends were watching them like a hawk. She was just so strikingly beautiful, with the long, blond ringlets brushing her shoulders of the simple, long-sleeved tee-shirt, jeans, and Nigel's old moccasins that she insisted on wearing to the party.

Chi came over to me and I had to laugh at his face, which was painted up like the kids, with a bunny nose and whiskers. He said, "So sorry, Denni, but François couldn't come today. He's in Vancouver on business. He says to give you his love."

Nigel was his happy and charming self, and every five minutes he would come over to me, slip his arm around my waist, and smooch my neck. Other times, I would look through the crowd just to check up on him, and I would see him looking for me as well. He would give me a little smile and a wink and continue with the person he was standing with, but by the end of the party, I knew that it had been too much for him.

Everyone had left by five o'clock, and I said that it was doctor's orders that we all were going to have an early dinner of leftovers with everyone in their pajamas. Nigel didn't argue, and Chi, Diep, still fully clothed, and the rest of us in our pajamas laid out all the leftovers on the new kitchen island. Nigel couldn't keep his eyes open and stretched out in the middle of us all, sleeping through all our after-party gossip and stories as Chi made a pot of coffee in the new kitchen for us.

We were all in bed early that night, and as I snuggled up to Nigel, he whispered, "Mrs. Royal, I had the time of my life today. Other than our wedding day, and the day I met the girls, today really was the best. Thank you for loving me so much."

"You make it easy to love you, Mr. Royal. How are you feeling?"

"Don't give me that patient talk. I want you to give me some wifey talk and a little action to go along with it."

"Honey, you need your rest."

"Fuck the rest. Are you saying for the first time in our three-year love affair that you have a headache?"

"Not exactly. I just don't want to overextend you."

He grabbed my hand down to feel his erection and said, "Sorry, baby, I'm already overextended. Can you do something about that for me?"

I couldn't resist him, although I knew he simply needed to rest and I was worried about him. I sighed and warned him to be careful. "Just lie there, baby. Don't move. I'm going to climb on top of you and make you feel so good; you'll sleep like a baby after this."

He was ready for me. My hands were on his chest and my legs were squeezing and pumping him. His hands were on my ass, dictating the rhythm. He cried out quietly as he rode his waves of pleasure.

He whispered, "Now you, baby. I need you to cum for me. I don't want it just for me, not this time. This is for you too."

I leaned over and held his beautiful face between my hands. "You want me to feel good, baby? Okay, I'm your girl and I love you." I leaned down with my breasts rubbing against his chest. He was kissing my neck as he heard me coming, calling out his name softly. It was the first time I had ever really lied to Nigel, and I did it just like most women have done at one time or another. I faked it, and I faked it like a pro.

***

311

Chi and Diep were over one morning for coffee, and I announced in my usual diva, take-charge way, "What do you think, guys? How about a little road trip to get the patient out of the house? How about the four of us go up to the old farm where I was born, just north of the city, and I'll tell you all about how my great-granddad and my dad are always there, or at least their spirits are, waiting in the clearing to say hello to me. Maybe you will be able to sense their presence like I do." I hesitated a little and lost a bit of my confidence. "Or I can just go by myself. It's really just a wreck of a place; it won't be of any interest to you at all."

Chi and Diep looked at each other and smiled. "We have been saying that we wanted to look for a piece of property ever since the day we met, haven't we, Chi?"

Chi was grinning and nodding in agreement.

"Well," I continued, "this is no Shangri la. It's actually just an old, overgrown bush with no buildings, and it's only twenty acres and good for nothing really. But there's something about it, and I'm compelled just to go there and stand in the clearing and drink it all in. It's kind of crazy actually," I admitted. "Now that I hear myself saying this, I know I'm going to regret it. Nigel will have something new to tease me about like he always does. This patch of bush was up for sale a few years ago, but I don't think it was sold, and the sign isn't up on the fence any longer."

Nigel leaned back in his chair, grinning from ear to ear. "My little enigma never fails to surprise me. Three years in, and she is finally letting me into her little world. Count me in. Let's go right now. No time like the present. No, wait. We'll go this afternoon, right after lunch."

We all met at 1:30 p.m., clad in boots and toques as if we were going to the North Pole. Nigel had dug out our old Hunter boots *château* for the excursion. I had to laugh; we were all such city slickers. Diep was armed with a bag of snacks and drinks for the drive up to the country. It amused me to no end that the boys, of course, wanted to ride up front, with us girls in the back. Men were such idiots when it came to their macho ideas about tooling around town in their big cars up front as if they were riding shotgun on the stage coach.

"Denni, I'll tell you the reason why I want Nigel up front with me," Chi offered.

"And why's that, Chi?"

"Well, Denni, I have to keep you two separate and apart. This big powerhouse of a truck has seen many wild times, but none as rowdy as a certain ride back from a certain airport one night, with you and Nigel getting it on in the backseat."

Nigel roared with laughter as I denied everything. "That's the most preposterous story I've ever heard! It's simply not true!" I interjected.

"Okay, Denni, okay. It never happened. The bra that I picked up off the floor of the backseat the next morning must have belonged to someone else. By the way, I put it along with the rest of the underwear in your laundry room the next day, just in case you were looking for it."

"You two men are such a pair, always teasing me. Just you wait. Diep and I will beat the pants off you next time we play cards. You'll see."

On our way, Chi re-told the story of the last time we went to my farm, the one down in Marlbank, and of his love for the farming life that had been introduced to him as a teenager when he first came to Canada and he became Québécois. At the end of the story, Diep quietly said, "God bless Stéphane," and we all murmured the same in response. As Chi turned off the 404, I said excitedly, "Okay, guys, we are exactly seven minutes away from my farm."

As we were all getting out of the car, Nigel grabbed my hand and said, "Honey, it's not deer hunting season up here, is it?"

I looked into his face to see if he was serious or making a joke. He had a big grin on his face, and I said, "The joke's on you, buster; you were the one that took the bullet as I remember."

We stood there in the clearing, Chi holding Diep's hand and Nigel holding mine. The silence was deafening. Whether it was the afternoon sunlight dappling through the bare, brown trees or the promise of the spring day, we were all spellbound. You could hear the rustle of the bush and the occasional bird calling out. We all jumped a little as a fat, bushy squirrel gave us a piece of his mind from his branch in a leafless, old chestnut tree.

Nigel put his arm around my shoulder and leaned down to kiss my cheek. No one said a word. I motioned with my hand to follow me, and we tramped over the dry brush and pine needles to the 'good' side of the property.

We stood in the new location, and I explained that exactly one half of the twenty acres was deemed flood plain, but this half where we were standing could be farmed and built on, and maybe that's why no one wanted it. You had to buy the twenty acres, but you could really only use half of it and keep the other half as conservation land. I pointed out a stand of magnificent old oak trees with their barren, black, gnarly branches. There were some American chestnut trees as well, towering over the clumps of pine, cedar, elms, and maples. You had to know your trees to be able to decipher the natural bush that was home to trees well over seventy years old.

Chi started the Benz, and we all buckled up, the boys in the front once again, with Diep and me sitting in the back.

"So, are we all in?" Chi asked but he didn't pull away from the side of the road. He just sat there looking at us all, one at a time.

"Yeah, Chi, we're buckled up," I responded.

Chi didn't move. Diep followed his clue and said firmly, "You mean, honey, are we all in to buy the farm? Is that what you mean, Chi?"

"That's exactly what I mean, darlin'."

Nigel and I both shouted at the same time, "Count me in!" and Chi smiled as he geared up and pulled the Benz out of the muddy soft shoulder that lined the deep ditch in front of the bush that used to be my farm.

We all chattered back and forth with ideas and plans for our new venture as we barreled back down the 404 when Chi threw out a soft little assurance my way. "Don't worry, Denni. We'll take good care of the oaks and the chestnut trees. It will take us many tramps through that bush to understand your vision, but we'll make it happen." He looked in the rearview mirror and smiled at me, adding, "Too bad your great-granddad wasn't home today. I would have loved to have seen him."

Nigel looked over at his old friend quickly and said, "Oh, Chi, you're so behind the times. Denni's great-granddad moved on quite a while back."

Chi continued his little quip, "What do you mean? Has he left the building, like Elvis?"

"Yes, you might say he has," Nigel said seriously. "George now lives with all of us, up on our mantle at home at 7 Russell Hill Road."

I had never loved him more than I loved him at that very moment.

***

Chi and Nigel visited the farm's local town hall to see who owned the patch of bush, and in less than a month, the twenty acres of bush was ours. Our short-term plan was to call my old friend, Tom Oliver, who was an arborist and had a sawmill. He would get the permits and begin to clean up the twenty acres, starting right away. He would work from our plan of where to clear, and we would all walk the bush to tag the trees that had to come down, according to his experience and the permits that he would arrange for. Nigel and I had no interest whatsoever in ever living on the property, but Chi and Diep planned on building their dream house there and running our apiary business.

Yes, the four of us were to become beekeepers. It gave Nigel something to research, as he had finished writing his book and was without a project to sink his teeth into. He reported back to us that there were all kinds of government grants for setting up an apiary and working with the environment with regards to ponds and forest management. We would have a nice, big mobile home installed temporarily on the cleared plot in order to be comfortable while we were up there acting like pioneers. Of course, little Martina's name came up again and again, as we made plans for the family's future at the farm. It was like my great-grandfather, George, was whispering in my ear through the whole process. He and his father had homesteaded that crown land back in 1850, when they emigrated from Ireland. Now I was following in his footsteps, just when I thought I couldn't be happier.

***

It was early May, and I watched her from my upstairs office window and smiled as I noted her carwash ensemble. Over the past two weeks, I had started teasing her about wearing her dad's clothes as much as he did, but I have to admit; she wore them well. It all started with Nigel offering her the infamous vintage Bob Marley tee-shirt that Brad had given him, and soon he had her up in his big walk-in closet, coaxing her to take whatever she wanted.

This particular day, however, she had on Nigel's old barn boots that he had brought home from the *château*. Her old, faded, baggy sweats were way too short on her long legs and wouldn't stay tucked into the rubber boots. Nigel's hand-me-down sleeveless Bob Marley tee-shirt was over her long-sleeved tee-shirt. She was wearing her hair natural these days, and the blond afro ringlets were clipped back with my art deco hair clips that Nigel had given me long before we were married. And still, as she stood there with the spring's sunshine lighting her up from top to bottom, the hose running and bucket of soapy suds in one hand and a big sponge in the other, she was the most strikingly beautiful young woman in the neighborhood.

She had jockeyed both the Benz and the Porsche out to the driveway so she could clean the two at the same time. All the car mats were out on the lawn, and everything around her was in disarray. You'd never know by the disorganized scene that she was a brilliant, organized, and focused mother, daughter, and lawyer who excelled at everything she touched.

She had looked up as the vintage Alpha Romeo spider convertible turned to pull in the driveway and then backed out again to park on the street.

François gracefully shut the door of his baby and strolled across the street with one hand in his pocket, moving across the pavement like a model working the runway. He was a good-looking thirty-something, taller than the older generation of Asian men, slim, confident, and well groomed. He had that classy, monied look about him. He wore his clothes well, and like his father, Chi, he always dressed in expensive Italian sportswear on the weekends when he would drop over to see Chi. He wore fine cottons and wools in subdued tones, but looked very sexy in a confident, European, take-charge manner. He too wore the Italian Ferragamo loafers than both Chi and Nigel wore. Nothing about him spoke to gym-wear or street-wear whatsoever. Today, he had on a pair of cream-colored pants with a navy tee-shirt that was way more than just a tee-shirt. It looked like a silk jersey fashioned with crew neck and the short sleeves that were a little tight over his biceps. I was reminded once again of the little thought that always crept into my mind whenever I saw François. He just looked like too much of a player for his own good. His eyes never left Nigella, and her eyes returned the voiceless communication. They were fifty feet apart, and I was only watching the scene as an indoor spectator, but anyone, anyone in the whole world, would have been able to sense that this sighting between the two strangers was going to change their lives forever.

He was about ten feet from her, and although I couldn't hear what he was saying, it was obvious that he was introducing himself. She dropped the soapy sponge and wiped her wet hand down her sweats to reach out to shake his hand. At that very moment, he was smiling and shaking his head back and forth and opened his arms to her for a family-style hug. Of course, I was watching this play out in silent pantomime, but I got the drift of good things to come from the two wide smiles that both parties were wearing.

She threw her head back laughing, just the way Nigel would have done. She stretched out her arms high to receive his hug, and from my vantage point of the second-story window, I could see it coming. I held my breath and I could almost feel it.

I gasped as the pail of cold soapy water that she held in her left hand tipped down against his shoulder as he pulled her in tight for the warm embrace. His spine straightened as the whole bucket tipped over and ran straight down his back. His mouth was opened wide as his arms flew up and away from her.

Nigella's long legs sprang back and her arms were still outstretched, still holding onto the now-empty bucket. Her beautiful face registered the horror of what she had just done. The empty bucket fell to the ground and her hands flew upward to land one on each side of her stricken face.

François did a couple of high steps and then he slowed right down. He reached up with one arm and pulled the wet silk jersey off in Chippindale-dancer style, up and over his head. He stood there, facing her, legs apart, with his pumped-up pecs and smooth chest peacocking for the beautiful klutz. They didn't move; they just looked at each other, four feet apart, their eyes holding. His little smile told her he was forgiving her for the debacle that she had caused.

I think that that was exactly the moment when François Tran and Nigella Hansson fell in love, right at that very moment, with less than ten words spoken between them. These two brilliant, sophisticated lawyers, the Vietnamese French Canadian and the Swedish Canadian Jew, knew without a doubt that they had met their respective soul mate.

Later that day, when Nigel was changing into a fresh shirt for dinner, I met him in our closet. I put my arms up around his neck. "Nigel, I have a quiet little story to tell you before we go down for dinner."

"What's up, honey? Everything okay?"

"I just want to forewarn you that there's yet another change coming to 7 Russell Hill Road."

"Not another reno. Please tell me we're not going to go through that again."

"Oh, no, no, baby. Something way, way more disruptive than that." I continued with my story now that I had his full attention. "I saw a couple fall in love today, right in our driveway."

"Is this part of your new book or have you been reading *The Blue Castle* again?"

"No, my handsome husband. This was happening real-time in real life. I just want to warn you that you can expect a request for a private conversation with your one-and-only godson, François Tran, any time soon."

"Is everything okay with Chi? Him? Wait. Back up. What are you talking about?"

"François met Nigella today, and I watched it all unfold. It was love at first sight. I think he will be asking you for Nigella's hand in marriage. As sure as God made little green apples."

It took a moment to register. Then his eyes opened wide and he exclaimed, "No! Are you kidding me? Are you sure, Denni? Really?"

We decided that we would leave well enough alone and let the kids take full control over their destiny in their own way.

When we came in from our nightly walk around the block, Nigella was waiting for us, sitting at the kitchen island. She looked a little distracted. Her face was flushed.

"Hi, honey. Something on your mind?" Nigel prompted.

"Yeah, Dad. Just wondering if I could ask you two a huge favor. I owe someone a dinner out to make up for a big mess I caused, and I'm wondering if you could possibly babysit Martina tomorrow night while I take care of this."

"Absolutely. Something about a possible job or work or something?"

"No. No, well maybe. I don't know. Oh, come to think about it, it may be. After all, he's a lawyer. Oh, maybe I've misread the situation altogether," she said in an uncertain voice.

"Well, do we know this person?"

"Oh, of course you do. It's your godson, François."

"So, it's family."

"No, Dad, not really. No, not at all. A girl doesn't feel this way about family."

She threw up her hands in mock despair and we all started to laugh.

"Denni, what am I going to wear?"

"Your very best silk La Perla lingerie. And pack an overnight bag."

"Honey, can I make a reservation or anything for you? Here, please take my card to pick up the tab. And first thing tomorrow morning, you and Denni run up to Holt's and get the most beautiful dress and shoes that they have in the store. My treat," the happy father added.

"Please, Dad. I can handle this. But actually," she confided, "when I invited François out for dinner to make up for my mess, he wouldn't hear of it. He told me just to be ready at 7:00 p.m. and he would take care of the rest." She laughed a little, and her face flushed. "As we were saying goodbye, he tugged down on my Bob Marley tee-shirt, you know, your old gym shirt, and he told me to leave Bob at home. He said he wanted to be the only man in my life. I'm feeling a little flattered by his attention." Her happiness, and finally being able to spit it out, ended with her clasping her hands together, jumping up and down, and declaring, "I think he likes me!"

"Well, I have to tell you, Nigella, your dinner date is one hell of a fine man. They don't come any better than that, honey."

"Yeah, Dad. So that's a yes to the babysitting?"

"Hell yes!"

***

As François pulled out a chair at the card table where Nigel and Martina were building a Lego robot, he looked right in Martina's face and said, "Hello, Martina. My name is François and I'm here to take your mom out for dinner tonight, but I'll bring her home in a few hours."

"Hello. I already know your name. Granddad told me that he knew you when you were a baby. You smell nice. Same as Granddad."

From upstairs, we heard Nigella call out, "Do I hear my dinner date down there?"

François scrambled to get out of his chair and just stood there, watching her slowly descend the stairs. No doubt about it, she knew how to work it. Her golden ringlets brushed the shoulders of the new, deep-blue dress. It had long sleeves, a deep *V* neckline and a deeper *V* at the back. It was just below the knee, very sophisticated, and very sexy. High heels tipped the outfit from just perfect to absolutely stunning.

He was waiting at the foot of the stairs for her to reach the bottom step.

She stood up close to him and laughed a little as she gave him a very slight peck on the cheek. "Do you like my new dress, François? I bought it especially with you in mind," she teased.

He couldn't move. He shook his head a little, grinning, and said nervously, "Blondie, you're killing me."

"And here you are, all dressed up and wearing my favorite boy scent."

"There's nothing boyish about me at all. I'm all man."

"That's a conversation to table for now, counselor," Nigella responded as she looked over at Martina.

I can safely say that neither one of them remember saying goodnight to the three of us as they floated out the front door. It wasn't just a spark between them. No, not at all. It was more like an eighty-hectare forest fire between the French-Canadian and the Swede – hot... very, very hot! Nigel and I looked at each other over Martina's head and laughed softly.

Nigel came over to the sofa and whispered to me, "Poor François. He's in the deep end. I hope to hell he can tread water. I think he's dealing with a woman who knows exactly what she wants."

I jumped up and leaned over Martina, who was sitting with two cushions on her chair to navigate the adult's card table. "Martina, I think we should have an ice cream party right now to celebrate."

"Yay! You too, Granddad. With those sprinkles, right Grandma? What are we celebrating?"

"We are celebrating you because you are remembering to speak English so nicely all the time, Martina. We're sorry we can't speak Swedish to you, and we appreciate all your hard work. Do you know that François also is an English-as-a-second-language person? His first language is French."

"Uh huh. Mommy told me all about François. Do you know that Uncle Chi is his dad? So, we're family. Right, Grandma?"

"Right, darling. We're family."

***

After their first date, the dinner table at 7 Russell Hill Road was always automatically set to include François, and occasionally, Chi would accept her invitation as well. Nigella cooked all the meals, and with Chi's blessing, raided the greenhouse daily. She used the departed Mrs. Himmel's best china and linens that I had incorporated into the dining room console, changing up the china at every chance, just like I would do. She took care of everyone and always wore an old-fashioned European apron over her clothes. She doted on

François hand and foot. She made up his plate for him and always saved him second helpings in the oven to keep everything warm. And he simply couldn't get enough of her. He arrived every night after work, sometimes just staying long enough to eat and then going back to work, and other nights, he would stay until after Martina went up to bed and Nigel and I would hear the two of them laughing down in the family room or in the kitchen, having a last coffee or a glass of wine long after we had went up to bed. Nigella was hesitant to ask us to babysit so they could get out a little more often, so they didn't have a lot of privacy. Martina took to the new arrangements like a duck in water, and Nigel and I made it a practice of going up to our room early, as Nigel had installed a television in our room to give us all a little space.

A few weeks after their first date, François said after dinner one night, "Uncle Nigel, can I speak with you for a minute? Can we just slip into Saul's office?"

Nigel settled down in Saul's old chair and said to his godson, "Allow me to start this conversation. First things first, son. All of this is just too weird."

François jumped up off the sofa, alarmed, "What do you mean? I thought you and Denni approved of me and Nigella!"

"Oh no, oh no! Sorry! Oh, no, I mean… I mean, you calling me Uncle Nigel. That's what's weird. If you're in love with my daughter, I can't be your uncle. And I can't be your dad. You already have a fine dad. Can you just call me Nigel?"

"Oh my God, Nigel. If that's all it takes to keep you happy, count me in! For Christ's sake, you almost gave me a heart attack."

"Good then. Now, what's on your mind?"

"It's her. It's Nigella. She's on my mind. I can't eat. I can't sleep. I'm a mess at the office."

"You've got it bad, son."

"Yeah, it actually started before I even met her. Dad told me all about her when he met her back in January, and I know it sounds crazy, but I think I knew then that this was going to happen. And then I saw her standing in the driveway with your old gym shirt on. I was a goner. But meanwhile, Dad has given me some good advice, and I want to run it by you."

"Shoot."

"Dad told me that you took Denni to Paris for your first night together, and he also told me he took Diep to New York for theirs. He said not to wait around – to just do it. I want to take Nigella away for the weekend, to ask her to marry me, but I wanted to clear it with you beforehand."

"I agree with your dad. Do it right away, this weekend if possible. Denni and I will be so happy to babysit Martina. Don't ever worry about that. But there is one thing that I've learned when dealing with strong-willed women like my wife and my daughter."

"What's that, Uncle Nigel?"

"Don't ask her to go to New York. Just tell her. Nicely. And don't wait. As Saul told me many years ago, 'Love recklessly, and love with abundance.'"

"Yes. Absolutely. But I want to reassure you about something though. This is kind of embarrassing and not the thing a man usually talks over with his father-in-law, but ours is a unique situation here, and I don't want you to worry about anything."

"Such as?"

"When I first laid eyes on Nigella, of course I thought she was the epitome of every man's fantasy Swedish sex goddess. You know, the hair, the body, the laugh, the wit. Oh my God, I was smitten. But once I got sitting beside her at the restaurant that first night, I realized that I was dealing with a beautifully wrapped present of pure sex that hadn't really been opened yet. I'm pretty sure she's still a naive and innocent girl in a real woman's body. I want you to know that I recognize who I'm dealing with here, and I don't want you worrying about her. My experience with women over the years tells me that while I'm not much in the looks department, I'm one hell of a good technician in the bedroom."

Nigel smiled at the younger man's claim of prowess. "Yes. I think you're right. She told Denni and me about conceiving Martina through a sperm bank, and I gathered there hasn't been a lot of, if any, sex in her life."

"I just don't want you to worry about her. I'll take very good care of her and I know I can make her happy."

"I know you will too. Thinking about her, though, there is a word to describe my daughter. I picked up on this over the first few days after meeting her last January. For all her brains, she's, uh, uh… she's guileless. Wouldn't you agree?"

"Exactly. That's it. Guileless. And it's a very strange trait to associate with a thirty-year-old female lawyer. But you've nailed it, Nigel. That's our girl. She's guileless."

The younger man stood up and walked over to where his godfather was sitting. "I love you, Uncle Nigel. I'm so blessed to have you and my dad in my life. Now the three of us all have our girls, plus our baby Martina to boot. Like you always say, 'how'd I get so lucky?'"

"And I love you too. I've always been so proud of you. But one last thing, son. Will you be getting married soon?"

"Oh! Of course! As soon as possible. But I know who I'm dealing with. Women like ours like the bling. I have to pick out the perfect ring for my princess, just like you and Dad did. You know how it is, Uncle Nigel. And we'll have to find a house, of course. Nothing but the best for my two girls. My condo is too small. I'll sell it and re-invest in a family home. Trust me, I'm working on all of it; I'm going to go to Tiffany's tomorrow."

"Whatever you need, please let me know how I can help. Denni and I have a little money set aside for the girls, and Nigella has already talked to us about moving into her own place by the end of the year, so finding a house may not be so far out of reach as you may think."

***

I listened to her whining and her intermittent tears for a full half hour before I pulled her back into the real world.

"Okay, okay, now it's my turn to talk. I want to recap what you've been telling me. You don't feel good about going to New York with your man. You say Martina will miss you. You say that you've never been away with a man before. You say that you haven't had any real experience with sex. You say that it's too early. You say you have never been apart from the baby. You say you have nothing to wear.

"Now I'm going to tell you the sad story of what happened to me a short few years ago when I was feeling exactly how you are feeling today. This is an ugly ending, Nigella, but you should hear this. I couldn't let love in and wouldn't accept Nigel's love at first either. I got cold feet, I had to be in control of everything all the time, and I had trust issues with men bigger than all of Lake Ontario, and I ended up in the psych ward of a hospital in the middle of France. And what's so scary? You are so much like me. You are all talk and no action when it comes to men. And you're also so sensitive and caring just like your dad. And your dad can tell you his own sad story of how my craziness and his own trust issues that have affected him as well. How do you think he broke his nose? He had a breakdown too. And we were apart for nine whole months. The way you are acting, you are going to end up in that same sorry state."

I continued, "Now. Run upstairs, wash your face, and put on some lipstick. Nigel and Martina won't be home for the afternoon, and you and I are going to go down to Yorkville to get you a bikini wax, a mani/pedi, and some very sexy lingerie. Trust me. I know what I'm talking about in this department. Men love neat and tidy lady-bits, and I simply can't have my beautiful Swedish princess going off to New York for a great love affair unprepared. And please, just trust François in all ways. He's a good man, and he wants you, and he loves you. He'll take very good care of you in the bedroom. He'll teach you to tell him what you need from him. Does he know that you had the baby with *In Vitro Fertilization* and that you have had little to no experience with men?"

"I just told him very briefly that I used a sperm bank to conceive Martina, but he doesn't know anything other than that. He probably thinks I know what I'm doing. But never mind that. Okay, Denni. You're right. I'm acting like a crazy person. I do want him so much, and I do love him. I just have to trust him. And I know I've used the English-as-a-second-language joke on you so often, but when you say the word 'lady-bits,' are you talking about down there?"

"Yes, little Miss Innocent. We can call your vaginal lips 'lady-bits' or 'vajajay,' but make no mistake about it; we need to be neat and tidy about it all. No Brazilian necessary – just a nice, little tidy-up."

She gave me a huge hug. "I love you so much. How can I ever repay you?"

"You don't have to repay family, baby. Just go get laid in the Big Apple and tell your man how much you love him. And have fun. Then marry him as soon as possible and be happy for the rest of your life just like your dad and me."

***

As I sat out in the wax bar lounge with all of our bags and boxes of tissue-wrapped lingerie waiting for Nigella to wrap up her bikini wax appointment, the receptionist, one other customer, and I heard a woman's European accent say loudly, "Ouch! Ouch! Does it always hurt this much or is it because it's my first time?"

Peals of laughter coming from the aesthetician wafted out of the procedure room as we all laughed along at the cute, little joke.

"Oh," the accent continued, laughing a little in a charming way, "that didn't come out quite right. You see, English is my second language."

That was our Nigella. She definitely knew how to work it. Poor François. She would surely give him a run for his money.

***

Chi and Diep were picking up the kids at the airport arriving on the Sunday-night flight, so we had Martina already in her nightie when we heard the side door from the garage open. I had prepared a cheeseboard and some snacks for everyone, and they all piled into the new family room in their haste to scoop up Martina and the dog. Nigel noticed her ring first.

323

"Something you want to tell us?" he said, waving his ring finger out in front of him.

François recounted the story of how he went to Tiffany's in Toronto, chose the ring, and took it with him to New York, unknown to his future bride.

"And I said yes!" Nigella happily exclaimed.

The ring was a beautiful, three-carat, round, brilliant gem mounted on an unusual, handcrafted, thick gold band. The two of them finally settled down on the sofa; François' one arm was around Nigella, and his other arm around Martina, who was on his lap as she sounded out the words in one of the storybooks he had brought back from New York.

François and Nigella made a touching toast to their parents, including their two deceased mothers, Duyen and Martina (senior), and we toasted their bright future ahead of them.

Nigella continued, "So it seems I have to buckle down and learn some Vietnamese pronouns. Chi and Diep, is it okay with you if Francois and I both address you with the Vietnamese language *mom and dad*, or do you prefer the old-school French Vietnamese?"

Diep answered, "We're old-school all the way. French is perfect. Right, Chi?"

"Yeah, French all the way. Mère or Mama and Père or Pops, just like François has always used," Chi added.

I held up my glass. "If Diep is Mère, I want to be Mom. How does that sound to everyone?" I added in.

Nigella was beaming and was the first to raise her glass. "Let's toast to our whole family!"

Even Martina, with her glass of sparkling water, called out a resounding, "Cheers, cheers for a thousand years."

Later, in the kitchen, Nigella hugged me and said, "Denni, oh, I mean, Mom, you were right. François just took care of everything. He even brought the birth control. You know, the safes as he called them. I'd never seen them before, let alone use one. It was so much fun. I laughed the whole weekend with all his showing off. The whole weekend was like a fairytale."

"Wait a minute. What did you say? You mean you aren't on birth control?"

"Well, no. I've never had to think about it before."

"Oh my God, baby. I'm such a lousy parent. I didn't even think about that issue. I'm sorry. Thank God for François. But we will get you down to the doctor right away and see that you get on some reliable birth control."

"But, Denni! About the sex! I'm so surprised at how much I loved everything he did to me. I can't stop thinking about it, although I must say I'm a little tender, you know where," she said as she pointed down to her crotch like a thirteen-year-old would do.

"You see what a bikini wax can do for a girl?" I joked with her.

"Yeah, he told me he loved it. Can we make our trip down to the Fuzz Wax Bar a monthly mother-daughter thing?"

"We sure can, baby. Hmm, so you're a big girl now."

"Oh, I certainly am! And I'm loving it!"

***

Over the next three months, everything came together. Nigel had regained a lot of his strength, and although he would never put his foot in the boxing ring again, he enjoyed his time at the gym with a modified work out. He napped during the day, and we still had our brisk nightly walks as if nothing had ever happened to him. He couldn't seem to gain any of his weight back, and that worried me. And his beautiful hair, just as the nurse had said, was still as thick and curly as ever, but was turning grayer day by day. As the nurse predicted, he had aged dramatically.

Chi and Diep, recently home from their honeymoon to Vietnam, filled us in with stories of their trip. They had missed their growing family so much they swore they'd never leave again without all of us in tow. Basically, they came back home very grateful that they were Canadians. What they really missed, they both admitted, was my old bush that we had all bought together. They called it 'the farm,' and they told us their new plans and ideas for the house they would build were almost ready for us to see.

Between trips up to the farm to oversee clearing parts of the land with Martina and the pup in tow, Chi was working every day in the backyard, coaxing it back into shape after the new addition had dug up some of his gardens. Diep was right beside him, arguing the point of the right mix of color and style of the plants. The old maple was professionally trimmed, and Martina's tree house was finally built and installed after it had had to take a backseat to Nigel's heart attack. Chi installed a long, narrow, shallow water feature all along the side fence and hedge, with a variety of tall, wheat-colored grasses behind it, contrasting against the dense, green hedge. This water would allow Patou to cool down in the hot summer months, and Martina could float her toys along the edge of it. The whole area was magic. Of course, all his planning was around the upcoming wedding. François and Nigella wanted their wedding to be exactly like ours, right in the backyard, with dinner at the Four Seasons afterward. Chi had saved our old chuppa, and Diep took the time to painstakingly embroider Hebrew sayings on it, right along with some

Vietnamese and French sayings as well. It turned out to be a real piece of Canadian-style art. I knew in my heart that Saul Himmel would have loved it and he would be so proud of Nigel and his multicultural and multiracial family.

***

It was the second time I had walked up the red carpet in the garden. This time, I was the mother of the bride. The groomsman sat me, according to tradition, last, just after mother and father of the groom, and just before the flower girl. Brad and Madison had slipped in at the last and taken their seats at the back of the other guests so as to not surprise or disturb the other guests. As I passed all the rows, I saw all our old friends and family already seated. There were a lot of thirty-somethings there, friends of François, and now of Nigella's too, all dressed to kill, sitting in the sunshine, basking in the love that always seemed to radiate from 7 Russell Hill Road, even right back into its big backyard.

Martina followed me up the red carpet, dressed in a white princess dress and wearing a little princess crown on top of her golden ringlets. She tossed the rose petals out to each side with aplomb. She stopped a few times to wave to someone that she recognized along the way. As she reached the chuppa, François scooped her up and held her in his arms with the Rabbi on one side of them and the best man on the other. They watched the father and the bride walk up the red carpet next.

Nigel and Nigella walked the red carpet to Mendelsong's *Wedding March*, and as they came into view, the music was overtaken by the ohs and ahs of the guests. She was the most beautiful bride any of us had ever seen, and she seemed to radiate a golden aura all around her. Nigel was the proudest father in the world and could barely suppress his joy as his trademark grin took over his handsome face. Nigella had chosen a long, scooped-neck, sleeveless white silk dress, cut on the bias, that showed her model's body off magnificently. She opted for no headpiece or veil and only wore one of my art deco hairclips that Nigel had bought me. That's all she needed. Her golden ringlets fell to her shoulders. She wore my mother's old triple-strand pearls and my vintage, ivory, hand-tatted, three-quarter-length gloves from Paris, with her engagement ring sparkling over them.

Once they reached the chuppa, Nigel took Martina out of François' arms, and they both stepped back to join me until it was time to stand under the chuppa with the bride and the groom.

Everyone laughed as Rabbi Klieman was so overcome with emotion under the chuppa that he had to wipe his tears and blow his nose noisily into his hanky before he could continue with the service. It was just as joyous as our wedding day, and I must say, I think that François appeared even happier than Nigel.

After the ceremony, and in front of the mike, François was every bit the statesman that the partners at his law firm had hired him for. He was charming, suave, and knew exactly what to say and how to say it, with no nerves at all – just a happy, confident man seriously in love with his new wife and daughter. He introduced his parents and then Nigella's parents without any of the complicated back stories of all our families. He introduced his family members, Brad and Madison as his Uncle Nigel's brother and his son who lived like gypsies, sometimes in France and sometimes in L.A. He told the guests not to try to work out the family ties; it was simply just too complicated.

He shouted out to the boys, "Yo, Brad, Madison, come on up here to represent the family and say hello to our guests." He then proceeded to tell the guests that around the house, his dad always called Brad 'pretty boy,' but not to try it, as Brad had just spent all night flying red-eye from the west coast with his son and was not up to defending himself.

Brad and Madison were quite a hit obviously, as everyone recognized who they were, but the famous duo kept it simple and to the point. Brad said that he was indeed related to both sides of the wedding party and that François was right; it was complicated. He had diapered François, the groom, as a baby and he loved his brother Nigel's daughter Nigella, the bride, like she was his own little girl. He said it was a match made in heaven and he asked the guests to all to pray for their happiness.

Madison continued, "And Mom and the other kids all send their love as well. And, although I am a little embarrassed to say so, François diapered me too, when I was a baby, just the same as Dad diapered him. I mean really, this backyard is good luck for all of us. Just look at Uncle Nigie and Denni; they are so in love with each other. There's enough love in this backyard for all of us. Like Denni says, 'Can you feel it?'"

François concluded his speech by saying humbly, "This is the best day of my life. May I present my beautiful, brilliant barrister and solicitor wife, Nigella Koffman Hansson-Tran, and my darling daughter, Martina Hansson-Tran?"

Nigella and Martina stood on each side of François. Nigella leaned over and said to Martina, "Martina, will you please introduce yourself and then introduce us?"

The little princess piped up immediately, "Hello, my name is Martina, and this is my mom, Nigella, and my dad, François. And I have a dog, Patou, but he's over at the dog-sitter's house right now. Oh. I forgot. Yes, and welcome to our wedding."

Nigella threw her head back and laughed as François scooped Martina up in his arms.

She looped her arm through François' and continued softly with her killer accent, "Thank you all for joining us on our wedding day. And thank you to our parents, Nigel and Denni, and Chi and Diep, for all your love and devotion to the family unit." She paused a little for effect and then added, "As François and Brad alluded to, our family structure is complicated. But really, I think my own story takes the cake for being complicated. Seven months ago, I lived in Stockholm, Sweden, with no parents, working as a lawyer and being a single parent to my beautiful daughter. I stand here today with two sets of parents who I love more than life itself, my daughter, and my handsome, sexy husband that I'm so madly in love with; I can't even tell you! Now that's complicated! But really, it's God's way of telling us all that fairytales do come true. I wish you all that same happiness."

The guests' clapping and cheering brought the speeches to an end, and the music amped up. The staff cleared the chairs away, just like they did at our smaller but just as lovely wedding the year before. You never know. You just never know.

***

I remember it was in September, and Martina had settled into school. She already had had her first birthday party at home in the new family room where Nigel had insisted that her whole class was to be invited. Nigel was very sensitive to the fact that his granddaughter was attending the very same school that gave him such a hard time when he was a young, black immigrant that couldn't fit in. Martina was, on all accounts, a Jew, and Nigel was going to make damn sure she was accepted into the neighborhood school without doubts raised about her African ringlets and light, tan-colored skin tones.

On the day of her party, the new family room was full once again with little children and all their parents, but this time, the guests were from our neighborhood along with Rabbi Klieman, who had officiated some of the guests' weddings as well as their parents' weddings many years before. Nigella and François and Nigel and I were the only mixed-race couples, and Chi and Diep were the only Asian couple. As I looked around the room, I had to ask myself if perhaps Nigel's concerns for his granddaughter's fitting in was simply not relevant in the neighborhood all these years later. I had an inkling that it was perhaps Nigel that hadn't moved on, and not the neighborhood at all. I smiled as I saw everyone mixing in, with the moms and dads keying in both François' and Nigella's cell numbers. I assumed that play dates for Martina and maybe even a little business would take place in the future.

I summed up the crowd the same as I had done at our first party. Nigella was the most stunningly beautiful girl in the room, and Nigel was the most handsome man, hands down.

I remembered our last party with the old crew from the trades was a good Canadian mix of cultures and color, such as the Italian husband with Asian wife, the black wife with the white husband, and the Muslim wife that wore her head covered, and the young, black single mother that was in her fourth year to become a licensed electrician. 'So what?' I asked myself. I was surrounded by happy, healthy, thriving new friends of all ages, and I decided that our next party's guest list would include both the trades and the neighborhood so that we could all enjoy the day together, just like the younger generations of Canadians do.

After the party, when Martina was in bed, the five of us agreed with Nigel when he commented that he was pretty sure that Martina would be invited to every birthday party for the school year and that he would be happy to take her to all the play dates that a lot of the parents had mentioned setting up. It was evident that my handsome, successful, sensitive husband still felt the sting of his own rejection so many years ago at that same little school in the neighborhood. It was the first time since I had met Nigel that I realized that he was ten years older than me in age, as well as experience and opinions regarding this particular segment of current Canadian culture. But what did I know? I didn't have a clue about the immigrant experience whatsoever. I stood there and suddenly realized that, other than François, I was the only non-immigrant in my entire family.

I snuggled into my husband's arms that night, and I knew by his voice that he had a smile on his face as he whispered,

"I'm just remembering what you did for me in bed after our first party, back in March."

"Is this your segue into sex, Mr. Royal?"

"No, not at all. I never want to experience that night again for as long as I live."

I bolted upright in bed and looked at him. "What do you mean?"

He reached out, laughing, and grabbed me to pull me down back into his arms and he said, "That was the first and only night you ever faked it with me."

I sprang back up out of his arms. "There you go again! Mr. Know-it-all! You think you know everything, don't you!?"

By this time, he was laughing out loud, and he sat up to try and kiss me before I could get away. "You're exactly right. I do know everything. Including you, my Irish faerie. I read you like a book."

***

I was sitting in front of the window in my office, thinking that I would be happy when the kids' house was ready for them to move into.

The newlyweds had been camped out in our basement apartment since their wedding, and although we all got along so well, I was dying to get back to just Nigel and me. It was entirely selfish of me, but I missed just us, and I knew that Nigel did too, although he never said so. I had gotten back to spending the mornings in my office, writing my third book, but it wasn't the same somehow.

They had found a beautiful, old house just two blocks away from 7 Russell Hill Road, but it definitely needed a major renovation, which was going to take time.

It was built around 1920 and in a totally different style than the formal brick center-hall plan 'Georgians' in our neighborhood. This house looked like a sprawling, hodgepodge Nantucket beach cottage somehow, with low eves and a circular porch that went around the whole house. The low eves were clad with cedar shakes, and they opened up to the second-floor dormers with big, expansive bedroom windows on all sides. The attic was open as well, with smaller dormers that crowned the quaint design. The layout seemed close to the ground, which added to the cottage feel, although there were three stories of living space. The backyard was a wide, deep bramble of overgrown shrubs and rubble from years of renters parking cars back there. Nigella said the overall design was very similar to seaside houses back home in Sweden and that it was the house of her dreams. We all agreed that the house was a lot like our Swedish princess herself; it was whimsical, charming, and had a fairytale aura about it.

We all encouraged them to get it, and between all of us, we had come up with enough money to float it. Forty-nine Parkwood Avenue was going to be lovingly restored to our Swedish princess' exact specifications, come hell or high water. Diep chipped in a big chunk from her insurance money that she had received when her first husband and son were killed in the car accident, François sold his condo, and I chipped in a good chunk of my inheritance from my mother. Nigel threw in the rest. Nigella paid for all the renovations out of her inheritance from Saul and Mrs. Himmel. Chi was putting in sweat equity as part of the construction crew and landscaping the deep backyard to perfection, as he had spent most of his savings on buying the farm.

I turned around as Nigel called me softly from the door, "Honey, can you just go down to see if Nigella is okay? I think she's sick."

"Oh my God, Nigel, yes, of course. I thought I heard François leave early this morning for work. Did Nigella take the baby to school?"

"Yes, but she came back and ran right downstairs."

I ran downstairs, calling out, "Nigella honey, are you okay? Dad says he thinks you're sick."

"I'm in here."

"Where? Where are you?"

"In the bathroom." She was leaning over the toilet, trying to put an elastic to hold her hair out of the way as she retched into the toilet bowl.

"Oh, honey, here, let me help you. Should I get you to the doctor?"

"No, Mom. I'll be just fine."

"Well, no, you're not just fine. Here, let me get your hair for you."

"Mom, really, I'm fine. It's perfectly normal."

"What's perfectly normal?"

"Mom, I'm pregnant. With twins."

"Nigel! Nigel!" I yelled up the stairs. "Come down here, quick! Hurry, honey, hurry! Right now!"

"Okay, girls, okay. I'm here. I'm here. What's wrong?"

"Nothing's wrong, Dad. Everything's right. I'm pregnant. With twins," Nigella said as she wiped her mouth.

Nigel was like a mother hen, making Nigella stretch out on the sofa, and he tucked her in with a throw over her long frame.

"Dad, please, Dad, you're smothering me!" she said as she threw the blanket over the back of the sofa. "I have an idea. Let's call François so he knows that you know. We were going to tell the four of you tonight, once he got home, and now I've spoiled his surprise."

Chi and Diep came over immediately, and François was home from his office in twenty minutes. It was champagne for everyone except the mother-to-be who had a glass of milk. They would tell Martina when she got home from school that she was going to have two little baby brothers to boss around for the rest of her life.

***

It was the most joyous Hanukkah and Christmas that any one of the seven of us had ever had. Nigella, being the adult Jew in the family, had enrolled in some Judaic classes through Rabbi Klieman and was cooking the Hanukkah meals, Christmas breakfast, and presents were at Chi and Diep's and then over

331

to our house for the Christmas dinner, and more presents, with the dog following along, waiting patiently for any little treats Martina could sneak to him. The year 2006 ended in a happy glow for all of us. None of us could believe it was exactly one year since Nigella had first reached out to her father. So much had changed for all of us at 7 Russell Hill Road.

***

It was spring by the time the kids finally got moved into their new house, and my husband and I settled down into what seemed to be our new normal. It had been a full year since Nigel's heart attack and he was managing well, but our nightly walk around the neighborhood was written in stone, and we never missed a step. We had settled into using this time as our sounding board, so to speak, and we both valued this little chunk of time to catch up privately, away from our growing family, just like married folks do.

Nigel and the dog walked Martina to school every morning, and I was happily ensconced in my office during that time, story after story pouring out of me.

Martina had sleepovers at both sets of grandparents and developed the first bit of independence from her parents. Between Chi, Mary the dog-walker, and myself, we had managed to train Patou into the perfect pet. Everyone loved him, of course, but I was secretly pleased to know that he had chosen me to be his favorite. He was my dog, hands down. Our busy life went on. In between entertaining our friends, there were family dinners at our house, at Chi and Diep's apartment, or two blocks over with the kids.

Our two grandsons arrived right on time, born downtown at Mount Sinai Hospital, with all five of us camped out in the waiting room while Nigella and François walked the halls and visited with us between contractions.

The babies were formally introduced to the world as Warren Saul Hansson-Tran and Noah Saul Hansson-Tran at their baptism, along with their sister Martina Hansson-Tran, who was also baptized at Diep and Chi's lovely interdenominational church on St. Clair Avenue West. Rabbi Klieman officiated, right along with Diep and Chi's Pastor, just the way Canadians do things these days. The two babies each had a different-colored ribbon wrapped around their ankle, as it was impossible to tell who was Warren and who was Noah.

***

I looked at Nigel and shook my head. "But please, honey, I want you to promise me that you will take it easy this weekend. I'm not kidding. I know you're doing well, and the new pills seem to be better for your energy level, but we can't afford to have a setback. We made a deal when I agreed to this weekend, and I need you to take it easy."

"Okay, my beautiful and devoted nurse. I'll take it easy, but really, what could I say when Brad called? He said that he and George just wanted to get away for a couple of days to have their kids all together. And they all go back to school next month. And I know he worries about me now too. Well, not only me, but when he heard about our little false-alarm kidnapping incident, he was beside himself, even though it turned out to be just a shakedown from the brothers. He deals with that kidnapping worry every single moment of his life. But on top of that, with all their crazy schedules and the paparazzi, their kids hardly know each other. And it's important to those two men that their children have cousins. You know how it is, especially now with our three babies thrown into the mix. All of a sudden, we have one hell of a big family. Thank God we have the new family room. So, our kids and the boys will join us here, but they will take the babies back home to sleep for the night, right?"

"Yes, you're right. It's all good, honey. Thank you. Now, about this weekend. I've got all the linens and everything sorted. The kitchen staff will be here from 8:00 a.m. until 8:00 p.m. to give us a hand with all the meals and snacks. Teenagers seem to eat every half hour, and the little ones are the same. So, as it stands right now, George is taking Nigella's old room, and his twins are going to bunk in with Martina in her old room. They're not bringing the nannie, as George says all you men are going to babysit all the kids for the weekend. Brad is taking the new guestroom by the family room, and all his tribe is sleeping downstairs in the apartment, with Madison more or less in charge down there."

He just stood there, looking at me.

"What is it?"

"Just you, sugar, just you. Kiss me. Kiss me slowly, the way I like it."

"Ever since the kids moved out, you are insatiable. If Dr. Gilbert knew how you carried on, he would be writing you up in the medical journal under the heading of *sex drives of older men*."

"Older men! Ouch! Here, feel this. Does that feel like an older man to you, baby? What about an afternoon nap? Yeah. I think I need to have a nap."

***

333

I had to laugh. I stood there in the doorway, looking over the family room. It looked like a bomb had gone off. George's four-year-old twins, still in their pajamas, were being coached by Martina how to ride the bikes around the sofas, sounding their bells as they turned each corner, just like Nigel had taught her to do out on the sidewalk. The older kids were in a very heated half-French, half-English debated monopoly game that was taking place at the big, burnished copper dining room table, with François speaking only in French and acting as banker.

George and Brad, sitting on one sofa with their feet up on the coffee table, each had one of our baby boys on their lap, giving them a bottle, with Diep interrupting them constantly, checking to see if the babies needed a fresh diaper. With each diaper check, she would take the time to rearrange their dark, curly heads of hair to her liking, delivering a final kiss as she reluctantly handed her grandsons back to George and Brad.

It seemed that our identical twins were going to grow up with the handsome Asian face of their father and the African curls of their mother.

Madison had fashioned a money bank out of a kitchen jar, and everyone that had a wrong guess as to which baby was Warren and which was Noah and had to put a quarter in the jar. The jar was half-full and it was not even noon.

Nigella had taken the opportunity to spend the morning at the hair salon, with a visit to the Elmwood afterward and a promise to be home in time for dinner.

Nigel was stretched out on one of the sofas, with Patou right up there with him, who was keeping a watchful eye on the other sofa where the babies were being fed.

François was asking George and Brad every five minutes if the boys were okay, and Madison and one of his brothers were playing a video game on a laptop. A basketball game was screening silently on the TV and Brad had amped up some country music on the BOSE system. Chi was behind the kitchen island with the kitchen help that the agency had sent to us, trying to accommodate all the kids' requests for this and that. Grilled cheese sandwiches reigned in the kitchen.

As Nigel was laughing at something George said, he looked up and caught my eye. He patted the sofa beside him to motion me to join him and I shooed Patou out of my spot. I took my station at the other end of his sofa, with our feet touching in the middle, as we usually did. Nigel promptly grabbed my foot and pulled me up toward him, rubbing my foot into his crotch.

Brad and George howled with laughter at his smooth move, and the babies both began to cry with all the noise and commotion. Diep immediately snatched one of the babies away in a huff as Chi came running to get the other.

Nigel sprang up and fell on top of me, kissing me all over my face while he groped my ass with his one free hand, and he shouted out in his big baritone, "How'd I get so lucky!? How'd I get so damn lucky!?"

Love was all around us as Saul and George, the two old white men, presided over the commotion from their big photographs on the brick wall at 7 Russell Hill Road.

***

It was autumn once again. Patou seemed to tag along everywhere we went and was completely happy and good-natured to let our baby boys crawl all over him. I was the odd man out on most occasions at the kids' house, as they had decided that French would be spoken at home, but I caught on to enough of the conversations to know when I was the brunt of the joke. Chi and Nigel loved to tease me, and I was a little slower on the uptake in French, to my disadvantage.

***

One morning, Nigel and Patou came in from walking Martina to school, as was their usual routine. He said to me, "The kids want to come over and have brunch with us all, here in the family room this Sunday. Okay with you, babe?"

"Sure, of course. What's up? Anything new? Oh – don't tell me. She's pregnant?"

"No, no, not at all. Nigella said they have a present for us."

"Oh. Okay, so it's a surprise, right? Or do you know what it is?"

"Nope. She's going to keep us guessing, I suppose."

"Okay, babe. Why don't we have a sleepover for Martina the night before to give the kids a bit of a break? She can go home with them after brunch on Sunday."

"Perfect plan, honey."

***

As we walked up the front steps from our walk that evening, I said to Nigel, "Honey, I have to admit you outdid me tonight. I'm tired. Do you mind if I just have a shower and hop into bed a little earlier tonight?"

He surprised me with a big bear-hug, and he was grinning from ear to ear. "Whatever you want, Mrs. Royal."

"No, no, don't get me wrong. This is not an invitation to a sexy shower with you; really – I'm pooped for some reason. I just need an early night. That's all."

I smiled a little as he eagerly joined me sans invitation in the shower. I had forewarned him that there was nothing for him here except maybe a halfhearted back scrub, but he had that eager little boyish look around his face somehow.

I don't know why I said it when I did; it was totally uncharacteristic of me, but it came out in a little, whiny voice. I was embarrassed with myself; I sounded like an unhappy, peevish wife that needed some attention. I blurted out, "Nigie, do you think I'm getting fat?"

He tried with all his might not to burst out laughing right in my face. He dropped his loofah and gathered me into his arms so I couldn't see his face, but I felt his chest heaving with suppressed laughter.

"Darling, darling, darling," he said as he struggled to compose himself, "you've got me walking on a landmine here. I'm really fucked here either way, aren't I? What's really going on with you, honey?"

By then, I was completely annoyed with myself for asking this ridiculous self-serving question and annoyed with him as well for handling it like it was a comedy skit or something. I responded with a little edge to my voice, "Nothing's going on here. I simply asked you a question. That's all. No need to roll on the floor laughing at me."

He was kissing me all over my wet face, and he decided he would meet the devil head-on, "Baby, baby. I love that your breasts are a little fuller these days. I love that your tummy is a little rounder. Your ass was always perfect, and it still is. You were a little too lean before, just like me. Ever since my heart attack, you were always so busy taking care of everyone else, including me, that you didn't take care of yourself, and you lost a little weight. Now you've gained it back, and baby, you're all woman. I can't get enough of you. I love you, I love you all the way, and I'll always love you no matter what."

Before I could even raise my eyebrows at his crafty but definitely affirmative answer, he kissed me on my mouth and said, "In fact, to prove my point, I went out yesterday and bought you a present. This present will show you how much I love your new curves."

"Oh. Oh," I said as I smiled. "I'm sorry, honey, for putting you in an impossible corner. Please forget that I ever said anything. What's gotten into me? I'm a little embarrassed, to tell you the truth."

I changed the subject, trying to bury my insecurities, and I said in an entirely different tone, "Hmm… did you just say you bought little old me a present?"

"Yes, and it's tucked away downstairs, in Saul's office. I want you to meet me there as soon as you get your robe on. Just leave your hair in your towel. This really can't wait."

I was smiling by then, and I met his enthusiasm with, "Okay, honey. See you in a sec."

***

I joined Nigel, hair up in my towel, with my big yellow diamond resting on my ring finger as usual. I settled into his lap in Saul's old office chair. That old chair had become our go-to spot for private, serious, or intimate conversations in the house for some crazy reason.

The gift lay on the desk in front of us. It was wrapped, surprisingly, in a plain paper with no ribbon or bow. It didn't look like one of Nigel's extravagant purchases he usually bought me. It certainly couldn't be this season's Hermes scarf or jewelry or lingerie looking like this. The gift was about six inches long and two inches wide.

He handed it to me, and with his trademark grin stretching from ear to ear, said, "Honey, I can't wait any longer. Open it. Just open it."

"Okay, darling, okay."

As I picked the gift up, Nigel urged, "Just rip the paper, honey. Just rip it!"

I ripped. Not understanding what I held in my hands, I reached over to the desk once again to grab Nigel's reading glasses so I could read the printing on the box.

My jaw dropped, and my eyes were wide behind his glasses that were perched on my nose. I was speechless with surprise. I literally couldn't utter a word. I looked into Nigel's face. He just sat there, grinning, not saying a word either.

We sat there in our quietness, neither of us wanting to break our little bubble even with a word. He kissed my hands. I kissed his face. He kissed my neck. I kissed his chest. Every kiss from both sides was delivered with a new tenderness that in our three years of loving each other, the moment seemed like yet another fresh start somehow.

As always, he took care of everything. After retrieving his reading glasses from my nose, he read the instructions out loud, A through Z, as he continued holding me on his lap.

Taking me by the hand, he led me back upstairs to our en-suite, and he sat me down on the toilet, hunkering down on his heels in front of me.

"Pee, honey, just pee!" was all he said.

As we both stood in front of the vanity, heads together, leaning over the stick, we traded his reading glasses back and forth with bated breaths.

The positive sign emerged and it was official. I was pregnant.

***

Sunday brunch came and once again we all congregated in the family room. We had moved the coffee table out of the babies' way, and they crawled and tottered this way and that way, as they navigated the choice of six pairs of legs to pull themselves up to, before falling over in a heap. Every time one of them would topple, Patou would be right there, nuzzling their face to check to see if they were okay. It was a race between us four grandparents to see who could scoop up the fallen soldier the fastest. "I got him. I got him."

"No, I got him."

"No way, you had him last time." We all agreed that Chi was nothing but a baby hog and he had to learn how to share.

Nigel wouldn't leave my side, even for Martina, and I must admit, both of us were literally glowing, all caused, of course, by our little secret. We had decided we wouldn't say a word to anyone until we had been checked out fully by the doctor. After all, as many people over the past ten years had reminded me, I was no spring chicken. The first pregnancy at age forty-six may require a little special handling.

Martina was dancing from one foot to the other, asking her parents over and over if it was time yet to give us the present. She excitedly helped Nigel and me unwrap the large, heavy package. Chi, Diep, and the kids looked on, watching our faces with anticipation. As the gift revealed itself, I was stunned. I said softly, "Oh, Nigel."

Nigel was blinking back tears as he looked up at the kids and said, "As Saul would say, 'I'm a little overwhelmed right now.'"

We were both so choked up; we couldn't even read the inscription out loud.

François said softly, "We can mount it under the portico, beside the front door, near Saul's old mezuzah. That way, everyone that enters the house can feel the love."

Chi took the large, engraved brass plaque in both hands and he stood up to read the words out loud:

7 Russell Hill Road

This is Saul's house.
We dedicate this property in his honor.

Nigel, Denise, Brad, Chi, Diep,
François, Nigella,
Martina, Warren, Noah,
and Patou

September, 2007

The End

Playlist in Order of Chapter

Chapter 1: Humble Beginnings
Ray Charles, *You Don't Know Me*

Chapter 2: My Day in Court
The Temptations, *Get Ready. Here I Come*

Chapter 3: Houseguests
Gretchen Wilson, *Redneck Woman*

Chapter 6: Paris
Leonard Cohen, *I'm Your Man*
Rod Stewart, *Tonight's the Night (Gonna Be Alright)*

Chapter 7: Addendum: Nigel
Pharrell Williams, *Be Happy*

Chapter 8: Single Again
Four Tops, *I Like Everything About You*
Jimmy Ruffin, *What Becomes of the Broken-Hearted*
Pharrell Williams, *Be Happy*

Chapter 9: Under the Maple Tree
Kelly Clarkson, *The Trouble with Love Is*
Kim Weston, *You Gotta Love Me All the Way*
Nora Jones, *Turn Me On*
Anne Murray, *Could I Have This Dance*
Roy Clarke, *Come Live with Me*
David Ruffin, *My Whole World Ended the Moment You Left Me*
David Ruffin, *I Wish It Would Rain*

Chapter 10: Addendum: Musings in The Kitchen
The Miracles, *Mighty Good Lovin'*

Chapter 11: On the Lam
Robin Thicke, *Blurred Lines*
Percy Sledge, *When a Man Loves a Woman*

Chapter 12: Nigella Hansson
Kelly Clarkson, *The Trouble with Love Is*
Tina Turner, *Simply the Best*
Tina Turner, *Better Be Good to Me*
Etta James, *Footprints on the Ceiling*

Chapter 13: 7 Russell Hill Road
Mendelsong, *Wedding March*

CPSIA information can be obtained
at www.ICGtesting.com
Printed in the USA
LVHW080134100421
684002LV00013B/504